<u>PRAISE FOR *TWO PERF[...]*</u>

"HILARIOUS . . . puts Performance Art's hairy [...] grand display. . . ."
—James Gautier, Kill Radio

"A well-written, hilarious adventure I'd recommend to anyone."
—Marc Wilmore, Writer & Producer for *The Simpsons*

"This book is a performance art piece."
—John M. White, Performance Artist, Painter, and Sculptor

"It saved my soul, just like it saved Bill's. Amen."
—John Fleck, Performance Artist & Member of the NEA Four

"Ridiculous and twisted . . . a heightened reality where
creativity brings redemption."
—Elisha Shapiro, Founder of the International Nihilist Film Festival

"Isn't it correct to retch, puke, and vomit while doing performance art?
I did that reading Scotch's book. . . ."
—Linda Mary Montano, Performance Artist &
Author of *Performance Artists Talking in the Eighties*

TWO PERFORMANCE ARTISTS

ARTISTS

WIC

KIDNAP THEIR BOSS

AND DO THINGS WITH HIM

A NOVEL BY

SCOTCH WICHMANN

FREAKSHOW
BOOKS

Two Performance Artists Kidnap Their Boss And Do Things With Him
© 2014 Scotch Wichmann

Freakshow Books
Attn: Rights Dept.
7510 Sunset Blvd #534
Hollywood, CA 90046
www.freakshowbooks.com

Special discounts may be available on quantity purchases by corporations, associations, and others. For details, contact the publisher at the address above.

"Freakshow Books" and its two-headed mascot are trademarks of Freakshow Books.

The mascot and "Bill Performing" cover art were illustrated by Alex Madrigal. For more, visit: www.alexmadrigal.com

Printed in the United States of America

First Printing, 2014

ISBN: 978-0-9910257-0-1
LCCN: 2013951733

This book is also available in E-Book formats.

Visit the *Two Performance Artists* website for the latest book, author, and tour news at www.twoperformanceartists.com

For Stephen "Tenafly" Taylor,
KayDee Kersten,
and all the performance artists John White made.

* * *

And for the organs you inspired in this work's guts: Nate Dryden, Clay Young, Gary San-Angel, Michael Mufson, Beth Stinson, Lee and Christy, Jude and Lindy, "Electric Shoes" Tim, Todd Ivers, "Honey Wall" Valerie, "Stilt Heels" Beth, Erin Feder, The Shrimps, Deborah Oliver, Jacki Apple, John Blough, William P. Fritz, The L.A. Live Art Forum, Randy Hostetler, Karen Finley, Tim Miller, John Fleck, Holly Hughes, Allan Kaprow, Linda Frye Burnham, The Kipper Kids, Bob & Bob, Richard Layzell, Fluxus, Joseph Beuys, Bas Jan Ader, Rudolf Schwarzkogler, V. Vale, Bobcat Goldthwait, David Lynch, and Elaine May.

And to my editors, K.D. Kersten and Charlie Wilson, for staring down the bull—thank you.

1

AN EVENING OF PERFORMANCE ART usually began with a pack of intrepid performers renting out an art gallery for a night in San Francisco's seedy Tenderloin district. They'd whitewash the gallery walls to cover up the bits of dirt, paint, fat, or blood left behind by the last show, tape up posters around town advertising an evening of unrivaled avant-garde acts, and then, on opening night, stand proudly at the door to collect a dollar from each patron for admission—and shoo away the winos who showed up to guzzle the free booze that flowed when it was all over.

Audiences were fickle. After years of watching performance artists scream, hurl, shimmy, and screw, crowds could quickly discern cliché from innovative material; they could sniff out the frauds from the talent, and were unforgiving if a piece stank. It wasn't uncommon for an audience to interrupt a show with a jaded barrage of catcalls, flying fruit, and sometimes, fists.

It was November. Rain pounded outside. I shifted in my chair beside a hundred other spectators in a bright white art gallery that reeked of fresh paint, our parkas and umbrellas dripping in the humid air.

The spotlights dimmed. I settled back into my seat.

A performer walks to the center of the floor. He's tall and thin in a black turtleneck and beret. He looks like a poet.

I frown. Occasionally, some joker tries to pass off poetry as performance art. I sigh, but decide to give him a chance. Maybe he'll remove his beret and spit in it—at least that wouldn't be poetry. Come on, man, dazzle us!

The man pulls out a piece of paper and begins reading. His voice is monotone.

It's a Kerouac poem.

I shift in my seat. What the hell is this?

Minutes pass. The poem goes on and on. People in the audience shuffle. I start to sweat. How dare he stand in front of a performance art crowd and read beat poetry in a floppy beret!

After five minutes I jumped up and threw my chair at him. It broke the performer's nose. Blood spattered on the whitewashed walls.

The audience applauded. Finally, there was something to look at.

Kerouac always left me nauseous. I headed for the men's room.

I opened the restroom door. A man was sitting on the tile floor, sobbing. He was skinny with a raggedy mop of hair, bellbottoms, and red cowboy boots. Tears rolled down his face as he scribbled line after line of text on the white bathroom wall in tiny letters with a black permanent marker in each hand. The pens squeaked with every stroke, so with both hands moving, the noise was tremendous.

"You must be a terror alone in bed with those hands," I said.

The man said nothing. The pens squeaked harder.

"What are you writing?" I asked.

"MY MANIFESTO," he cried, "AND I HOPE THAT KEROUAC RIP-OFF SEES IT!"

I stepped closer and read from the top:

PERFORMANCE ART MANIFESTO

Performance Art should not be confused with the performing arts, namely drama, dance, comedy, circus, or music. Performance Art has its own distinct history that began in the 1950s when civil unrest and the remains of Surrealism and Dada merged with the desire of radical artists to turn the commodity art establishment on its money-grubbing head. Artists began staging Happenings—today called Performance Art—which amounted to informal gatherings where spectators went to watch an artist do something, and each "performance" was considered art simply because the performer said so.

And so, given its unique history, it's no surprise that Performance Art accumulated its own language, its own rules, and its own clichés that are different from those of other art forms. It is, for example, a Performance Art cliché to throw dishes against a wall. It is a cliché for a woman to sit on a stage and invite audience members to come up and rip off pieces of her dress while she sings opera and pulls turnips out of her buttocks. It is a cliché to slap oneself silly and wail about how Daddy spent his evenings in the living room snorting lines. It is a cliché to shoot one's friend in the arm or leg, or nail oneself to the back of a Volkswagen. Didactic Performance Art manifestoes like this one are clichés also. All of these things have been done and redone by imitators; thus, imagination and invention are the rare marks of true Performance Art. Reading poetry at an evening of Performance Art is not a cliché—it's just stupid.

"That's beautiful, man," I said. "What's your name?"

"Hank," the man sniffled.

"I'm Larry," I said. "So what else do you do besides watch performance art and write manifestoes?"

"I program computers," said Hank.

"No shit? So do I!" I said.

Hank sputtered a little laugh and wiped his nose. I studied his face, and then his head.

Phrenology—the study of head shapes—was codified in the late 1700s by Franz Joseph Gall, an Austrian physiologist who believed that a person's race, psychological tendencies, latent intentions, and future fate could be known by examining the shape of his or her skull. Gall's science was abused over the years as a profiling tool, first by Viennese quacks, then later by the Nazis, but Victorian showmen did well by it, adding it to their palmistry, fat lady, and snake oil acts that traveled in wagon caravans across England and North America in the nineteenth century.

Ringed by carnival tents, folk musicians, and sword swallowers, the phrenologist talked up the supernatural and medicinal benefits of his art with pomp and circumstance until the crowds that had flocked from nearby towns were begging to have their heads read. A student of psychology, astrology, telepathy, scatoscopy, necromancy, and numerous other mystery sciences, the phrenologist would take off his top hat, twirl his handlebar mustache, roll up his sleeves, and take their money fast, rubbing his hands over their skulls, feeling their warts, their bumps, their scalps, eye sockets, brows, noses. Despite the hoopla, phrenologists' cranial divination was terrifyingly accurate; they had the power to see inside people's heads.

Seeing inside a man's head isn't easy—it requires steady nerves and a detailed mental topography of the subject's facial features, but I certainly had the genes for it. I'd inherited the skill from my father, who'd inherited it from his father, who'd inherited it from my great-great-grandfather, who'd run a traveling show out of Kentucky called Professor John's Medicine Show which featured jugglers, tattooed nymphs, and The Mystery Man from Virginia. So it was with some authority that I could say that anyone with a decent phrenological eye would have taken one look at Hank's head and concluded that he fell somewhere between high-strung and sheer lunacy. First there was his skull's overall shape: rectangular and long, suggesting intellect and extreme creativity, but with a proneness to unhinged manic flights. A tall forehead descended to a classic Cro-Magnon brow, symptomatic of sexual anemia and a tendency toward jealousy. Thin lips on an oversized muzzle signaled narcissism, cyclical depression, and various impulse-control disorders. A blocky-toothed overbite betrayed wanton co-dependency. Miniature feline ears warned of epileptic seizures. And then there were the eyes: colossal, forward-set orbital sockets under a permanently furrowed brow that hinted at protracted bouts of nihilism, depersonalization disorder, hysteria, pubic fungi, constipation, acne, hemorrhoids, acrophobia, and crying.

The man was obviously a genius.

"THIS is really what I should be doing," he whispered, caressing his manifesto. "Performance art. I have a lot of ideas—"

"I've always wanted to do a performance with roller-skates," I offered.

"Or meat," said Hank.

"Or both," I said.

Smiles slid across our faces.

And that was how we started.

2

HANK AND I BOTH LIVED in the Tenderloin, San Francisco's decrepit maze of rat-infested alleys, litter-strewn streets, low-rent flophouses, strip joints, and massage parlors. Overrun by passed-out bums, toothless whores, pickpockets, two-bit dealers, and psych-ward escapees, the hilly neighborhood had been named in the 1920s by cops who'd gotten fat on bribes from the Loin's pimps and hustlers; if you were on the take, it was a choice cut of meat.

In a breath, the Tenderloin was San Francisco's cheap seats. If you wanted angel dust, acid, or smack, you went to the Loin. If you wanted a bar with a jukebox and jug wine for a buck, you'd find them there. Straight, gay, or transvestite hooker? He, she, or he-she was there. Alleys reeking of vomit and piss? There. Scads of mentally ill who defecated on the sidewalk while panhandling you five blocks straight before pausing to retrieve a flattened cigarette butt from the gutter that could be re-lit for a short-lived-but-pleasurable smoke? They were there too.

Sherry, Hank's wife, didn't believe two computer programmers could randomly run into each other in a restroom at a performance art gallery in the Tenderloin. It was too coincidental . . . it was suspicious . . . and it didn't help that the Loin was San Francisco's hotbed of underground gay action.

One night Hank invited me over to dinner.

I walked to their apartment on O'Farrell Street. The building was a tall wooden Victorian job, dingy gray and spitting splinters with rusty fire escapes, broken windows, and graffiti.

I rang the buzzer. Sherry came down and opened the lobby door. She was a bony blonde with long legs and crooked teeth. A half-empty wine bottle dangled from her hand.

"Hi, I'm Larry," I said.

"You're the one who's going to perform with my husband," she said flatly, taking a slug of wine.

"I—yes."

"With meat," Sherry snapped.

"And roller-skates," I said, forcing a smile.

Sherry snorted, turned, and led me up nine flights of stairs to their apartment.

The three of us sat down at the kitchen table to wine, beans, and rice.

"So, you got a girlfriend?" asked Sherry.

"Not currently," I said.

"I see." She shot Hank a look.

"How's work?" I asked Hank.

"Gone," said Hank. "Budget cuts. They laid me off yesterday—"

"BECAUSE ALL YOU TALK ABOUT IS PERFORMANCE ART!" Sherry yelled, then she turned to me. "So. Where do *you* work?"

"I don't."

Sherry's nostrils flared.

"I mean—not right now," I said. "I'm in-between gigs." I looked at Hank. He exhaled. "Sorry to hear you got laid off," I said. "My timing is terrible. I was going to ask you for a job—"

"You mean a blow job?" Sherry sneered.

"HOLY SHIT, SHERRY!" Hank screamed, spitting beans out of his mouth.

"Come on, Larry." Sherry jumped up and waved her dinner fork at me. "I know you've been getting into my husband's pants. ADMIT IT, YOU LITTLE FAIRY!"

I laughed and took a gulp of wine. "I knew you'd understand. What can I say? Your husband's got a great ass."

She stabbed her fork into my hand.

It took ten stitches to sew up the gash. Sherry apologized at the hospital, but I knew she'd never fully trust me after that.

3

HANK AND I DECIDED TO make performance art our careers. Sherry didn't like it, but since she didn't have any legally marketable skills herself, she reluctantly agreed to let Hank have a go at his dream.

We began putting on performance art evenings. We rented storefronts. We whitewashed walls. We pasted up flyers and posters.

Our shows took off. Although Hank and I typically performed on stage together, sometimes we'd mix it up with a solo piece, or even invite another artist to join us. Before long we were making enough money for rent and more. Hundreds of people showed up each night to see what we'd do next. Art critics called us "inspired" and "prolific." The Tenderloin was ours. We avoided Kerouac like the plague, and nobody ever threw a chair at us.

We lived like kings for two years—then the economy began to sour. Crime was on the rise. Drugs and prostitution spilled into the streets. Junkies were mugging tourists in broad daylight. Performance art audiences dwindled—our fans were afraid to visit the Tenderloin for shows. Locals still came, but mostly only hookers and druggies; they loved our work, which we genuinely appreciated, but they could never afford to pay more than a few cents for admission.

We started drinking. I drank because our dream of living performance art lives was slipping away, and Hank drank because Sherry was driving him insane.

* * *

Hank and I stripped down to our underwear. After months of performing little pieces on street corners for tourists' extra change, we'd managed to book a paying show. It was a five p.m. matinee gig, but we didn't care.

We were backstage at Linoleum, the Loin's oldest performance art gallery, and the name was fitting: the stage was nothing more than a square of yellow and brown kitchen linoleum glued to a concrete floor. Ten feet away was Julio, Linoleum's owner. He was struggling to control the leash of a barking black dog named Bitch. The animal was a Presa Canario—one hundred and twenty pounds of muscle from the Canary Islands with an engine block for a head and a maw of jagged teeth.

Holding onto Hank for balance as I pulled off a sock, I looked up at the ceiling. It was covered with show posters from all the famous acts that had graced the linoleum before us. There was Mary's Singing Tilapia . . . Sam Sammy's Seminal Flying Sauces . . . and even Ling-Ling Johnson, who'd impressed San Francisco's mayor with his somber act, Shaving My Ling-Ling to Pomp and Circumstance.

Hank wriggled into a sticky vest he'd made out of duct tape. Chunks of raw steak dangled from it on little pieces of fishing line.

Julio made a face. "You're really going to wear that?"

"Do you like it?" asked Hank, modeling.

"The smell is driving the dog crazy," said Julio, gripping the leash a little tighter.

"I hope so," said Hank. "We've been wanting to try this piece for two years."

Their banter made me chuckle. I jammed my feet into a pair of roller-skates, adjusted my tighty whities, then checked myself in a mirror. A wiry, gap-toothed forty-year-old man with bloodshot blue eyes, dirty blond hair, and an overbite smiled back. Not bad.

I opened a bottle of wine, took a swig, then handed it to Hank. He guzzled it, then parted the curtains and peeked out at the crowd. Six prostitutes, three junkies, and a kid reporter waved to him.

"That's the audience?" Hank whispered.

"That was all I could get," said Julio. "Regulars are still staying away—civilians are getting mugged left and right. You're lucky I got ten people out there."

"The crowds will come back," I said, stretching my hammies like a veteran. "You should've seen our last performance, Eating Mud on Stilts. There was this newspaper reporter—"

Bitch lunged and ripped a chunk of steak off Hank's vest.

"I can't hold her," Julio hissed, wrestling with the leash. "Start the show!"

"Ready?" I whispered to Hank.

Hanks nodded.

"GO!" I yelled.

Hank runs onto the stage and lies down on the floor beside a tattoo machine and a microphone. He flips a switch and the tattoo needle begins buzzing. People in the crowd laugh and cover their ears—the noise, picked up by the microphone, is deafening. Hank takes the needle and begins tattooing a line down his forearm.

Julio stumbles onto the stage with Bitch, ties her leash to a steel plate that's screwed to the floor, and beats a sweaty retreat.

Bitch growls, walks to Hank, and sniffs the meat dangling from his vest. Food. She tears off a hunk. Her movement makes Hank's tattoo line waver. He pauses to steady himself, then starts the needle going again, scrawling out a shaky letter D in black ink while the microphone broadcasts

Bitch chewing.

Bitch pulls off another hunk of meat—but this time a piece of the vest rips off with it, exposing Hank's left nipple. Hank whimpers. The hookers in the crowd clap and hoot.

I skate out on stage in my underwear, stumble, wheels clacking, regain my balance, and begin circling Hank and Bitch. As I come around, Bitch chases me, then lunges at my ass. I tense, ready for the pain, but her leash snaps taut, jerking her back. The audience howls.

Bitch returns to Hank and tears another piece of meat from his vest as he keeps the needle moving—he's inked the letters DE so far.

I skate faster. Julio steps out from the behind the curtains and waves his arms to get my attention. He yells something like, "HEY—MAYBE THAT'S ENOUGH!", but over all of the tattoo-buzzing and Bitch-growling it sounds like, "HEAT—A MEATY HAT'S ROUGH!" It makes me laugh and I skate faster.

Bitch clamps down on Hank's vest. Hank tries to push her off, but she takes a step back and discovers she's able to drag him across the linoleum. She retreats again—Hank slides across the floor. Reaching the end of her leash, she rails against it, digging in, jerking her muzzle—then there's a clang of metal. Hank lifts his head just in time to see the steel plate rip loose from three of the four screws anchoring it to the concrete. Bitch sees it too. She throws her head against her leash again and tosses Hank like a rag doll. I circle and try to grab his hand, but it's too late—the metal plate spins on its one remaining screw, then tears free. The bitch is loose.

She lets go of Hank, raises her head, and curls her dark-pink lips at me.

"Hey, I think she's smiling!" I laugh.

Bitch lunges at my crotch but I dart right, skating around Hank and the stage in widening concentric circles as the crowd screams and scatters for the exit. Teeth snap at my knees, calves, then clamp down on a skate. I stumble and fall on my ass, sliding. The bitch is closing fast.

"THROW SOME MEAT!" I scream, and Hank does, ripping off some steak and hurling it across the stage. Forgetting me, Bitch chases the steak down, snatches it up with her canines, chew, chew, swallow, then keeps on chewing, down to the linoleum. She finds a curled piece of flooring, pulls at it, tearing up a three-foot section, and starts eating it.

Julio emerges, waving a broom for protection. "GET OUT OF HERE! ALL OF YOU!" he screams. "YOU'RE FUCKING CRAZY!"

I grab Hank and we dart for the exit, trailing meat.

The kid reporter was outside scribbling notes. "I wouldn't have believed it if I hadn't seen it!" he said, giving us a thumbs-up.

Hank cried tears of joy and showed us his tattoo. It said DECOYY in scribbly letters. I doubled over laughing.

Julio came out. "WHAT THE HELL WAS THAT?" he yelled.

"Performance art!" I sang.

"When do we get paid?" asked Hank.

Julio slapped himself in the face, pulled out some change, threw it at us, spat on the sidewalk, then went back inside while Hank and I scrambled to pick up the coins.

Suddenly, Hank froze. I looked up. Sherry was standing across the street with her arms crossed. She ambled over to Hank on her clacky heels and held out her palm.

Hank dropped the coins into her hand.

Sherry looked at them. Her nostrils flared.

"You're getting a fucking job," she slurred, drunk. She turned and clacked away down the sidewalk.

Bitch walked out of the gallery with a hunk of steak dangling from her maw. She looked at us, sniffed the air, then trotted off.

"What should we title tonight's piece?" I asked.

"Decoy Tattoo with Meat—and Bitch," said Hank.

Perfect.

4

I **WALKED TO MY APARTMENT** building on Post Street. Built in 1890, the six-story structure reeked of urine and mold, and it was nothing to look at with its flaking gold trim, but city rent control kept it affordable.

I unlocked the security gate out front, entered through the building's glass doors, crossed the lobby, climbed the six flights of stairs to the top floor, walked to the end of the hall, stole my next-door neighbor's newspaper from his doormat, and let myself into my apartment. The living room wasn't much—a leaky twelve-foot ceiling, three cracked plaster walls, and a fourth wall of red brick. A threadbare couch where I slept sat in the center of the room, facing the brick wall. A coffee table stood before the couch. An alarm clock, TV, and VCR sat on the table. Off to the right was a tall double-hung window with a view of the street below. I wiped my brow. The living room was warm. Fading sunlight burned across the empty wine bottles, old newspapers, dirty clothing, and performance art props that littered the yellowing oak floor.

My stomach growled. I went to the kitchen and opened the fridge. Empty. I grabbed an open bottle of wine off the counter and gave it a whiff—not bad. I walked to the bathroom and yanked on the pull chain that dangled from the bare bulb overhead. The bulb flickered to life. The john was simple—toilet, tub, sink, mirror, and a rusty old steam radiator that chugged and sputtered.

I unzipped my pants and let the day loose as I drank. It was my emptying-while-filling, my scatological yin and yang. When I was finished, I zipped, exited to the living room, flopped down onto the couch, took a hit of wine to numb the hunger pangs, and opened the newspaper to the classifieds. I scanned the first page of employment ads—nothing—then I turned the page. The paper had included a sponsored listing of jobs for computer programmers who knew how to program Portalia. I took another slug of wine. I'd never used Portalia myself, but I'd read about it plenty. It was the world's most popular operating system—the software that made a computer work by coordinating its memory, disk drives, and other hardware.

Portalia was manufactured by Redsoft, a cut-throat multinational that had risen to dominate the operating-system market. Almost every new computer in the world came with Redsoft's Portalia pre-installed on it at the factory, which was more a result of Redsoft's infinite money supply, marketing prowess, and army of lawyers than anything revolutionary Portalia supplied; in fact, the great irony of Redsoft's success was that Portalia had a reputation for being buggy and unstable in spite of its popularity.

Programs designed to run on Portalia were written by programmers fresh out of college who were lured by Redsoft's endless parade of TV ads that sported bikini-clad women mouthing heady slogans like COME GET SOME AT REDSOFT. The programmers didn't have much experience, but Redsoft didn't care; it was willing to cough up serious dough for anyone under thirty years of age who was green enough to spend eighty hours per week wrestling with the operating system's idiosyncrasies. I'd heard that programming Portalia was a nightmare; if a program refused to run, it was impossible to tell whether the program had a bug or it was simply Portalia crashing again.

But none of this bothered Redsoft's freshmen programmers; they'd become America's nouveau riche and they loved it. They banded together like Redsoft fraternity members and sang the praises of Portalia every chance they got, climbing the corporate ladder, slapping backs at parties, and cashing fat paychecks for blow. They had a good thing going and couldn't care less if Portalia crashed—the money was just too good. Most of them were too young to remember life before Portalia anyway, so crashing seemed perfectly natural. Old-time veteran programmers like me and Hank were disgusted by the young coders' hubris and luck, but even more by Bill Kunstler, Redsoft's squeaky-voiced co-founder and CEO who was now worth billions despite his company's flawed flagship product.

The next morning I went to the public library and found a book about programming Portalia. Bill Kunstler's face graced its cover. I sat down at a table and thumbed through the pages. The operating system was pretty-looking and seemed like it would be easy to master; I could probably fake my way through a Portalia job interview, then learn how to program it after-hours on the sly.

The library had old typewriters that were free to use. I sat down at one, pulled my résumé out of my pocket, and carefully unfolded it. LARRY FROMMER, PROGRAMMER was printed at the top. And just below that, I noticed, was an orange pizza stain. Shit. I rubbed the grease off as best I could, then rolled the paper into the typer. I typed PORTALIA right above PROGRAMMER. It looked great. I zipped the paper out and folded it back into my pocket. I was good to go.

I went home and rooted around for something to wear. A plaid polyester tie, stained tuxedo shirt, and wrinkled pair of brown slacks were the best I could find. I took a hit of wine, tore one of the Portalia listings out of the newspaper, and walked downtown to interview. When I arrived, the office waiting room was already crammed with programmers half my age—fresh-faced Ivy Leaguers wearing pinstriped suits and Rolexes, their hair perfectly slicked.

"Can you even work a computer, Gramps?" muttered one at me out of the corner of his mouth with an oily Harvard twang. All the boys laughed.

A door opened and a manager with a clipboard entered. He looked twenty years old. He scanned the room—then spotted me. He motioned for me to follow him out into the hall.

"May I help you?" he asked, eyeing my wrinkled slacks.

"I'm here about a Portalia job," I said, starting to pull out my résumé.

"How old are you?" asked the manager.

"Why does that matter?" I asked, breathing old wine on him.

"Most applicants over thirty haven't even *seen* Portalia, let alone programmed it," he said smartly. "And you . . ." The manager paused to take in my receding hairline. "This might not be the right culture—"

"Sure, got it," I said, nodding. "Got one thing to do before I go."

I spun, walked back into the waiting room, and punched Harvard in the mouth.

* * *

Hank called. He was drunk.

"Find a job yet?" he slurred.

"No. But there are a ton of Portalia gigs—"

"Sherry says she'll leave me if I don't find a job," Hank sobbed.

"HANG UP THE PHONE!" I heard Sherry scream in the background.

"She wants a new area rug for the living room," Hank whispered.

"I'll find us a job," I said. "Don't worry. Tell her—"

There was a click and the line went dead.

* * *

Later that night I walked to a local diner and ordered soup. A waitress brought out a bowl of split pea and a basket of crackers. I dumped the crackers into my pockets for later and dug into the soup.

A burly truck driver walked in. He was four hundred pounds of grease and soot in a blue flannel shirt, roomy jeans, and a baseball cap. He sat down, ordered a steak and baked potato, finished half his plate, then left. I nearly killed myself running over to his table.

I'd wolfed down the rest of his steak and started on the potato when he returned—he'd only left to use the john. I spotted him when he was ten feet away, his fists clenched, face red and cheeks puffing. I jumped up and circled behind a table.

"You ate my steak!" said the trucker.

"I thought you were finished," I gulped, swallowing potato.

"YOU'RE PAYING FOR THAT STEAK!"

I tried to run for the door, but the trucker was too fast.

I decided to try a performance art defense maneuver.

Performance art is a shaman's game. A performance artist can manipulate his perceptions until he self-induces a real psychosis so dense that it takes on mass, building in gravity until he tears himself open and spectators fall in. In imploding he becomes like radiation that spreads his mind to other minds. Sometimes he spreads like a gas, or suddenly, like an apple placed in your hand; other times he explodes like glass that sprays shards into brains like diamonds. Later, after the theater houselights snap on and people in the audience awaken, some can't recall what their bodies were doing while their heads were away. Where was I just now? How long was I out? What happened while the performer was up there on stage talking about wigs and making slow-motion kung fu moves? Why is my shirt wet? Why are my shoes in a pile across the room? Performance art like that leaves a trace, a mark, an impression on audiences—a choreographic score passed from performer-hands to spectator-brains where it can resonate, spread, heal, or incite. Take a man who watches a performance art piece about fish.

The next day at lunch, the man raises his tuna sandwich for a bite, then stops, recalling something funny the performance artist said the night before. The man repeats the performer's lines to the other fellows at the table, pulls tuna out of his sandwich, and flicks it onto the floor. The man looks at the tuna on the floor while the other lunchers gape and think, hey, this guy's got some pretty bad manners. But there it is—tuna on the floor. The flicking was a beautiful act, a reproductive act, and transformative. How did it get into the man? Why, the performance artist put it there—the choreography, the instructions, the score; the man played them out, extending the performance in time and space until others fell in.

"I'm an Amazonian tree frog," I screeched, retreating behind tables. "A *Phyllomedusa vaillanti*, to be exact."

"PHYLLYO MY ASS!" screamed the trucker, flipping over a chair.

"The *Phyllomedusa vaillanti* is a green arboreal poison-dart frog, famous for its ability to secrete biologically active polyamino acids that are thousands of times more potent than pharmaceutical morphine," I sputtered. "Amazonian shamans of the Matsés tribes cut themselves and rub the poison into the wounds to induce digestive failure and accelerated heart rhythms, which are followed by spells of hyperawareness and hallucination. Would you like to experience a little hyperawareness right now?"

The trucker, still running in circles after me, was flabbergasted I'd managed to utter all of that while eluding him in figures of eight around the tables. "I'M GONNA WRING YOUR LITTLE NECK!" he roared.

I ran at him, crackers falling out of my pockets, jammed a finger down my throat, and sprayed poison-dart frog vomit all over his boots. He jumped back and screamed that I was crazy, then looked down—his boots were dripping soup and steak. He stared at them—he couldn't look away. "Ph-phyllo?" he mumbled. He was suddenly hyperaware as hell. I took a step toward him, but he retreated, shaking like he might cry. There was no way he was coming near me again, ever.

5

NIGHT FELL. I PLOPPED ONTO the couch, turned on the TV, and cracked open a bottle of vermouth.

The evening news came on. The top story was about Software International, a company downtown that produced a popular line of software products for Portalia. SI was facing an age discrimination lawsuit because it had refused to hire an elderly programmer.

I watched SI's CEO make a reconciliatory speech in front of shareholders. He said the company would revamp its hiring policies immediately so that hardworking programmers of every age would receive a fair shake. He said he knew the courts were watching—and they'd look favorably on SI if its hiring practices could be turned around.

I went to SI the next morning and applied for a programming job.

They called me in the following day. I was to interview with a Mr. Belly in the company's Portalia Applications Department. When word reached SI's CEO that an old-timer was coming in, he insisted on joining the interview too, much to Belly's chagrin.

We sat down at a conference room table. The CEO looked like a male model with his expensive suit, perfect white teeth, manicured nails, and hair so blue-black it looked like plastic.

Belly was thirty and quite possibly the fattest man I'd ever seen. His gut was so big that he couldn't push his chair up to the table—only his fingers reached. There wasn't much for them to do, so he just folded them over his breasts.

Belly read my résumé quietly to himself. His lips moved as he read. Spittle appeared at the corners of his mouth.

"So. Larry," said Belly. "I see here that you've done a lot of programming over the years—but what experience do you really have with Portalia?"

"Well," I said, "I've seen pictures of it. It looks fancy—"

Belly started to laugh. The CEO raised a finger, stopping him. Belly's mouth shut.

"Yes," said the CEO with all seriousness, "Portalia *is* fancy. That's why SI makes software for it. Bill Kunstler did it right."

"Bill Kunstler is a genius!" I squealed.

"Ah-ha! I see we've got ourselves a Bill Kunstler fan!" the CEO said.

"He's just so—"

"Inspiring?" said the CEO.

"Exactly," I said.

"You know," said the CEO, leaning in, his voice low, "he owns the majority share in SI."

"He—wait—Bill Kunstler?"

"Yes!"

"You mean . . . Bill Kunstler would be my boss?" I asked.

The CEO chuckled. "Well," he said, pausing to do some quick math on his fingers, "technically speaking, Kunstler would be your boss's boss's boss's boss's boss's boss's boss's boss's boss. But yes."

"Oh wow!" I yelped. "Oh wow. I feel like I almost know him already!"

The CEO laughed. "You know what, Larry?" he said. "I like your style. You're refined and mature. I understand you don't have any Portalia experience, but you know, we could pay to have you trained."

"Are you—really?" I said.

The CEO continued: "I think bringing someone aboard with solid legacy programming experience like yours, Larry, would be healthy for Software International's bottom line—not to mention inspiring for our younger programmers. Don't you think so, Belly?"

Belly nodded and flashed me a murderous smile.

"You're hired," said the CEO, rising. He walked over and threw open the conference room door. Reporters ran in and began taking pictures.

I took the opportunity to mention that Hank was also a "mature" programmer looking for work. The CEO smiled, shook my hand for the cameras, announced that Hank and I were both hired with full benefits, and commanded Belly to start us on Portalia training right away.

* * *

Hank and I stepped into SI's classroom on our first day of training. Ten rows of hard plastic seats faced the front of the room where a lectern, projector, and screen were set up. All of the seats were taken except for two in front. We shuffled toward them down the aisle, taking it slow like veterans.

The instructor came in. He couldn't have been a day over twenty. He marched to the front of the room, removed his suit jacket, rolled up his sleeves, and powered up the projector. The screen glowed white, then a picture of the SI building appeared with text underneath: PROGRAMMING PORTALIA BY KLAS. Klas gave his suspenders a smart snap and addressed the class in a guttural German accent:

"Hallo, mine name is Klas. Velcome to Portalia Programming 101. I vill be your instructor and here is vut you should know: I wrote my first program at age five, graduated from Harvard at twelve, and am now a multimillionaire, all of vhich means I am doing something right and vhatever I say goes."

Hank shifted around in his seat. "Here comes the bullshit," he whispered.

"Let us begin now," said Klas. "Who can tell me whose face this is?" He pressed a button on the projector. A slide of Bill Kunstler's face came up in full color. Somebody at the back of the room began clapping, then somebody else. Soon the whole room was applauding. Klas grinned and shook his fists like he'd just been elected president. People stood up. It was a standing ovation to the face, our boss, indoctrination to the hilt, though I had to admit the face was impressive. It filled the entire screen from top to bottom and from ten feet away we could see every wrinkle, every freckle, every mole. It was a facial map of failure and success, a flesh-topology of flagrant greed.

The room settled down. Klas began his lecture. It lasted four hours, then it was time for lab. Klas divided the class into teams and each was given a photocopy of the day's assignments.

We filed down a hall to the computer lab, which turned out to be a blindingly white meat locker of a room—ten feet by eighty, with shiny anti-static walls, buzzing florescent lights, and ceiling vents that whistled a steady torrent of frigid air. The room was filled with desks, and on each desk a computer sat waiting with Redsoft's Portalia logo displayed proudly on its screen.

We found a desk and got settled while Klas went around the room and helped each team write its first program.

"Hallo," he said when he came to us. "Your first assignment is to make a message pop up. It is very easy." Klas grabbed our computer's mouse and jerked it around, pushing little blocks around on the screen. Each block was a module that contained pre-packaged programming code from Redsoft. The trick was knowing what each module did; if you knew that, you could figure out how to arrange the blocks to form a program.

Klas clapped his hands when he was done. The program was finished, represented by a small stack of blocks. He clicked on a block to start the program running. A message appeared:

HELLO YOUR NAME IS FOOBAR.

Klas clapped his hands again.

Hank pointed to one of the blocks. "I don't understand this one," he said.

"That module controls the output," said Klas. "It makes the pop-up message appear."

"Yes, but how?"

"Vhat do you mean, 'how'?"

"How does it control the output?"

"I do not understand your question."

"This little block—it contains programming code?"

"Yes."

"May I see the code? You know, how it's written, how it works?"

"The module is made by Redsoft. You cannot open it. There is no need to open it. Vhy do you need to open it?"

"So I can look at the code inside—maybe even modify it."

"Vhy would you vant to modify it? It is designed so you cannot open it. Do not vorry about how it works—only vorry about what it does."

Klas erased the program from our computer with a click of the mouse and walked off.

Hank and I stared at the screen. Real programming was dead. Anyone with a mouse could program Portalia. Gone were the days when programmers could only type commands into their machines, clawing code from the folds of their brains, just them and the chips, forging order where there had been none before, arranging language into austere logic for the fullest effect, summoning courage to push the computer's speed and efficiency to their bloody limits. Gone was the poor man's classical rhetoric in the modern age, the dialogue in the computer's native tongue that had once called for a profoundly symbiotic understanding of the machine's heart, all murdered by Bill Kunstler's popularization of pre-fabbed modules. The art of coding had been reduced to simian assembly-line work.

I'd heard that the biggest problem with Portalia was that its pre-fabricated programming modules were, in the name of flexibility, stuffed with code for every conceivable use, making them cumbersome, slow, and unstable.

Rumor had it that when Redsoft needed a new module, it divided the labor between low-wage sweatshops in Singapore and India. Working in parallel, the overseas teams were given bonuses for finishing ahead of schedule, plus the low-stress benefit of Redsoft's black-box programming approach: it didn't matter how a piece of code worked, so long as it did. Bloated programming ran rampant; there was no incentive for programmers to painstakingly optimize a hundred lines of code down to thirty. Even worse, Redsoft's sea of non-disclosure policies forbade teams to communicate with each other, so they often duplicated each other's efforts, producing thousands of lines of redundant code, all of which found their way into Kunstler's best-selling programming modules.

Once the sweatshops were finished, their snippets of code were shipped back to Redsoft, where they were assembled into polished modules by the real slave labor: recently graduated Computer Science college majors who desperately wanted a piece of the computer industry's boom. Unmarried men were mostly hired for the job. These "Bachelors of Science," as Bill Kunstler called them, worked long hours at night when Redsoft's offices were otherwise dormant. Gangly and antisocial, saddled with staggering college debt, emasculated by genderless corporate politics, angry they weren't millionaires yet, and generally aimless with too much free time on their hands, they spent nights alone in their cubicles, pounding caffeine like water, riding their keyboards like jockeys, killing each other in video games, cussing over the office speakerphones, but most of all, fantasizing about sex.

They needed outlets. Sexual outlets. They were cooped up. Neophytes quickly discovered that night jobs didn't afford much opportunity for meeting women. Alone with their computers in their cubicles at three in the morning with their reflections staring back at them, they fantasized . . . consumed mass quantities of pornography . . . exchanged innuendos via electronic mail . . . masturbated in the restroom stalls. . . . They wanted to reach out, to spread out, to make contact with women—and preferably ones with breasts.

The Bachelors began hiding secret messages and pop-up surprises in the Redsoft modules that came across their desks. The hidden messages were designed to activate only if a user performed—entirely by chance—certain actions in sequence, such as typing a special word at a particular time of day, clicking on a certain part of the screen while printing, and so on. The module men competed against each other in games of one-upmanship to see who could produce the cleverest message.

At first it was only a hello with the Bachelor's phone number. Then it was bad poetry. Then someone had the idea of including a picture of his face. Someone else recorded his voice. Animation and video soon followed, all carefully squirreled away to be unleashed on unsuspecting users weeks, months, or years down the line—or maybe never.

Each man prayed his message would be discovered by a female who, moved by its content, would pick up the phone to learn more about its mysterious—and surely well-endowed—master. Known in the programming industry as "Easter eggs," these messages were, in the minds of their makers, seminal jewels capable of carrying forth to millions the Freudian mark of their creators—a teste-ment to a programmer's procreative virility that would be obvious to anyone with plumped lips and porno tits.

Since Portalia programs wouldn't run without Redsoft's modules, Hank and I were forced to include them in our code, which meant our programs would always be slow and inefficient. Our hands were tied.

Maybe we were wrong, I told Hank. Maybe computers had become so powerful that it didn't matter if the modules were bulky; maybe the machine's brains could chew through them just as fast, if not faster, than tighter code could have sprinted five years earlier.

My words gave Hank confidence. He took the mouse, pushed a block across the screen, and let go. The block snapped into place. It was, I had to admit, a little exciting; we'd just written our first piece of Portalia code.

"Do another one," I whispered.

Hank steadied himself, then began dragging another block, but this time, halfway through, the computer froze. What the hell? I pressed a key on the keyboard. The computer didn't respond. Hank wiggled the mouse. Nothing.

A Portalia message popped up:

YOU HAVE PERFORMED AN ILLEGAL ACTIVITY.

Hank spun around and looked for any sign of the cops, but there wasn't a badge anywhere. Other students were busy writing their programs. The air conditioner blew. Florescent lights buzzed. Apparently, no one had noticed our illegal activity, whatever it had been.

Hank raised his hand. Klas came over.

"Vhat did you do?" asked Klas.

"I don't know," said Hank. "I was moving the mouse—"

"This is an error message," said Klas, pointing at the incriminating text on our screen. "This means you did something BAD."

Before we could protest, Klas pressed our computer's reset button, sending the machine spinning into its reboot cycle and instantly wiping the work we'd begun. We'd have to start our program over.

"Maybe we just need a fresh start," I said.

Hank nodded.

The computer finished its startup cycle and the Portalia logo reappeared on the screen. Hank handed me the mouse. I dragged one of the blocks to the center of the screen. We held our breath. The machine didn't freeze. Everything was OK. I dragged some more. Blocks snapped into place. I gained confidence. Soon we were finished. There it was—our first Portalia program. We sighed with relief.

"Try it," Hank whispered.

I clicked a command to start our new program running. The computer's disk drive clacked and whirred, then a message appeared:

ERROR: OUT OF MEMORY

The computer froze. I raised my hand. Klas came over.

"What is this 'out of memory'?" I asked.

"I can't remember," joked Klas. He pressed our computer's reset button.

"Shit," said Hank.

It was going to be a long night.

* * *

I opened my eyes. We'd fallen asleep in the lab. My head was on the keyboard. I sat up. Hank was snoring on the floor. The other students had left. I shivered—the room was freezing. I looked at the clock—seven a.m. I checked the computer and saw we'd finished all of the programs in our first assignment. I woke Hank and we grabbed some breakfast.

We returned to the classroom for the second day's four-hour lecture, then headed to the lab with a new list of assignments. It was a repeat of the day before. Portalia crashed. Klas ridiculed us in front of the class. We worked through the night, fell asleep in the lab, then it was back to the classroom the next morning.

We were zombies by Friday. We slept through the weekend, then started the training cycle all over again on Monday.

Weeks passed. Our computer continued crashing. It wasn't uncommon for it to crash five or ten times per day. Some days it crashed hourly. The morphology of each crash varied. There was the random-gibberish-spew-ing-across-the-screen crash, the flickering-display-just-before-the-machine-freezes-up crash, the sudden-restart-without-warning crash, and countless others. Sometimes the crashings ordered themselves in serial or simultaneous combinations for variety: gibberish, then flicker . . . flicker-freeze . . . gibberish-flicker-freeze-restart. . . .

Klas accused us of causing the crashes. He said our programming was obviously crap, and we started to believe him. He told us to study our programs harder, and we did, combing them for anything that might make the computer halt. We found nothing, yet the crashing went on. Klas took to kneeling during lab to pray for us, begging the Lord to crash-proof our coding, and if that was impossible, then to at least have mercy on the users of the programs we wrote.

We studied the crashings. We became crashologists. We discovered that our machine crashed a lot while we were programming, but Portalia crashed a lot when we weren't programming, too. Sometimes it crashed while the computer was starting up or shutting down. Sometimes it crashed while we typed or moved the mouse. Sometimes it crashed when we weren't doing anything at all.

We developed superstitions and compulsive tics. Don't touch anything until the computer has started up. Don't type too fast. Knock on the desk before rebooting. Lick your finger before inserting a disk. No triple-clicking. Don't breathe on the screen. No coffee on Wednesdays.

We invented sick games. Who would predict the next crash? How would it go? A freeze-up? A gibberish-reboot? Would it take the computer's hard drive with it or bring down the network? Would it be a big bang or an insidious memory leak that slowly propagated through the chips, quietly corrupting files as it went, a one becoming a zero, a spreading cancellation, a cancer growing black with random data from the inside out?

The training lasted eight weeks, during which Klas took every opportunity to flash Bill Kunstler's face on the projection screen. People gave a standing ovation every time, but Hank and I would have none of it. We sneered at the face. It was the face indirectly responsible for the sleepless nights, the hard plastic chairs, the fading of our careers, and the new generation of programmers who knew nothing about the computers they programmed.

Klas held a little graduation ceremony on the last day of class. "You are all now Portalia programmers!" he said. "Vell . . . some of you more than others." He gestured to me and Hank. The class laughed.

Each student received a certificate of completion with Bill Kunstler's face on it.

Hank and I took ours to the restroom and put them to good use.

6

THE WEEKEND ARRIVED. I LEFT my apartment and started the walk uphill to my favorite liquor store a few blocks away.

The hot June sun beat down on my neck. I passed a herd of tourists struggling up the hill. Tourists were easy to spot. We locals had technique—we pushed forward with our hips, heads down, arms pumping, while the tourists grazed, aimless, flat-footed, and upright, like cattle.

The hill grew steeper. My knees clicked and popped. I pumped harder. My thighs burned. I squatted low and marched bow-legged like a Sisyphean midget pushing a boulder. Sweat ran into my eyes. I cursed the local rags that called San Francisco a pedestrian-friendly town—a Paris or New York where a flâneur with a good pair of shoes could supposedly uncover tucked-away alley shops, little espresso cafes, walk-up automatiques serving tomato panini encrusted with brie....

Sometimes the comparisons were accurate—mostly in late summer when warm breezes turned Market Street into our own Champs Elysées. Pubs barbecued steaks outdoors and drew cold beer from wooden kegs. Hookers giggled and flirted on the sidewalks. Ex-cons played checkers on makeshift tables. Office workers streamed out of high-rises in search of two-hour lunches. Parades and political demonstrations marched to wild applause. High-class women clacked along in high heels and short skirts. Children ran around with ice-cream cones. Card sharks and grifters ran Monte games on card tables at a dollar per hit. Sideshow performers contorted for donations. Tourists stood in line for a trip on a cable car bound for the wharf. Grizzled hobos drank and sang bawdy Barbary Coast songs about all the old San Francisco names: Lotta Crabtree, Luisa Tetrazzini. . . .

But winter was a different story. In winter all of the Baudelairean flâneur shit went right out the window. Flowers died. Animals died. People died. There were actual carcasses—winter rains washed them out of alleys and down the hills. Pigeons, cats, rats, and the occasional bum floated down to Market Street. You couldn't go three blocks in February without seeing a taxidermist picking through the freebies.

Of all the San Francisco places to be in winter, Market Street was the worst. Rainwater left the streets and cable car tracks lethally slick. Mud slid down into intersections from surrounding hills. Waterlogged drunks gurgled for pennies. Cigarette smoke choked the air. Umbrellas jabbed at eyes. Steaming throngs of human misery packed the sidewalks. High-rises blocked out what little sun there was. Pedestrians splashed through puddles six inches deep and flattened drowning flora under their boots. Taxis skidded around corners mere inches from sopping tourists. Tires spun. Water sprayed. Drains clogged. Traffic cops globbed around knee-deep in sludge to direct traffic lanes into converging patterns of honking gridlock. And don't forget the wind . . . winter weathermen gave two wind forecasts: one for the city at large and another for Market, where gusts howled twenty knots faster, rains went horizontal, umbrellas flipped inside-out, exhaust and particulate carcinogens swirled into babies' mouths. It was insidious. Criminal. In winter on Market even Baudelaire slips and falls splay-legged, breaking his hip as his cane shoots out into traffic and gutter water races up his pants.

I reached the top of the hill. A frigid wind blew.

I looked east. I could see the high-rises downtown. SI stood among them, glinting in the sunlight.

I shivered. It might have been June, but I felt a cold winter coming.

7

I **REPORTED TO WORK ON** Monday. Hank called in sick.

I found Belly's cubicle and said hello.

Belly dropped a hefty stack of paper in front of me. "These are your programming assignments," he barked. "They're due Friday. Get to work."

I flipped through the stack. It was eight inches thick.

"There are a lot of assignments in here," I said. "Do you think Friday's a reasonable—"

Belly leaned forward. "Shut up. I've worked here a long time and I'm not about to take any crap from old timers."

I swallowed and looked at the stack. "Which of these should I do first?"

"The VPPs."

"VPPs?"

"Vital Programming Projects." Belly grabbed the top page from the stack and held it up so I could see. The letters VPP were stamped on it in red. "VPPs have priority," he said. "As long as there's a VPP on your desk, you don't get breaks. You don't get vacation time. You don't get anything . . . except get it done."

I lifted the stack. It was heavy.

"My God. How many VPPs are in here?" I asked.

"They're all VPPs."

I left Belly and went in search of my cubicle. SI's windowless building was a half mile long in a straight line. Rows of cubicles ran from one end of the office to the other. Each row had a number, as did each cubicle in each row. I passed row after row. All of the cubes were the same—three carpeted walls with a regulation desk, chair, computer, phone, filing cabinet, and garbage can.

A worker looked up at me as I passed. He seemed startled at the presence of another human so close, then relieved when I didn't stop to say hello.

Some cubes were decorated. I saw gold-framed photos of loved ones . . . calendars with pictures of kittens, dogs, and birds . . . stuffed animals . . . baseball caps . . . action figures straining in battle . . . stained coffee mugs bearing slogans like IF YOU HAVE TO ASK, DON'T. . . .

I found our row. It had five cubicles. I walked along them. Each was identical to the last, and all were unassigned—Belly had put me and Hank in a row by ourselves.

The last cube in the row was mine: number 1070. I set my VPPs down on the desk, flopped into my chair, and tried phoning Hank. He didn't answer.

I slid open my desk drawer. The previous occupant had left behind a single black marker. The ink was still good. I wrote my cubicle's number across my palm so I'd remember it, then left my cube and went in search of the restroom. There was a framed map of the office on a wall. I looked at it and saw the men's room was at the other end of the building—a full half mile away.

I began walking down the building's central aisle. When I'd passed ten rows of cubicles, a man came into view at the aisle's far end. He was walking in my direction. I wondered if he was on his way to a cubicle near him, or if he'd walk straight toward me long enough for us to pass. I couldn't see his face, but I thought he might be watching me watching him and wondering the same thing—whether I might turn and vanish down an aisle, never to be seen by him again.

The man was closer now—just a quarter mile away. I could almost see his face. He seemed to be looking at the path where his trajectory would take him, but not at me, as if I wasn't there at all. I wondered if he was self-conscious about our approaching. The more I thought about it, the more self-conscious I became. Was I supposed to look at him? And if I did, would he think I was staring? Should I look down at the carpet instead?

The man and I grew closer. He continued staring straight ahead. My throat went dry. What was wrong with him? Was he drunk? Was he high? My eyes darted between him and my own trajectory. It was a real timing problem. If I caught his eye too early, I'd have to smile or nod or say hello early, then hold it until we passed, grinning like an idiot. If I eyed him too late, I might miss the opportunity to say hello if he said it first, and then I'd appear nervous.

At thirty feet I could see he was young. Maybe twenty-five. And muscular. What if he was aggressive? What if he decided to start a fight? I tried to relax. It was better not to put him on guard. My arms felt stiff. Were they swinging unnaturally? I tried to time them so they'd look casual. Look at me walking... I haven't a care in the world! Here I am, just strolling along. I walk this hall every day; how about you, pal? I haven't seen you around here before. Welcome to my building, fucker!

At twenty feet I couldn't take it anymore. My paranoia was ridiculous. I decided to take it on the jaw. If he started something, so be it—I'd clamp down on him like a chimp and bite his damned nose off! I burrowed my gaze into him. I looked him up and down, his hair, his face, his shirt. He might think me gay, but never mind; I couldn't take the tension any longer. Come on, look at me, you nervous twit!

He was ten feet away. Couldn't he see me? Was he blind? I screamed out in my brain as loud as I could: IF YOU CAN READ MINDS, LOOK AT ME! I'M SENDING YOU A MESSAGE! YOU LOOK LIKE A FOOL, STARING STRAIGHT AHEAD LIKE THAT! LOOK AT HOW NATURALLY I AM WALKING!

At five feet, still nothing.

At two feet, his eyes moved. He saw me. "Hello," he said elegantly without mussing his stride. I nearly tripped as I tried to return the salutation—I moved air but my lips stuck together as the sound came, mumbled and drowsy as we passed:

"Hellufhh."

I glanced over my shoulder and saw the man continue his trek away down the aisle to Lord knew where, maybe to circle the earth, while I stumbled on with my lips caked with spit. I started to sweat at the thought of it, that this stranger would think me a total idiot . . . to him I was just some old bastard who probably couldn't control his bowels, maybe some employee's senile father . . . and what if he was a manager? He'd think I was totally incompetent! Sweat poured down my face. Here I was, a veteran PERFOR-MANCE ARTIST, purveyor of all things experimental in front of live audiences more numerous than the hairs on my head, and I was sweating over a single word fumbled to a total stranger who probably couldn't care less if he never laid eyes on me again.

I entered the restroom, locked myself in a stall, and sat down. I grabbed some toilet paper and wiped my forehead before noticing the floor was a repeating tile pattern of the SI logo:

SISISISISISISISISISISISISISISISI

The letters made me dizzy. I steadied myself against the stall wall, spat on the floor, stood up weakly, flushed the pot, and got the hell out of there.

* * *

I returned to my cubicle to find a short man puffing on a pipe and typing furiously on my keyboard. He had disheveled white hair and a frail, malnourished build. A cardboard box filled with computer disks sat on his lap.

I said hello and he jumped, spilling his box of disks all over the carpet. He smiled and stuck out a hand. "Well, hello," he said, puffs of cherry-scented smoke floating out of his mouth. "I'm Rudy, SI's head programmer. I'm just installing some software on your machine. I'll be out of your hair in two shakes."

Rudy crouched and began gathering up his disks. I studied him. He was a salty little dog with tobacco-stained fingers, a grimy SI polo shirt, and tattered deck shoes. Something about him seemed familiar.

"I didn't know we're allowed smoke in here," I said.

"Oh, we're not—it's strictly forbidden," said Rudy with a wink and a mock elbow to invisible ribs.

"How long have you worked at SI?"

"Five years," he said.

"And before that?"

"Here, there. I've been a programmer forever," said Rudy, smiling.

That was it—of course. Something passed between us—familiarity, maybe, like a wife in flannel and curlers after thirty years of marriage—and then I felt it, our secret handshake, revealed as software code in my head as sure as anything:

```
if (

        HeIsProgrammer and
        IsOverForty and
        IsntManagement and
        ProbablyDrinks

)


then

        MutualTrustEnabled = TRUE
```

I gave a slow nod to indicate I understood. Rudy nodded back, then put his finger to his lips and looked up at the ceiling. It was a signal to be careful—the office had ears.

"Well, it was nice meeting you," said Rudy, standing. "I'll see you around."

He picked up his cardboard box and made to leave.

I noticed the stack of VPPs I'd left on my desk was gone.

"Did you see some papers on my desk?" I asked.

"Oh, sure. A facility engineer came by a few minutes ago."

"Facility engineer?"

"Janitor. He put them away in your filing cabinet."

I opened my cabinet. There were the VPPs, neatly stacked.

"You're not supposed to leave anything on your desk when you walk away from your cubicle," said Rudy. "The first time you leave something out, the engineers will put it away for you. The second time, they'll throw it away. You'll get used to it." He started off, then came back, pulled a wall calendar out of his cardboard box, and handed it to me. "I almost forgot—here's your free gift from Redsoft. It's a ten dollar value!"

"Thanks," I said.

"Do you have a pen?" Rudy whispered.

I opened my desk drawer and showed him my fat black marker.

"Good," said Rudy, walking away. "You'll need it for December."

I opened the calendar. January featured a picture of Redsoft's head-quarters.

February showed a photo of Redsoft's products.

I flipped to December. There was Bill Kunstler, grinning in a Santa suit at a Las Vegas computer trade show and flanked by an army of elf-eared porn actresses in red thong bikinis.

I pinned the calendar to my cubicle wall, took up the marker, and went to work.

8

HANK SHOWED UP TO WORK the next morning. He took the empty cubicle just over the wall in front of mine, dropped his VPP stack onto his new desk, and came over. He peered over the tops of the cubes, saw nobody was around, ducked low, pulled a bottle of wine out from under his shirt, and took a swig.

"Belly reamed me for missing work yesterday," he said, wiping wine off his chin. "You should see my VPP stack. It's huge."

Hank noticed the Redsoft calendar on my wall. It was open to December. Santa Bill's head was unrecognizable—I'd scribbled it out with angry black marker.

Hank studied the inky mess.

"Is it . . . Santa's head on fire?" he guessed.

I shook my head.

"Is it cancer? A tumor?"

"Closer."

"Is it . . . Bill Kunstler?"

"You're perceptive for a morning drunk," I said.

Hank surveyed my desk. It was bare except for my keyboard and the stack of VPPs.

"I've never seen a desk so clean," he said, guzzling vino.

I told him the story about Rudy, the facility engineers, and SI's clean-desk policy.

"You're telling me that if I leave even a single piece of paper on my desk, a facility engineer will run over here and put it away in my drawer?" asked Hank.

"That's what I'm saying."

"I don't believe you."

We went to Hank's cube. He positioned his VPP stack squarely in the middle of his desk and we went off to the men's room.

When we came back, the VPPs were gone.

Hank opened his filing cabinet. The VPPs were inside, neatly stacked.

"This is crazy!" he said. "Let's try it again with something else!"

Hank went away, then returned a minute later with a garbage can from the breakroom. He dumped the trash onto his desk. Banana peels, coffee grounds, burger wrappers, milk cartons, cola cans, and a Styrofoam container of wet Chinese noodles slopped into a runny mound. We snickered, left the mess behind, and went for coffee. When we came back, the garbage was gone—even the milk had been wiped up.

"They're not supposed to throw anything away the first time," I said, "so that slop should still be around here."

Hank opened his filing cabinet's top drawer and there they were— milk cartons, banana peels, and even the noodles, all neatly packed into a plastic bag. I opened the bag and dumped the contents back onto Hank's desk. We left for another round of coffee. When we came back, everything was gone from the cube—it had vanished completely, every last drop.

"How do they know when we leave?" asked Hank.

"Maybe they patrol the aisles."

"Impossible," said Hank. "We'd see them. Maybe they have us bugged?"

"Or cameras, maybe," I said. "I wouldn't put anything past Belly."

Hank searched his cubicle. "I don't see cameras."

"I bet they're up there," I whispered, pointing at the ceiling.

Hank climbed up onto his desk, then froze. His legs were shaking.

"What's wrong?" I asked.

"I don't like heights," he whispered.

"You're already up there," I said. "Just take a quick look."

The ceiling was a patchwork of acoustical tiles. Hank bumped one of the tiles upward and pushed it back, revealing a dark crawl space above. He stood on the wall of his cube and raised his head up into the black.

"Nothing," he said. "Just air conditioning ducts." He stepped off the cubicle wall and back down onto his desk, then stopped.

"What is it?" I asked.

Hank didn't answer. He was staring over his cubicle's wall at something off in the distance.

I scrambled up onto his desk and looked. A sea of five hundred cubicles stretched out before us as far as we could see. There was movement everywhere—workers typing, stretching, staring off into space, sauntering down aisles in search of copiers or shredders or coffee. It was teeming and repulsive in the way that vermin packed into a tight space are repulsive: swarms of ants, of flies, of rats, flocks of dirty pigeons rising and falling, eating, shitting, spitting up . . . we were all of that and more.

We climbed down from Hank's desk and never went up there again.

* * *

We went to work on Belly's VPP stacks. Portalia crashed repeatedly, but we gritted our teeth and pressed on, programming one assignment after the next, eager to beat Belly or die trying.

We slowly settled into a routine. The office became familiar. Even the long haul to the men's room ceased to be intimidating. We walked it like everyone else—mute, with our eyes locked straight ahead on infinity. I was an island. My co-workers did not exist and it was mutual—they ignored me right back.

By Wednesday we were beat; we'd worked until midnight the night before. We guzzled coffee and dragged our mice around like crazy. Without sunlight it was impossible to tell if it was day or night. The clocks on the office walls were battery powered and unreliable, so we told the time by our computers' clocks. Portalia told us when to work, break, eat, and sleep—we were running on Redsoft time.

Thursday came. We slaved bleary-eyed over the diminishing VPP stacks, ate soggy vending-machine sandwiches at our desks, and squinted under the florescent lights.

Belly made a surprise appearance in the afternoon. He watched Hank awhile, then looked in on me. A minute passed. I felt him burning a hole in my head. I dropped my mouse, turned, and looked at him.

"Yes?" I asked.

"What are you doing?" he asked.

"What are YOU doing?"

He motioned for me to get back to work. I didn't move.

"Work," he said.

I flared my nostrils.

Belly waddled into my cube. "Why are you looking at me? You should be looking at THIS!" he hissed, mashing his fat hand onto my keyboard. Letters flew across my screen and obliterated the program I'd been coding.

Belly laughed and walked off. I was too tired to fight.

* * *

Friday came. Our VPPs were due. We dragged, clicked, and typed as fast as we could. We didn't answer the phone. We skipped lunch. We held our bowels.

We finished around four p.m. I couldn't believe we'd beaten Belly and lived to see a weekend. Hank and I met up in the aisle. How we'd celebrate! We drank a little coffee and razzed each other . . . contributing honey to SI's swarm felt good. Maybe Portalia programming wasn't such a bad gig after all.

Sitting at his desk a half mile away, Belly began verifying our work over SI's computer network at five o'clock sharp. We watched as he checked each program we'd written, one by one. He was probably surprised that we'd finished our impossible workload on time, and when he saw that our programs ran perfectly, he'd have no choice but to offer us a little recognition, a token, a congratulatory remark. . . . How would it come? By phone call? Electronic mail? Maybe he'd stop by to harass us in person. His capitulation would be subtle—something to let us know we'd done well, that we'd been accepted into his fold, that he'd gained confidence in us, that we'd made him look good, and, though we'd never see eye-to-eye, that maybe old-time programmers weren't useless hacks after all.

We waited. Two hours passed. No word came.

We decided to seek comfort in a few pitchers of beer at a local pizza joint. We packed up our belongings and readied to head out for two well-earned days of relaxation.

We stepped out of our cubicles. SI's postman was heading toward us. Hank and I beamed. Here it was! We were going to get it—congratulations at last!

The postman was pushing a hand cart with two enormous reams of paper on it. He rolled up to Hank's cube and stopped.

"I'm the postman. Are you Hank?"

"I sure am!" said Hank.

"Here are your new VPPs," said the postman, pointing to a ream. "They're due in two weeks." Hank stared at the stack. It was three feet high.

"You're joking," said Hank.

"I just deliver 'em," said the postman. He dropped the stack onto Hank's desk, then looked at me.

"You Larry?"

"No."

"Bullshit."

"All right."

"Thought so."

He lifted the other stack from the cart and dropped it onto my desk with a thud.

"Asshole," I said.

The postman flipped me the bird and pushed his cart away down the aisle.

Hank's eyes were red. "This is bullshit," he whispered.

"Calm down," I said. "You know this is just what Belly wants, to wind us up—"

"He's not going to break me!" Hank hissed. He walked to his cube, sat down, and started on his new stack.

I fell into my chair.

My phone rang.

"Hello?" I answered weakly.

"Larry Frommer?"

"Yes."

"Hello, my name's Dick Jenkins—I ran into Hank earlier this week and he gave me your work number. Say, I own a small art gallery in the Tenderloin where I'm holding a reception for a local painter, and I wondered if you two might like to do a little performance art beforehand in our lobby. I saw your work a while back and—"

Dick's speech went on. A performance. It was something about a performance. Hank and I hadn't done a performance in weeks. Or was it months? I eyed my VPPs.

"And best of all," Dick continued, "we have a budget. We can pay! The painter is Wolfe Henderson—maybe you've heard of him?"

Pay. Dick was willing to pay us . . . in money.

"Did you hear that?" I muttered, covering the phone. "Dick Jenkins wants to pay us."

"Pay us for what?" came Hank's voice over the cube wall.

"For a performance," I said. "He has a gallery opening coming up."

"A performance?" asked Hank.

"Performance art," I said.

"I don't remember what that is."

Hank's words hung in the air. The VPPs stared at me. My wretched bones sagged.

"So, what do you say?" asked the voice on the phone, tender like a devoted lover in bloom, unaware I was about to send her away.

"We just don't have the time," I said softly before hanging up.

9

MONDAY WE DRAGGED OURSELVES INTO the office and tore into our VPPs. I had no idea how we'd finish them in two weeks. There were constant interruptions. Sherry called Hank just to yell at him. The CEO came by with his entourage of photographers. Portalia crashed. By the time I looked at the clock it was already six in the evening and we'd only finished a handful of assignments.

Tuesday came. We worked nonstop. Hank's fingers bled. I took two breaks: one to eat a burrito from the breakroom vending machine, and another to set it free.

As I left the restroom, I passed a group of workers gathered around a pompous executive named Maurine. She and her millionaire husband had just returned from the Caribbean.

"Oh, you wouldn't believe how lovely St. Thomas is this time of year," she told the crowd. "So lush . . . so exclusive. My husband Charles and I toured it from end to end on horseback, then chartered a boat. You simply MUST charter if you plan to fish. The yellow fin were jumping like mad. We used hundred-pound line and nabbed six forty-pounders in thirty minutes. I'm not kidding. The secret? Never let your captain troll faster than four knots. Do ten in a swell and you'll be dribbling champagne on your cardigan."

I ran to my cube and threw up into my trash can. Hank offered me a mint.

We went back to work. I programmed until I couldn't keep my eyes open anymore. I looked at the clock. It was two in the morning. I crawled under my desk to sleep. My dreams were punctuated by facility engineers collecting trash from two until three, vacuuming from three to five, then window washing and dusting until seven.

I don't remember when we stopped showering; it could have been Friday—or maybe Saturday. By then we were sleeping at the office every night. I hadn't changed my underwear in days.

* * *

One afternoon a skinny young man in sandals, a nose ring, and a Redsoft T-shirt walked past us sipping fancy espresso from a tiny cup. I'd seen him around—he was a new employee. People called him Spreadsheet.

"Welcome aboard," I said with a smile. "You're new, right?"

Spreadsheet sniffed. Apparently, I'd interrupted his delicate coffee business.

"I'm hardly new," he said. "I've been programming for two years."

"Impossible," laughed Hank. "How old are you? Eighteen?"

"What kind of programming is it you do, exactly?" I asked.

"I'm a spreadsheet programmer."

Hank and I laughed.

"How do you program a spreadsheet?" I asked.

"I put the numbers in there."

"That's not programming," said Hank. "It's data entry."

"No, it's not," Spreadsheet said.

"You're a secretary!" Hank snarled.

"Call me what you want, Gramps, but I bet I have more stock options than you two."

Hank and I looked at each other.

We didn't have stock options.

Hank clenched his fists. I had to hold him back.

Spreadsheet strolled off down the aisle, stirring his espresso.

* * *

The months passed. Belly was convinced that we were up to no good, so he made Rudy install Redsoft's dreaded Megamonitore on our computers. The monitoring software recorded every program we ran, every click of the mouse . . . Megamonitore got it all.

Megamonitore displayed a bloodshot 3D eyeball in the lower right-hand corner of our computer screens to remind us it was watching, and thanks to a bug in the programming, it twitched whenever we pressed a key; the faster we typed, the faster it twitched. It was unnerving. The eyeball monitored us day and night for illegal moves, contraband, foul language, porn, terrorist manifestoes, and who knew what else. For fun Hank and I began sprinkling our electronic mail with inflammatory words we thought might trigger the software's alarms: Redsoft, SI, Belly, loudmouth, blubber, stoolie, rat, sneak, prank, sedition, coup, donkey show. . . .

I covered the eyeball with a piece of duct tape. I knew it was still under there, twitching, but at least I wouldn't have to look at it.

Belly spotted the tape, peeled it off my screen, and told me never to do that again.

The eyeball was back.

* * *

Portalia crashed hard.

I dialed Belly's phone number.

"It crashed again," I said.

"Call Redsoft," Belly hissed.

I cringed. Redsoft support technicians were trained to deny that Portalia had any faults.

I dialed Redsoft. A male voice answered.

"Redsoft Programmer Hotline. How may I help you?"

"Hi, I'm a programmer at Software International."

"Yes?"

"I'm trying to write a program with a code module we bought from you, but it crashes every time I use it."

"May I have the module's serial number, please?"

"I don't have a serial number."

"Of course you do."

"No—really. I don't."

"You must've received one when you bought the module."

"My boss bought it and he didn't say anything about a serial number."

"I'm not authorized to help you unless you have a valid serial number."

"I don't understand. This call is costing sixty dollars—isn't that enough?"

"I can't help you without that serial number."

"How about this: one-two-three-four-five."

"Thank you very much, sir. Now, how may I help you?"

"What? I just made that serial number up!"

"That's fine with me, sir."

"Oh my God—"

"How may I help you?"

"I told you: your module is crashing Portalia."

"I find that hard to believe."

"Believe it."

"I guarantee our module is a hundred percent stable."

"How do you even know which module I'm talking about?"

"I . . . well . . . which module are you using?"

"Your database module for Portalia, version two."

"That module is perfectly stable. No other customers have reported any problems."

"If I run my program WITHOUT your module, the program runs fine. As soon as I use your module, my computer crashes."

"Your program probably has a bug."

"What kind of bug?"

"I don't know, sir. I'm not a programmer."

"But this is the Redsoft Programmer Hotline."

"Yes, but none of us are programmers."

I hit myself in the forehead. "Let me talk to one of your senior technicians."

"Sure."

I waited. Ten seconds passed. Nothing happened at the other end.

"Well?" I asked.

"That would be me, sir. I'm the senior technician."

"GET A PROGRAMMER ON THE LINE RIGHT NOW! I WANT A PROGRAMMER FOR MY SIXTY BUCKS!"

The technician put me on hold.

Fifteen minutes passed, then a new voice came on.

"Hi, I'm a programmer. What's your question?"

"It's about your database module for Portalia—"

"What about it?"

"It crashes whenever I try to use it."

"Really? Sounds like your program must have a bug. Ha ha ha."

"My program is fine—"

"What kind of crash are you experiencing? Do you see an error message?"

"Yes. Portalia gives me error forty-seven. It says the module is causing a memory overflow."

"Our module is causing the overflow?"

"Yes. YOUR module. Overflow."

"That's error message number forty-seven? Overflow? Portalia says that our module causes it? Error forty-seven comes up?"

"YES! ERROR FORTY-SEVEN! YOUR MODULE!"

"Interesting."

"Exactly. It sounds like your module is the one with the bug now, doesn't it?"

"I wouldn't call it a bug."

"What would you call it?"

"I'd call it a feature."

"Crashing isn't a feature."

"Sure it is . . . because . . . look at it this way: if our module crashes when the memory overflows, that's a good thing—a crash prevents the memory from overflowing even more."

"But your module's causing the overflow in the first place."

"Yes, but by crashing, it keeps the overflow from getting out of hand; too much overflow would be bad, don't you think?"

I hung up the phone before I murdered somebody.

10

IT WAS A FRIDAY NIGHT. Hank and I were sick of work. We decided to hit the town for a little performance art.

We left the office and walked ten blocks to the Tenderloin. The old neighborhood was becoming a ghost town. Half of the performance art galleries had been boarded up or replaced by liquor stores and massage parlors.

We stopped for drinks at a pool hall at Sutter and Polk, an intersection famous for the male transvestite hookers who strutted the sidewalks in fishnet stockings, short leather skirts, and Bette Davis make-up.

We ordered a few drinks, then a few more. Hank began swinging a pool cue and yelling something about being a Rolling Stones Hell's Angel. I fell on the floor, laughing. The bartender threatened to call the cops, so we stumbled out of there and headed for another bar.

A deep voice yelled after us. We turned around and saw Fredina Sooterkin, a performance art groupie and homeless transvestite hooker wearing a blue bra, a silver metallic skirt, and a fake pregnant belly. She wasn't the best-looking broad that a john could get with her bare feet, toothless mouth, and bushy mustache, but what she lacked in looks she made up for with gummy libidinal verve.

"Well, if it isn't the performance art twins!" she gummed, hugging us both.

"You smell like the sewer," slurred Hank.

"Well, where do you think I've been sleeping, honey? And you don't exactly smell like scrubbed cock." She paddled Hank's can and he laughed his head off.

"So," Fredina said, "where you two been off to?"

"Working," I said.

"You mean performance art?"

"No—we had to get jobs."

Fredina clamped her hands over her ears, screamed, and ran around in little circles, her bare feet slapping. "I don't want to hear it!" she screamed. "You sell-outs! I thought you two were for real!"

"We didn't sell out!" said Hank. "The whole neighborhood sold out! There's not a lick of performance art anywhere! Nothing!"

"Well, what do you expect?" said Fredina. "You two weren't around to keep it going. The excitement died down. Nobody can afford to do anything anymore. Everybody's gone. Highball and Billy went to Seattle. Looty and Farmer went to Los Angeles. Fat Joe and Pillsfarm are dead, and believe me, honey, you don't want to know how. As far as I know, you're the only two left. You're extant, baby, and you know what that means: the last ones, the prequel to the sequel. And by the way, Larry," she finished, pointing at my feet, "do you want those shoes?"

Fredina's words sank in. Extant. The last ones. I untied my shoes and handed them over. Fredina put them on. They clashed with her silver skirt, but at least they were something. We said goodbye so she could get back to hustling.

Hank and I strolled on. All of the neighborhood's old haunts were closed. How long had we been gone? Was it just months? It felt like years. I tried to catch my reflection in a dim storefront window but it was too dark.

We gave up looking for some action. The night was over. Seeing how the weekend was shaping up to be worthless, we headed back downtown to SI. Maybe we'd get some VPPs done.

My bare feet were cold the whole way over.

* * *

Hank and I started taking coffee breaks to keep our stamina up. The breakroom was bright with florescent lighting and warm from the coffeemaker. There was a refrigerator, a microwave, a sink, a table, and a vending machine dispensing sandwiches, burritos, cola, candy, and gum. Hank and I talked on occasion, but more often we stood in silence, staring at the ceiling or the floor or the company bulletin boards that were plastered with posters detailing minimum wage rules, health and safety laws, recycling tips, and notices of upcoming Redsoft seminars. It was a place of solace and recovery, a demilitarized zone where even Belly in his worst mood wouldn't think of trying to rattle us.

Sometimes other programmers ambled in to socialize with each other. They were a sorry bunch of physical extremes—either grossly overweight with sleep apnea or skeletal with terrible acne. There were the incessant stutterers, the ones who smelled like shit, the ones with teeth brown from too much cola, the unwashed shirt club with the fast-food grease stains. . . . We listened to them make small talk amongst themselves, yapping on with mind-numbing prattle:

> "Have you seen Belly lately?"
> "No, why?"
> "I think he's getting fatter."
> "Really? You think so? Heh heh heh."

> "Hey. The coffee here is really bland."
> "You're telling me."

"Have you tried the stuff across the street?"

"No. Why? You know something I don't?"

"It's stronger."

"Really?"

"A LOT stronger."

"Hey—thanks, pal. I'll give it a try."

"Did you see the game last night?"

"What game?"

"You know—the game."

"Oh. The game. No. Why? Who won?"

"We did."

"Oh . . . well . . . good!"

"Have you been in the men's room today?"

"No. Why?"

"There's a real log in there—first stall on the left."

"Really? I have to use the crapper right now. I'll be sure to have a look at that floater!"

Breaktime always ended with mumbled goodbyes all around and a slow somnambulist walk back to our fluorescently lit cubes, unsure of what day it was, sliding past co-workers as they slid past us, our minds idling, eyes straight ahead, plodding through recycled air, dragging our feet, cubicle aisle after cubicle aisle, bad coffee filling our gray heads with nausea as we grew increasingly, brutally bored.

One day I asked Hank if he thought boredom was dangerous.

"Sure," he said, biting down on a cold, brown, shrink-wrapped, oxygen-starved taco freshly birthed from the vending machine. Grease ran down his chin. "It can be. It can make people destructive. Look at the Communists. They're bored stiff. The government takes away all of their creative outlets. Oh sure, the neo-Marxists might rally for some fairy State-sponsored art because it arouses a new need—simulating Marxism's self-feeding cycle of production, synthesis, and revolution on a microcosmic scale—but in the end, creativity that serves no utilitarian purpose is crushed. Everyone over there wears gray. Everyone owns the same clothing. Everyone eats the same slice of bread for dinner. That's utopia? Ha! They're all cogs bored out of their minds! Too dazed to revolt! Hopeless!"

Hank went on: "I went into a Communist bar once. A real USSR bar. I sat down. Everyone was bored. There was no music playing. No TV. No radio. Flies buzzed in the air. The people were going crazy. You could see it in their eyes. Even their beers were flat. It was a dangerous scene. Then, with zero fanfare, a little man named Oleg stood up, walked over, and broke his beer bottle over my head. He was standing over me when I woke up, all five feet of him, with no expression whatsoever—I mean, his face was totally blank. He wanted me to hit him, give him a run for his money, maybe even kill him. When I saw that blank face, I just stood up, walked back to my barstool, and ordered him a new beer. I knew he didn't have anything against me personally, and he sure hadn't been looking to spill his drink. I was just there. I was something to do—entertainment—a little relief for everyone in that joint. I'm sure all of them went home that night and told their wives how crazy Oleg had cracked an American in the head. It was something to talk about. They probably theorized for hours over why I hadn't retaliated, or whether the Americans were getting soft, or if I'd suffered a concussion. They probably talked about it for weeks, spinning new conversations and yarns off that single act. How can you blame them? Their Commie brains were bucking for some action."

That's when we realized SI was Communist with its mind-control techniques and subtle influences that reminded us of its omnipresent sovereignty at every turn, homogenized us through cubicalization and superior janitorial science, hastened our bowel movements with uninviting men's room stall walls of cold, clinical steel. . . . We even had Belly, our very own

Russian-style dancing circus bear.

If SI was Communist then Redsoft was our papa, a Karl Marx comprising equal parts operating system and propaganda. The posters in the breakroom, the Bill Kunstler slideshows, the flyers over the men's room urinals, and the calendars in our cubes were designed to transform us into a working class of Redsoft devotees who would tacitly accept Portalia's instability as the norm, and it worked: we'd lowered our standards until we wept with joy whenever an hour passed during which our machines didn't crash.

Job dedication was measured by a man's software programming and his obedience to SI's culture of ceaseless work, but most of all by how earnestly he embraced Redsoft, our father. Loyal workers followed Redsoft's stocks. They talked up Redsoft products in the halls. They read Redsoft books. They mobbed the Redsoft trainers and representatives for the latest secrets and tidbits about the company, its strategies, its freebies and giveaways, the mugs, the T-shirts, the hats emblazoned with Redsoft logos. Redsoft is throwing a party, Redsoft is sponsoring a free trip to Cabo, a Redsoft exec is speaking at a computer convention in Los Angeles and everybody gets free tickets....

With SI and Redsoft working so hard for our affections, it felt only natural to accept indoctrination like good Communists should.

I shaved my head. Hank began wearing blandly gray Oxford shirts buttoned all the way to the neck. I grew a Lenin goatee. Hank started a Marxist beard. We said "Greetings, comrade" to strangers in the halls. We ate day-old wheat loaves for lunch with nothing on top. I concentrated on producing as much as I could, but even more, on the minutiae of producing. I sniffed the office air. I investigated carpet fibers on the walls. I counted phone rings. I read Redsoft posters aloud. I meditated on copier hum. And when the receptionist walked by from time to time with the gape in her skirt that showed a sliver of muscular thigh, I obediently took it in, knowing it was probably just another Redsoft orchestration, a choreographed move to supply us with our every need—even subtle sexual stimulation—in the name of helping us evolve into Very Producing People.

We managed to remain Communists for a week.

In the end, the revolution never came, at least not in the way we thought it would. Our minds drifted. The harder we focused, the harder focusing became. We pressed our faces against our monitors. We sat in our chairs until our legs went numb. We skipped meals to finish more VPPs, which were growing increasingly detailed in their hundred-page specifications, diagrams, and flowcharts.

The Redsoft propaganda men must have sensed our growing fatigue; to help bolster us, new posters appeared in the cubicle aisles and in record numbers with catchy slogans like SI AND REDSOFT: TOGETHER WE CAN DO IT, all mounted at perfect right angles to each other as subliminal reminders to keep vigilant and pursue communal consistency amongst ourselves. But even with the posters we could only pretend for so long that the coffee wasn't causing diarrhea and the carpeting on the walls wasn't itchy and the ringing phones weren't shrill and the copier's hum didn't sound a little rickety.

Worst of all was the Portalia programming, which had become the basest of all rote activities—like writing the same ten-thousand word sentence again and again for hours, days, weeks. I'd become a living stupor, a drugged lobotomy with legs, falling asleep and waking up on my desk in drool while my fingers worked on. There were times when I didn't even know what I was clicking on or why, except that the programs falling out of me somehow contributed to SI's perpetuation. Little code blocks lined up across my screen for days on end like empty strands of DNA flickering sixty times per second, hypnotizing me into dull illiteracy.

My goatee gave me a rash. Our backs hurt. Hank had indigestion from all of the bread. Performance art thoughts streaked through our brains in hallucinatory flashbacks, an automatic defense, I was sure, against Communism's prescribed numbing, and then the rustle of the receptionist's skirt as she walked by, flashing her muscular thigh. . . .

Hank's mind was the first to go. It was a Wednesday. His voice slogged over the cubicle wall like mud.

Larry

Yeah

You dead over there

Yeah

It's been a long time since we've done anything

Yeah

So

So

Do you think we still have it

Have what

The performance art thing

Maybe

Let's do one

One what

A performance

Where

I don't know . . . the elevators

When

Now

We met up in the aisle. Hank looked pale and malnourished, like death with a beard.

We headed for the elevators. They were at the far end of the building. It was hard for me to tell if my legs were moving. I could feel the performance machinery in my head stirring, coughing, smoking oil. It had been so long. What had we been doing with ourselves?

We passed aisles of cubicles. As we walked by workers looked up from their keyboards with blank expressions devoid of anything resembling personality.

We arrive at the elevators. Nobody's around. Hank pushes the call button. We hear a ding and an elevator door opens. We step inside. The doors shut. Hank presses the button for the lobby. The elevator begins to move.

The elevator's walls are mirrored so secretaries and executives can check their hair. Hank and I adjust our manes, then press the elevator's stop button. The elevator stops between two floors.

Hank pulls out a pair of screwdrivers, hands me one, and we go to work on the elevator buttons, prying their tops off and rearranging them. Three becomes six; five becomes two. All the floors are mixed up by the time we finish.

I press start. The elevator descends toward the lobby. I go into a handstand with my toes high against the back wall.

The doors open. Two executives step in. I watch them in the mirrors. They have no idea what to make of me. One of them laughs; the other looks horrified. Laugher presses the ten button. Horrified hits twelve. The doors close and the elevator ascends.

I start walking in place against the mirrored wall. Each time I take a step, Hank squeezes his eyes shut and wheezes like an asthmatic. Step and wheeza, step and wheeza. My shoes squeak. Laugher grins. Horrified looks ready to pry the doors open with his fingernails. "Why don't you get down from there?" he scolds.

I move my feet faster. Hank is huffing and puffing, foaming at the mouth, opening and closing his eyes, squeezing his fists, and staring straight ahead. Horrified tells Laugher we must be on drugs. The elevator dings. The tenth-floor button lights up. The doors open. I look out. By the looks of the lobby I can tell we're really on the eighth. Laugher steps out. The elevator doors start to shut. I see him look around, confused—where's his office? Isn't this the tenth—?

The doors shut and the elevator ascends. I move as fast as I can. Hank is sweating. Horrified swallows. He doesn't know what to do—it's a goddamn madhouse!

Ding. Twelve lights up. The doors open. Horrified steps out. I can tell we're really on eleven. The doors start to shut.

Horrified looks around, confused—this isn't his floor! He spins and jams the doors with his briefcase. They open and he steps in. Hank and I freeze like two mannequins drenched in sweat. Horrified hits buttons at random in the hope they might take him up to his floor. The elevator begins moving down. "DAMN IT!" he yells. He puts his face up to Hank's. Hank stands motionless except for the sweat dripping off him.

"You're fucking disturbed," Horrified says.

Hank's mouth makes a clicking sound. Horrified blinks.

Ding. The elevator doors open. Horrified steps out. I can tell by his unsure exit that he knows he's on the wrong floor, but he doesn't care. The elevator doors close.

We name our performance Stationary Running in an Elevator with Transposed Buttons Makes Businessmen Nervous.

It was almost like old times.

11

HANK AND I KNEW OUR performance art stamina would need
months of rehabilitation, so we took it easy at first, with anonymous little
performances to ease us back into shape without drawing too much heat
from Belly. We traded performance art ideas via electronic mail, whispered
about performance art in the breakroom, practiced maneuvers in the aisles
while crouched low, under the radar of supervisors scanning the office for
employees idling time. . . .

Workers realized something unusual was happening around the office. It was impossible to miss our effects, the anthropological evidence, the
performance detritus we left behind like piles of fresh dung.

People started spinning wild theories in the halls and debating over
clues. Was it a conspiracy? The work of a single disturbed mind? A political
statement? Who was posting the messages on SI's public network accusing
Redsoft of performing lobotomies? What about the postage-stamp-sized
porno pictures stuck all over the office under pieces of scotch tape? Or how
about the colossal toilet overflow in the men's room that ran under the door
and down the hall, a catarrh that soaked the office carpet ten feet in every

direction, and the little paper boats which, when the facility engineers in rubber boots opened the restroom door to clean up the mess, floated out in the brown-water flotsam?

* * *

It was lunchtime. Hank and I headed for the breakroom.

We passed Rudy's cube. He popped his head out. "Come here!" he whispered, exhaling cherry pipe smoke.

Rudy's cubicle was a disaster zone. He was a compulsive information junkie; it didn't matter what kind of information it was, he had to have it. His desk was buried under a mountain of pulp paperbacks and tabloids, newspapers in three languages, conspiracy mags, and computer printouts.

When he wasn't busy maintaining SI's networks, Rudy created viruses. His tiny, artificially intelligent software programs were his hobby and they had but one goal: to infiltrate computer systems in order to bring home information for Rudy's own gluttonous consumption—especially if it was of the unpublished, private, illicit, classified, or inflammatory variety. Once unleashed, a new virus would replicate itself a thousand times to better its chances of survival in the wild, then quietly spread out like kamikaze robots, infecting floppy disks and computers, traversing networks, dialing into phones, and diving deep into data. Capable of interacting with each other, the viral siblings collaborated on penetrating secure systems, engaged in hot sex to produce smarter offspring, disguised themselves to avoid detection, fought if attacked, and, if captured, disfigured themselves or even performed seppuku—Rudy had programmed the digital guts to go "guhhh" as they all gushed out.

Self-determination was one of Rudy's rules, so even he never knew where a virus might go once released into the wild, nor what juicy secrets it might uncover. The unpublished chapters of some writer's new novel? Nuclear missile secrets from the Ukraine? Diary entries confessing murder? The President's bank balance? Photos of a cheating spouse? Rudy's virii returned it all in volumes, at all hours, from the most insular and highly guarded fortresses of knowledge that other hackers only dreamed of mining.

"I'm about to launch my latest virus," Rudy whispered. "I've been working on it for months!"

"What does it do?" asked Hank.

"Remember the physicist Heisenberg?" asked Rudy. "In nineteen twenty-seven he came up with quantum physics' uncertainty principle, which says you can't observe events without affecting them. The greater the watching, the greater the watcher's influence is on what is being watched." Rudy chuckled and puffed on his pipe. "I named this virus Heisenberg because it's perfectly safe to observe its effects—its trail, the evidence it leaves behind, the systems it penetrates—but if it detects you watching, it'll respond."

"Respond how?" I asked.

"Slow your computer to a crawl, set your screen resolution to ten by ten, change all of your files into photographs of my ass, print solid pages of black until your printer runs out of ink, telephone your credit card numbers to North Korea, and mail invitations for sadomasochistic sex to everyone in your address book," said Rudy.

He clicked a program labeled HSBRGVRS. A digital counter on his computer screen began stepping backward from ten to zero. Heisenberg was about to start.

"The virus can see you with this," said Rudy, pointing to a video camera that was connected to his computer, "so whatever you do, don't look at it."

Hank and I nodded.

The countdown reached zero. Rudy stepped back. "OK. There it goes . . . look away! Look away!"

We all looked away. We waited. A minute passed. I had to look. I peeked at the computer. The screen was black. The machine didn't appear to be doing anything.

I stared—then I felt it, a presence watching. The virus was looking at me looking at it—Heisenberg!

The computer started beeping. As numbers streamed across the screen, its resolution changed to a blocky ten by ten, the machine's mail program fired up and began sending out sadomasochistic sex invitations, the printer started ejecting black sheets of paper, and we heard the modem dial North Korea.

"Who's peeking?" Rudy cried, covering his eyes. "No peeking! You'll piss it off! Turn your backs on it! Turn your backs!" We all turned our backs. After a few seconds, the computer quieted down, the printer quit shooting paper, and the mail program stopped sending sex invites.

We waited, then Rudy peeked. The coast was clear. The computer was fine and there was no sign of Heisenberg—it had escaped into the network, and from there, the world.

Rudy puffed on his pipe and beamed like a proud father.

* * *

Weeks passed. Our performance stamina was slow in returning. Small, anonymous pieces around the office were nothing like our fading Tenderloin days when we played for wild crowds. Setting a performance in motion days in advance for random audiences we never saw was solitary, sober, and sexless, but as much as we yearned to perform for live blood-and-guts spectators, we knew SI management would never sanction performance art. And so we performed in silence, creeping down the aisles, reorganizing desks, reciting text under our breath, wearing trash cans like boots, humping chairs with our pants down, or computer "antiquing"—a new and potentially dangerous little act that involved sawing a co-worker's computer cables into rubber and metal bits with a fingernail file, then re-assembling them with duct tape ripped from a roll by our teeth.

Then one day my phone rang. It was Belly.

"You two come to my office right now!" he said.

I walked over to Hank. He was busy cutting a stamp-sized penis out of a porno picture with a pair of scissors.

"Belly wants to see us," I said.

Hank put down the penis. "Did he say why?"

"No."

Hank let out a long exhale, then popped a handful of vitamins.

Belly was eating a hamburger at his desk when we arrived. He was red-faced and breathing hard and his underarms were soaked with sweat. He pointed to two empty chairs. Hank and I sat.

"The CEO called me into his office," said Belly, chewing.

"Why?" I asked.

"TO FUCK ME!" Belly yelled, knocking his burger to the floor. "I'm getting fucked! He's going to personally watch every single move I make from here out! The heat is on! The game is up! You fucked me, just like I knew you would!"

"Wait a minute," I said, "we didn't—"

Belly held up a computer printout. "Do you know what this is? It's the report from Megamonitore. Porno? Performance plans? It's all right here! Don't you KNOW who reads this report? The CEO! He knows everything! Your conspiracies! Your sloth! He knows you Lenins are behind the pranks and overflowing toilets, and since I'm your manager, I look like a jerk! The CEO wants my head on a stick!"

Hank laughed. "Come on, the CEO wouldn't—"

"WHY WOULDN'T HE?" Belly screamed. He was clearly going mad—dribbling, fat waddling, waving his hands, crumpling the printout. . . .

"The messages you sent! Libelous electronic mail! Dozens upon dozens! Repeatedly! Pranks! Hours wasted! The proof's right here! Megamonitore caught it all! The CEO wants reimbursement! Do you KNOW how many attorneys SI has? Hundreds! All champing at the bit! They'll take away your houses! They'll rip the clothing from your pimpled backs! You'll be in arrears for millions! Your wives will leave you if they haven't already! SI will own you! They'll take every last scrap unless you MARCH right back to your desks and work like you've never worked before! You've outlived your usefulness as our PR puppets! You're my slaves hereafter! You'll earn back every red cent! You'll work more VPPs than you ever imagined! Portalia is your new first name! You'll be here seven days a week! I'm gonna ride your asses like a two-ton cellmate! You'll do whatever I say because I speak for the CEO now, and if you screw me, you screw him, and if you screw him, he'll pick up the phone and the lawyers will screw you for MILLIONS! If you ignore my orders, if you goof around, if you pull another prank, if you cut another computer cord or paste up a single postage-stamp titty, the attorneys will be all over you and that's it, that's all, there's no negotiation! My ASS is on the line, my family's FOOD is on the line, which means YOUR asses are on MY line, capeesh, kaput, fuck off, and bye-bye!"

Belly jerked his thumb at us to get out. Hank and I rose and slunk back to our cubicles.

We arrived at our aisle to find the SI postman pushing an empty cart past us with a smirk on his face.

We came to Hank's cube and stopped. A four-foot stack of VPPs sat on his desk.

I ran to my cube and saw my own four-footer.

I felt sick. I looked at Hank. His eyes were red. He was shaking. He started to faint. I grabbed him and held him up.

"Please," he whispered.

"What do you want to do?"

"I can't—no more," he said as he started to cry.

Workers watched as I helped Hank along the central aisle to the elevators, down to the lobby, and out the front doors into the foggy San Francisco air.

I walked Hank back to his apartment. Sherry began interrogating him sourly as she gathered him inside. Why was he home from work early?

Why had he been crying? Had he taken his vitamins? I knew she'd throw a fit when she heard we'd just quit our jobs, so I got out of there.

12

I WALKED UP POLK STREET to a bar called The Honkey Donkey. The sign over the entrance read GET YOUR WHITE ASS IN HERE.

I went in and sat down. It was the usual crowd.

Hans, the bartender, came over.

"How're you doing, Larry?"

"Hank and I quit our jobs today."

"Good for you. Have some wine."

"You're a good man, Hans."

Hans poured me a glass. I downed it. Hans poured another, then set out a plate of chicken wings. I ate a wing and studied my reflection in the mirror behind the bar. My hair was matted. I looked a little on edge . . . dangerous. . . .

"Are you going to do a performance tonight?" asked Hans.

"Maybe with a little encouragement," I replied, holding out my empty glass.

Hans filled it.

"Do it," said a petite woman from the end of the bar. She had braided black hair and green feline eyes. "I saw one you did a while back—the thing with the tuba and the goat."

"Hey, you liked that?"

"Not really. But I saw it."

That was good enough for me. I stood up and pulled out the rubber doll's head I carried for impromptu performance art occasions. It was androgynous with glued-on eyes, ears, and hair. In the wrong hands a doll's head was a performance art cliché—an overused symbol of youth, play, or perversion—but in the hands of a master it became an alter ego, a tongue-in-cheek metaphor for the Everyman, a doppelgänger that parodied the performer and reflected the audience without judgment.

I begin bouncing the doll's head against the bar mirror. Drunks gravitate toward the show. Boing, boing, boing, the little head flies. The doll's hair loosens, then flutters down to the bar top while I sing:

YOU CAN'T COME CLOSER
THAN I LOOK
AND THROW MYSELF
AT GLASS—
ENCEPHALITIS FLIES
LIKE RACEHORSE GLUE,
I SWALLOWED ME DOWN
LIKE A BOA

I bounce the head one last time, catch it in my mouth, and swallow. The lump passes slowly down my throat. I take a bow. The drunks clap.

"Thank you," I say, "but it's not over yet. Stick around until tomorrow and see how it comes out, The End."

People groaned and applauded. Hans returned the doll's hair to me. It was sticky. I stuck it to Hans's ass. "That can stay right hair," I punned, "asss sculpture." Hans snorted and poured me a free round.

I christened the performance I Swallow the Bouncing Baby Head After the Hair Falls Off, then ambled over to a stool beside the woman with the cat eyes.

"That wasn't bad," she said, "but some little girl's probably missing that head and crying her eyes out."

"Maybe I need it more than she does," I whispered.

The woman smiled and rolled her eyes. She was dressed in a tank-top, olive pants, and combat boots, and her skin was pale with freckles. Her arms were sinewy and muscular. A purple shiner under her left eye was headed toward black.

She extended a hand. "My name's Mouse."

"I'm Larry."

"Hello, Larry."

"You have pretty eyes."

Mouse laughed. "Thanks. They're my mother's. She was Irish. And a palm reader—the best in all of Dublin."

"Will you read mine?" I asked, wiping a hand on my pants and holding it up.

Mouse crinkled her nose. "I might catch something."

She was flirting. I coughed and sucked down some wine.

"I don't know palms, but I'm pretty good at reading heads," I offered.

Mouse raised a brow. "And what does my melon tell you?"

"Well," I said, studying her, "your ovoid skull—"

"Did you just call me an egghead?"

"Yes, but with your wide cheekbones, it means you're sympathetic. And charitable."

"Ah—so I'm *not* allowed to kill you."

"Your dimples and laugh-line nasolabial folds say you're sensual—"

"Please don't harass my folds."

"Your ears protrude a little—"

"This gets better and better."

"—So you're curious and intuitive. Your nose's wide dorsal base in-dicates you're reliable—and athletic—but. . . ."

"What now?"

"Your jaw has a steep gonial angle, so you *might* have a temper—"

"No fair—I told you I'm part Irish."

"You *might* even be violent."

"Oh wow, violent too?"

"Accurate?" I whispered.

Mouse smiled and took a sip of wine. "Maybe."

"What line of work are you in?" I asked.

"I'm a kickboxer."

"Sure you are."

Mouse raised an eyebrow. She was serious.

"Any money in that?"

"If you're good."

"Are you?"

"No, but I could kick your ass," she said, socking me hard in the arm. She knew how to use her knuckles. I felt blood congealing into a bruise under my shirt.

Seeing I was impressed, she pulled up a pant leg and flexed her calf for emphasis. It was like a steel ball. "Holy shit," I whispered. I wanted to give her calf a little squeeze, but didn't, remembering the knuckles.

Told you so, her smile said.

* * *

I went to the bar's payphone and dialed Hank's number. Sherry an-swered.

"Hi, Sherry. Is Hank in?"

"Yes, but he can't come out. I sent him to bed. He's completely fatigued. He needs rest. And thanks a lot for encouraging him!"

"What does that mean?"

I heard Hank yelling in the background. The man was suffering.

"You egg him on, Larry. You make him do things."

"I didn't make him quit his job, Sherry. It was Portalia—"

"Hank said you two flooded the men's restroom."

There was a scuffling sound on the phone, some yelling, then Hank.

"She's holding me prisoner!" he yelled. "Call the cops!"

"Hank! Come to The Honkey Donkey!"

There was more scuffling for the phone, but Hank managed to hang on.

"I only have a second. Have you read tonight's newspaper?" he asked.

"No," I said.

"Go buy it," he said. "Go buy it and laugh your head off!"

Sherry wrestled the phone away from Hank. I could hear him laughing hysterically in the background—or maybe he was crying. Or both.

"I'm hanging up now, Larry," Sherry said.

"Wait," I said. "Give him a message."

Sherry sighed. "What?"

"Tell him I'm going to drop off our performance demo tape at 347. Maybe we'll get a gig."

"What's 347?"

"A theater in the Tenderloin that showcases performance art one night a month," I said. Performers had to submit a sample videotape of past performances to land a slot in the showcase. If Favio Smelter, 347's flamboyant owner, liked our work, he'd put us in his lineup—and he paid cash.

"Well, I'm not holding my breath. You haven't seen a paying gig in months!"

"Oh, come on, Sherry, that's not fair—"

"Bye, Larry."

She hung up. I went back and sat down beside Mouse.

"Everything all right?" she asked.

"No," I said.

"You should take up kickboxing. It relieves stress."

"I'd probably kill somebody."

"Sure, but it'd be sanctioned. Come see for yourself," she said, slipping me a napkin with an address written on it. "I train tomorrow at noon."

"Maybe I'll come check it out," I said as Hans poured me another wine.

* * *

I drank until The Honkey closed, then stumbled back toward my apartment. Passing a newspaper rack, I put in a quarter, took out a paper, and flipped through it in search of whatever Hank had seen.

Turning to a section called "People in the News," I saw a small Bill Kunstler item:

BILL KUNSTLER HONORED WITH
MILLENNIUM AWARD

COPENHAGEN, DENMARK—Denmark's highest technology honor, the Technology Man of the Millennium Award, was presented to Redsoft CEO Bill Kunstler on Wednesday. Berns Kohhlvidder, Denmark's Minister of Technology, said in a speech that Kunstler was chosen for his role in bringing Redsoft's revolutionary Portalia operating system product to the world.

"Portalia has brightened our lives and brought easy-to-use computing to every desk. More than any other technology in the last thousand years, it's changed our world forever," said Kohhlvidder.

The award purse included one million dollars, an honorary doctorate, and a gold statuette bearing Kunstler's likeness.

I couldn't believe Bill was off winning awards while Hank and I were suffering. If anyone deserved an award, it was us.

I pried open the newspaper rack, grabbed the unsold papers, and threw them into the street where the morning traffic would run them over, but it wasn't enough—not nearly. I shoved my finger down my throat and threw up, covering the papers in chicken wings and wine, then unzipped and pissed back and forth until every last paper was soaked. My only regret was not needing to shit.

I walked home, let myself into my apartment, sat down on the couch, took up a black marker, and wrote BILL on the sole of my shoe. It was an old performance art trick and a black magic curse. I blew on the ink to help it dry and smiled, knowing I'd walk all over him for days to come.

* * *

That night I dreamed a performance art dream.

"YOU HAVE PERFORMED AN ILLEGAL ACTIVITY," Hank yells.

He's performing on a stage. A tight spotlight illuminates him. A close-up video camera transmits the scene to a large TV screen for the audience to see.

Hank writhes on the floor with his arms behind his back, then rolls onto his belly. A computer keyboard sits beside him. He puts his mouth on it and starts chewing on the V key. He manages to bite the V off with a click, then swallows it down.

"YOU HAE PERFORMED AN ILLEGAL ACTIITY," he hollers.

The audience giggles. Hank puts his mouth on L and works on it, his lips and teeth a blurry mess on the TV, and then it goes—he pries L up, gnaws it off with a click, and swallows.

"YOU HAE PERFORMED AN IEGA ACTIITY."

The crowd laughs. Hank continues eating until the remaining letters are gone, then he stands. He picks up a microphone, holds it to his stomach, and starts jumping up and down. The audience hushes. The clatter of keyboard keys tumbling in Hank's stomach is audible over the theater's loudspeakers.

The lights dim to black. Hank continues jumping in the dark. The clatter in him grows softer, until finally . . . nothing.

The lights come up. The audience roars and gives a standing ovation.

Hank bows, then shuffles backward into the dark.

I woke up. My sheets were wet.

13

THE NEXT MORNING I WALKED up Turk Street to drop off our demo tape at 347. The theater was an ugly building sandwiched between an alley and a liquor store. It had been painted red once, but traffic exhaust and soot from bums' midnight barbecues had turned the façade a dull brown. There were steel bars over the windows, but vandals had still managed to spray paint GAY SEX SEX SEX across the glass. A purple mural of a crouching naked man was painted on 347's front door. The man was bent over, grabbing his ankles, with his pants pulled down, ass fully exposed. I couldn't see his face, but I could certainly see his ass: the mail slot was right in the middle of it.

I apologized to the videotape for the indecency as it slipped through the gaping hole. I heard it hit the floor inside.

An unshaven bum lying on the sidewalk a few doors down smiled and said I had nice hair.

I hurried away before he could get up.

* * *

I walked to Mouse's kickboxing gym. It was south of Market Street in an old brick warehouse. A sign over the entrance read MUAY THAI KICKBOXING, and in smaller letters, NATIONAL SPORT OF THAI-LAND.

I went in. The humid air reeked of sweat. Kickboxing bags dangled from the ceiling. Weightlifting equipment crowded the floor. I headed for the center of the warehouse, passing bags and equipment until I found the boxing ring.

In the ring was Mouse—a lot more Mouse than I'd seen the night before. She parried and ducked, then fired a barrage of kicks, punches, and elbows into a canvas bag her trainer was struggling to hold out in front of him. He was six feet tall and thick, but Mouse had him winded—each strike knocked him backward, powered by her white equine thighs that were bare-ly contained by her silver kickboxing shorts. Her cut-off tanktop revealed a washboard stomach rippling with sweat as she dodged and spun, breasts tight like fists heaving under the cotton as she got the punches out, quick hands hands hands and then WHAM, she laid into the bag with her shin like a cleaver and her trainer stumbled four feet back.

My legs felt like rubber. I sank into a chair.

Mouse's trainer was dying but he came back for more, slowing, breathing hard, face flushed, knees wobbly. Mouse's knuckles were taped, but from where I sat they looked a little bloody as she threw a blur of set-up jabs and then WHAM, her trainer went down.

I felt an erection coming on.

The trainer got back up with the bag as Mouse padded back and forth in her bare feet like a tiger, her real speed just getting started now, her hair pulled back and swishing like a tail, her shins burning red but holding and her thick, hard ass, my God, it was invincible, such quick hands and a knee to his balls in a nice variation, then a push-back and WHAM, he was down and clutching his stomach, the canvas bag resting beside him like a newly dead appendage.

I looked down. My pants were raging.

Mouse put her hands on her hips and waited. She bounced her rear foot playfully on the mat a few times, thump thump thump, toes spread wide, hamstrings and calves dancing lightly with each bounce, muscles rippling and vanishing, all of her a hardy mix of round and hard and flat.

She flicked a finger at the trainer to get his ass up.

He couldn't.

"Shit," she muttered.

I eyed her arms, her stomach. She was an animal, pure instinct, all muscular curve . . . I'd had no idea bodies like hers existed. I wiped my forehead. I'd worked myself into a frenzy.

Mouse spotted me. She smiled and walked to the ropes, slowly unwinding helical coils of bloody gauze from her hands. "Hey," she said, breathing hard. "I'm glad you showed up. I'll meet you outside."

I went outside to wait. She emerged after a minute with a gym bag slung across her back. She wore a mid-thigh-length green dress and clunky black boots. Her shins glowed bright red from the kicking.

"So, what'd you think?" she asked, bouncing up and down and socking me on the arm.

"You pummeled him!" I gasped. "I . . . I want you to kick my damned head off!"

Mouse laughed, then saw the bulge in my pants.

"What's that?" she asked, pointing.

I coughed, turned, and tried to adjust the lump.

"Oh, I . . . it's nothing serious . . . I . . . these pants are starched and they—"

"Starched?"

"Yeah, sometimes they poke out in front . . . they're like cardboard. . . ."

"You should try softener—it'd fix them right up."

"Oh, right, good idea. I'll try it."

Mouse started walking up the street. I followed.

"You're ferocious in the ring," I said.

"I'm training for the lightweight division Muay Thai Kickboxing Championship world title," said Mouse. She pulled out a yellow flyer advertising the fight and handed it to me.

"Will you only be fighting women?" I asked.

"As far as I know," said Mouse. She stopped walking. "Do you think it matters that I'll only be fighting women?" She put her face right up to mine. "You don't think I could beat a man?"

She arched a brow and her green eyes waited, daring me to reply. I could feel her breath on my face. I swallowed.

"You'd better be careful," she said, throwing a knee to my groin. She stopped just short of contact, but it was enough to make my balls retract, bending me at the waist as if I'd been hit, chin forward, my body tensed and waiting for the gnawing testicular pain to begin, though it didn't. I was lucky. Her precision was stunning.

"You could've crushed my balls," I coughed.

"See?" she giggled. "Softener fixes that stiffness every time."

I laughed while nonchalantly trying to protect my groin.

She scribbled her phone number on the back of her flyer and handed it to me.

"Call me sometime," she said, then she turned and jogged off down the street, her calves and thighs flexing. I stood and watched her go.

When she reached the corner, she stopped and looked back.

I gave her a wave.

She flipped me the bird, then skipped off around the corner.

It was the most beautiful gesture I'd ever seen.

I walked back to the Tenderloin. When I was halfway home, it occurred to me that Mouse could prove seriously dangerous to my health if I managed to piss her off. I needed protection. I took out my wallet. I had ten bucks. It was enough.

I ducked into a sporting goods store and bought myself a groin cup.

14

A **WEEK PASSED WITH NO** word from Hank. I tried calling, but each time Sherry answered and said he was unavailable.

The Bill on the bottom of my shoe was wearing off. I retraced the letters with black marker. I hoped the curse was having an effect. Maybe he'd catch the clap from one of Redsoft's board members, or worse, lose value in his stock portfolio.

I finally passed the doll's head. I washed it off, glued on new hair, and slipped it back into my pocket.

* * *

One night I returned home to find an answering machine message waiting. I played it. Out came a sing-song faux-French voice:

"Hallo, this is Favio from 347, mm hmm. I have seen your demo tap and you can FORGET EET. My God, your performance on that tap is SHEET! Why don't you wash your clothes? You look like a couple of slobs. My friends told me you were SHEET and this tape proves eet. So, I do not want you for my show. I plan to feature a spastic man with the shakes instead. Come pick up your demo tap. This is Favio."

The machine beeped. So that was it—no performance gig for us and no money.

I paced the apartment, then sat down on the couch. I looked at my forearms to pass the time . . . then my elbows . . . then I pulled down my pants and played with my legs. I liked looking at the skin and the hair up close. I licked my knee. It was salty. I lifted my shirt next and eyed my nipples. There were two. I pinched one. It felt good—

I jumped up. I had to keep my hands off myself. My body's details were petty and trivial; whittling away the hours with my hands all over me was a disgusting waste of time, especially when I knew that in the end my self-indulgence would achieve nothing.

I tried to stay busy. I did push-ups. I read. I paced the living room. I avoided the bathroom mirror. I watched the clock hands move. I drank eight glasses of water. I kept my shirt tucked in. I talked to the air. I stood at the window and watched pedestrians pass by on the sidewalk below.

Unemployment begets leisure and solitude, which beget casual self-inspection, which begets vain self-obsession over one's corporeal minutiae.

I swallow more water and run my finger along the curve of my throat. I laugh at the thought of a flâneur who strolls only his apartment. I catch myself staring at the dark entrance to the bathroom and thinking about the mirror in there. I do more push-ups so I can watch my arms bend. Tucking in my shirt means having to handle my smooth belly and ass, and I do, albeit more slowly than I should, and then whoops, there go my clothes. That's all I can take: I'm flipping the bathroom light on and pressing my face and nipples flat against the mirror like magnets—hello, how I missed you.

I examine every inch. There are new freckles on my shoulders. My hair needs a trim; so do my armpits and balls. I use a straight razor. My chest needs it too. I remove every hair until I'm napless as a sphynx, nubile and impish, balls perfect and shining, anus as smooth as my performance art mouth. I turn sideways and flex my skinny arms. Like stars in heaven, muscle is a function of light and contrast. Muscular curves cast shadows that set them off as distinct, pleasurable bodies to be admired. Without shadow, shoulders mush blandly into arms, calves fall into featureless broom-handle legs, and abdominals lie flat without definition, like putty in the gut.

I'm only satisfied after hours of prodding and picking and smoothing. When the excitement finally wanes and the heat dies down, I click the light off, my constellations rest, and the disgust over my self-indulgence settles right back in.

* * *

The next day I ran into Mouse downtown. She was on her way to the boxing gym in a pink dress. Her hair was pulled back in a ponytail.

"I thought you were going to call me," she said.

"Sorry—my job search has been killing me."

"I bet they're beating down your door."

"Sure. I'm on my way to an interview right now," I said, pointing to a beer stain on the front of my shirt.

Mouse laughed. "Don't worry. You've found jobs before."

"Nobody wants an old-time programmer."

"Not one so mopey, anyway."

We started walking toward her gym.

"Why did you get into kickboxing?" I asked.

Mouse shrugged. "I just like to kick ass, I suppose."

"A sadist, eh?"

"Maybe," she said—then she leaned in close. "Have you ever kicked ass before?"

"I've broken a nose or two."

"Sure you have," she laughed. "Oh, look at the tough performance artist!"

"I have broken noses," I said.

"With your legs?" She made a tight fist and held it under my chin. "With your legs you broke noses?"

"No."

"You really should try it. I think it would fix you."

I gave her a doubtful look. She put down her gym bag and gave me a push. "Go ahead," she said. "Kick me." Was she serious? I wasn't the most limber man. She stuck out her chin and pointed to it. It was a beautiful chin. "Go ahead. Right on my chin." I knew I couldn't get my foot that high. Then again, she was short—

"Don't think about kicking a woman," she said. "You're just kicking another human being. Go on. Really, go ahead. Kick me. See what it's all about."

"I shouldn't kick a woman."

"Pretend I'm a man."

Indecision squatted on my face.

"Pretend," she said. She deepened her voice and thrust out her chest. "Hi, my name's Mouse. I'm a man with a big, fat dick. Please kick me in the head."

"I couldn't. . . ."

"Come on, you BITCH!" Mouse yelled.

I reared back and kicked her jaw as hard as I could—CRACK! She went down hard on the sidewalk and started jerking and foaming at the mouth. Oh God, she was having convulsions! I knelt and checked to see if her head was bleeding or if I'd broken her neck or—

It was a trick. She grabbed my hair, flipped me head-first onto the ground, jumped up, and kicked me straight across the jaw—CRACK!— in one oiled move. I saw stars. Pedestrians paused to watch. Passing traffic stopped. Birds froze in flight.

Recovering, I grabbed her ankle, dumped her, flipped her over, and straddled her—God she was firm. She tried to get up, but too slow—her head came up first and I caught her across her jaw with my fist.

We giggled. She grabbed my heel and twisted. I lost my balance and fell. She jumped up. I tried to stand, but only made it as far as my knees before it was too late, her kick was coming and CRACK!—her shin connected with my eye. I sailed sideways into the gutter and slid into sludge.

Mouse wiped off her mouth, straightened her dress, and picked up her gym bag.

"See?" she said, barely winded. "Sometimes you just have to get back to basics."

I smiled. I couldn't move. One of my eyes was swollen, so I just looked at her with the other.

She laughed, flipped me the bird, and walked off. From the gutter I watched her calves flexing off into the distance.

She was my muse.

* * *

One night my toilet clogged. I called the landlady. She was a stout Swede named Sorevag who lived just down the hall.

Sorevag knocked. I opened the door and saw her standing there in a frumpy gray dress with a plunger in her hand. She had a wrinkled round face, a white mustache, a mop of gray hair, saggy teats, and two plump legs encased in stockings that pooled around her ankles.

She gibbered something in Swedish like a Minnesota hen, pushed me aside, and headed for the bathroom. She switched the light on and lifted the toilet lid. The seat was spattered with dried urine. She sighed with disgust and gave me a look. I shrugged.

Sorevag eased the plunger into the bowl and began pushing and pulling with grunts. The plunger sucked. Water sloshed, turning brown. Droplets flew up onto her dress, but she didn't seem to care. More water slopped out of the bowl and onto the floor. Sweat patches appeared under her arms as she leaned into the plunger, full weight against the handle, really heaving it in, her stockings slipping and sliding under her weight. She pinched her lips tight. Push and pull, push and pull, then it was over—the toilet gurgled and the water went down. Sorevag stood up straight, rubbed her sore back, then let me have it.

"YOU DON'T URINE ON SEAT NO MORE!"

I nodded, unsure if she'd understand anything I had to say.

She pointed at the bathroom's rusty radiator.

"YOUR PEE SPRINKY ON THE RADIATOR?"

I scratched my head. "Well, maybe sometimes if I'm drunk—"

"THEN YOU ARE REASON IT IS RUSTING. LOOK AT IT. IT IS RUSTING RIGHT THROUGH. YOU MUST PEE SITTING DOWN FROM NOW ON!"

"Listen, Sorevag—"

"MY NAME IS SOLVEIG! YOU LIVE HERE TEN YEARS AND YOU DON'T KNOW THAT? ALL RIGHT THEN, I DON'T KNOW YOUR NAME EITHER. I WILL CALL YOU RADIATOR. NOW YOU SIT DOWN WHEN YOU HAVE TO GO. YOU UNDERSTAND?"

"You can't tell me how to pee—"

Solveig shook her plunger at me. "IF I FIND MORE RUST ON THAT RADIATOR, I WILL MAKE YOU BUY NEW ONE!"

She grunted and slammed the front door on her way out.

* * *

I decided to go watch Favio's man with the shakes perform at 347. I called Hank to see if he wanted to go, but Sherry said no.

I walked down to 347. Favio was taking tickets at the front door when I arrived. He was tan in a tight muscle shirt that showed off his chest hair. A thick gold chain dangled around his neck. He smelled of cologne and male juices. I was glad to be wearing my cup.

He took the dollar admission from my hand with a sneer and handed me a photocopied program that listed the evening's performances. A photo of Favio in a muscle pose was printed on the cover.

"I heard your message on my machine," I said.

"Good for you," he responded in a faux-French accent.

"You'll be sorry."

"Screw you! I don't want your performance here, old white man!" he spat. He reached into his pants. What would it be? A knife? A gun?

He pulled out the demo videotape I'd left. A foot of tape dangled from the cassette's opening.

"Here is your tap," he said. He dropped the cassette into my hand with two fingers.

"What the hell did you do to it? Why's it hanging out like that?"

"I like it hanging out," he said, glancing at my crotch.

"Stay the hell away from me."

"Oh, you are punchy," he sneered.

I sat down in the theater. There were a hundred people in the crowd—a full house.

The lights dimmed. A shrill voice came over the loudspeakers:

"HELLO. I AM HERE NOW AND I HAVE THE SHAKES. IT IS A DISORDER THAT MAKES ME SHOUT PROFANITY. SOME CALL IT TOURETTE'S SYNDROME. I CALL IT THE SHAKES. THERE IS YOUR DEFINITION. NOW I'LL GET ON WITH IT SO YOU CAN SEE WHAT IT IS ABOUT—SO SHIT! SHIT AND CRAP! CRAP AND SPIT!"

A spotlight came on and illuminated the shaky man. He was naked and standing on his head in the center of the stage's wood floor. His penis was thin and flaccid.

An old computer screen sat beside him. The screen flickered to life and glowed green as it warmed up.

"SPIT AND SLIT! SLIT AND SHIT! LOOK AT ME, I'M GO-ING FULL CIRCLE!" the shaky man yelled as he scissored his legs back and forth. The scissoring caused his body to undulate in little circles, which slowly rotated him around on his head. He made a complete rotation—we saw his hip, his ass, his other hip, and then his penis again. A thin line of drool ran from his mouth.

It was too much to take. I turned my attention to the computer screen where a dumb little animation was playing. It showed the shaky man dancing in a field of flowers—then something in the upper right-hand corner of the screen. It looked familiar. I squinted. What was it? Then I saw: the Portalia logo. Shaky was using Portalia. Shitty, crappy, spitty Portalia.

I had come full circle.

I took off my Bill shoe and threw it at the man. He caught it between his feet and, seeing BILL written on the sole, flipped it around with his toes so the audience could read it.

"BILLY, BILLY, TOUCH MY WILLY!" he screeched. The audience laughed.

I screamed and ran all the way home.

15

I GAVE MOUSE A CALL and she invited me over for dinner.

I washed my T-shirt in the bathroom sink, slicked my hair back, bought a bottle of wine at the liquor store, and rode the bus across town to the hippie Haight-Ashbury district near Golden Gate Park.

Her house was a small one-story Victorian. I knocked. The front door opened and there was Mouse in a yellow summer dress with her hair piled high. She was barefoot and holding a Chihuahua.

"Hi, Larry," she said, smiling.

"Hey, baby," I joked, offering her the wine.

She blushed and traded her dog for the bottle. The Chihuahua squirmed in my arms. "Don't worry," said Mouse, "he's harmless. Say hello, Blanche."

Blanche licked my nose.

"Why'd you name him Blanche?" I asked.

"It was my mother's name."

"You must've loved your mother," I snorted.

Mouse laughed. "Keep him company while I finish up," she said. "I have to take the pasta off the stove."

She headed for the kitchen. I ogled her legs as she walked away. She reduced me to a slobbering animal. I deserved to eat my pasta out of a trough.

Mouse's living room was sparse. There was no furniture, save for a couch and coffee table. Framed family photos sat on a mantle at the far end of the room. The main attraction was a mammoth kickboxing bag hanging from the ceiling. I walked over and gave the bag a kick, but it was so heavy that it didn't move an inch.

Blanche followed me to the kitchen. Mouse had a stove, a fridge, a sink, a table, and two wooden chairs. A windowed door offered a view of the backyard. I looked out and saw a manicured lawn ringed by sunflowers.

We ate and drank, then left the dishes and stepped outside. The warm night sky was clear. We stretched out on the grass. Mouse let her hair down and reclined with her arms propped up behind her, legs straight out, feet bare, toes spread. Her dress stopped just above her knees. I could see her legs in the dark. Her quadriceps bulged like a linebacker's from the thousands of kicks she'd fired.

"All right," she said, "I have a confession to make. Remember when you asked me why I started kickboxing?"

"You said you liked to kick ass."

"Yes, and that's true, but. . . ."

"There's more than just kicking ass?"

"Yes . . . well, I didn't tell you the whole story because—"

"You had plans to kick my head off."

"Ha. Exactly. And I didn't want you to accuse me of being sappy—"

"I doubt 'sappy' would've come to mind as you were kicking me in the head."

Mouse laughed. "All right. The truth is: I started because my father was a boxer and I wanted to be just like him."

"Gentleman Jim" Sullivan, she told me, had been a squatty American with tree-trunk legs, bushy eyebrows, and a husky smile. He drank an olive martini on his porch each evening at dusk and always left the olive, sharpened his straight razor with a leather strop, toted a hanky in his pocket in case his daughter sneezed, and dreamed of traveling to Spain—though he never did—to rough it in the countryside where he'd smoke cigars and talk to manzanita bushes under the hot sun before stopping in for a drink at a pub where the flamenco dancers would stomp it out on top of the bar.

Jim had been all business in the ring, but he'd always dealt a square deal and the other fighters knew it. Rookies underestimated him because he was short, but any misunderstanding vanished the moment he landed his first gut-hit with such taurine ferocity that freshmen paused to wonder whether they'd lose the round, consciousness, or a kidney from the flat-footed gentleman with the steel forearms. He always left the ring with a smile, even when he lost; the other fighters called him the last of a breed, a regular "Gentleman Jim" Corbett, a classic.

"I grew up watching him fight," said Mouse, "so while other girls were asking their fathers for dance classes, I begged mine for boxing. We were poor, but there was a Muay Thai kickboxing school downtown that offered cheap lessons twice per week. It seemed exotic. My dad didn't even know what Muay Thai was, except that it involved kicking, and oh, I liked to kick—walls, cars, him, you name it. He took a second job so we could afford it and I loved it from the start. I was flexible and quick, my shins were sharp, and I healed fast. I still do. See where you kicked me?" She pointed to her face. "No bruises."

I looked. It was true. There wasn't a mark on her.

"He came to every one of my fights and yelled until he was hoarse—sometimes the refs had to tell him to pipe down, he was so loud. He didn't leave a single enemy behind when he died last summer. Even the fighters whose ribs he broke loved him," said Mouse, wiping away a tear. "The day before he went, I promised I'd be a champion just like him—and he said he knew I would."

"And here you are, fighting for the title," I said.

"It'll be at the War Memorial gymnasium," said Mouse. "I'm going up against Raylene 'Razorlegs' Kitty. She's the reigning world champ. I've seen her on TV, but we've never met in the ring. Do you want to come watch?"

"I'm busy that weekend."

"Oh," said Mouse, looking down at her lap.

"I think I'm getting a haircut," I finished.

Mouse laughed. The moonlight made her dress glow. She flexed her toes. How this sultry creature could be interested in me was a mystery.

"All right," she said. "I told you a secret; now it's your turn."

I tried to think of something juicy. I dug my fingers into the lawn. My pulse quickened. My legs began to sweat. An idea came. It was tempting, but what would she think of me? Would she take offense? Would she think I was a freak? Was it kinky? Was I about to complicate everything? I looked up at the sky, around the yard, at her, and thought, what the hell; I could always blame it on the wine.

"All right," I said, "I'll tell you one. But you can't hold it against me."

"I won't," said Mouse, shaking her head.

"Even if it's about you?"

"Even then."

I took a breath.

Mouse waited.

"Well . . . I . . . I didn't know what to expect when I came over tonight. . . ."

"Yes."

"And I saw how you demolished your trainer in the ring. Your elbows, your knees . . . my God, you almost killed him! And your shins—"

"Like baseball bats?"

"Like bats! And . . . well . . . I have this history of angering women. I could only imagine what you might do if you were upset."

"You look harmless."

"Well, harmless mostly, usually . . . most of the time. But I didn't know if I'd piss you off somehow, so . . . I took precautions," I said, glancing at my crotch.

Mouse pondered this for a moment with a raised brow, then began crawling toward me to investigate, slow and serpentine, her dress gaping, breasts hanging low, her eyes locked on mine, until she was so close I could feel her heat. Biting her lip with a wry smile, she reached out as if to caress my shoulder, but her hand descended instead, floating lightly down my chest before coming to a stop an inch above my pants—

Then she did it, quick as a rabbit—rapped my cup with her knuckles as if she'd known it had been there from the start. She fell back on the grass, laughing. My face flushed. I covered it and rolled away across the lawn, which only made her laugh harder.

It was time to go. Blanche didn't want me to leave. He tried to hump my leg but, being too short, settled on my foot. I patted him and said I might be back. Mouse kissed my cheek and agreed that I might.

I pulled out my doll's head and offered it to her. "For good luck," I said.

She laughed and took a step back. "I've seen what you do with that," she said, wrinkling her nose.

"I washed it!" I promised, dancing it around.

Mouse smiled, unsure, but took it gently in her hands. "Why, I'm honored," she said.

With that, I turned, walked away down the path, grinning, and gave quiet thanks to my cup.

16

I DECIDED TO VISIT HANK. If I had to wrestle Sherry to see him, so be it.

I entered Hank's apartment building, climbed the spiral stairs to the ninth floor, and knocked on his door. It opened. I braced myself for Sherry's usual verbal assault, but hallelujah, there stood Hank.

"HANK!" I yelled.

"Sshh," he whispered. "Get in here. Sherry's gone to the grocery store." His eyes were wild.

He stepped aside and quietly let me in. I looked around. Although they'd had me over to dinner—the night Sherry stabbed my hand—I hadn't paused to take it all in. The air was musty. The living room had fetid blue carpeting and a window that looked out on a narrow alley. Off to the right were a kitchen and a bathroom, and behind me, a small den.

"Where have you been?" I asked. "I thought you were dead."

"I was—but then I had The Idea."

"What idea?"

"You'll see."

He motioned for me to follow him. We tiptoed into the kitchen, poured two whiskeys, and drank them down.

"I have some bad news," I said. "I tried to get us a gig at 347, but—"

"I don't want to hear it," said Hank. "Don't tell me. It's of no consequence."

"Fair enough," I said.

Hank poured us two more whiskeys. We clinked our glasses together and drank.

"What happened to your face?" he asked.

I touched my cheek and felt the bruises from Mouse's kicks.

"Woman named Mouse," I said. "We got it into it a little on the sidewalk."

"Say no more," said Hank. "Sherry and I pounded the shit out of each other when we started dating. Look, I still have this scar," he said, unbuckling his belt.

"I believe you," I laughed, stopping him. "Really. And for the record, Mouse and I aren't dating."

"Sure," said Hank, "and my cock's a foot long."

"In that case, keep unbuckling," I said.

Hank giggled and poured us two more whiskeys.

A thick coil of red rope sat on the floor in the corner of the kitchen.

"What's the rope for?" I asked.

"It's an old fire rope. The building was built before fire escapes were mandated, so most of the apartments still have them. Sherry's burning to throw it out, but I want to use it in a performance—maybe climb it and set myself on fire."

We exited the kitchen and walked to the den. The den's door was padlocked shut.

"High security," I said.

"I don't want Sherry going in there," said Hank. "So, are you ready?"

"Ready for what?"

Hank removed the padlock and we went in. It was dark. Candles flickered. I smelled incense and wax. I saw piles of books about Redsoft. Magazine articles about Bill Kunstler were taped to the ceiling. Newspapers clippings were stacked on the carpet. A video of Bill Kunstler giving a speech at a computer trade show blared on a TV in the corner. There were pamphlets, computer disks, T-shirts, and promotional giveaways everywhere; if it existed in the world with a Redsoft logo or the name Bill Kunstler on it, it was probably in Hank's den.

Most disturbing of all was Hank's desk. He'd pushed it against the far wall and built an altar on top. Burning black candles sagged in dripping puddles of wax. Miniature Bill Kunstler figures stood at attention around the candles, all carefully cut out from newspapers, pasted onto cardboard, and propped upright on toothpicks with their eyes poked out. The wall behind the desk was plastered up to the ceiling with newspaper photos of Bill. In some places the pictures were four or five layers deep, taped and glued and stapled on top of each other. Bill's eyes were missing in all of them.

I shuddered with excitement. Here was Bill, the devil himself, pasted up and under our control, even if only in effigy. We could defile him to our hearts' content. By God, I was going to defile him now! I began to unzip my pants—

"No, not like that," said Hank, reading my mind. "I've had a better idea. I can't tell you now, though. Sherry will be back in five minutes. Meet me tomorrow morning in the alley outside at seven."

"Seven—in the morning? Are you serious?"

"I want to get an early start," Hank said, smiling. He looked excited, yet there was a Zen calm draped over him. He shuttled me toward the front door. "You won't believe what I've come up with. Just meet me down there."

I stepped out into the hall, then paused. "One thing," I said.

"What?"

"All those pictures of Bill—what did you do with the eyes?"

Hank smiled and stuck out his tongue. It was covered with little

Bill Kunstler newspaper eyes dissolving in saliva.

Hank shut the door. I wanted to kick it down and demand to know what the hell he was planning, but it was better to leave before Sherry came home.

I turned and headed down the stairs.

Seven wouldn't come fast enough.

* * *

I returned to my apartment, opened a bottle of burgundy, killed the lights, and sat down on the couch to watch the demo tape Favio had rejected. There was no accounting for taste, but I couldn't understand why he'd hated our work; Hank and I weren't any worse than the man with the shakes.

I wound the loose tape back into the cassette, slid it into the VCR, and pressed the play button. Scratchy black and white sixteen-millimeter film leader rolled up the screen, then a title:

"FEAR OF HEIGHTS." HANK & LARRY, 1986

The title cuts to a small white clapboard house—an old single story with a plank porch and a grass lawn in front. The house's pitched roof slopes down over the porch under a bright, cloudless sky.

Hank enters the frame from the left. He's skinny and wearing underwear, a dirty white tanktop, and cowboy boots. He walks along the spine of the roof to its midpoint, then lies down on his back.

I enter from the right, walking in a straight line across the grass down below. Wind blows my hair around. My arms are extended straight out, parallel to the ground, palms up. I'm looking up at the roof's edge as I totter forward across the lawn, wearing dirty white underwear and boots like Hank's.

Still on his back, Hank starts rolling down the roof. It's slow at first, but only slow in the way that watching an accident unfold is slow as the brain gathers but cannot analyze—then gravity takes over and he accelerates, parallel to the porch, rattling down the shingles, sun beating off his forehead in flashes with each revolution, arms at his sides, all the way down to the roof's edge, then over. He falls.

It looks like I'm supposed to catch him—my arms are outstretched and my palms and eyes are up—but I've gone too far across the lawn; I don't see him tumbling horizontally through the air ten feet behind me, spinning in space, a body dropping twelve feet to the grass, parallel to the ground, stiff, uncontrolled, unchoreographed. There is no cushion. There is no net. His shadow races to meet him from across the grass until it's right under him when he hits.

His body bounces. It undulates in the air on the way up because it's soft, then again on the way down. He comes to a rest on the ground. He doesn't move. Maybe he's unconscious. Maybe his back's broken. Maybe he's dead.

The film ends. The piece had been brutal, surreal, a puzzle—in short, gorgeous.

I sat on the couch drinking and tried to fathom how Favio or any other human could possibly reject what Hank and I had made that day.

17

I AWOKE THE NEXT MORNING at seven, threw on pants and a T-shirt, and ran out the door.

A frigid wind blew. San Francisco mornings were freezing in summer. Wind whipped across my face as I ran down the street.

I ducked into the narrow alley beside Hank's building. Hank wasn't there. I looked up at his apartment window and saw it was dark. I squatted beside a dumpster to wait.

The air was still. Pedestrians walked past the alley's mouth. A few may have sensed my presence, but none looked in; there was an unspoken rule to leave a man in an alley alone. The best part of the city was here, in-between; this forgotten, fetid womb of soiled mattresses, trash bags, and abandoned tires was where new dreams were born.

Hank showed up. He sat down, produced a flask, took a sip, then handed it to me.

"All right," I said, taking a hit, "you made me wait all night. You made me run over here in the freezing wind. Now spill it. What's this big idea?"

Hank started right in: "You know we haven't had any gigs in months," he said. "The performance art scene has changed. The neighborhood's changed. We've done a few small pieces here and there, but nothing big enough to put us on the map. Am I right?"

"Yes, yes, get on with it!"

"So," he said, quieting to a hush, "an idea came to me for a performance—the *ultimate* performance—"

"Give it to me!" I begged.

"All right," he whispered, "here it is. First: we get into the car."

"We don't have a car," I whispered.

"Good point. First: we find a car," he said. "We find one and we get into it. We drive it to Bill Kunstler's house. We drive right up onto his lawn. We park. We go into his house and—" Hank made little walking movements with his fingers. "We kidnap him—just like that!"

I laughed so hard that bourbon came out my nose. "Just like that? That's more of a crime than a performance."

"Don't get high-handed on me now. Keep an open mind. Don't start driving home distinctions between this and that. Performance art's subversive—that's why people fear it. Let's make it real! Bring performance art to the people! Make life imitate art!"

"Let's get arrested and spend our lives paying Bill Kunstler's attorney bills."

"Have you forgotten how those SI corporate robots raped us?" asked Hank. "They're just prostitutes for Bill Kunstler's shitty product! He could've killed us! He almost choked us to death! He made cash on our backs! We gobbled his mediocrity and added to his billions! He doesn't deserve it, Larry, not a dime of it."

"His attorneys might quibble with you on that point."

"There won't be any attorneys," said Hank.

"He's the richest man in the world. I think he can afford lawyers."

"Not after we're done with him," Hank whispered.

The plot had suddenly thickened. "Please continue," I said.

"So, we kidnap him. And we take him to your apartment."

"Why mine?"

"Because you don't have a Sherry"

"Ah, right."

"We take him to your apartment and we put him in a cage and—here it is—" Hank looked around to make sure we were alone, then said it: "We turn him into a machine."

"A machine?"

"A performance art machine. We make him do performance art. Piece after piece. We transform him into a performance artist."

Transform him. I tried to imagine Bill in our grasp—hell, in my apartment—at our command, churning out performances. Could it be done? A shudder ran through me. The idea was almost too exciting—and fascinating purely as a bona fide performance art challenge.

"And that's all he does? Performance art?"

"That's all? That's everything! We take it all away—his money, his power, his wife—until he's left with performance art, and nothing else. That's the performance. We dedicate a man to performance art. Bill Kunstler: he *transforms*."

"He transforms," I repeated. The sound was so soothing—but could it be done?

"He *deserves* it," said Hank, sensing my hesitation. "Portalia alone—"

"I know," I said. "But—"

"What?"

"It's just this: why do you think one of the richest men in history isn't constantly surrounded by bodyguards, motion detectors, cameras, and guns? You know his car is bulletproof. You know he probably wears Kevlar underwear. You know—because criminals have all of that, terrorists have all of that, politicians have it—so you know he must have it. There's no way we could get within ten feet of him without a dozen bodyguards tackling us like rabid dogs."

"Don't worry," said Hank with even more enthusiasm. "We'll figure out the details!"

"And what about his house?" I asked. "I don't even know where he lives. You really want to drive—"

"We don't have to go there," said Hank.

"I thought we were going to drive the car onto his lawn."

"No, I just said that for emphasis, you know, to sell the idea. We don't have to drive anywhere."

Hank pulled out a newspaper and showed me an ad for an upcoming tradeshow called the Computer and Software Super Expo that would be held at the convention center downtown. The show was only a week away.

He pointed to the name of the scheduled keynote speaker.

"Bill Kunstler," I whispered.

"See? Billy's coming to us in the flesh."

I rose and started to pace. "It could work," I said. "It could really work!"

"I know!"

"We should make a kidnapper's manifesto," I said, "if we're going to make this art."

I started running around while singing an impromptu song. Hank pulled out a piece of chalk and transcribed my words onto the alley wall:

BILL KUNSTLER WILL BE OUR LITTLE SHAMAN BOY
WE'LL MAKE HIM SPEAK A NEW LANGUAGE
WE'LL MAKE HIM LOSE HIS MEMORY
WE'LL TAKE OUT HIS BOWELS AND PUT THEM BACK
WE'LL REBUILD HIS SKELETON
WE'LL REMOVE HIS BRAIN,
WASH IT IN A BASIN, AND PUT IT BACK IN

Then Hank added a line of his own, laughing:

(AND THE SINGER HERE IS A LITTLE CRAZY)

We wrote THE BOSS IS OURS on the soles of our feet and walked in clockwise circles until the chalk wore off. It was our magic pact and there was no going back.

We were going to make a performance art machine.

We were going to kidnap Bill Kunstler.

18

WE WALKED TO THE HONKEY Donkey. I found us a booth in a dark corner of the bar while Hank brought over a pitcher of beer, two pint glasses, a napkin, and a pen.

"The office is open," he said, pouring beer.

"All right," I said, grabbing the pen. "Let's divvy up the planning. The preparations will go faster if we each take a few tasks."

"Our first task should be to drink this beer," said Hank.

"Agreed!" I said, raising my glass. We toasted, downed them, then drank two more.

"I can't believe nobody's thought of kidnapping Bill before," I slurred. "If you wanted to kidnap someone, why wouldn't you choose somebody with money? And why not one of the richest men alive?"

"Kidnappers should aim higher," said Hank.

Hans, the bartender, brought over another pitcher. It was time for work.

"All right," said Hank, "let's start with weapons."

"I'll take care of that," I said.

"You sure? We may need some serious firepower."

"I'll do it. It'll be fun." I wrote my name down next to the word WEAPONS on the napkin. "All right. What's next?"

"Getaway car," said Hank.

"What about Sherry's car?"

"That piece of shit? She sold it. What about your new woman?"

"She has one."

"Think she'd let us borrow it?"

"I could ask."

"Good. All right. Since you have weapons and the car, I'll figure out how to grab Bill," said Hank. "The specifics: the convention center layout, the breakdown of the actual operation, the execution."

"Fair enough," I said. I wrote down HANK: GRAB.

"I'll figure out how to hold him," I said.

"I think we should put him in a cage like an animal," said Hank.

I wrote LARRY: CAGE.

"What about the other thing?" I asked.

"What other thing?"

"His money—taking it."

"Right, so he can't afford attorneys."

"Exactly," I said.

"I'll take care of it," said Hank.

I wrote HANK: MONEY.

"How are you going to do it?" I whispered.

"I have a plan," said Hank. "I don't want to get into details here, but I think we'll need some help from our old pal Rudy—Rudy the programming genius."

"I like it," I said.

"Set up a meeting with him," said Hank. "I'd call him myself, but with Sherry around. . . ."

"Done," I said, writing LARRY: CALL RUDY.

19

THE NEXT DAY I RODE a bus to Mouse's house. I knocked on the door.

"COME IN!" she yelled.

I went in. Mouse was doing sit-ups on her living room floor.

I watched her go. She was wearing her silver boxing shorts and a cut-off tanktop. Her stomach was a six-pack of muscle—maybe even a twelve-pack.

"How many do you have left?" I asked.

"Five hundred," she huffed. "I'm shaping up for fight camp."

"When is that?"

"I leave Saturday. It's in Vegas. Only have two months to get me in shape for the bout," she gasped.

I wandered over to the mantel to look at her family photos. There was one of a bare-chested boxer with a gap-toothed smile and bushy eyebrows in a fighting pose—her father, no doubt. Her mother, Blanche, was in a frame beside him. She had jet-black hair, freckles, and exotic feline eyes—Mouse's eyes.

Mouse finished her sit-ups and I followed her to the kitchen. She turned on the faucet, stuck her mouth underneath, began gulping like an animal, then giggled. Water ran across her face and down her tanktop. She turned off the water, grabbed a towel, and tried to dry herself off.

"You're staring at my tits," she said, smiling, then lifted her top to reveal two perfectly round breasts that defied gravity. She pulled her top back down. "And now your mouth is open," she said, laughing. I felt my face turn red. "Which for some reason reminds me," she continued, "I still haven't met your pal Hank."

"Or Sherry. That can be arranged."

"Let me invite them over for dinner."

"You really want to open that can?"

"What do you mean?"

"They don't always get along."

"Lots of couples don't always get along."

"They REALLY don't always get along."

"Oh, come on. Don't hog them. You think you have a monopoly on fascinating people?"

"Not at all. Go ahead. Call them. Be fascinated."

Mouse hopped up onto the kitchen counter and picked up the phone. I recited Hank's number. Mouse dialed. Sherry answered. Mouse introduced herself and said she wanted Sherry and Hank to come over for dinner. Sherry was delighted. The women tittered, made their plans, then said goodbye.

"It's done," said Mouse. "We're set for Friday."

"I'll be there," I said.

"By the way, how's the job hunt going?" asked Mouse.

"I've decided to take a little hiatus," I said. "Hank and I are going to focus on performance art for a while." Thoughts of SI tore through my brain as I finished my sentence. My mouth went dry and my shoulders tensed.

"My God, you look terrible," said Mouse. "I'm sorry, I didn't mean to bring it up—"

"No, it's fine," I said. "I guess I'm still uptight over SI."

"You need therapy. Come here."

I walked over to her. She turned me around and gave my shoulders karate chops.

"Your shoulders are like cement."

It was true—they were up around my ears. I tried to relax them, but they only tensed up more.

"You know what you need?" said Mouse, hopping down from the counter. "Role-playing. A little role-playing to get that old job out of your system—"

"Oh, please no," I said.

"Come on, it'll be fun. Who do you blame most of all for what happened—for the torture you've told me about, the ridicule, the harassment?"

"Bill Kunstler," I said dryly.

"Bill Kunstler. Good. Then THIS," she said, pointing to one of her kitchen chairs, "is Bill Kunstler, mastermind of all the shit you were made to eat over the past . . . what was it . . . six months?"

"I lost track," I muttered.

"No matter," said Mouse. She turned and addressed the chair with her hands on her hips. "Hello, Bill. My friend Larry here has something he'd like to say to you."

"I have nothing to say," I said.

"Oh, you must have SOMETHING," said Mouse. "Oh . . . oh, I get it, you're more a man of action. You don't just have something to say—you have something you'd like to DO. Is that it?"

My teeth clenched and my nostrils flared involuntarily.

"Bill," said Mouse to the chair, "I'd like you to meet Larry. Larry, this is Bill. Bill, Larry here would like to DO something to you. What's that? You say you'd like to fuck Larry in the ass? Well, that's not very nice! Did you hear that, Larry? Bill said he misses fucking you in the ass. What are you going to do about THAT?"

I grabbed the chair, swung around, slammed it against the kitchen wall as hard as I could, then let go. The chair stayed—all four legs had punctured six inches into the drywall.

I looked at Mouse. She was smiling and not surprised at all; she looked pleased, in fact.

We stared at the chair frozen in space.

"Feel better?" asked Mouse.

I did.

She opened a bottle of wine and handed it to me. I took a hit, then she grabbed the bottle and had a gulp herself.

"Hey, easy there," I said, "you've got your training—"

Mouse took another swallow. "Screw it. I'm probably not going to win the fight anyway."

"The hell you're not!" I said, grabbing the bottle.

Mouse laughed and thrust out her chest as far as it would go in her best sexy pose.

I'd corrupted her already.

20

I DIALED RUDY'S WORK PHONE, but an automated recording said his number was invalid. I called SI's receptionist and asked for Rudy's extension. She checked the company phonebook, but couldn't find anyone named Rudy. I asked her to transfer me to Bob, a programmer whose cubicle I remembered had been right beside Rudy's.

"This is Bob Wilson," Bob answered.

"Bob! It's Larry Frommer."

"Larry! What you been up to?"

"Drinking."

"Lucky you," Bob laughed.

"Sorry to be all business, but is Rudy around?"

"He's gone."

"Gone where?"

"Belly terminated him."

"What? Why?"

"Who knows?" said Bob. "Rudy stopped by my cube, said congrat-ulations—that I was now the senior programmer instead of him—then left with his belongings in a cardboard box. Belly followed right behind him and practically pushed him toward the elevators."

"Was anyone else fired?"

"No, but I wouldn't be surprised if there are more."

"Why do you say that?"

"Something strange is going on."

"What do you mean?"

"The FBI is here," Bob whispered.

"What?"

"There are men in suits all over the place—interviewing people, walking out with computers. It's some kind of investigation."

"About what?"

"Nobody's talking. My phone's probably tapped—"

"Do you have Rudy's home number?"

"I don't."

"Who might?"

"Belly, I imagine, but I doubt he'd give it to you."

"You're probably right. Thanks, Bob."

"No problem. Say hello to the bottle for me."

"I will."

I hung up and dialed Hank.

"Make it quick," he whispered. "Sherry's on the war path."

I told him about Bob and the FBI.

"That's ridiculous," said Hank. "Rudy was SI's best programmer. Why would Belly fire him? And the FBI—"

"I know. I say we go down there tomorrow and make Belly give us Rudy's number."

"All right. But I'll need to run an errand first."

"What errand?"

"I have to pick up some wine. We're dry over here."

"I'll go with you."

"Come by in the morning."

"See you then."

We hung up.

* * *

I met Hank on the sidewalk outside his apartment building the next morning.

"Where are we going for the wine?" I asked.

"The Biggity Baggin discount warehouse on Fifth. They sell food and liquor in bulk. I've never been, but Sherry shops there all the time."

We started walking. Hank was hungry, so we stopped off at a fast-food joint called Sexy Chicken. He ordered a bucket of Hot Thighs, Dewy-Drizzle Drumsticks, Creamytime Mashed Potatoes, and Lickety Thick Coleslaw to go.

The cashier slid the bucket across the counter. Hank lifted the lid and looked inside. The food had already congealed into a greasy gray mound.

We left Sexy Chicken and continued down the street. Biggity Baggin was only a few blocks away.

Hank glanced over his shoulder.

"What's wrong?" I asked.

"I don't know," he said. "I feel like we're being watched."

"Right now?"

Hank nodded.

I looked up and down the street. There were parked cars, delivery trucks, bums, apartments, shops . . . nothing out of the ordinary.

"Have you sensed this before?"

Hank nodded.

"When we're in public or all of the time?"

"Most of the time."

"I think you're just antsy about nabbing Bill."

"I didn't think of that. You're probably right," he said.

We reached Biggity Baggin. A mob of eager shoppers pushed toward the main entrance while the hundreds who'd already finished shopping struggled to exit. Hank and I joined the mob entering. We shuffled forward as departing shoppers elbowed past us, pushing shopping carts crammed high with groceries in gargantuan quantities; I saw one lady in flip-flops balancing twenty tampon boxes and ten gallons of bottled spring water on top of a new lawn chair.

An attendant in an official orange vest asked to see my Biggity Baggin membership card when we reached the entrance. I didn't have one, so the attendant directed us toward a membership counter where sixty people waited in line to sign up. Hank and I pretended to head for the counter, then changed direction when the attendant wasn't looking, tossed the chicken bucket into a cart, and rolled away into the aisles.

Biggity's warehouse was a half-mile square. Aisles were stacked to the rafters with bulk items in oversized boxes. Laundry detergent came in twenty-pound tubs. Oranges came in crates. Mustard was available in yearly editions.

People pushed and shoved. Carts collided. Aisles jammed with shoppers and carts and children. A man halted right in front of us to search for his glasses. Women fumbled with their pocketbooks. Little girls pulled the legs off dolls. The flow of shopping cart traffic forced us through Biggity's central aisle, which led straight to the twenty checkout stands at the front of the store where crowds waited to pay with their carts in vague, disorganized lines. Shoppers jostled. People argued. Am I in line? Yes, you are, but I'm ahead of you. . . .

We rolled to the aisle marked LIQUOR. Beer came in kegs. Wine was bottled in gallon jugs. It looked like heaven—until we saw the prices. The numbers seemed high. Could they be right? We calculated, dividing quarts by dollars, pleasure by pain, then realized the booze wasn't cheaper in bulk at all.

"We might as well have gone to the liquor store," I said.

Hank hung his head. "I guess we came up short."

"Guess so," I said, picking up a gallon jug of a coastal Merlot from New Jersey. Fancy. I spun the cap off and drank. Hank laughed and kept a lookout. When I came up for air, he grabbed the jug and took over, then me, until it was empty.

We moved on to a Cabernet Sauvignon without bothering to check if it was coastal or not. As Hank guzzled, I looked out across the crowd. Beer-bellied slobs fought over ten-pound steaks, fat mamas slapped their kids' faces, married men ogled hot ladies in line while pretending to read checkout tabloids . . . between the jostling, the blaring loudspeakers, the bright tiled floors, the refrigeration, the aisles reaching to infinity, and the glaring florescent lights, the warehouse struck me as a mental hospital in a middle-class-level of Dante's hell.

A manager wearing an orange vest hurried over and wanted to know if we planned to pay for the wine we'd downed.

Hank grinned like a madman. His teeth and lips were Bacchus red and wine was caked all around his mouth—he looked like a bloody savage caught eating a corpse. The manager took a step back, unsure, then ran off toward the security booth.

There was an emergency exit at the end of our aisle. We grabbed our chicken bucket and ran through the door with a jug of Chardonnay. Alarms began to ring.

We stumbled across the parking lot, then caught a bus to Software International.

"WE ARE DRUNK OUT OF OUR MINDS," I slurred as we hurried through SI's lobby, past a receptionist, and into an elevator with the chicken bucket.

"DON'T WORRY, IT'LL PASS," announced Hank to the entire building.

We rode the elevator up, exited, and staggered toward Belly's cube.

A facility engineer saw we were drunk and offered us a plastic garbage bag, just in case we got sick. I took it and thanked him as we charged onward down the hall.

We passed Rudy's cubicle. A clean-cut man in a suit was watching another clean-cut man in a suit crawl on the floor behind Rudy's computer. The first suit saw us and approached with a flashlight in his rubber-gloved hands.

"FBI," he said. "Where are you two going?"

"We're visiting a friend," I said, trying to sound coherent.

The suit shined his flashlight in my face. "Is this your friend's cubicle?" he asked, pointing to Rudy's cube.

"Yes," I said.

The agent raised an eyebrow.

"What he means," said Hank, "is that our friend's cubicle looks just like this one. They all look the same, don't they? Carpet on the walls, a desk, a chair—"

"Is your friend Rudy Schwartz?" the suit asked.

"No," said Hank, shaking his head.

"Lying to a federal agent could subject you to fines and jail time," said the suit.

"Oh, we'd never lie," I laughed.

"Are you drunk?" the suit asked.

"Maybe," I said.

"We only drink socially," said Hank.

"And we're always social," I slobbered.

The agent eyed us with disgust and waved us along.

* * *

"LUNCHTIME!" yelled Hank, sliding the bucket across Belly's desk. Belly jumped out of his chair and put up his dukes.

"We come in peace, you crazy beast!" said Hank. "Look! We even brought you an offering!"

"You two are drunk off your asses," said Belly. "There's wine all over your faces!"

"We shopped at the warehouse." I burped, waving my new plastic garbage bag around. "And drank—drunked? —at the warehouse."

"I'm not interested in your Pig Latin spatter," said Belly.

"It's not Pig Latin spatter, you derelict!" I said. "It's Pig Spätzle—you don't know what the hell's in the slop, but it satisfies because it expresses the eneralgay ideayay." I smiled, then fell to the floor. I had a feeling I was drunker than Hank.

"Get the hell out of my cubicle!" Belly growled, jerking a thumb toward the exit.

"But we brought you chicken!" said Hank.

Belly opened the bucket and looked inside. "Is it poisoned?"

"WE JUST BOUGHT IT!" I sang from the floor. "We wouldn't try to kill you!"

Belly bit into a thigh. "This chicken's cold."

"Since when did that stop you?" I asked.

Belly ignored me and took another bite. "Don't think for a second that I'm hiring you back here."

"We just want to find Rudy," Hank said.

"I'm not his keeper," said Belly, chewing thigh.

"That's not what we heard."

"What does that mean?"

"We heard you fired him."

"So what? I fire a lot of people. I wanted to fire you."

"But why Rudy? He was the best programmer SI had—"

"None of your business," mumbled Belly through a mouthful.

"Why is the FBI searching his cubicle?" asked Hank.

Belly pointed a finger at us. "That's enough. You can—"

"FBI! FBI!" I yelled at the top of my lungs.

Belly ran over to me and clamped his fat hand over my mouth. "YOU SHUT UP!" he squealed, his eyes wild and red like a rat's. "Shut up! They're questioning people right now!"

He removed his hand. My lips tasted like chicken grease.

"Tell us where to find Rudy, or we'll really start yelling," said Hank.

"Why do you want him?"

"We need him for a job."

Belly was sweating. He took a breath, walked to the cubicle's entrance, checked the aisle for agents, then came back. "Rudy's just lying low for a while," he whispered.

"Lying low where?" asked Hank.

Belly wiped his brow. "I still don't understand why you—"

"WHERE?" I yelled.

"The Flamingo Motel on Lombard."

Hank and I made faces. The Flamingo was a roach-infested flophouse down near the water.

"Which room?" asked Hank.

"Not a room," whispered Belly. "He's under it."

"What do you mean, under it?"

"There's an old fallout shelter under there. Go in through the basement door on the side of the motel and look for Pink Floyd behind the furnace."

Hank and I just looked at him. It was crazy talk. I was sure Belly was lying.

Belly shrugged. "That's what Rudy told me," he said, his mouth full.

I rolled onto my side and threw up into the garbage bag.

21

I OPENED MY EYES AND found myself sprawled on a pile of dirty laundry and performance art props on my living room floor with the garbage bag full of wine vomit beside me. I stumbled to the living room window, saw nobody was looking, pushed the barf bag out, shuffled to the kitchen, splashed water on my face, and dried off with a dishtowel.

On the kitchen wall there was an old photograph of my parents posing in a bar. My father, Abe, was smiling. My mother, Marilyn, was not.

Abe had met Marilyn in Nebraska in 1946, where he managed to knock her up on their first date. Fearing her father's twelve-gauge, the lovers boarded a bus and fled. They lived awhile in Kansas, but Marilyn was restless. She'd always wanted to be a showgirl, so we made our way to Las Vegas, where she prodded Abe into taking odd casino jobs—bellboy, change man, porter, shoeshine—to fund her budding career.

Marilyn began auditioning, but Vegas was a hard town. Nobody wanted a five-foot dancer with child-bearing hips. She came home dejected nightly. She started drinking—"Gin takes the sting off," she said—and she smoked; two packs a day, then three.

Months passed without a lucky break. She pounded the pavement, but show directors refused to acknowledge her innate talent. She took to berating Abe. "IT'S YOUR FAULT I GOT KNOCKED UP," she'd scream, "AND YOUR FAULT I DON'T HAVE THE DOUGH TO MAKE MYSELF UP BETTER FOR AUDITIONS!"

The brow-beatings left Abe black and blue. Sometimes he cried, but in the morning he'd whistle and tap dance around the kitchen like nothing had happened. "Sorry, Mr. Abe," Marilyn would say in her robe, kissing him on the cheek, to which he'd say with a smile, "Forget about it, Mubsy," and cook us up a flurry of eggs before riding the bus across town to shine the high rollers' shoes.

Abe liked the casinos. He began putting a few bucks down here and there during lunch . . . nothing serious, just a few coins to make Lady Luck smile. Soon it was a five spot after quitting time, then a ten, then rattling the dice with his pals after work. He stayed out later and later; soon he was gambling away half his pay. Marilyn guzzled gin and beat him until he begged for mercy. In the morning he'd laugh it off in the kitchen and cook me oatmeal while she lay passed out on the couch. "Don't worry, Larry," he'd say, "she's just frustrated. You have to understand, she wants to be a dancer, and me, well, it's hard for your old man to quit the tables. You'll see someday." Then he'd dance across the linoleum like Fred Astaire with a spatula for a cane and sing a made-up song that made me laugh so hard the oats came out my nose:

> *From Vegas we have come,*
> *And to Vegas we will go,*
> *For every time we try to leave*
> *The car does seem to slow*

After countless tryouts, Marilyn finally made the second round of auditions for the topless show Dancing Baubles in Heaven, but when she showed up for the cut, Abe busted in drunk, threw a blanket over her tits, and punched the director flat out. She tried again, and after another year was cast as the gymnastics girl in a variety act, The Flying Splits. The gig was on speculation—it had no money—so she had to buy her own costumes. It ate up most of my parents' savings, but we managed. The newspapers liked the show; one article even mentioned Marilyn by name. *I'm dancing in Vegas*, she wrote her friends back home. The engagement was booked for six weeks, but after two she came home and found Abe had gambled away her costumes at the craps table. She gave up dancing after that and never let him forget it. He felt so bad that he swore off betting and moved us to San Francisco.

Marilyn became a bartender at Clinch, a boxing-themed saloon in the Tenderloin, and told anyone with an ear how Abe had ruined her chances in show business. He took it on the chin for a year, then moved out—he'd finally had enough.

I went to live with him in a flophouse on Sixth Street. He made the rent working for the railroad. It was honest as hell. Every night he came home with blackened fingers ground to the nub. Sometimes he cried, but he always danced it out in the morning.

Abe took me to see Marilyn at the bar every Saturday night. She looked haggard, but patrons liked her because she told dirty bartender jokes with a cigarette dangling from her lips. Abe and I would sit at the back table until the place closed, then go up and sit on the stools. "How're you doing, Larry?" she'd ask in a raspy voice, pushing me a Shirley Temple and serving herself and Abe for free.

Her teeth were falling out. When they were half gone, the dentist pulled the rest and gave her dentures. She didn't like wearing them—she said they made her nervous—so she kept them in a glass of scotch behind the counter. It made the patrons laugh . . . she played it up with blowjob jokes . . . the barflies guffawed and clapped . . . it became a running gag. "For heaven's sake, put your teeth in," my father would say, and she would, but just long enough to suck the scotch off, then clink, back in the glass.

She chain-smoked brown slims that made her cough. She hucked the phlegm into a paper napkin. "Your father killed me, Larry. He took away my career. It'll be a miracle . . . cough . . . spit . . . if I don't die of obscurity this very night. I was going to be a dancer but he ruined it. I would've been a star. . . ."

Marilyn died. We drove to the mortuary. It was an open casket. Abe put her dentures in the coffin—he couldn't afford flowers. A few barflies showed up. The preacher spoke, then we drove her down to the cemetery where she and Abe had plots beside each other.

It was sunny. The air smelled of cut grass. Men with shovels lowered the casket into the ground.

Abe and I stood beside the grave. He threw in a handful of dirt, then broke down sobbing. We walked to the car and got in. He took a hit from a flask, then threw the rest out the window. He died the next summer.

* * *

My phone rang. It was Hank.

"Let's go see Rudy," he said.

"I'll meet you in an hour," I replied.

"And bring some tools," said Hank before hanging up.

I put on a pair of jeans and a T-shirt, then rummaged around for tools. All I could find was an iron mallet. I slid it down my pants.

I met Hank outside his apartment. He was dressed in plumber's overalls and red cowboy boots. A toolbox was in his hand. I snickered at his overalls.

"Oh, you should laugh," he said, pointing at my mallet bulge.

We started walking toward The Flamingo, just a couple of low-rent repairmen.

* * *

It would be some time before I would learn that the U.S. Office of Civil Defense had started a nationwide program in 1961 to transform public buildings into fallout shelters for civilian use in case of a nuclear attack. Millions of shelter sites were identified, licensed, marked with yellow Fallout Shelter signs, and stocked with food, water, medical supplies, radios, Geiger counters, and other equipment.

Designed by hotelier and science-fiction nerd William Argot in 1962, The Flamingo Motel's populuxe space-age geometry, pink stucco, and sparkly crushed-quartz façade clashed with the salty nautical charm of the surrounding neighborhood, so it wasn't a surprise that locals hated it. They nicknamed it Argot's Asshole, picketed on the sidewalk during its construction, and vowed never to set foot inside—which meant they were unaware that Argot's architect had included a Civil Defense bunker twenty feet beneath The Flamingo's basement. William ignored his critics because he knew that in the face of a nuclear attack, he'd be sauntering down to the basement, unlocking the shelter's four-inch lead door, and descending thirty-three steps into a watertight den protected by one thousand cubic yards of concrete and stocked with enough food, water, and filtered air to keep three city blocks alive for weeks while his detractors were outside getting vaporized.

The Civil Defense shelter program was eventually dissolved. Russian missiles had become so powerful that a civilian-grade bunker was about as effective against a nuclear blast as a cardboard box. Some decommissioned shelters were repurposed, but most were boarded up in the name of superstition, their emergency supplies and Cold War fears forgotten behind fresh drywall.

When Argot died in 1971, he bequeathed The Flamingo to his acid-tripping son Francis. Young Francis wasted no time. He tore down the yellow Fallout sign, hid the bunker's basement entrance behind a Pink Floyd poster, and, with the help of a long-haired stoner assistant everyone called Reindeer, transformed the shelter into a psychedelic LSD-manufacturing lab that turned a profit overnight.

Bored with pushing acid, Francis graduated to selling PCP out of The Flamingo's parking lot, then Mexican heroin out of the motel rooms, then primo Colombian blow from behind the lobby's front desk until cops busted him in 1974.

Francis served time in San Quentin for a year before a cellmate stabbed him to death with a bed spring. With no heirs in sight, the city auctioned The Flamingo to a Japanese buyer, who in turn hired a U.S. management company to run the motel.

The new management never bothered to look behind the Pink Floyd poster. Argot's bunker lay cold, dark, and forgotten by all but one: Francis's old LSD lab assistant Reindeer—or Rudy for short.

* * *

Hank and I arrived at The Flamingo. Its quartz façade glittered in the sunlight. We crossed the parking lot and found the metal door on the side of the building that led to the basement. Hank grabbed the door's handle and pushed. The door wouldn't move.

Hank studied it. "I don't see a lock or a keyhole anywhere," he whispered.

"Must be a slide bolt on the inside," I said. "Stand back." I pulled the mallet out of my pants, did a full batter wind-up, and let the door have it. There was a terrible metallic crash and the door shook, but it didn't budge. I hammered again, then again harder, but nothing.

"You're denting the shit out of it!" Hank laughed.

"Gotta break the bolt," I whispered, panting. "Here, you try." I handed him the mallet. He did a wind-up and swung, but missed by a foot, clobbering the side of the building. Bits of pink quartz stucco sprayed across the parking lot.

"I'm the manager—may I help you?" a young woman asked.

Hank and I turned. The motel manager was standing ten feet away.

"We're here to fix the tankard," I blurted in a Southern drawl.

"Tankard? What is that? Who called you?" she asked, eyeing her dented door.

"You did."

"Oh," said the manager.

Hank gave his toolbox a shake. The manager looked at it. The toolbox was the perfect distraction, the working man's classic calling card that gained him access anywhere—buildings, basements, the works. People in power never asked questions when they saw a toolbox was involved; nobody with a brain wanted to stand in the way of repairs that kept toilets flushing, elevators running, and vending machines dispensing.

"Well, keep the noise down," said the manager. "Guests are still sleeping."

"Sure thing, ma'am," said Hank.

"And," said the manager, "it opens outward."

I grabbed the door handle and pulled. The door swung open.

The manager smirked at Hank's red cowboy boots, then turned and walked back to the motel lobby.

We stepped through the doorway into the basement. There were gas valves, water meters, rusty lawn furniture, gardening equipment, rat droppings, and, off in the corner to the right, a belching oil furnace.

We looked behind the furnace and there it was: a dusty, nine-foot-tall Pink Floyd concert poster hanging on the wall. Hank moved it aside, uncovering a heavy lead door underneath. We swung the door open, stepped through the entrance, and descended a long metal staircase into the bunker.

The sub-basement was a concrete warehouse with a twenty-foot ceiling and walls painted in swirling psychedelic purples and pinks. The shelter's central aisle was bounded on both sides by wire mesh cages filled with survival supplies. Each cage was twelve feet wide by thirty feet deep and crammed with dull brown fiberboard barrels stacked to the ceiling in rows. Each barrel was marked OFFICE OF CIVIL DEFENSE with a list of contents. MEDICAL KIT barrels contained aspirin, isopropyl alcohol, penicillin, phenobarbitol, gauze bandages, and purified cotton, while FOOD SUPPLY barrels offered a dry-bowel feast of crackers, biscuits, bulgur wafers, and hard candy.

We continued down the aisle past more cages, then stopped.

"Do you smell that?" I asked.

Hank sniffed the air. "Cherry pipe smoke," he whispered.

"RUDY!" I yelled. "IT'S HANK AND LARRY!"

Rudy poked his head out of a doorway at the end of the aisle. "Well, hey, how have you two been?" he asked, hurrying over to us with his pipe in hand. He looked like he'd lost twenty pounds. "You scared me—I thought you were the FBI. How in the world did you find me? Here, step inside and have a look at my lair."

We followed him into a small office. It was the shelter's old Civil Service command station. The room was stacked with ham radios, radiation detectors, city maps, and defense protocol handbooks, all under a blanket of dust. Rudy had set up a couple of powerful computers that were busy chewing through world news stories and stock reports. The computers were connected to a cable that ran along the floor, out the door, and down the hall, where I suspected it joined up with the motel's network backbone for undetectable access to the outside world. Rudy was a hacker's hacker if ever there was one.

"What brings you around?" he asked. "I haven't been out of here in—what's it been? A week? Two? I can't go out during the day because I might be spotted, and I can't go out at night because the night clerk turns the alarm on. Have I lost weight? Bulgur doesn't exactly pack on the pounds."

"We should bring Belly down here," I said. "We could put him on the bomb shelter diet—"

"Don't mention that jackass!" Rudy growled. "You wouldn't believe how he screwed me; he's the reason I'm down here!"

Hank opened his mouth to ask how Belly had screwed him, but Rudy was already into it, full steam ahead.

"Belly approached me with a loony plan," said Rudy, biting into a salt cracker from a food ration barrel. "He said a Canadian friend of his worked at a bank that processed high-volume credit-card transactions. One day, while investigating a string of unusual deposits, the Canadian uncovered serious money being transferred to accounts in Colombia—Bogotá, to be exact."

"Money laundering?" I asked.

"For the cartels," said Rudy, lowering his voice.

"Which ones?" asked Hank.

Rudy shrugged. "All of them. Moving wads of paper cash has always been dangerous, so cartels have modernized—they use credit cards now. It's easier to hide. Whenever this dirty bank encountered a drug transaction, it would simply break it up into thousands of tiny transactions factored through offshore accounts, making tracing them practically impossible."

"How did you fit in?" I asked.

"Belly wanted me to write a sniffer program to monitor all of the credit card transactions running through the bank. The Canadian would in-stall it and we'd cherry-pick the transactions belonging to the cartels, then divert a few bucks from each one into an account the Canadian had set up under a fake name. It sounded fun and the amounts were small, so why not?"

Rudy continued: "The Canadian installed my sniffer and the money started rolling in. But there was a problem: Belly neglected to tell me that this so-called 'bank' wasn't just processing cards for mom-and-pop shops in Omaha; it was a national clearinghouse for some pretty big-name credit cards. We were sucking in numbers from TEN MILLION transac-tions per hour. The Canadian panicked—the data was filling up the bank's hard disks—so he altered my sniffer to electronically mail the data out of the bank so it could be processed offline."

"Mail it where?" I asked.

"To my mail account at SI."

"You're joking," I said.

"EXACTLY!" Rudy yelled. "THANK YOU! TEN MILLION PIECES OF MAIL PER HOUR! SI's mail system choked! Managers came running! What the hell are all these credit card numbers doing in all of this mail to Rudy blankety blank? Hello? FBI? We've got a real deal on our hands, a real stinky deal!"

Rudy took another bite of cracker. "So, I showed up to work on Monday. Belly took me aside and said the FBI was coming to see me. I asked him what the hell he was talking about. He said the Canadian had changed my sniffer. That was stupid, I said; why would he do that? Belly said sorry, that it was actually his own idea; he hadn't known it would amount to TEN MILLION PIECES OF MAIL PER HOUR. So I hurried to my cubicle, grabbed what I could, and ran. I couldn't go home—the FBI was probably already there—so I came here. So far I don't mind sub-basement living. My friend Francis and I used to cook acid down here back when we were hippies."

"What now?" asked Hank.

"I don't know," said Rudy. "Lie low. Maybe hitchhike to Mexico."

"I guess this is a bad time to ask you for a favor," I said.

"What favor?"

Hank and I smiled.

"Oh, please," said Rudy. "I can only handle one manhunt at a time. I'm curious, though; you two don't seem like criminal types."

"It's a performance art piece," said Hank. "But if we tell you what it is, there might not be any turning back; you might have a hard time letting go once the choreography's in your head."

"I'll risk it," said Rudy.

"It involves Bill Kunstler," said Hank.

"What about him?"

"We want to take his money."

"A get-rich scheme, eh?"

"No, better."

"What could be better than stealing his money?"

"Deleting it."

Rudy took a puff of his pipe. His eyes narrowed. I was pretty sure he was thinking about how if he hadn't written his sniffer, he wouldn't be in trouble, and he wouldn't have written it if the Canadian hadn't offered to install it at the bank, and the Canadian had only offered because the bank's computers were insecure, and they were only insecure because they were running Portalia, which meant Kunstler was probably as culpable as some—and maybe more culpable than most—since his product was earning billions while Rudy was sitting in a bomb shelter eating bulgur.

"Tell me more," said Rudy.

We told Rudy everything. He listened to our idea with nods and chuckles. When we were done, he couldn't put it down, just like Hank had said.

"What do you need from me?" Rudy asked.

"Full access to Bill's stock accounts," said Hank.

"I might have just the person to help you," said Rudy. "Let me talk to him and I'll let you know."

As Hank and I rose to leave, I noticed the office's wallpaper was pink with little dancing reindeer printed all over it.

"That's some crazy wallpaper," I said.

"It's LSD blotter paper," said Rudy. "Each reindeer's a dose."

"Is it still good?" asked Hank.

"Probably. Acid can last for years."

Hank walked up to a reindeer and licked off an antler. Rudy laughed and offered us each a salt cracker on our way out.

Hank and I climbed back up the stairs, exited the basement, and crossed the sunny parking lot. I knew Rudy would come through—our choreography was in him.

22

HANK AND I WALKED TO a hardware store called Lodell's to buy supplies for the kidnapping. Lodell's housed forty aisles stacked to the ceiling with tools, electrical, plumbing, and lumber, plus it delivered—a necessity since I had no car.

When we arrived, a cook was grilling up free hamburgers in the parking lot to promote a new line of barbeques. We ordered two burgers rare, grabbed a large shopping cart, and went inside.

Hank pulled out a shopping list and we started down the aisles, tossing supplies into our cart as we went: rope, chain-link fencing, aluminum fence posts, foam bedrolls, duct tape, plastic tubing, padlocks, superglue, a speakerphone, steel wool, staple gun, extension cords, power strip, dimmer switch, white porcelain toilet, a drill, bolts, ratchet set, mountable C-clamps, canvas camping tent, earplugs. . . .

Hank stopped in the aisle and looked at his hands. They were shaking.

"Is it the LSD?" I asked.

"I think it might be the lights," he said.

I looked up. The lights hanging from the ceiling were florescent and buzzing. Their flickering induced hystero-epileptic reactions in some people, and Hank had always been susceptible; symptoms could include tremors, dry mouth, cracked lips, hyperactivity, and dizziness.

A young man in a blue Lodell's apron approached us. He had acne and a pubescent mustache. His nametag identified him as the store's assistant manager.

"Help you find anything?" the kid asked.

"We're doing fine," I said.

"Wow," said the kid, eyeing our shopping cart. "What's all this stuff for?"

"A kidnapping," said Hank.

The kid blinked.

Hank mimicked the kid's blink in slow-motion with his tongue hanging out. The kid grinned as he realized he was dealing with a couple of jokers who were just out to have a little fun.

"A kidnapping," Hank repeated more slowly, his lips drying out.

Hank and I were usually cautious about putting choreography into people because the results weren't always predictable, but right then I was pretty sure that Hank was thinking of using some to kick the tenderfoot's ass—who knew, maybe the kid would learn something. I watched the kid's head, its shape, the way he held it with one ear out, and I could see Hank's choreography going in . . . an inkling of our performance plans . . . obsessive thoughts of kidnapping . . . a becoming-score in the urchin's unseasoned brains. . . .

"A kidnapping," Hank said again with a hypnotic hand flourish that was quite beautiful.

"Are you serious?" the kid whispered, stepping closer. He wiped his mouth. Hank's choreography was definitely in him. Here comes a performance, I thought.

"Who will you kidnap?" asks the kid.

"Maybe you," says Hank.

The kid's mouth opens to speak; he looks like he might drool.

Hank's eyes are watering. He licks his lips and asks if the kid wouldn't mind turning off the store's florescent lights—the buzzing's unbearable. Hank wipes sweat off his brow and I see him swallow down some stomach acid. He burps.

"You look awful," I tell him.

"Will you turn off the lights or not?" Hank asks the kid.

"Why don't you kidnap them?" mumbles the kid, mesmerized. Thanks to Hank, he's got kidnapping on the brain. "Why don't you climb up there and kidnap the lights if you want them off so bad?"

Hank looks up at the lights. He swallows. I know he'll never go up there with his fear of heights . . . but I will.

I set my burger down, run to a stack of shelves, grab hold, and start to climb, one shelf after the next, all the way to the top, twenty feet off the ground, until the florescent lights are flickering and buzzing right above my head. I jump and try to grab a light, miss, slip, and knock down a stack of electric fans. Hank and the kid scatter as the fans crash to the floor. Customers look up and see me on the shelf. An assistant manager comes running. Suddenly, our performance has an audience—people are amassing from the store's four corners with burgers in their hands.

I jump up again, catch the light fixture this time, and hang on. The buzzing's intense. I tighten my grip. The light sways. My legs dangle. Customers laugh.

"IT'S KIDNAPPED!" I yell down to the kid. "HOW MUCH WILL YOU GIVE ME FOR IT?"

"I—I don't know," the kid fumbles.

Seeing he needs encouragement, I make a fist and punch the light, cracking its fixture. The bulb flickers.

"HOW MUCH?" I scream. The kid doesn't answer. Like a chimp, I kick my legs, swinging the light fixture back and forth with my body fully extended—

"All right, all right!" says the kid. "Ten bucks!"

"HA!" I scream. I see another light five feet in front of me. I swing and try to kick it. The kid gasps. The assistant manager commands me to come down, but I build momentum and kick, smashing the light with my boot. Glass rains down.

"HOW MUCH?" I scream.

Our choreography spreads. Customers get kidnapping on the brain. People take out their wallets.

"I'll give you fifteen bucks!" says an old man.

"THAT'S MORE THAN YOU!" I yell, pointing at the kid.

"All right!" the kid says. "Twenty!"

"AND I WANT YOUR APRON!"

The kid looks down at his official Lodell's apron.

"I can't," he whimpers.

I get back to swinging and manage to kick the light in front of me again, raining more glass.

"Twenty-five!" says the kid.

"YOUR APRON!" I scream. I see a light behind me and begin swinging for that one. I kick it, knocking it askew. Its bulb buzzes angrily. The next kick will break it for sure—

"ALL RIGHT!" screams the kid.

I let the light go and climb down from the shelves.

"I guess I asked for that," said the kid.

"People usually do," I said, retrieving my burger.

The kid smiled. My words had gone right into his head. We suddenly had a convert who saw there were times when kidnapping made sense—that in truth, we'd kidnapped him—his mind—and not the lights above. I worried for a moment that maybe now the kid was a potential danger to others, but enlightenment is cheap without gamble.

The kid untied his apron like a snake shedding its skin and handed it to Hank. Hank grabbed a box of plastic bags from our cart, tore it open, took out a baggy, and stuffed the apron into it as if it were an archeological specimen.

"Be careful with that," he said, pointing to the choreography in the kid's head as we rolled away toward the cash registers.

The checkout clerk looked over our purchases: duct tape, sound-proofing, rope. . . .

"My, what are you boys into?" she asked.

"Covert operations," I said to her, chewing into my burger like an animal.

23

HANK, SHERRY, AND I CAUGHT a taxi to Mouse's for dinner. I knocked on the front door. Mouse emerged wearing a skirt and a pink silk blouse that showed off her arms and shoulders. Sherry looked intimidated by the fighter's muscles, but she smiled and hugged Mouse hello anyway.

"And you must be Hank," said Mouse, extending a hand.

Hank laughed nervously, shook her hand, and looked right at her tits.

We went inside. Mouse gave Hank and Sherry the grand tour of the living room with its couch and punching bag, the bedroom with its attached bathroom, then the kitchen with its view of the backyard.

We sat down on the couch. Mouse brought out salmon appetizers, then brushed past me hard on her way back to the kitchen. I saw her nipples were erect. I crossed my legs and smiled.

Sherry nibbled salmon and got down to the business of hen-pecking Hank: "I still can't believe you almost made us late with your silly insistence on taking a bath. It's a wonder we made it here on time. I wish we could afford a house like this. And—oh heavens, Hank, chew with your mouth shut!"

Hank waved her away, popped a vitamin, and swallowed it with salmon.

Mouse stepped out of the kitchen holding a butcher knife and told us no fighting or she'd start hacking off body parts. Hank and Sherry looked at each other and laughed. The hostess was always right. . . .

Mouse brought out two bottles of wine and we drank them down. Hank and Sherry started to loosen up.

We polished off the salmon, then out came the main course: a minimalist dish of sprouts sprinkled over concentric circles of beans—lima, kidney, black, white, soy, mung.

"If there are beans, they're in here!" said Hank, inhaling a lentil.

"It's very gourmet," Sherry purred with a smile.

We sat eating beans. Blanche ran around like a clown and begged. I tossed him a kidney bean. He caught it in the wrong pipe, but managed to cough it up and then eat it again. We all laughed.

We finished the beans and drank some more; Hank sipped a vermouth, Mouse and Sherry opened another bottle of wine, and I poured an old single malt into a weighty crystal glass.

The women went to the kitchen to clean up.

I pulled Hank aside.

"So, what do you think of Mouse?"

"I'm not sure about those beans," slurred Hank, "but her legs are muscular as hell—she could kick the shit out of a crapper!" He looked down at my glass. "You know, there's lead in that crystal."

"So?"

"Lead will shrink your cock," he whispered.

"It will not!" I laughed.

"Hey, no secrets in there!" yelled Sherry from the kitchen.

Hank and I tittered and sucked down our booze.

We all regrouped in the living room. Sherry perused Mouse's family photos on the mantle, pausing on a black and white picture of a young woman who had long dark hair and freckles.

"She looks like you," said Sherry.

"My mother," said Mouse. "She was Irish—"

"And a palm reader!" I blurted.

Sherry's eyes opened wide. "Really?"

"Really," said Mouse.

"Can *you* tell fortunes?"

"Of course," said Mouse. She took Sherry's hand and studied it— the lines, the whorls, the bone structure—then she took Hank's and read it next to Sherry's, side by side, comparing.

"You're going to have a wild sex life together," Mouse concluded.

Hank yelped and grinned at me . . . he was practically hopping on one foot. I couldn't tell whether he was excited by Mouse's legs or the possibility of wild sex with his wife.

"Wild sex, eh?" said Sherry. "When is THAT supposed to start?"

"Ha ha," Hank deadpanned, "how about right now, you slippery slut?"

He grabbed for her ass. Sherry jumped up and ran. They giggled and chased round the couch with the vermouth in his hand and the wine in hers and the dog yapping at their heels until Hank stumbled face-first into Mouse's hundred-pound punching bag, knocking himself unconscious.

Sherry ran to him. "Oh, Hanky!" she cried.

Hank grabbed her tits. Sherry screamed and fell back, laughing.

We move the party to the kitchen. Mouse cracks open a bottle of port. I look at the clock. It's two in the morning and the women are just getting started. Hank passes out on the floor. I sit down on the kitchen's one good chair; the other is still sticking out of the wall right where I left it.

Sherry studies the chair.

"What is this?" she asks, seeing how its legs are embedded in the drywall.

"It's art," Mouse answers.

"I like it," says Sherry. "It's very Postmodern."

"Sit on it," says Mouse.

"Oh, no," says Sherry with a gasp, "I couldn't. . . ."

"Really," says Mouse. "Try it."

Sherry giggles and starts to climb up, but as her rear hits the seat, the chair slips out of the wall and takes a chunk of drywall with it. She crashes to the floor. Her head bounces on the linoleum, but she doesn't spill her drink—she holds her glass straight up in the air like a caught touchdown pass.

"I am so sorry," Sherry slurs. "I think I broke your art."

"Oh, no," says Mouse, "it's supposed to do that. It's functional."

Sherry stands up. "That was so much fun!"

"Try it again," says Mouse.

Sherry holds her drink while Mouse picks up the chair and shoves the legs back into the wall. The chair stays. Sherry climbs up slowly, and this time manages to get all the way into the seat with her back parallel to the floor and her eyes toward the ceiling. The chair's more precarious than before, but it holds.

"I love this!" she says, slurping wine.

"OK, do the thing," says Mouse.

"Here I go," says Sherry. She wriggles. The chair begins to loosen in the wall.

"NOW!" yells Mouse.

Sherry slams her feet hard against the wall and the chair shoots straight out like a rocket, flies halfway across the kitchen, and lands on the floor with a crash, waking Hank out of his stupor.

"That was fantastic!" says Sherry. "My God, Mouse, my GOD, you have the best taste in art!"

Mouse and I fall over, laughing.

* * *

Mouse called a cab for Hank and Sherry. When it arrived, Hank groped Sherry's tits all the way out to the car. She giggled, pulled off his belt, unbuttoned his pants, and went down on him as he shut the rear door. The cabbie smiled, waved to us, and pretended not to watch the fried blond hair bobbing in his rearview as he drove off. It was going to be a good night for them. Mouse and I went back inside.

Mouse grabbed my shirt and dragged me toward her bedroom. "I like your friends," she said, locking her lips onto mine.

I grabbed the bottle of single malt, lifted Mouse, and carried her through the dark to the bed. She smelled of lavender and her ass was rock-hard.

She put her hand on my pants. "Think I can swallow it whole?" she asked.

"No one's ever tried," I said.

"I want it!" she said.

"Take it!" I said.

"Let me love your locust!" she cried.

I stopped. My . . . locust?

Mouse laughed and began working on my pants. "Did you know that there are different kinds of locusts?" she said. "There's *gazam*, the lopping locust; *yelek*, the licking locust; *solam*, the bald locust . . . which one are you? By God, I must know!"

I grabbed the whiskey and ran for the bathroom.

"Hurry back," Mouse sang, undoing her blouse.

I flipped the light on and shut the door. Locust! What was she insinuating? I took off my underwear. My balls were hairless, the result of a solo session at home with the scissors.

I looked at it. It was still soft. I played with it a little, offering encouragement. It grew—some. It looked smaller than I remembered. I gave it a flip. I jiggled it. I checked it in the mirror, then saw Mouse was right. It did look like a locust. I heard her laugh in the bedroom. I couldn't get the thought out of my head. Locust! A pearl of slime formed at the tip. I wiped it off. Disgusting.

I tried to control my breathing but visions of men with micro-penile conditions in gym showers filled my head with dinky cocks that looked more like cysts than dicks. Maybe Hank was right about the lead in the crystal—maybe it had shrunk my penis, shriveling the flesh like a poison. . . .

Claudius died of poison, and rumor had it that he'd suffered from a small cock. He was fifty years old when he became Rome's fourth emperor in the first century AD despite being a drunk and a gambler with a stammer and a tendency to dribble. His mother hated him. She called him a monster of a man after making him suckle until he was nine.

Claudius had many children. Most were unsuccessful. One son, Drusus, threw a pear into the air and caught it in his throat, choking to death the day before his own wedding. Another, Britannicus, was poised to inherit the throne despite being a tittering, sickly boy who masturbated in the halls of the court at all hours.

Being a family man, Claudius married his niece, Agrippina the Younger. Agrippina wanted Nero, her son from a previous marriage, to become the next emperor. At his wife's urging, Claudius adopted Nero, who, being older than Britannicus, became joint heir to the throne.

Britannicus masturbated harder. Claudius fell ill. Agrippina was impatient for her husband-emperor to die, so she hired Locusta the Poisoner, a female contract killer of legendary proportions, to lace Claudius's mushrooms with belladonna at dinner. Claudius shit his robes, but lived. Locusta tried again and succeeded the second time, soaking Claudius's favorite dietary aid—a feather he used to induce vomiting—in a steamy broth of arsenic.

Nero leapt onto the throne and had his masturbating step-brother poisoned by Locusta. When Britannicus convulsed and slumped into his soup bowl, Nero nonchalantly reassured his dinner guests not to worry, that his poor brother had a long history of fainting. Years later, to punish Locusta for her crimes, a new emperor had her torn apart in the ring by wild animals, but only after she'd been raped by a specially trained giraffe. . . .

I screamed.

"What are you doing in there?" asked Mouse.

"Nothing."

"Come out here and give it to me!"

I looked down. I still wasn't hard enough. I needed something to get my mind off of locusts and poison. I remembered a story Hank had once told me about Siberian spas where Russian guests would step into an igloo steam hut, flog themselves with medicinal tree branches until their backs bled, run outside and roll in the snow naked, then run back inside for a shot of vodka to invigorate the body and clear the mind. It was worth a try. I took a hit of the single malt, grabbed a towel, and began flailing my back as fast as I could.

"What are you doing in there?" yelled Mouse. "I'm writhing for you!"

"I need to work up to it!" I gasped, whapping myself faster. "Every performance needs a build-up!"

"You're obsessed!" she cried. "Come perform for me, mister!"

I turned and looked at my back in the mirror. It was bright red. I was invigorated as hell! I busted out of the bathroom, dove onto the bed, and slid into her all in one move. She was hot and wet and light as a feather—I rolled back and lifted her by the ass. She smiled and closed on me like a fist. "I'LL JUICE YOUR LOCUST!" she growled, squeezing, suckling, pulling like a gummy clam, a vagina dentata with the teeth knocked out, undulating her insides until, gritting and sweating booze, we exploded together. We tumbled off the bed, still joined at the hip, and took all of the blankets down with us.

As my eyes closed, I saw her pull one of her father's old boxing gloves out from under the bed and tuck it under her ear like a pillow.

24

I OPENED MY EYES. IT was still dark outside.

"Mouse?" I whispered.

Mouse groaned. Her face was buried in her father's boxing glove.

"Do you mind if I borrow your car?" I asked.

"The keys are on the dresser," she mumbled.

"No, I mean borrow it while you're gone—while you're at kickboxing camp. I need to run some errands."

"You're drunk, Larry. You shouldn't drive."

"While you're at camp, Mouse."

"Oh—then, sure. Take it—"

"Thanks," I said.

I smiled. That was easy.

"—if you'll feed Blanche while I'm gone," said Mouse.

Shit.

"I'm not very good at house-sitting," I said. "I'm accident-prone, I water the lawn too much, I forget to lock the front door—"

"Feed Blanche, Larry. Feed him."

"All right. Feed Blanche."

"And water the plants."

"And the plants."

"I leave for camp tomorrow."

"Tomorrow."

"The keys are on the dresser."

With that settled, I wrapped my legs around Mouse and slept like a baby.

* * *

Morning came. Mouse flopped her arm over my belly.

"My head's killing me," she moaned. "Does yours hurt from the drinking?"

"No. Hank and I practice a lot."

"I dreamed you wanted to borrow my car in exchange for watering the plants and feeding Blanche."

"That wasn't a dream."

"Really? You'll feed Blanche?"

"Sure."

"Thank you. So, why do you need the car, again?"

"Hank and I just need to run some errands."

"Errands, eh?" said Mouse, sitting up a little. "What sort of errands?" She poked me in the gut.

"Ugh! Don't poke my gut."

She poked me again. "Tell me!"

"We're planning a performance and we just need some wheels."

"A performance? Really? When? I don't want to miss it."

"It'll be ongoing—a long piece if we're lucky. It might still be happening when you get back from camp."

"What kind of performance is it?"

"Bill Kunstler," I said, still a little drunk.

"I should've known," she laughed.

I told her about the scheme.

"You're not serious—you're joking, right?" Mouse was really sitting up now. "Tell me you're joking."

"We're not joking."

"You're going to turn him into a performance art machine."

"Yes."

"Look me in the eyes and tell me you're serious."

"We're serious."

"You were going to try something like this without telling me?"

"It's a recent development—"

"You can't just grab him. His bodyguards will come after you."

"He might not have bodyguards."

"You're dead if he does. They don't mess around. I had a friend who was a bodyguard and he carried a .45 with him all the time."

"We'll work it out."

"You'd better have at least one gun between the two of you."

"I don't know. . . ."

"You'll get your asses shot off!"

"It'll be over before they know what hit them."

"I know where we can get one."

"One what?"

"A gun. I know a guy."

"What guy?"

"He owes me a favor. He sells things."

"Guns?"

"Whatever you want."

"Guns."

"Yes."

"Really?"

"Let me call him. I don't want you getting killed."

She reached for the phone. She was crazy.

"Are you sure?" I asked, feeling her ass. "It might be dangerous—"

Mouse flipped me the bird. End of discussion.

* * *

Mouse and I climbed into her car. It was a retired police cruiser—an old Chevy Impala built like a tank. She rolled her window down and floored the accelerator. "HANG ON!" she yelled as we tore out into the street, missing a taxi by an inch. She gunned it for a mile, then screeched to a stop outside Hank's building.

Hank was waiting on the sidewalk with his toolbox. He jumped in back and Mouse took off for the Mission District.

"How's your head after last night?" I asked.

"Good as new," said Hank.

Mouse screeched around a corner and hit the accelerator, narrowly missing a bus.

"YOU DRIVE LIKE A MANIAC!" yelled Hank over the roar of the wind.

"I'M HUNG OVER SO YOU SHUT UP!" Mouse screamed, flipping off the oncoming traffic.

"So who is this guy?" Hank asked.

"He sells things," I said.

"Guns?"

"Whatever we want."

"How much will it cost?"

"Don't worry about it," said Mouse. "He owes me a favor."

The Mission District was San Francisco's Latin Quarter, a rich mélange of Churrigueresque architecture, Diego Rivera-inspired murals, tapas bars, vegetable markets, tequila saloons, bakeries, and vendors hawking everything from donkey piñatas to silver belt buckles inlayed with turquoise.

For two thousand years, the Mission's fertile, damp land had been home to California's Ohlone—a peaceful native people known by their intricately braided hair, dot-and-line tattoos, masterful basket weaving, and soft tribal tongues—that is, until Spanish Franciscan friars arrived in 1776 to burn the natives' culture, convert them to Catholicism, and enslave them to build what would ironically survive as San Francisco's oldest building: the Mission San Francisco de Asís, or simply, Mission Dolores.

Thousands of Ohlone died of exhaustion and European disease. The Spaniards buried them right beside the mission—so many bodies, in fact, that when a bullfight ring was erected there in 1840, fans had to duck the flying bones the bulls kicked up with their hooves. I looked down at the asphalt road rushing past and said a prayer for the Ohlone buried underneath.

Mouse parked and we got out. Mexicans, Nicaraguans, Guatemalans, and Brazilians chatted in the streets, their staccato Spanish and Portuguese rising up past the sun-drenched billboards above. The sidewalks bustled with flirty belles in dramatic rouge and eyeliner, day laborers in cowboy shirts and handmade boots, aproned shopkeepers smoking two-dollar cigars. . . . I saw flashes of gold teeth, a tricked-out low-rider sedan with carpeting on the dash and a Jesus hanging from the rearview, stooped old women cooking tortillas on rolling fry grills, filling the air with the scent of corn, smoky beans, and salsa. . . .

Everywhere I looked, no one was idle; even if they were only standing around, nobody was just killing time; everyone seemed *busy*—busy waiting for social interaction. It was a shared, expectant waiting, with everyone waiting together. I smirked at the thought of a New York or Parisian flâneur trying to blend in while searching for conversations to overhear or fascinating characters to observe. A dandy pedestrian swollen with the intoxicating, solitary romance of his own languid stroll would be quickly outed as a voyeur, a parasite, a thief, taking in without giving back, while the locals gave and gave.

Mouse led us into a shop called GRASS OR ASS—YOU PICK! One half of the showroom was a pot smoker's dream with lighters, bongs, and pipes, while the other offered aisle after aisle of sex toys: blow-up dolls, testicle weights, cock rings, gel dildos, dick pumps, ball gags, solo jerks, anal probes....

Nelson, the shop's owner, was busy helping a woman pick out a vibrator behind the sex counter. He was a real hippie leftover—a fifty-year-old Deadhead with long, stringy hair, jeans hanging off his hips, a shirt unbuttoned to his pot belly, and a self-styled tribal string necklace with a pair of kitchen tongs dangling at the end.

"Nelson!" Mouse called.

"Mouse!" Nelson boomed. "I'll be right over. Look around—everything's twenty percent off!"

"How'd you meet this Nelson?" I whispered.

"I used to work here," Mouse said.

"Here?" I croaked, eyeing a vibrating Ben Wa ball display.

"I worked the pot counter."

"Why does he owe you a favor?"

"He was selling a little dope under the table. I was working when cops busted in. While they were busy reading him his rights, I went to the back and flushed four pounds of weed down the toilet. The DA had to let him go."

Nelson came over. "Mousey!" he said, hugging her.

"Nelson, meet Larry and Hank," said Mouse.

"Nice to meet you, Nelson," I said, shaking his hand.

"Only Mouse may use my birth name," Nelson said. "To you I am Monochrome Rainbow Serpent Under Clouds."

"Monochrome," said Hank, shaking Nelson's hand.

Nelson led us through a beaded curtain to the shop's breakroom. There were cardboard boxes stacked to the ceiling, a sink, a microwave, a couch and a coffee table. We sat down. Nelson pulled out a bong, lit it, and passed it around.

"What line are you guys into?" asked Nelson.

"Performance art," I said, puffing.

"Really? Where do you perform?"

"The Tenderloin, mostly."

"Wait—didn't you play Smelly Joe's place a while back?"

"That was us."

"I saw you every Friday night!" Nelson said, slapping his thigh. "I still remember that thing you did with the toaster and the rubber hose. Holy shit, you guys are LEGENDS!"

"Thanks," said Hank.

"Hey, you know," said Nelson, "I've been getting into performance art a little myself."

"It's nice to know we're not the only ones," said Hank.

"I haven't done any gigs yet, but I've been working on a piece. Do you want to see it?" Nelson asked, taking another hit of the hubbly-bubbly.

"We're sort of in a hurry," said Mouse.

"It'll just take a minute. I'd love to get your opinion—see if I'm on the right track. Let me do the intro for you at least."

Nelson reached into a box and pulled out a specimen jar filled with brown liquid. He walked over, set the jar down on the floor in front of us, and removed the lid to reveal a dead cat floating in formaldehyde. Mouse scrunched up her nose.

Nelson pulled down his pants and underwear, then used the kitchen tongs hanging from his neck to squeeze his testicles. He began jumping up and down. "THE KITTY! THE CATTY! FLOATING IN THE BATTY!" he shrieked. He repeated it several times, then bowed.

"That's the intro," said Nelson.

All of us clapped.

"You're right on track, man," I said.

Nelson beamed. He zipped up his pants, put away the cat, then clapped his hands. "Now," he said, "how about some GUNS?"

We followed him to the rear of the breakroom where he unlocked an old Army trunk. He reached in, lifted out an oilcloth, and handed it to me. I unwrapped it. Inside was an old rifle that had been scratched and beat to hell—it looked like someone had used it as a baseball bat, then maybe a can opener.

"THIS is your gun supply?" I asked.

"What do you mean? Do you even know what this is?"

"No."

"It's a Soviet Kalashnikov AK-47 automatic rifle, lady and gents," said Nelson like a spokesmodel. He cocked the gun. "Famous for its ease of manufacture and amazing reliability, the 7.62 millimeter caliber *Avtomat* takes a thirty-round cartridge, fires six hundred rounds per minute, and sports a muzzle velocity of seven hundred meters per second with a kill range of fifteen hundred meters. The thing's indestructible."

Nelson scooped up a handful of dusty brass rounds from the trunk and offered them to Hank. "Go ahead," said Nelson, "check out this ammo. These babies will ricochet off bone and keep on clicking."

His words made Hank's face go pale.

"I think you need another hit of the grass, master," said Nelson, spitting out a brass round he'd hidden under his tongue. The cartridge fell to the ground with a clink and bounced around. Hank hopped up and down frantically to avoid it, sending Nelson into hysterics. I pulled Hank out of there and back to the couch. We sat down. Color slowly returned to his face.

Nelson's cell phone was sitting on the coffee table. Hank looked at it. I knew what he was thinking: we could use a phone for our Bill operation. I looked over my shoulder. Mouse and Nelson were busy gathering up ammo in back. I gave Hank a nod and he grabbed the phone, switched it off, and shoved it down his pants.

Mouse and Nelson returned with the gun and ammo in a garbage bag.

"Do you have any more guns, Monochrome?" I asked.

"I could get you some," said Nelson.

"Let me get your cell phone number, just in case."

Nelson wrote down his number.

Mouse checked her watch. "I have to catch my bus to fight camp," she said.

"To fight camp!" Nelson roared, raising his tongs high.

* * *

Mouse drove us to the bus station. Hank stayed in the car while I grabbed her duffel bag from the Impala's trunk and walked her to her bus.

I grabbed her hands and kissed her knuckles. "Don't get hurt," I said.

"I won't," she said. "Don't forget to feed Blanche."

"I won't," I said.

Mouse leaned in close. "You're not really going to kidnap Bill, are you?" she whispered.

I smiled.

"I didn't think so." She laughed, pulled me close, kissed me on the lips, pinched my ass, hopped aboard the bus, found a seat in back, pushed open the window, and stuck her head out. "I'll see you in a month or two!" she said.

I threw her a kiss as the bus pulled away.

I walked back to the Impala, got in, and started her up.

"We're on," said Hank.

25

WE PARKED IN FRONT OF the convention center downtown, grabbed Hank's toolbox, and headed for the entrance. Automatic lobby doors slid open and we stepped into a madhouse of frantic trade show coordinators, booth contractors, equipment movers, technicians, engineers, middle management, marketers, ad men, sign builders, janitors, and executives yelling and running in every direction with display booth sectionals, signage, computers, video equipment, overhead projectors, tools, and cleaning supplies. There wasn't much time left—the center would close at five o'clock sharp so union workers could move in to test electrical systems, roll out hundreds of trash cans, stock the snack bars, and clean the restrooms before the show opened.

We joined a crush of people pressing toward South Hall. South was the prized jewel of all the convention center's exhibition spaces—it had the highest ceiling, the lushest carpet, the most popular exhibit booths, and, most importantly, the stage where Bill Kunstler would step out to address five thousand reporters, users, programmers, hackers, critics, and competitors.

South Hall's gaping entrance loomed ahead. The crowd pushed forward through its twenty-foot-high doors, then thinned as people fanned out to the left and right in a hurry.

The hall was cavernous. Views in every direction were blocked by massive booths—some reached fifty feet into the air with faux-wood walls, metal catwalks, hanging signs, and laser beams. Redsoft was everywhere, from colossal banners and Portalia posters to lunchboxes and iron-ons featuring Bill's face.

We turned a corner and happened upon fifteen Redsoft fans waiting in line to receive a free Redsoft T-shirt from a Redsoft representative. The fans were all male and malnourished with bad teeth and poor posture. The Redsoft rep was a woman, which was always a crowd-pleaser at a computer convention. The fact that she was wearing a tight Redsoft polo shirt heightened the tension, to say nothing of her blond hair, double-D breasts, black slitted mini-skirt, and sprinter's porno calves.

Hank and I waddled to the back of the line like pigs. A teenager ahead of us turned and eyed us through half-inch-thick eyeglasses. "She was a Playboy Bunny, you know," he said, jerking a thumb at the T-shirt woman.

Two skinny debaters stepped into line behind us and ran through Bill trivia like their lives depended on it.

"I heard he makes sixty million in interest per year," said the first.

"It's five-fifty mil," said the second. "*Financial Journal Daily*, March fourth."

"March fourth? Your numbers are old. Mine are from yesterday's issue."

"East or West Coast edition?"

"East."

"Watch out—I heard East fudges numbers to placate Wall Street. Fifty-five's probably more accurate."

The bespectacled teen in front of us turned around. "Fifty-five mil, sixty mil, who cares? What difference does it make?" he snapped.

The debaters were aghast at so brazen a challenge, and in the Bunny line no less. Everyone in line turned to watch. The debaters came out gnashing.

"You must be KIDDING!" screeched the first.

"The difference is *five million*—almost a hundred thousand per week!" yelled the second. "You'll never see that much cash in your whole miserable life! And who let you in here, anyway? Stinking heathen! Mind your own business!"

People in line chuckled. Red-faced and exposed as an infidel, the four-eyed teen cowered while the debaters finished him off with catcalls and whining baby cries to his back.

These were the show's real characters—the die-hards, the obsessed, the cult followers of Bill. They loved him because he'd validated their potential long ago: that even a whiny-voiced milquetoast man with no college degree, no ripped abs, no Hollywood looks, and no discernible fashion sense of any kind could transform himself into an omnipotent technology hero of celebrity status and power.

Defending Bill's name, his company, his products, and the veracity of his biographical minutiae was his rabid followers' sport of choice. They memorized facts, practiced rebutting at lightning speeds, and if challenged, stood at the ready to rip a challenger's Redsoft knowledge and information sources to shreds in a show of all-out oral warfare. Battles grew louder the longer they lasted, especially at Redsoft-sponsored tradeshows, which were considered hallowed ground. Men traded snipes in the parking lot, in autograph lines, in tradeshow aisles, and even in the restroom in escalating cycles of intensity and volume, as if they believed Bill himself might step out of a stall after overhearing an impassioned defense of his character and, being suitably impressed with the loyal subject's bulldog tenacity and oral precision, offer up a position at Redsoft while making small talk at the sink. They walked like Bill, whined like Bill, cut their hair like Bill, used Bill's software, took Bill's certification classes, read Bill's interviews, bought Bill's books, and secretly fantasized about stroking billion-dollar Bill cock.

Hank and I reached the front of the line.

"Well, hello," purred the T-shirt Bunny. She winked and glanced at our crotches. "And what size are you two?"

"Extra-large," we said in stereo, grinning.

Bunny handed us each an extra-large T-shirt. We put them on. They reached down to our knees like bibs, presumably to catch drool, breast milk, or semen, whichever came first.

"Very nice," Bunny whispered. "Feels good inside there, doesn't it?"

We nodded, giggled like idiots, then stepped out of line so the debaters could have their turn at her.

* * *

Hank and I walked the length of the hall until we came to the last of the booths. We slowed our pace. The speaking area lay ahead. Thousands of empty metal folding chairs sat arranged in neat rows on a vast expanse of blue carpet that ran from where we stood to the foot of South Hall's grand stage. Blood-red curtains hung behind the podium where Bill Kunstler, Mr. Redsoft himself, would deliver his keynote.

A red velvet rope blocked access to the stage's side stairs, and behind the rope stood a muscled security guard in a navy-blue suit.

"How are we going to get past him?" I whispered.

Hank shook his head—he had no idea.

A voice boomed over the hall's loudspeakers: "ATTENTION. THE TIME IS FIVE O'CLOCK. BOOTH SET-UP IS OVER. THE CONVENTION CENTER IS NOW CLOSED. PLEASE MAKE YOUR WAY TO THE NEAREST EXIT."

Security guards fanned out to remove non-essential guests. The Bill fanatics at the Bunny booth took off running.

We tried to blend in. A janitor had left a vacuum and garbage can nearby. Hank grabbed the vacuum, flipped it on, and started moving it back and forth while I busied myself with adjusting the trash can's plastic liner.

A security guard started toward us. We avoided eye contact and focused on our work. The guard walked by, then bolted after some Bill fans who were pretending not to see him.

"That was close," said Hank.

"Hey!" came a burly voice.

We turned and saw a union foreman approaching with a cardboard box.

"Why aren't you wearing your union shirts?" the foreman asked, eyeing the Redsoft shirts Bunny had given us.

"We forgot," said Hank.

"I'm not surprised," said the foreman. "It's been busy. Here, I have extras." He pulled two yellow union T-shirts out of his box and gave us each one. We put them on.

"Say, have you seen Joe around?" the foreman asked.

"Er . . . earlier," I bluffed.

"How about Jack?"

"Haven't seen him."

"Chuck?"

"Half an hour ago."

"All right," said the foreman, "keep up the good work." He gave us a salute and walked away in search of more union men in violation of the dress code.

Hank grabbed his toolbox and we headed for the stage. The security guard behind the rope watched us approach with his legs spread wide to make room for his brains.

"Backstage is off limits," he growled, holding up a meaty hand.

"Since when?" I asked.

"Since now. The hall's security sweep has begun."

"We have to check the fuse box."

The guard looked us over. "Where are your badges?"

"We're union," I said, pointing at my T-shirt.

"You need badges," the guard grunted, pointing at his own badge that had his name, a barcode, and the Redsoft logo on it.

"Look," said Hank, "Bill Kunstler is speaking tomorrow, and if the fuse box blows—"

"Not my problem," the guard snapped.

"Who do we see about getting a badge?" I asked.

"Nobody. They were issued in limited numbers. Everybody with a badge underwent a security check, and as far as I know, they aren't issuing any more. If you didn't receive one, it's probably because you weren't deemed important enough."

"Who's your boss?" I snarled.

"Redsoft."

"What's your manager's name?"

"Redsoft. That's the only name you need to know, lackey. The sound of that name means turn around, go find one of your union brothers who has a badge, and send him over here to do your work for you while you take your usual two-hour lunch, because you sure as hell aren't going backstage without a valid badge. Have a nice day."

"I'm going to maim him!" I whispered as Hank pulled me away.

"Not now," said Hank. "Let's go steal some badges."

"From where?"

"Redsoft."

* * *

We hurried through the maze of booths until we came to Redsoft's. It was three stories tall with new products on the ground level, a conference area on the second, private executive suites up top, and computers every-where.

Redsoft employees were working frantically to put the finishing touches on the booth's signs and lighting. A woman with a clipboard directed them from the ground. She seemed to be in charge. I pointed her out to Hank.

"She has a badge," I said.

"I see it too," said Hank. "Follow my lead."

We started our approach. All of the computers in the booth were networked together with cables, and all of the cables converged at a tall blue box that stood in the middle of the booth's ground floor. Hank was leading us straight toward it.

"You want to steal that thing?" I asked. "It must weigh three hundred pounds. How will that get us badges?"

Hank shushed me. We strolled onto the booth's plush carpet. The blue box was alive with flickering lights. We stepped behind it and Hank examined its electrical cord; it was a custom design that snaked from the box's chassis to a high-voltage electrical wall socket where it was plugged in.

"May I help you?" the clipboard woman asked, marching over to us.

"Who's in charge?" Hank grunted.

"I am," said Clipboard.

"Glad to hear it," said Hank, "because I'd like to know who plugged *this* box's electrical cord into *that* electrical outlet."

"Why? I don't know. One of my engineers, probably."

Hank shook his head. "Nope. You can't do that. Union rules clearly state: only union may apply AC power to a stand-alone appliance if said appliance draws in excess of two hundred watts."

"You're joking. It's just a power cord."

"It's just a five-hundred-dollar fine," said Hank.

"I've had about enough of you union jerk-offs," said the woman. "Redsoft practically owns this building. We bring in more crowds than anyone else at this show. I seriously doubt the convention center will give a damn—"

"Five hundred bucks," said Hank.

"Why don't I give you five hundred of these instead?" said the woman, flicking her chin at us. She spun and walked off.

"Cover me," whispered Hank. He crouched, pulled out a pair of wire cutters, cut the cord from the back of the blue box, jerked the other end out of the wall socket, rolled the cord up, and shoved it down his pants. "Let's go," he said.

We started walking away.

"What the hell was that?" I whispered.

"Just wait," he said.

Five seconds passed.

"Hey, my computer just froze," said somebody in the booth.

"I think the whole network's down," said another.

"I'll check on it," said a third.

We continued walking. I looked back at the booth in time to see an engineer jog over to the blue box. He pressed the box's reset button. Nothing happened. He checked the network cables going into the box. They looked fine. Then he saw the box's display lights were off. Maybe it was unplugged? He stepped around behind the box, looked down at where the cord had been cut off, and screamed.

Clipboard ran over, asked what was going on, looked down, and saw the cord was missing. It only took her a second to realize what had happened. She scanned the aisles, left, right, then straight ahead. We locked eyes.

"HOLD IT RIGHT THERE!" she yelled, running over to us. "Do you know how much that cord cost? Where is it?"

"Cord?" asked Hank, scratching his belly.

"You ass! Give me my cord right now or I'll call security!" she huffed.

"Go ahead," said Hank. "Call security. We'll see you later. We're on our way to the incinerator—"

"No, wait! Stop. I'm sorry. Please. That cord was custom-made for the box. It's a heavy gauge and shielded with a special plug—it's irreplaceable. We need it to make the box run, and we need the box to make our network run."

"Sounds serious," Hank yawned.

"Please," said Clipboard, "please, this is so ridiculous—"

"Hey, maybe one of my jerk-off union pals has seen a cord," said Hank. "I'll ask around."

We sidestepped the woman and started walking. She jumped in front of us.

"All right, I get it, I see what's going on, I'm a little slow today. You want money, right? Just tell me how much, we'll go back to the booth, and I'll write you a check right now. Five hundred, was it?"

"I can't take your money," said Hank. "Union rules. If you want to pay your fine, you have to mail a check to the union office in New York."

Clipboard was close to tears. "I—look, about what I said back there—today has been so frustrating. There are so many rules . . . it's my first trade show . . . I honestly didn't know we weren't supposed to plug in the cord . . . it was an honest mistake. Please, there have been so many screw-ups already: I spent ten thousand more than I should've on the booth, half my crew didn't show, our booth signs have typos, and if I don't get that cord back, my VP's going to fire me, I just know it; he's a hot-headed bastard—"

"I suppose I could ask around," said Hank. "Maybe one of our guys has an extra cord that would fit."

"Please?" Clipboard begged. "What do you want? Just tell me—"

"An apology is a start."

"Yes! I am so sorry," said Clipboard. "I am so, so sorry, you have no idea. I feel terrible. I was very unwelcoming—"

"And?"

"And whatever you need—"

"Well," said Hank, "the truth is that we're big fans of Bill Kunstler."

"HUGE!" I bubbled, gesturing wildly.

"Oh! That's so flattering!" said Clipboard, blushing as if I'd complimented her personally. "Thank you so much—"

"And," continued Hank, "we didn't have time to buy tickets for Bill's keynote speech tomorrow, so we were hoping—"

"You want to see his keynote. Of course! Yes! I can do that! I have tickets at the booth!"

"Well . . . actually . . . we were hoping to meet him."

"We're his BIGGEST fans!" I gushed.

Clipboard's face fell. "Oh. I—I don't know if that's possible. He has very tight security—bodyguards and all of that. I don't even think I could get close to him."

"BACKSTAGE AUTOGRAPH!" I screamed, clapping my hands.

"Maybe you could give us a couple of badges?" asked Hank, pointing at hers.

"You want to go backstage," said the woman slowly, as if trying to determine whether this violation of protocol and common sense could somehow be justified.

"Just to see him up close!" I burped. "I—I—I just want to touch him!"

Hank stifled a laugh. I was becoming more moronic by the second.

Clipboard smiled as she realized I was a simpleton, just some yokel lucky enough to land a union gig that would pay my mental health bills; and Hank here was just my union buddy who'd taken me under his wing. The two of us had only the best of intentions and we'd simply gone about things the wrong way. She'd been unkind, flipping her chin at us like she had.

"You know, I probably don't need my badge anymore anyway. I'm almost done setting up the booth, and I plan to drive home tomorrow, so if you really want it. . . ."

She unpinned her badge and gave it to me. I leapt into the air with a whoop.

"Let's go back to the booth and I'll get another for you," she said to Hank. "How would that be?"

"Perfect!" said Hank.

"Yesss!" I hissed.

"And then you'll find my cord?"

"It's a deal," said Hank.

We walked back to Redsoft's booth. Clipboard asked her lead engineer for his badge. He handed it to Clipboard, and she handed it to Hank.

"And look at what I found!" said Hank, reaching down his pants. He pulled out the cord and handed it to the engineer, who accepted it gingerly.

Hank fastened Clipboard's badge to his shirt, then the engineer's to mine. He pointed at the name on my badge. "NOW YOU'RE TODD, THE NETWORK ENGINEER," he said with a smile.

I pointed at his badge. "AND NOW YOU'RE JENNIFER, RED-SOFT SENIOR SPECIAL EVENT AND TRADESHOW COORDI-NATOR," I screeched. Hank laughed.

We waved goodbye to Clipboard and the engineer, who watched with open mouths as we headed for the stage with our toolbox.

"You found badges," said the security guard behind the rope as we approached.

He checked mine. "Looks fine. Thanks, Todd," he said. Then he checked Hank's.

"Jennifer?" the guard asked.

"Hennifer," said Hank. "It's German."

"All right," said the guard, stepping aside.

Hank and I climbed the stairs, parted the curtains, and slipped backstage.

* * *

It was dark. Our eyes slowly adjusted to the light. We were standing in the center of the stage. It was bare except for a few props, ropes hanging down from the rafters, and a skirted table that would be adorned with refreshments when Kunstler arrived.

"I see the fuse box," Hank whispered, pointing to the stage's rear. We walked to it and saw the box was mounted on a concrete wall sandwiched between a restroom, a payphone, and a loading dock roll-up door.

Hank opened the toolbox and scattered a few screwdrivers around on the floor so we'd look busy if anyone happened by.

"All right," he said. "Where do you think Bill will enter?"

I scanned the stage. There were three entrances: a hallway to the left, another to the right, and the loading dock door.

"The loading door seems unlikely," I said.

"Let's try left," said Hank. We walked down the hallway. It ran forty feet, turned a corner, and dead-ended at a glass door that looked out on the convention center's courtyard. The yard would be crammed with thousands of tradeshow visitors on the show's opening day.

"He won't enter here," I said. "It's wide open—no security. Let's try the other one."

We doubled back. The other hallway ran forty feet, turned, and ended at its own glass door that looked out on a small parking lot with five stalls marked VIP.

"This is it!" I said. "His limo will pull up here—he'll step out and come right inside."

"Pretend I'm Bill," said Hank as we walked back to the stage. "I enter and walk up the hallway. What do I do next? Where do I go?"

"You shake some hands," I said, "then stop at the refreshment table. You drink a little water, maybe eat a few pretzels. . . ."

"Then what?"

"You have a forty-minute talk coming up, so you probably pull out your notes, stroll, try to focus, then it's time—you go out on stage, give your speech, take a bow, shake some more hands, then head back to the limo and leave."

"So when do we grab him?"

"We certainly can't get him when he's coming in," I said. "His bodyguards will be watching."

"And the same when he leaves," said Hank. "Fans will be talking to him, clapping, slapping his back . . . we won't be able to get near him."

The stage curtains parted and the security guard stuck his head through.

"How much longer?" he asked.

"We're almost done," said Hank.

The guard nodded and left. I went to the restroom while Hank started picking up the tools.

I turned on the restroom light. There was a toilet stall, a sink, and a maintenance closet. I used the toilet, washed my face, dried off with a paper towel, shut the light off, and opened the door to leave.

I stopped. A crack of light was visible under the maintenance closet door. It looked like sunlight. I turned the restroom's light back on, walked to the closet, and tried the door. It was locked.

I jogged out of the john, grabbed two screwdrivers, and handed one to Hank.

"What's this for?" he asked.

"Follow me," I whispered.

Hank followed me into the restroom. I showed him the light under the closet door.

"Where's it coming from?" he whispered.

"Let's find out," I said.

We pried the pins out of the door's hinges, lifted the door off, set it aside, and stepped into the closet. There was a bucket, a mop, bleach, and something else: a steel door with a band of sunlight shining underneath it. I touched the door. It was warm.

"Kill the lights," I whispered. Hank ran out, flipped the restroom's lights off, and came back. I felt around in the dark, found the door's bolt lock, and slid it open with a click. I opened the door a crack. Sunlight rushed in. We looked out. The door opened directly onto the stage's rear loading dock.

"We could take him out this door, across the dock, and load him into the car," I whispered. "Nobody would see us."

"There'll be equipment and catering trucks out there," said Hank. "And maybe security cameras. It's risky."

"It'll be fast. Nobody will see a thing. We'll be out of here before anyone knows he's gone."

"How are we going to get him into the restroom?" asked Hank. "And if we get him in, how are we going to convince his bodyguards to politely stay outside while we hustle him out back?"

"I don't know," I said, "but I see no other way."

We returned the door to its hinges, walked back to the car, and drove home in silence, racking our brains for ideas.

I dropped off Hank, drove to my building, parked at the curb, went up to my apartment, and flopped down on the couch.

Our plan's uncertainties were worrisome. Kidnapping a man whose veil of celebrity made him unknowable, and hence unpredictable, made the risks incalculable. The smartest robbers studied their targets—casing joints, calculating odds, running scenarios and counter-scenarios—and even after all of that, many were still caught.

And look at us. We'd never even spoken to Bill, never seen him in person; we only knew him through the media. Yet in less than two days he would be in our clutches, our hands literally on him, putting him in the car, applying violence if needed, then into the cage, and after that, caring for his daily needs like a couple of mothers. What if he turned out to be a real pain in the ass? A tooth-and-nail fighter? Incessantly demanding? What if he screamed like a baby? Or had special dietary needs? A diabetic? A claustrophobic? A chattering epileptic?

The more I thought about him, the less real he seemed—a chimera of archetypes: Weakling Warrior, Financial Genius, Corporate Vampire—while the blood-and-bones Bill remained an enigma.

I recalled reading an article once that had portrayed him as a tiger—a carnivore that killed and ate his competition without remorse because his genes were simply coded that way: hunt, attack, chew, digest, repeat. His mind was better equipped than his competitors' for this function because he'd grown a brain capable of identifying the gestalt in an enemy's moves; not just what road the enemy would travel, but what direction the road would take—before the road was even paved—or even how the paving would be affected by subtle factors like sun and lay of the land, while somewhere in a nearby bush, Bill waited, crouched and ready to pounce when his prey finally passed by.

His critics tried to rewrite him into something less threatening and more manageable, but without success. He was an indefinite article, sexless, like an economy rolling forward with weight and direction but without form—one can check its indicators, its pulse, its position, but it can't be controlled, except maybe by force. Bill would always be described in similes by the media because it was the only way they *could* describe him—Bill is like this, Bill is like that—but the comparisons never added up to much. He evaded their summations effortlessly. He was beyond similes; he was more like like, or as as, a simulacrum of similes, of endless comparisons that ultimately gave way to nothing but a collection of forces and vectors. As I drifted into sleep, I realized he was like a baseball pitch, with Hank and I being what would come between the mound and the catcher—an unnatural wind that would alter the ball's course—and the next stop for Bill as he flew toward our outstretched mitts.

26

HANK SHOWED UP AT MY apartment in the morning with a case of beer, two burritos, his video camera, a beat-up tripod, and a videotape called *Ten Keynote Speeches by Bill Kunstler* for us to study.

We ate the burritos, drank the beer, and then went to work, clearing the dirty laundry, old newspapers, and wine bottles from the middle of the living room to make space for the cage. When we were finished, the room was bare except for the couch, the TV and VCR on the coffee table, my performance art props, and the sun shining through the window.

My phone rang. The Lodell's deliveryman was downstairs with our kidnapping supplies. Hank and I ran down to the lobby and began hauling the chain-link, fence posts, foam, duct tape, and other supplies up to my apartment.

Building a cage that doubles as a stage for a captive performer who's looking to escape is no trivial matter. For best results, construct a cube using aluminum posts and rails no less than three inches in diameter each. Fasten heavy-gauge chain-link of medium mesh to all six sides, including the bottom. Make the cage's dimensions roomy enough to allow the performer to move in all directions, yet not so large that the occupant can build up a running start to break out; six feet high by eight feet long by four feet deep is ideal.

The cage's location in the room is important. A corner is an excellent choice because the chain-link and posts can be bolted to wall studs on at least two sides.

Sound can be a problem, especially in an apartment. A performer jumping up and down may draw the attention of other tenants, especially if the apartment's floor is wood. To avoid this, slide a thin, noise-dampening foam pad under the cage before bolting it down.

The apartment's walls should be soundproofed. Professional soundproofing tiles are expensive and unnecessary; layers of clothing work just as well for the budget-conscious kidnapper. Hang or nail shirts, pants, and blankets two articles deep onto the walls to absorb screaming and yelling—which, it should be noted, are sometimes the hallmark of a powerful performance, and not necessarily cries for help. Also consider purchasing a canvas camping tent. Cut it so it can be lowered over the cage as an emergency light-proof muffle if needed.

After completing the cage's assembly, fashion a small hatch in the chain-link so food and other items can be passed to the captive. Double up on the fencing surrounding the hatch so it can't be kicked out during escape attempts.

The average human produces three pounds of solid and fluid waste every two days, so be sure to equip the cage with a toilet. Connect its plumbing to the apartment's sewer line. The captive may try to overflow the toilet to attract attention, so only open the water supply when the cage can be monitored. Provide a bucket for times when the toilet is inoperable.

Mount a video camera on a tripod outside the cage to record performances. Recordings may be viewed later for sentimental value or as a possible source for future performance material. Place the tripod no closer than ten feet from the cage. Keeping a safe distance is important to prevent the performer from grabbing the camera with a makeshift grappling hook or, worse, urinating on it; urination is a common attack because it's one of the few subversive weapons available to a captive that's actually effective against a camera through chain-link.

Set up audience chairs in front of the performance cage. For reasons already stated, the chairs should be at least ten feet from the cage unless contact with urine or other subversive instruments as wielded by said occupant is desired. A couch may be substituted for chairs.

The set-up took six hours. When Hank and I finished, the chain-link cage was bolted to the living room's brick wall and the perfect size for a captive performer. The cage had a toilet, a bucket, a large hinged door for entry, a little hatch for inserting food, a noise-dampening foam pad underneath, a lightproof cover cut from a canvas tent—and all of the living room's walls were soundproofed with layers of clothing.

"Would you do the honors?" I asked, opening the cage door. Hank crawled inside. I closed the door, wrapped a chain around the door's post, and padlocked it. "Do the breakout test," I said.

Hank jumped up and down. Between the pad underneath and the bolts holding it fast, the cage barely moved at all. Hank kicked at the doors. They rattled, but held fast.

"Urine test," I said.

Hank unzipped his fly and pissed through the links. The urine spattered a safe distance from the couch and tripod.

It was time for the yelling test. I stepped out into the hallway, shut the apartment's door, and counted to thirty. I didn't hear a thing.

I went back inside. Hank said he'd yelled at the top of his lungs. I hadn't heard a peep. The cage was perfect.

The phone rang. It was Rudy.

"I've got some info," he said. "Meet me at Hotel Lucky around the corner."

I wrote down the address and hung up.

"Who was that?" asked Hank.

"Rudy," I said. "He has something for us at Hotel Lucky."

Hank hung from the cage's ceiling and whooped like a banshee.

I smiled, knowing nobody else in the world could hear him but me.

* * *

Hank and I walked to Hotel Lucky, a bug-infested dump on Turk Street where male prostitutes took their johns.

We went in. The dim lobby reeked of cigarettes and sour wine. Music thumped in a room somewhere overhead. A hairy, fat man wearing gold hoop earrings sat behind a desk and guarded the elevator door behind him.

"Room twenty-nine," I told him.

"Your pretty boys are already up there," said Fat. He rose and slid open the elevator door. Hank and I stepped in. The elevator walls and ceiling were mirrored. Fat punched the second-floor button for us, then offered some friendly advice: "You'd better clean the carpet if you dirty it."

"We're not going to dirty it," I said.

"That's what the last ones told me," said Fat, "and I made them go back up there and eat it." Hank and I digested his words as the door shut.

We stepped out on the second floor and walked down the hall to room twenty-nine. I knocked. Rudy opened the door and let us in. The room was dank with a sagging bed, yellowed curtains, a lamp, and a dingy bathroom.

A bone-thin man with a blond mohawk sat smoking a cigarette in the corner. He looked familiar.

I sat down on the bed and leaned back on the bedspread. My hand touched a glob of something wet and slippery. I gagged, ran to the bathroom, washed my hands, and came back.

"Stay off the bed," said Rudy.

"Thanks for the warning," I said.

Rudy introduced us to the smoking man. "This is Roman. He's a programmer at SI. Maybe you saw him around the office."

"I do less programming these days," said Roman in a faint Russian accent. "Portalia ruined my hands with all of that clicking and dragging of the mouse. Look at them—they are useless now!" He held up his hands. They looked like two heads of cauliflower. Roman leaned forward and pointed his cigarette at us. "Bill Kunstler is a monster. Rudy says you plan to ream him as some kind of art project. That is fine. How you ream him, I do not care, but when you do, I want to be the one holding the stick!"

"The stick's all yours," said Hank.

"Rudy said you have information," I said.

"Have you heard of Billfold?" asked Roman. "It's Redsoft's financial service."

"It sounds familiar," said Hank.

"It should. Millions use it, including Kunstler. It offers your typical banking products for the unwashed masses—checking accounts, credit cards, and so on. But if you're a billionaire and a friend of Kunstler's, you receive a special prize: an invitation to use Billfold's private brokerage, where you can park or trade shares with impunity. Kunstler had it built because he didn't want to trust his fortune in Redsoft stock to some Wall Street firm . . . plus he was tired of the SEC monitoring his every move . . . which is why the service uses recursive proxies, aggregation, a private transfer agent, and offshore accounts to make tracing stock transactions practically impossible."

"Is that legal?" I asked.

"If you own a thousand lawyers like Redsoft does, then of course," said Roman. "And as you'd expect, Billfold's network is a fortress—heavily segmented with firewalls and intrusion detection. When a billionaire wants to pull up his accounts on his computer, he has to dial in over a phone line using a custom high-speed modem and Billfold's encryption software. Every transaction is monitored for signs of theft or fraud; if an alarm is triggered, the questionable account is instantly frozen until it can be investigated, no fooling around."

"How are we supposed to get past all of that?" I asked.

"I will tell you how," said Roman, taking another hit of cigarette. "If Billfold sounds familiar, it's because SI has a contract with Redsoft to provide nightly financial forecasting analysis to big-ticket Billfold customers. Every morning at two a.m., a secure Redsoft computer dials into a computer host at SI and transmits a summary of the stock buys made by Billfold customers during the previous day. SI's host calculates forecasts for the purchased stocks and transmits them back to Redsoft, then Redsoft's computer hangs up and posts the forecasts to customers' accounts before the markets open."

"Where do you fit in?" asked Hank.

"I maintain the host program at SI," said Roman. "If there's a problem when Redsoft tries to dial in, they call me."

"Get to the good part," Rudy urged.

Roman took another drag. I could barely see his face through all the smoke.

"An engineer at Redsoft was running tests with me to confirm that SI's host was receiving Billfold's numbers correctly," said Roman. "When the time came for SI to transmit its forecast data to Redsoft, the program got caught in a loop and transmitted an oversized stream of data over the line. Redsoft's machine couldn't handle it—it choked and crashed. Redsoft's engineer called me angry as hell because I'd overflowed his computer's buffer."

It was too good to be true. A buffer overflow vulnerability was dangerous in a hacker's hands. If a computer could be made to gag on too much incoming data, it was sometimes possible to attach a string of rogue programming instructions to the end of the data stream; if the computer processed the instructions accidentally, it could be made to do almost anything.

"If Redsoft's system still has this vulnerability," said Roman, "we should be able to slip it some code the next time it dials into SI, then take control of it. Redsoft monitors mainly for attacks originating from outside the Billfold subnet; I doubt they'd suspect their own computer could be hijacked while dialing out on its own phone line."

"If the overflow works," said Rudy, "it's only a matter of time before we find Bill's money."

* * *

Hank and I returned to my apartment, opened a bottle of wine, sat down on the couch, and slid *Ten Keynote Speeches* into the VCR. It was time to study our target.

We watched all ten speeches. They all looked the same: Bill speaking behind a podium at a computer tradeshow . . . Bill looking harmless in his glasses, tousled hair, pasty skin, and saggy Redsoft polo shirt . . . Bill stroking his double chin . . . Bill gesturing calmly . . . Bill pointing to a projection screen beside him . . . Bill cracking computer jokes . . . Bill drinking a glass of water, then pouring another from a pitcher . . . Bill pausing to answer questions from the audience. . . .

And then there were the bodyguards: two hulks in suits flanked Bill at all times with bulges under their jackets that could only be guns. Each speech started with Bill already on stage, so we never saw his arrival, but it was safe to assume that his guards were right beside him from his car to the podium and back.

We finished the videotape, then watched it again: podium, glasses, messy hair, pasty skin, saggy shirt, double chin, sips of water, then questions and answers.

"There has to be something we can use," said Hank.

"Fast-forward it," I said.

Hank rolled back the tape and hit the fast-forward button. Speeches flew by. All of Bill's repetitive gestures became obvious at high speed. We saw he preferred using his right hand to point, he played with his double chin after mentioning Redsoft's competition, and he slouched while answering easy questions.

But most noticeable of all was how frequently Bill drank water. A full pitcher and glass sat on a table beside his podium during every speech at every venue. A glass lasted about fifteen minutes, and when it was empty, he refilled it from the pitcher.

"He sure drinks a lot of water," said Hank, reading my mind. "Which means—"

"He has to use the john sometime," I said, sitting up on the couch. "We could wait in the restroom for him backstage."

"What if his bladder's enormous?" asked Hank. "We can't be sure when or if he'll use the john."

"We could slip him some ipecac—that syrup you give kids to make them vomit," I said. "Then he'd have to use the restroom."

"How long does it take to work?"

"I don't know. Five minutes? Ten, tops. We could put a little in his water. He'd start speaking, then take a break to go puke—that's when we'd get him."

"What if he doesn't drink the water?"

"He always does. You saw the tape," I said.

"What if the guards enter the restroom with him?"

"The man can't throw up by himself?"

"I'm just saying it could happen."

"No way. The restroom's too small and Bill's too proud—I bet he'd make them wait outside. What's the danger? It's just a john, right?"

"How do we get ipecac into his water?" asked Hank.

"We'll just walk out on stage and pour it in. We could even add some lemon to mask the taste."

It sounded crazy, but we had good luck with crazy.

"Just walk out there," said Hank.

"Just walk out there," I repeated.

"I think we have a plan," said Hank, cracking open a fresh bottle of wine.

27

I LOOKED AT THE CLOCK. It was midnight—only fifteen hours until the keynote. Hank and I grabbed an oversized pillowcase and set out across the Tenderloin on foot to gather performance props for Bill.

Props were vital. A burgeoning performance artist might sift through a three-foot-high mountain of junk for hours, triggering memories and mental associations until a prop suddenly took on new meaning for him in the funhouse of his subconscious—a teacup became a gun, or a shoe became a mouth, both figuratively and, sometimes, literally. Where thirst might motivate a stage actor's character to drink water from a cup, the performance artist was free to ignore nature, performing outside the predictable laws of probability, necessity, and cause-and-effect.

Hank and I ran through the alleys, pausing at each garbage dumpster to dive in and dig for props. Some dumpsters had already been picked over, but no matter; by the time we finished, we'd packed our pillowcase with old newspapers, a mannequin arm, dance tights, a gorgeous purple can of hairspray, a soccer trophy, duct tape, plastic scissors, a soggy cardboard sign with I SUCK YOU FOR MONEY scrawled on it, a ladle, a trash can, an old pair of size-thirteen shoes, a light bulb, electrical wire and tape, slightly used litter-box sand, a three-foot section of ventilation shaft, a tooth, a kitchen timer, a broken dildo, and more.

We passed a grocery store. I went in, grabbed a lemon, then found the ipecac syrup in the medicine aisle. It was sold in one-ounce bottles. I read the label:

ADMINISTER ONE TEASPOON TO IN-DUCE VOMITING. IF VOMITING DOES NOT OCCUR WITHIN 15 MINUTES, ADMINISTER A SECOND DOSE. IF VOMITING STILL DOES NOT OCCUR, INDUCE MANUALLY WITH FINGER. SYRUP MUST NOT BE ALLOWED TO REMAIN IN STOMACH ONCE INGESTED.

"You sure this stuff works?" asked Hank.

"Maybe we should test it," I said.

We bought two bottles and went outside. There was a little park with grass and trees. We sat down on a bench.

"Do you want to try it?" I asked.

"No."

"Me neither."

A drunk bum stumbled past us, ran a few steps, and fell down. We hurried over to him and helped him up.

"You okay, buddy?" I asked.

"I'm all right," he slurred, weaving.

Hank held out a bottle of syrup. "We'll pay you a dollar if you'll drink some of this."

The bum's eyes lit up. "Booze?"

"Ipecac."

"I-kak-kak?"

"It's vomit syrup."

"But I don't wanna vomit."

I took out a buck.

"All right," said the bum. He took the dollar, opened the ipecac, gave it a sniff, then drank the whole thing down.

"Holy shit!" I said.

"You're going to vomit," said Hank. "You're really going to vomit!"

"I bet I am!" said the bum.

We all stood around. Ten minutes passed. A plane flew overhead. Crickets chirped. The bum didn't vomit.

"How do you feel?" I asked.

"Fine," said the bum, "just dandy."

With that, he bent over, puked all over the grass, and passed out.

Hank and I slunk away.

* * *

The phone rang. I opened my eyes. It was dark outside. Hank and I had passed out on my living room floor.

"Hello?" I answered.

"Hello, Larry," said Sherry. "Hank hasn't come home yet. Is he over there?"

"I think so," I said, looking at Hank. He was still passed out.

"IT'S THREE IN THE MORNING! DO YOU KNOW HOW LONG I'VE BEEN AWAKE WORRYING?"

I went over and roused Hank. "Sherry's on the phone," I whispered.

Hank stumbled to the receiver.

"Hello? Yeah. Sorry I didn't call. Oh. All right."

Hank hung up.

"What'd she say?"

"As retaliation, she's going to buy a new area rug for the living room immediately."

"Right this second?"

"Well, once the sun comes up."

It was time to get ready. Hank and I spread a bed sheet out on the floor and packed up our kidnapping supplies: four yards of cotton rope, an oversized heavy-canvas duffel sack, a bandana, duct tape, the lemon, the bottle of ipecac, the AK-47 with ammo, and Nelson's cell phone.

"I'll load up the car," said Hank. I threw him the keys. He hoisted the bed sheet over his shoulder and headed out the door.

I padded to the kitchen and made some toast. Ten minutes passed. I went to the living room window and looked out. Hank was pacing back and forth under a streetlight in front of the apartment building with the bed sheet. I slid open the window.

"What are you doing?" I whispered loudly.

"Looking for the car!" he whispered back.

I went outside. Hank was squinting in the dark at the cars parked up and down the block.

"Where'd you park it?" he asked.

"Right here," I said.

"When did you drive it last?"

"Yesterday—I drove it home from the convention center."

"Maybe you parked on a different street?"

"It was here," I said. "I'm sure of it."

I let out a long sigh. In San Francisco, old beaters like Mouse's Impala weren't popular with thieves. If one disappeared, there was usually only one explanation.

As if on cue, we both looked up and saw a no parking sign right beside where the car would have been. I shut my eyes.

Hank slapped my back. "I think you got towed, pal!"

* * *

The walk to Bryant Street took thirty minutes. A cold wind blew. White cumulus clouds raced overhead against a black sky. We were headed for San Francisco's Hall of Justice. Built in the 1950s, the gray cement monolith rose seven stories into the night. Giant fir trees rustled and creaked out front as we approached. A twenty-six-foot coiled bronze sculpture squatted on the grass beside the Hall. It looked like intestines squirming—a nervous warning of the thieves, rapists, and murderers teeming in the hall's uneasy guts just five yards away.

The city's open-air tow yard was around back. It sat in the shadow of a freeway overpass and was guarded on all sides by a slatted, fourteen-foot chain-link fence draped in vines and capped with helical razor wire.

We walked along the fence to the yard's main driveway. A weary-looking guard with a clipboard was trying to calm an attorney who was awaiting the release of his car. Hank and I waited our turn and listened to the cars rushing above on the overpass while the attorney talked himself into a frenzy—he threatened to sue the guard personally if there was so much as a fingerprint on his brand new BMW.

A tow truck rumbled up to the driveway with a yellow Ferrari dangling from its chains—fresh meat. The guard pressed a button and the yard's rolling chain-link door slid open on rubber wheels. The truck driver floored it, bottoming the Ferrari out and scraping its tailpipe all the way up the driveway until he was through the gate. The attorney cursed and stomped around, certain that his BMW had probably been bottomed the same way.

I approached the guard. He looked jaundiced and haggard under the streetlights.

"Help you?" he asked.

"I think our car was towed," I said.

"You pay yet?"

"No."

"You have to pay inside," said the guard. "Room one-twenty."

As we left to go pay, the tow truck that had arrived with the Ferrari came roaring out of the gate, stopped, and waited to make a right turn into traffic. The attorney shot the tow truck driver an evil look. The driver pulled his hat down over his face so he couldn't be recognized, then floored it, disappearing into the night in search of his next haul.

Hank and I walked around to the Hall of Justice's main entrance and went inside. A guard ushered us through a metal detector, then directed us down a madhouse corridor teeming with shackled brawlers, screaming bailiffs, powdered cokeheads, and singing drunkards.

The insanity spilled into room one hundred and twenty at the end of the hall, where a line of sad sacks stood waiting to pay their tow fees beside a row of handcuffed prisoners, a fetid bum catnapping on the floor in the corner, and two leggy hookers sitting on a bench with their teenage pimp between them.

Five men waited in line ahead of us. They stared off into space, whistled with their hands in their pockets, and stole peeks at the hookers' legs.

The tow clerk sat at a counter behind bulletproof glass. A sign over the window read PAY BY CASH ONLY. One by one, each man stepped up to the clerk, talked through a hole in the glass, pushed his money through a shiny metal tray, and shuffled off with his receipt to the lot out back to retrieve his vehicle.

I pulled out what cash I had—eighty bucks. I started to sweat.

"The fee can't be more than this, can it?" I muttered.

"I have no idea," said Hank.

"We're cooked!" I said. "How are we going to grab Bill without a car? I'm such an idiot!"

"Calm down. We'll take him in a damned taxi if we have to," said Hank with a timbre of doubt that I instantly found annoying.

I swallowed bile and waited for our turn. A steel plate had been installed under the bulletproof window to protect the wall from kickers. It hadn't stopped the graffiti artists, though; someone had scribbled KILL HIM IF YOU CAN in black marker on the plate and aimed it at the clerk's head with a curving, jagged arrow. It made me laugh. I pointed it out to Hank.

"Sounds like a good idea, doesn't it?" I said.

"Easy there," Hank whispered.

"Hey, you want some?" said a voice.

We turned around. It was the teen pimp on the bench. He was wearing jeans, a black muscle shirt, and a black fedora with a purple feather in it. He couldn't have been a day over fifteen.

"What did you say?" I asked.

"Pussy, man. I got the good stuff," he said in a low voice while stroking a non-existent mustache.

"What are you talking about?"

"My sisters, man!" The teen nodded to the hookers sitting beside him. They smiled at us. "You'll like them! Only fifty bucks." The pimp laughed a crazy laugh and lifted up their dresses to show us what they had underneath.

"Next!" yelled the clerk. Hank and I stepped up to the window. The clerk was a low-rent city drone with tattoos, receding hair, bad acne, and a scraggly mustache—and she was a woman.

"Our car was towed," I said.

"License plate?" the clerk asked.

"I don't know it," I said.

"Make? Model? Year?" she asked.

I described Mouse's car. The clerk typed something on her computer keyboard.

We waited. The clerk picked at her pimples.

Text appeared on the clerk's computer screen. "Your Impala's here," she said. "Total fee including citation and towing is one seventy-five."

"ONE SEVENTY-FIVE?" I hissed.

"Will you take eighty bucks?" asked Hank.

"Sorry," said the clerk. "One seventy-five."

I hauled off and kicked the steel plate. The clerk jumped. The hookers whooped.

"Please don't kick the wall," the clerk whined.

Hank pulled me out of there, but not before I managed to spit in the clerk's shiny metal tray.

We began walking home. The wind whipped the trees around. Old newspapers blew past us in the street. The whole city was howling.

We'd gone half a block when the teen pimp in the fedora came running up behind us.

"Hey, wanna get your car?" he asked.

"It's not happening tonight," I said.

"I can help you get it."

"Sure you can."

"I'm serious, man!"

"What's your name?"

"Freako."

"How much, Freako?" I asked.

"Eighty dollars."

I looked at Hank. He shrugged. It was probably a con, but we had nothing to lose. I gave Freako our eighty bucks. He laughed and took off running. "Follow me!" he said.

We followed him around the Hall of Justice to the tow yard, jogged along its slatted chain-link to a dark corner, scrambled up a dirt embankment, and crouched outside the razor-topped fence as cars rushed by on the overpass above.

We peered through the chain-link slats. A field of knee-high yellow weeds ran three hundred yards to an asphalt blacktop where towed cars were parked.

"All right," I whispered. "How do we get our car?"

"Sneak in there," said Freako, "and find it. Start it up with the headlights off, then drive it across the field and come out right here," he said, pointing to the razored fence that was right in front of my face.

"Come out where? You mean ram the fence?"

"No," said Freako. "Here! Look!" He reached down, grabbed the bottom of the fence, and lifted it up. Vertical seams had been cut into the chain-link so it could be raised like a garage door. Freako was able to raise it three feet, but a fully grown man could probably pry it as high as five or six—plenty enough for a car to slip under.

"Got it?" asked Freako.

I nodded. Freako laughed and ran off to bail out his sisters.

Time was wasting. I lowered myself to the ground, raised the fence up a foot, and slid underneath with Hank right behind me.

I raised my head and looked across the field. The parking lot was dimly lit by a single spotlight. Weedy thorns burrowed into us as we began moving forward on all fours, crawling through the grass, keeping an eye out for guards, dogs, lasers, video cameras, chiggers, and snakes.

We reached the edge of the blacktop and kept going, slithering low under the light from one parked car to the next until we found the Impala.

The doors were unlocked. Hank and I crawled in. Our union T-shirts and toolboxes were on the back seat where we'd left them. I handed the ignition key to Hank. He slid it in and gave it a turn. The engine roared to life. He pressed the accelerator. The Impala rolled forward. We inched past the other parked cars to the edge of the blacktop, then into the weeds. Grass brushed the Impala's undercarriage. We were vanishing into the dark, leaving the spotlight behind, flattening a path in the weeds to the corner of the lot. I looked back. Nobody was chasing us. The guard with the clipboard at the front gate had to be deaf.

We drove until we reached the fence, then I jumped out, wriggled under the chain-link, and lifted it high. The fence's steel barbs dug into my hands, but I bit my tongue and nodded to Hank. He began driving toward me. The Impala's front bumper traveled under the fence, then the first few feet of hood. I struggled to lift the chain-link higher so it would clear the hood's slope, but the fence wouldn't budge. My arms gave out—I had to let go. The fence sprang down onto the car's hood and bounced, leaving little scratch marks on the paint. Hank hit the brakes. I ducked under the fence and motioned to him that the fence was too low. He motioned for me to raise it higher. I cursed, ducked back under the fence, and gave it another try. Hank inched the car forward. I felt my grip going. The barbs began clawing at the hood, metal on metal, like fingernails on a chalkboard. I panicked and nodded at Hank to stop, but it was too late—the front tires had already slipped forward and down the slope of the dirt embankment. The car picked up speed. I let go and jumped back. The barbs ripped pinstripes all the way up the hood, up the windshield, tearing off the wipers and then over the top, shearing off the antenna, then down the back window, the trunk, and the rear bumper as the Impala's rear end bounced down the embankment, over the sidewalk, and off the curb, clear.

I ran to the fence, pushed it back into place, and squinted through the slats for any signs of a chase. All was quiet. The weeds were already standing back up as if we'd never been there.

I scrambled down the embankment and tried to ignore the flakes of paint peeling up all over the car. I got in and shut the door. Hank drove. The windshield was raked with scratches. Mouse would kill me. I swallowed and watched the Hall of Justice grow smaller in the rearview until the city swallowed us up and we disappeared in the dark.

* * *

Hank and I were itching and dirty but there was no time to clean up; we had to get into position behind the convention center before security blocked off access.

We stopped at the apartment, grabbed the kidnapping supplies, threw on our union T-shirts, removed the license plate from the Impala for anonymity, then drove across town to the convention center's back lot. Hank pulled up beside the loading dock. Catering vans were already arriving for the show. Hank backed the Impala in tight behind a van and cut the engine. We were only three feet from the dock with plenty of room for our escape. The car's clock said six a.m.—only nine hours before Bill's speech.

The sun was rising. I eased my seat back and fell asleep while watching Hank dig thorns out of his socks.

* * *

I opened my eyes. The sun was high overhead and the car was sweltering. Hank was asleep. I sat up in my seat and looked out. Catering vans and TV camera trucks were parked all around us. I looked at the clock.

"Hank!" I said. "Wake up! We only have fifteen minutes!"

Hank jerked awake. "Let's go," he said. We put on our Redsoft badges, scrambled out of the car, grabbed the toolbox and bed sheet, and ran to the backstage VIP side entrance.

A mob of fans awaited Bill's arrival. Hank and I pushed to the front of the crowd, showed our Redsoft badges to a security guard, and went inside.

The backstage area was bustling. Production assistants ran around wearing radio headsets. Caterers prepped champagne and caviar on the skirted table that bowed under the weight of a four-foot ice sculpture of Bill's head. Video technicians installed a TV monitor so everyone could watch Bill speak. Reporters and photographers jostled to be first in line when Kunstler walked in. The tension was heightened by the muffled roar of two thousand spectators already seated on the other side of the curtains.

Hank and I walked to the payphone, opened the toolbox, and scattered some tools around, then I grabbed a screwdriver and the bed sheet and headed into the restroom. I locked the door, turned the light on, went to the maintenance closet, pried out the hinge pins, set the door aside, and stepped into the closet. The sunlight beating against the outer metal door had pushed the closet's temperature to what felt like eighty degrees. I wiped my brow, opened the bed sheet, and took out the kidnapping supplies. Canvas sack, cotton rope, bandana, duct tape, and AK-47 went on the floor; lemon, ipecac, and Nelson's cell phone went into my pants pocket.

I replaced the closet door, made sure it was unlocked, shut it, exited the restroom, and walked back to the payphone.

"He still hasn't arrived," said Hank. "Let's pour the ipecac."

We grabbed a few tools, pushed past the reporters, parted the big red curtains, and stepped out on stage. The ubiquitous water pitcher lay dead ahead on a table beside Bill's podium. We started toward it. Time seemed to slow. I looked out at the sea of people. Some watched us intently. I steadied my breath. Did we look suspicious? Did they know what we were planning? Had some of our choreography slipped out? Were we inciting others to crime this very second? Would we be held responsible if a rabid Kunstler fan ran out and kidnapped himself a billionaire?

We reached the podium. My hands were shaking. I picked up the water pitcher and set it down on the floor so Hank could lay out his tools on the table.

Hank picked up a wrench and pretended to adjust the podium's microphone while I crouched down behind him, slid the pitcher close to me so nobody could see it, poured in half of the ipecac, then pulled the lemon out of my pocket. I'd forgotten to bring a knife. I gouged my fingers into the fruit and squeezed. Juice and seeds dripped into the water. I picked the seeds out, stirred the concoction with my pinky, and gave it a sniff. It smelled like lemon. I stood and set the pitcher back onto the table. It was done. We grabbed our tools and headed back toward the curtain.

A sound engineer stopped us.

"Everything all right with the podium mic?" he asked.

"Condenser element voltage," Hank grunted.

"What was wrong with it?"

"Current waffle due to condensation," Hank bluffed. "I bounced the tube to reset the arc, then burned the draw off—that seemed to fix it."

The engineer cocked his head, confused, but let us pass.

The reporters backstage pushed and shoved. A limo had just pulled up outside, and sixty seconds later—right from the VIP parking lot entrance as we'd predicted—in strolled Bill Kunstler in his glasses, brown loafers, and Redsoft polo shirt. The people backstage cheered. It was hard to look away from him. He had a celebrity aura, though I couldn't tell if it was an innate quality or just a product of his constant publicity. Two armed bodyguards in suits flanked him as he mingled, joked, and shook hands all around. He stopped for a bite of caviar at the skirted table and chuckled at the ice sculpture—the big Bill face was melting in the heat.

The stage manager announced that his crew was ready. He uttered a command into his headset and music started thumping in the hall outside. The roar of the audience grew louder. Hank and I watched the presentation unfold on the backstage TV monitor.

A master of ceremonies emerged from the curtains, thanked the crowd for coming, told a few jokes, then introduced Bill.

Kunstler stepped out and waved. Fans jumped to their feet with deafening applause—it was their big chance to hear fame speak. A lady in the second row fainted to the floor and the crowd let her lie right where she was.

The audience settled down and Bill began speaking. He looked the same as he had on the videotape: the same gestures, the same repetition. I found myself anticipating what he'd do next—how he'd move, when he'd adjust his glasses, or when he'd build for a joke.

Bill reached for the pitcher, poured himself a glass of water, sipped until it was gone, then poured another.

"Get ready," Hank whispered. "I'll call you from the payphone when he's coming."

I stepped into the restroom, felt my way through the dark to the maintenance closet, stepped in, locked the door, then crouched and felt around to make sure the supplies were still there. My hand touched the AK-47. I picked it up. Its rusted trigger felt gummy.

Nelson's cell phone rang. I pulled it out and answered.

"Here he comes!" Hank whispered.

I slide the phone into my pocket as I hear the restroom door open. This is it. I grip the Kalashnikov tight, pick up the bandana I'll use as a gag, and take a deep breath.

I hear the squawk of a radio—it sounds like a walkie-talkie. Why does Bill have a radio? I hear footsteps. They sound like boots—how's that possible? Bill is wearing loafers. And why don't I hear vomiting?

Suddenly, whoever's out there grabs the closet doorknob and tries to turn it, but it's locked. I grit my teeth. The knob jiggles a few more times, the toilet stall door opens and shuts, then a deep male voice—

"The restroom's clear. Send in Kunstler."

Of course—one of Bill's bodyguards is doing a security sweep.

I hear the bodyguard exit. Ten seconds pass . . . then the restroom door opens again. Someone enters, locks the door, hurries to the toilet. I hear the bang of the stall door, then a rush of vomit. It's Bill. The retching continues for a minute, then a flush, then more vomiting. Kunstler is really emptying out. I unlock the closet door and peek out. My God, there he is— Bill on his knees with his face in the bowl.

What if he fights? Or worse, what if he screams? He might decide that drawing his bodyguards' attention is the only defense he has.

Bill flushes the toilet one last time, stands, and wipes his mouth with toilet paper. In a moment he'll step out of the stall, wash his face, and go back to finish his presentation.

There's no more time. I step out of the closet and swing the rifle like a baseball bat, cracking him in the back of his head. His glasses tumble as he slumps to the floor. He's out cold. I double-check that the restroom door is locked, grab the duct tape from the closet floor, wrap his wrists and ankles, stuff the bandana into his mouth, slide the canvas sack over him, tape it shut, jam his glasses into my pocket, drag him into the closet, shut the door, lock it, unbolt the metal door leading out to the loading dock, and bust out, dragging the sack. I make it across the dock and jump down to the asphalt. Hank jumps out of the car and helps me hoist the canvas. It's awkward—Kunstler is saggy like a doll—but we manage to load him into the backseat through the right rear passenger door.

I climb onto the loading dock and run back to shut the maintenance closet door. As I reach for the handle, I hear knocking on the restroom door and the bodyguard's voice: "Mr. Kunstler? Sir? Everything all right in there?"

I shut the closet door, run across the loading dock, climb down, jump into the car, and scream for Hank to floor it, but the car's boxed in—a semi-truck is backing up past us, blocking our only exit. Hank lays into the horn but the truck continues backing. This isn't good; we could be blocked for minutes. There's a concrete wall behind us, a catering van in front, the loading dock on our right, the semi on the left—

The maintenance closet's metal door opens in a flash of light and Bill's bodyguards run out with their guns drawn. They look around—left, right, then straight at us.

"FLOOR IT! MOVE THE VAN!" I scream. Hank hits the gas. We rocket forward and smash into the catering van. It rolls forward as our tires spin in place and smoke billows up. We open ten feet of clearance. Hank cranks the wheel left and guns the Impala into the opening.

I look back and see the bodyguards chasing after us with their arms pumping—then one of them skids to a stop, raises his Glock, and draws a bead on my head. I wince and wait for him to pull the trigger, but he doesn't.

Maybe he can't. Maybe our desire is so strong that we've become a force of inevitability—a causal agent so indomitable that the bodyguards are as helpless in the passage of our destiny as a pig squeezing through a boa. They never had a chance, not a single one of them. I wouldn't be surprised if the bodyguard in his aim suddenly grew arthritic in the shooting hand . . . or if the gun jammed because the manufacturer's mean times between failures had suddenly been breached . . . or that the heart murmur his doc told him ten times to ignore suddenly went staccato.

The Impala swings, squeezes past the semi on one side and the van on the other with metal grinding, me screaming, bodyguards yelling—then breaks free.

We burn rubber and climb to twenty, thirty, forty, then fifty, busting out from behind the convention center and into the street, barely making the turn, skidding, screeching, flying, fishtailing, then straighten out toward busy Van Ness Avenue while the bodyguards radio for backup somewhere in our past—but of course for them it's too, too late.

28

HANK DROVE IN CIRCLES AROUND the city while I watched out the back window to make sure we hadn't been followed. Neither of us heard a peep from the back seat.

Night fell. Hank drove to my apartment, pulled the car up to the curb, and cut the headlights. We jumped out, reattached the Impala's license plate, then opened the backseat door.

The sack was on the floor. Bill had thrown up—the canvas was wet with vomit and his legs had poked out of its mouth. I pushed them back in, wrestled the sack out of the car, and grabbed one end. Hank grabbed the other, and we muscled it into the apartment lobby and up the stairs.

We were panting and sore by the time we reached the sixth floor. We lowered the sack onto the carpet and dragged it down the hall toward my apartment. The vomit stench was overpowering.

We heard Bill groan.

"He's waking up!" whispered Hank, dragging faster.

We reached my apartment. I jammed my key into the lock and kicked open the door. The living room was pitch black. I let Hank go in first, then started pushing the sack in after him.

I heard a door open down the hall. I looked and saw Solveig step out of her apartment. I froze. She looked at me, then the sack. I smiled weakly. She made a face. She was only four doors down and could reach mine in the blink of an eye.

"What are you doing?" she asked.

"Just a little laundry," I said. Out of the corner of my eye I could see Hank crouched in the apartment, holding his end of the sack with white knuckles, ready to jerk the canvas inside if she started toward us.

Solveig sniffed the air. "I smell something," she said.

I sniffed. "Smells fine to me," I said, but it didn't matter—she was already padding away down the hall to investigate.

I gave Hank the nod. He jerked the sack into the apartment. I followed and locked the door behind us. We were home.

I felt around on the floor in the dark, found a flashlight, and flicked it on. The cage jumped to life as I moved the beam, casting ten-foot shadows of Hank dragging the sack toward the chain-link. I went ahead of him, removed the padlock, and opened up the cage door as wide as it would go. I climbed inside and Hank handed me one end of the sack. I grabbed it and pulled while Hank pushed. The sack squished through the cage's opening. We untied its mouth, walked to the other end, and lifted it straight up. Bill slid feet-first out of the sack in a wash of sweat. His hands and feet were still secured with the duct tape and the gag was still in his mouth.

I pulled his glasses out of my pocket, dusted them off, hooked them onto the roof of the cage where he'd find them, then pulled off his socks and shoes. Hank handed me a pair of scissors. I pulled the gag out of Bill's mouth, then cut off his polo shirt, pants, and underwear. Despite the indecency, it was impossible to look away as we stripped him naked; he'd brought his fame with him like a blanket.

We stepped back to look at him. Bill's nude body glowed wet and shiny like a fetus. I moved the flashlight beam from his dull executive haircut matted with fresh blood to his pale face, down past the nipples, across the rising and falling paunch, past the shriveled penis perched on two testes, down the soft, white thighs running reluctantly to a pair of dimpled calves—

Bill stirred. I shined the flashlight on his face.

"Doctor?" asked Bill dreamily without opening his eyes.

Hank motioned for me to answer.

"Yes?" I said.

"Could you ask the nurse to turn down the lights?"

"Of course," I said, moving the light from his face.

"And nurse?" Bill asked.

"Yes?" said Hank in a woman's voice.

"Tell the doctor to be careful."

"Of course he will," said Hank. "Careful as can be."

Bill began to snore. I pushed the gag back into his mouth, then Hank and I shimmied out of the cage like eels, padlocked it tight with the chain, tiptoed to the kitchen, opened some wine, and guzzled straight from the bottle. We didn't say a word. We just drank and breathed, walked in circles, and looked at each other and the walls and the bottle and the dark doorway that led to the living room. The reality was sinking in—the realization—the gravity—holy shit—

"Bill Kunstler is in OUR living room!" I whispered.

"I can't believe it!" Hank squealed, clenching his fists.

"Do you think he has brain damage?" I asked with a giggle. "There's blood on his head where I cracked him."

"He'll be all right. He probably lost a few brain cells."

"Do you think we'll get into trouble? How much do you think one of his brain cells is worth?"

We tried to figure out. Hank was quicker at the math. A trillion brain cells divided by a fortune of ten billion was only a hundred dollars per cell—not at all unaffordable for the average man!

I opened a second bottle of wine. Hank rooted through the fridge.

Passing over rotten vegetables, old condiments, and dried-out pizza, he emerged with a jug of expired milk. I found a rusty bucket under the kitchen sink and poured the milk in.

We shut off the kitchen light, carried the bucket and wine back to the living room, and sat down on the couch to observe Bill like a pair of ethnologists in the wild.

I felt around on the floor, found the dimmer switch we'd installed, and turned it up to full.

The spotlight over the cage lit up with a hum. I squinted. The chain-link glowed a stark and searing white, plunging the rest of the room into total darkness. The spotlight's bulb hummed. Dust flowed under it. The cage glared with harsh beauty. It was a brutal territory, a panopticon, a man-made desert, incapable of bias or weakness, like a boxing ring before fight night— old blood frying clean under the lights with a new drama of meat and bone waiting in the wings.

We look at Bill. He's naked, save for his tape and gag. It's performance time.

Hank whistles.

Bill wakes. We hear him breathing through his gag. He listens— then looks down and sees he's bound. He panics, fights to free himself, stops, rests, fights some more, then stops to rest again.

He rolls onto his side and surveys the cage. He can't see us—we're in the dark. He squints, trying to identify his surroundings, but the intensity of the spotlight is so direct, and his infamous myopia so severe, that he can't see beyond the chain-link.

He calls out as best he can through the gag:

"Hwwwo?"

He listens.

Nothing.

Using his tongue and teeth, he works at the gag, biting it, wetting, and pushing until it finally falls out of his mouth, then he calls again in a voice that's parched and raspy, yet unmistakable in its trademark high squeak:

"Hello?"

No one answers. He rolls onto his other side and starts working the duct tape from his wrists. He slides his arms under his ass, down to his knees, then under his legs to his front. He bites at the tape, gnawing through the adhesive until his hands are free.

He feels his way around the cage on his knees. Hank tries to assist by pointing at the eyeglasses hanging from above, but of course Bill can't see us. I try not to laugh.

Bill's hands move over the prop piles in the cage—the doll's heads, old rags, bowling ball, greasy chowder fork. They must feel strange. He starts to cry a little.

"Hhhhh . . . hhhhhh. . . ."

He drags himself forward to the front of the cage with his ankles still taped, grabs the chain-link, and gives it a few hard tugs. It doesn't budge.

Holding on, he slowly climbs the links, hoisting himself up hand over hand until he's standing. He puts his face up to the metal and looks out, cupping his hands around his eyes.

We sit in the dark. Will he see us?

"Hello?" Bill's voice is quiet. He touches his head, looks at his hand, sees blood, lets out a little cry, then begins hopping forward along the chain-link, following its circumference, looking for weak points, rattling the metal. He goes all the way around until he comes to the cage door. He feels the padlock—it's solid.

He squats, falls backward, and begins working the ankle tape. He's remarkably quiet for a man who's just been kidnapped. I wonder why he doesn't scream for help. Maybe he figures yelling is useless. If his kidnappers have any brains, they probably drove him to a rural location where nobody will hear him. How long was he unconscious? Two hours? Three? And who are his captors? Maybe he doesn't want to know. If he yells for help, we might come running, and we're probably dangerous . . . uneducated . . . rash . . . prone to flashes of violence . . . maybe even sexual predators.

I giggle. Hank smirks and slaps a pillow over my mouth.

Ten minutes pass. Bill finally works the ankle tape off. He stands and re-checks the cage door. He feels the padlock, gives the door a rattle, then takes a little run and hits it with his shoulder. The door flexes, but doesn't give; the whole cage barely moves at all. He hits it again, but it's hopeless.

Bill begins walking in circles. He mutters something about being claustrophobic; it looks like he's having a panic attack. We watch him go. He yells for help, but the clothing on the walls keeps his voice from escaping the apartment.

"HELLO?" Bill yells. He's white as a sheet and shaking all over. He puts his hands on his cheeks.

"I think he's gonna throw up," Hank whispers.

"No, he's not," I whisper back. "He's fine."

Bill clutches his stomach. He's breathing fast. He peers out at the dark living room for signs of movement.

We wait a beat, then I switch the spotlight off. The room's pitch black. Hank sneaks up to the cage with the bucket, aims at Bill's last known location, and pitches the milk through the chain-link. Bill screams, runs around, trips, fumbles, bounces off the fencing, throws some props at us in self-defense, then retreats to a dark corner, shaking, crouched, ready for the next attack.

"WHO'S THERE? HELLO?"

Hank and I remain silent. I imagine what Bill's thinking. Why isn't anyone answering him? Is it possible he's in the room alone? Could this all be automated somehow? Some kind of sick Rube Goldberg machine?

I flip the spotlight back on. The cage is dripping in milk.

Bill vomits.

29

HANK NUDGED ME. I OPENED my eyes. It was morning and I was still a little drunk. Sunlight streamed through the living room window. Hank pointed at the cage. I sat up and looked. Bill was snoring peacefully.

"Sleeping like a baby," said Hank through gritted teeth.

"HOW DARE YOU SLEEP!" I screamed, pulling off a boot and throwing it at the cage.

Bill started like he'd been drilled in the ass, scuttling backward on all fours, half-blind, butt cheeks waddling, then managed to spot his glasses hanging from the cage's ceiling. He jumped up, grabbed them, put them on, looked down at the mess of props under his feet, then saw he was buck naked with dried milk and vomit stuck to his chest. He tried to brush it off, grimacing at the sight of it, then looked up and saw what must've looked like a pair of real nutcases sitting on the couch grinning at him. Hank ran at the cage and leapt onto the chain-link like a gorilla in heat while I jumped around on the couch like a countertenor diva on PCP screeching, "IT'S MISTER BILL AND HIS BILLION-DOLLAR BUTT!"

Bill shrieked, flattened his naked body against the cage's back wall and visibly tightened his sphincter.

"Oh, don't act so delicate," I sneered.

"WE were the delicate ones!" Hank screamed. "WE were the delicates until YOU!"

"I'M SORRY!" Bill screamed.

Hank and I stopped. Bill's apology had caught us off guard. It hung in the air like a milky wet rag.

"That wasn't sincere," said Hank. "Sincerity is always feigned under duress. You have no idea what you're even apologizing for."

Hank moved along the chain-link, slowly, menacingly, then jerked his head forward like he intended to somehow pass right through the metal and take a bite out of Kunstler. Bill jerked backward so hard he hit his head on the wall behind the cage. It was obvious he had no physical self-control, no coordination, no depth perception whatsoever thanks to years of physical inactivity. He started crying.

"Are you experiencing trauma?" asked Hank, with a silly tilt of his head.

"Tra-ma?" I repeated.

"Tra-ma?" repeated Hank. We sang it over and over and danced a little jig.

"WHAT DO YOU WANT?" Bill pleaded.

I rifled through Bill's wallet. I saw his driver's license, lunch receipts neatly preserved for tax write-offs, credit cards, a condom . . . condom? Most unusual. I held it up inquisitively. Bill blinked. "For fucking people like us?" I asked. Bill had no response. I put the condom back and continued: discount club cards, a picture of Bill's trophy wife, and, in a fancy zippered compartment, a wad of cash in hundred-dollar notes. I took out a Franklin and held it up to the light. It was real.

"There's some more where that came from!" Bill bleated.

"Some?" Hank simmered. "You've been kidnapped, your head's

bleeding, you're naked and reeking of milk, and you're only going to tempt us with SOME?"

It was time for a performance art demonstration. I slid the Franklin back into the wallet, strolled to my personal pile of performance art props, rooted around, and came back with a bucket of tar and a pair of rubber gloves. I set the bucket down on the floor where Bill could see it, snapped the gloves on, removed the lid from the tar, and unceremoniously dropped his wallet in with a splat. Bill shrieked. Hank laughed. I pushed the wallet down until it was submerged, rolled it around until it was pretty well globbed up, then picked it out and began shaping it into a gummy tar ball.

Bill looked at me wide-eyed and struggled to interpret my gesture. Maybe we were telling him that he'd insulted us by not offering us his entire fortune—his entire wallet—right up front.

"I didn't mean to offend you," he begged. "Please! I—I can make you millionaires!"

"We don't want your money," said Hank flatly.

Bill blinked. How could Hank and I possibly not want his money? What, if not millions of dollars, could a man possibly have that would be of so much interest to another? Money was all Bill had. In his mind, money was the only logical target, the only rational reason we could have for risking life and limb to kidnap him. Any other reason would be illogical—or irrational—

Or personal.

Bill's mind seemed to settle on this last possibility. Events had taken a serious turn. This was no ordinary kidnapping, and Hank and I were no ordinary kidnappers. He pressed himself against the cage's back wall as far as he could go and covered his torso with his arms. He swallowed. We had his full attention.

"I—I'm sure I must have something you want," Bill whispered.

"We want you to be our performance art machine," I said, packing another layer of tar onto his wallet.

Bill's lips repeated my words silently. I could tell he'd heard of performance art before—maybe he'd even seen some on his travels to Milan or Paris or New York, though it had likely been of the poetry-in-a-beret variety.

"I don't understand," said Bill.

"Performance art machine." I said. "*Performa arta machina.* Not money. Performance art machine—"

Bill shook his head. "But I don't know how."

"You will," I said. "We'll put the choreography in your head."

"What choreography? I—"

I sang a few bars of the shaman song: "*Bill Kunstler will be our little shaman boy / We'll make him speak a new language / We'll make him lose his memory. . . .*"

Bill started shaking. Hank chuckled, walked to the video camera, and pressed its record button. Nothing happened. He opened the camera's tape compartment. It was empty.

"I forgot to grab a videotape," he said. "Let's run over to my apartment and pick one up."

Hank and I headed for the door.

"Wait!" called Bill. "Please—"

We stepped out into the hall and locked the apartment before Bill could finish.

"He's freaking out," I whispered, shaking the nerves out of my hands.

"I know," said Hank, "but we have to stay strong. He's probably just afraid we won't come back."

It was a sentimental thought indeed.

* * *

We walked to Hank's building, up the spiral staircase to the ninth floor, and down the hall to his apartment. He unlocked the door and we entered just in time to see Sherry down on all fours with her breasts falling halfway out of her dress over a set of carpet samples while a greasy rug salesman with a handlebar mustache and a bad toupee grinned at her hungrily.

"Well, hello!" said the rugger.

"Who the hell are you?" grunted Hank.

"HANK!" Sherry yelled. "Behave yourself! Choosing the right area rug is important!"

"That's surely right!" the rugger warbled with a twirl of his mustache and a ha-ha grin that said, too late, Bub, I'm working my way in here, and your wife with the swell rack likes it. The rugger adjusted his toupee, then returned his attention to Sherry.

"Now try this one," he said, removing a new sample from his briefcase and laying it on the floor. He took her hand and glided it over the sample. "It's a double silk shag."

"Mmmm . . . that's nice," Sherry cooed. "And it's real silk? Worms make this?"

"Mmm hmm. Big worms," the rugger chuckled suggestively. "Real big."

Sherry giggled. Hank glared at her.

"HANK, STOP GLARING!" Sherry snapped.

Clenching his teeth, Hank walked to the bedroom and grabbed a blank videotape from the closet. Then he went to the kitchen, opened a bottle of whisky, and downed a shot.

"AND HANK!" Sherry yelled from the living room. "I'M TIRED OF STEPPING OVER YOUR FIRE ROPE! PLEASE FIND ANOTHER PLACE FOR IT!"

Hank sighed, took another whisky swig, handed me the bottle, gathered up his prized red fire rope from the kitchen floor, carried it to the living room, and set it down in the corner.

"THAT ISN'T THE PLACE FOR ROPE!" Sherry screamed.

Hank ignored her. "Let's go," he said.

We stepped out into the hall. As Hank closed the apartment door behind us, I heard the rugger ask:

"THAT'S your husband?"

To which Sherry responded: "That's just Hank."

* * *

We descended the stairs, crossed the lobby, and stepped outside. Hank paced the sidewalk with his fists clenched.

"Who does that rugger think he is?" he growled.

"Let's go kick his ass," I said.

"No," said Hank, shaking his head. "It's better if I perform it out."

"That's a great idea," I said, "we'll rent a space and—"

"No," said Hank, shaking. "I need to perform it out right now."

I followed him to a drugstore. He bought a tin of hair-removal wax, a lighter, a propane stove, a wool cap, and a pint of peppermint schnapps, then led me down a few blocks to the popular intersection of Powell and Market where tourists liked to watch arriving cable cars reverse direction on a rotating wood turntable.

A hundred tourists stood waiting for the next car when we arrived. They pointed and smiled as Hank stepped out onto the turntable, set up his propane stove, opened the schnapps, and guzzled half the bottle.

A bored cop watched the scene from a nearby sidewalk. He'd seen his share of wackos using the turntable for performances and proselytizing, and one more kook wasn't going to ruin his day, even if the lunatic was lighting up a stove only ten feet away from a gaggle of open-mouthed tourists.

Hank stokes the fire, throws the tin onto the stove, and removes his shirt. Bums and shopkeeps stop to watch. The tourists ready their cameras; some even take out a dollar so they'll be ready to tip if the performance is good.

Hank begins skipping backward in circles around the stove and yelling, "THIS IS WHAT I THINK . . . THIS IS WHAT I THINK . . . THIS IS WHAT I THINK. . . ."

The wax melts, then liquifies, then begins to smoke. Hank grabs it from the stove, pours it over his head, throws the tin aside, and rubs the burning wax into his scalp and eyebrows like shampoo. The crowd groans. That wax has to hurt.

Hank skips and rubs and chants faster: "THIS IS WHAT I THINK . . . THIS IS WHAT I THINK. . . ."

Flashbulbs pop. Children giggle. Bums cheer him on. Hank is a blur around the stove now, around and around, skipping and rubbing like a madman until finally, hitting his crescendo, he skids to a stop and finishes:

"THIS IS WHAT I THINK . . . OF YOUR GODDAMN TOUPEE!" he screams, and in one violent tug, rips all of the wax and his hair clean off and throws them to the ground.

Tourists hold out dollars. A bum throws up. The cop snorts.

Hank walks over to me with the schnapps and the empty tin. He's bloody and bald. A little piece of scalp hangs down from the side of his face.

"Missed a piece," I said, pointing.

"I feel better," said Hank.

* * *

Hank slipped the wool cap over his head so he wouldn't scare anyone else and we walked back to my apartment.

Bill's eyes were puffy and red when we arrived. He reeked of sour milk.

"I thought about the song you sang," he said, pushing his face against the chain-link. "Machines . . . brains . . . memory . . . language . . . this is all about computers, right? You don't like my products? You don't like Redsoft? That's why I'm here? Well, I just wanted to say: you have every right to feel that way."

He began to cry. "You have me! I'll confess it all! My products are filled with bugs! They don't work as promised! Some are terrible, even though we have a chokehold on the industry—monopolists, every last one of us! We've ruined whole economies! Guilty as charged! Greedy beyond belief! I know it's true. I've used people; thrown them away like garbage after taking their ideas and their time—"

Memories of SI flooded my brain. I felt myself stiffen involuntarily. Bill caught my reaction and turned his attention to me.

"You—wait—I saw that—when I said that I've used people—"

Bill was a fast study. I glanced at Hank. His eyes were burning.

"Did I use you?" Bill asked me, his voice softening. "Did I—wait—is that it? Did you work for me?"

"No," said Hank.

Bill looked at him. "No?"

Hank pointed at Bill's face. "Performance art machine."

Bill nodded and tried to go with it. "Exactly," he said, "I've acted like a machine! Without heart! Without humanity! I was an automaton—"

Hank shook his head again and repeated more firmly than before: "NO."

Bill looked at me, then Hank. "No?"

Hank pointed at him and said it again: "Performance. Art. Machine."

"Performance art machine," Bill repeated, gearing up for the mental challenge. What did Hank mean? Was it a code? An anagram? There had to be clues. He looked down at the performance props on the floor of the cage, then up at the spotlight overhead, then at how the couch had been set up so Hank and I could watch the cage like an audience might watch a theater stage; maybe he was thinking too hard.

"I . . . you . . . want me to perform?" he asked.

Hank smiled. Bill's eyes widened.

"You're serious? This really is some kind of 'art' thing?" Bill asked, making quotes in the air with his fingers. The gesture was insulting. Hank and I realized he was only planning to humor us. He'd labeled us a pair of crazy artists, maybe revolutionary-types, even Communists, and he thought if he went along with the game, we'd let him go after using him in some crackpot Marxist propaganda escapade.

Hank put his face up to the cage. "You are the 'art,'" he said.

"How long do you think the performance will take?" asked Bill.

"AS LONG AS IT TAKES!" yelled Hank, pulling off his cap to reveal his bloody scalp. Bill screamed. Hank took out the schnapps, swallowed a gulp, and modeled his skull for Bill. "What do you think? Barber take a little too much off the top?"

Hank pushed the empty wax tin into the cage. Bill picked up the tin, saw what it was, and suddenly understood: Hank had done that thing to his head all by himself.

30

THE PHONE RANG. I ANSWERED. It was Rudy.

"We're in, damn it! We overflowed the hell out of Redsoft's machine and we've got a command prompt, baby! Come meet us for some eel!"

I hung up.

"Did they get in?" asked Hank.

"Let's go, cowboy," I said.

"Yeehaw!" whooped Hank. He put on his wool cap and we stepped out.

Bill shivered and watched us leave. He didn't say a word.

* * *

Hank and I walked to Yankee Noodle, a separatist Taiwanese diner a few blocks away. We arrived just in time to see a cook sing an ode to Chiang Kai-shek, then chop the head off a greasy three-foot Shanghai eel. The head clung for a second, then dropped into a dirty bucket on the floor.

Roman and Rudy were seated in a corner booth. They waved us

over and we sat down. Rudy slid us the morning newspaper. It was open to a wire story:

REDSOFT CEO FLEES AUDIENCE

SAN FRANCISCO, CA—Midway through his keynote speech at San Francisco's Computer and Software Super Expo yesterday, billionaire and Redsoft CEO Bill Kunstler departed abruptly, leaving audience members scratching their heads.

"I'm excited to announce that an incredible new business opportunity was extended to Redsoft just moments ago," said an unnamed Redsoft official to the thousands of tradeshow attendees, many of whom paid $25 to hear Kunstler speak.

"I'm not at liberty to reveal details," said the official, "except that it represents a brand new investment direction for Redsoft. Bill extends his sincere apologies for having to cut his speech short."

Shares of the software maker's stock gained three points at closing.

"Redsoft's PR machine is hard at work," said Rudy. "I guess they had to tell the crowd something after you grabbed Bill."

"You think they've already gone to the cops?" I asked. "Or the FBI?"

"No way," said Rudy. "A kidnapping would've been leaked in ten minutes flat—it'd be all over the news by now. My guess is they'll try to keep the cover story rolling as long as possible—investors hearing he's missing is the last thing they'll want."

"Redsoft will likely hire its own army to hunt you," grunted Roman with a self-assured shrug. "Same as in Russia. Mercenaries. Ex-military. Maybe CIA. Or better, KGB—"

"Roman, please," said Rudy.

Roman leaned in and looked me in the eye. "I still can't really believe you did it," he whispered.

"Just like we can't really believe you broke into Redsoft," I answered back.

"You will see for yourself soon enough," he bristled.

"It's true," said Rudy. "He had their machine on its knees in thirty minutes."

"I can't wait to ream him," said Roman, making the best fist he could with his crumpled hand. "I want that maggot eating out of a dumpster!"

A waitress came over. Roman ordered us an eel while Rudy took out a pen and diagrammed Redsoft's computer network on a paper napkin.

"The buffer overflow worked exactly as planned," said Rudy. "Roman was able to bring up a command prompt and install a back-door terminal program that'll let us dial into the machine whenever we want. Using that as our base, we spoofed the machine's network address to bypass Redsoft's intrusion detection sensors, then poked around until we found the primary transaction database server where Billfold's customer-account data and transaction records are stored. All of Bill's stock accounts are in there. Fiddle with those, and you're fiddling with his wealth."

"Tell them about the archives," said Roman.

"Yes, that's the catch—the archives. The transaction server is archived onto a backup array every night. The archives go back years; every transaction Bill's ever made is probably stored on there. If you make a change to the transaction server, you'd better make it in the archive too, or you'll set off an alarm. Roman's working on a program to keep the two synchronized so that if you modify one, it'll the modify the other."

"Destroy this," said Rudy, handing the napkin to Roman. Roman stuffed it into his mouth and began chewing.

"Are you sure it's safe to dial into Redsoft's machine?" asked Hank. "Won't they be able to trace our call?"

"No," said Roman, his mouth full.

Rudy took another napkin and wrote a phone number on it. "This is the magic number," he said. "It's a direct line to a server at SI. You dial this, and SI's server will dial Redsoft on another line and patch you through. If our hack is discovered, the phone company will only be able to trace it as far as SI. SI's phone system is a rat's nest—I've seen their wiring closet. Nobody will figure out where the call originated from."

"When will it be ready?" I asked.

"Tomorrow," said Rudy. "We'll drop off the equipment at your apartment."

"I wish I could see Bill's face when you do it," said Roman, swallowing napkin.

"I'm curious," said Rudy. "You still haven't told us what you plan to do about his wife."

"What about her?" asked Hank.

"You don't think she'll notice the Kunstler family fortune disappearing?"

"Are you kidding? After years of putting up with Bill's lust for money? I bet she'll welcome it," I said.

"You'll videotape it, won't you?" Roman whispered.

"Absolutely," said Hank.

Our eel arrived. Roman cut us all a hunk.

31

WE LEFT YANKEE NOODLE AND started back to my apartment.

Hank looked over his shoulder. "I think we're being followed," he whispered. "Redsoft can't pretend Bill is off on some business trip forever. They're searching for him already—I can feel it."

"Stop. You're making me nervous."

Hank stole another glance behind us. "I thought about what you said earlier, about finding a performance space and putting on a show. I think we should do it."

"You're on," I said. "But right now I think it's feeding time."

We entered my apartment. Bill was sitting in the middle of the cage. His eyes were red.

I went to the kitchen and returned with a hamster water bottle and a loaf of bread. Hank clipped the bottle to the side of the cage while I wadded the loaf into a ball and poked it through the chain-link until it fell inside.

Bill looked at the bread ball at his feet.

"You want me to eat that?" he squeaked.

"That's dinner," said Hank, "and maybe breakfast too."

Bill started crying.

"What now?" asked Hank.

"I want to make a phone call."

"Why?"

"I need to check on the market. My stocks—"

"Unbelievable!" said Hank.

"Please?"

"No!"

Bill swallowed. "Could I at least have some clothes?"

"Make your own! You have plenty of props."

"But—"

"Improvise," I said. "Make a performance out of it."

Bill clutched at his belly as if in pain.

"What's wrong with you?"

"I need to go to the bathroom."

I pointed to the toilet in the corner of the cage.

"There?" said Bill. "In front of you?"

"That's it," said Hank.

Bill whimpered. "I can't."

"You will eventually," I said.

Bill cried harder and began rooting around in the cage for something to wear.

Hank took me aside. "I don't like how he's being so resistant to performance art," he whispered.

"We just have to train him," I said. "I read somewhere that sleep deprivation makes a captive more impressionable. The CIA calls it the poor man's mescaline. All we have to do is keep him awake until he wears out."

We looked around the room for something that would keep a man awake. Hank pointed to my record player. I hadn't used it in years. We plugged it in and turned it on. The platter spun. It still worked.

"Where are your records?" asked Hank.

"Here," I said, pulling a record out from under a pile of clothing. "It's my only one. It came free with the player."

Hank took it and read the title: *Yoga for Everyone*. He put it on the platter and lowered the arm. A man's voice began speaking about the joys of yoga.

"This won't work," said Hank. "I don't think it would keep an insomniac awake."

I walked to my performance prop pile, found a screwdriver, came back, and raked it over the record's tracks until they were scratched to hell.

"Now try," I said.

Hank played the record. The voice came on in the middle of a yoga workout with a jarring skip: "AND HERE COMES THE DUH-DUH-DOWNWARD DOG. FLATTEN YOUR YOUR BA-BACK AND DON'T LET YOUR RI-RI-RIBS SI-SINK."

The record skipped, then started over with the downward dog. Hank and I put earplugs in our ears and turned the player's volume up.

Bill winced. "WHAT ARE YOU DOING?" he yelled over the noise. The record played the downward dog passage, then started over. We shut the apartment's lights off, turned the cage's spotlight up full, and sat down on the couch.

The record started over. Bill covered his ears and glared at us. It was a stand-off.

Hank and I went to sleep.

The record started over.

32

MORNING CAME. THE RECORD WAS still playing. We turned it off and removed our earplugs. Bill lay on his side in the middle of the cage. The dark circles under his eyes told us he hadn't slept. During the night he'd fashioned himself a skirt from cellophane and duct tape. It was very short, revealing a little ass.

"Nice," I said.

Bill grimaced and clutched his stomach.

"What's wrong with your gut?" asked Hank.

"I still have to shit," Bill grunted.

"Then shit," I said.

"No."

"You will eventually," I said.

"Not in here I won't!" Bill snapped, adjusting the skirt to hide his rear.

There was a knock on the door. Hank looked through the peephole. "It's Rudy and Roman," he whispered.

I grabbed the cage's canvas cover, slid it down over the chain-link to keep Bill out of sight, then gave Hank a nod.

He opened the door. Rudy and Roman hurried in with a second-hand computer, two keyboards, two monitors, and a mountain of cables. They set the equipment down on the coffee table.

"It reeks in here," said Roman, covering his nose.

"Never mind that. Get a load of the fancy decor!" said Rudy, taking in the layers of clothing hanging on the walls.

"Is the computer all ready?" I asked.

Rudy nodded. "I finished the coding last night. He's in for a real surprise."

Roman eyed the cage's canvas cover. "He's really in there?"

"That's right," I said.

"I want to see him."

"We're only here to set up the computer," said Rudy.

Roman shot Rudy a glare but turned his back on the cage, and we all went to work.

Cutting a small flap in the canvas, I attached a keyboard and monitor to the outside of the cage while Hank set up a second keyboard and monitor on the coffee table. Both keyboards and monitors would be connected to the computer at the same time so we'd be able to watch everything Bill typed, and if necessary, take control of the machine from the couch.

Rudy ran a telephone cord to the apartment's phone jack, started up the computer, and confirmed it was able to dial into SI, and from there, Redsoft.

Roman tapped me on the shoulder.

"He's really in there?" he whispered, nodding to the cage.

"You're obsessed!" I laughed.

Roman licked his lips and waited for an answer.

I forced a smile.

"WHO IS IN THERE?" he yelled.

"It's Kunstler, Roman," I said.

"Did you tell him about my hands?" Roman asked. "How he ruined them?"

"No."

"THEN I WILL!" Roman screamed, pulling a pistol from his waistband. The rest of us froze. Roman ran to the cage, lowered the gun, raised it, pointed it at the canvas, then at the floor, then at himself, then at us, then back at the cage.

"Roman," said Rudy, "please, put it away—"

"HE'S REALLY IN THERE?" Rudy asked. "YOU REALLY HAVE THAT MAGGOT?"

Before I could answer, Rudy whipped the cage's canvas off to reveal Bill shaking in the far corner.

"WHO—WHAT THE HELL IS THIS?" Roman yelled. He shook his head to clear his vision, then looked again, and saw that, sure enough, it was Bill Kunstler in a cellophane skirt.

"YOU RUINED MY HANDS!" Roman screamed.

Bill opened his mouth to ask how he'd managed to mangle the Russian's hands, but he was shaking so hard that all we heard was his teeth chattering.

Roman cocked his gun and aimed at Bill's head.

Bill whimpered and pulled his knees up to his chin, inadvertently exposing a little flank.

Roman grimaced with revulsion. "YOU SICK, SELFISH LITTLE—"

"Don't do it, Roman!" Rudy begged. "Please—"

Sweat poured down Bill's face. He pinched his eyes shut. We all waited for the shot.

Roman slowly lowered his piece. "I just can't shoot a man in a skirt," he said.

Bill jumped up and ran for the toilet.

"I told you you'd shit," I said.

Bill looked up and, in his first defiant act, flipped us an uncoordinated bird.

Hank and I applauded.

* * *

Bill paced the cage like an animal after Rudy and Roman left.

"You almost got me KILLED!" he cried. "That Russian was going to shoot me!"

"Make a performance out of it," I said.

"I WISH HE'D SHOT YOU!" Bill screamed, kicking the chain-link with his bare foot so hard the recoil sent him crashing to the floor.

"That wasn't very nice," I said.

"My toe's bleeding—and it smells like shit in here!" Bill cried.

"Imagine how we feel," said Hank.

Bill flipped us another bird.

"Don't be angry. We bear gifts," I said, gesturing to the computer. "This computer is for you. It's connected to the screen and keyboard that are mounted on your cage, and look!" I ran to the cage and powered up Bill's monitor. The screen flickered, then came to life. "IT'S PORTALIA!" I sang with glee, showing him the Redsoft Portalia startup screen. "Here's your keyboard. Go ahead! Type something! Try it out!" I backed up to the couch and sat.

"This is some kind of trick," said Bill.

"How could it be a trick? It's just a keyboard. Use it or don't use it—it's up to you. We'll just sit over here in the audience."

Bill paused, unsure, then wriggled a hand through the chain-link. He touched the keyboard. It felt good. He pressed a command key to see what programs were available on the machine.

"I don't see any programs on here," said Bill.

"We removed them all," said Hank.

"Except for mail," I said. "Press F1."

Bill pushed the F1 key. An electronic mail program appeared.

"You're going to let me send mail?" asked Bill.

"That's right."

"I don't believe you."

"Try it," I said.

Bill opened a blank mail form and typed a short message to Redsoft's chief financial officer.

From: Bill
To: CFO@Redsoft

This is Bill. Help! I've been kidnapped!

Bill pressed a key to send the mail. The message disappeared as the computer sent it off.

A second later, a new piece of mail appeared in Bill's inbox. Bill pressed a key. The new message opened. It was the note he'd just sent.

"The mail came right back to me," said Bill.

"Exactly!" said Hank.

"You can only mail yourself!" I said. "Anything you send comes right back!"

"I knew it was a trick," said Bill.

"You can mail yourself ideas!" said Hank. "What a great way to generate performance art material! It's like a diary—"

"I am not going to WRITE MYSELF!" yelled Bill. He punched his keyboard. A string of random numbers and letters spewed across his monitor—then the screen froze.

"You crashed Portalia," said Hank.

"Well, what do you expect?" said Bill. "This old computer is junk!"

"Don't worry," I said. "A friend of ours installed some special software that'll automatically restart it when it crashes."

We all watched our monitors while the computer restarted. The machine went through its usual warm-up diagnostics, then paused before starting Portalia.

A status message appeared at the top of the screen:

DIALING. . . .

The computer dialed a phone number. After a few rings, a remote computer answered and began exchanging data with our machine. We were connected to SI. We heard a series of clicks as the SI machine dialed into Redsoft's network and patched us through.

The status message on the screen changed:

CONNECTED. RECEIVING ACCOUNT RECORDS. . . .

We were in. A list of account records scrolled up the screen. Each record showed an account number, and next to it, the total number of shares held in that account.

"What are these?" asked Bill as the numbers flew by.

The list ended and the accounts stopped scrolling, giving Bill just enough time to read some of the numbers.

"These are my Billfold stock accounts," he said flatly, his voice as distant and plain as the soldier who looks down at his belly in the heat of battle and says he never knew intestines looked like that.

The status message changed again:

DELETING SHARES. . . .

The accounts began scrolling again from the top, but slower this time. As each account's share total scrolled into view, there was a pause while it counted down to zero. The shares were being deleted account by account. A thousand shares here, five thousand shares there. . . .

"This is can't be real," said Bill.

Hank and I smiled.

Bill hit the keyboard, but the program ignored him. The account share totals continued decrementing. Five hundred here, ten thousand there. . . .

"STOP IT!" Bill shrieked.

The numbers stopped. The status message changed.

500,000 SHARES DELETED. REPLICATING CHANGES IN ARCHIVE. . . .

"NO!" Bill screamed. Once the account totals were reflected in Redsoft's archive database, they'd be permanent; our changes would be consistent across all of Redsoft's systems of record and irreversible. Bill scrambled to yank out the keyboard's cable, the monitor cable, anything, but it was too late:

ARCHIVE SYNCHRONIZED. DISCONNECTING. . . .

The computer's modem hung up and Portalia's startup screen reappeared on our monitors.

"THOSE WERE WORTH MILLIONS!" Bill cried.

"Only a few billion left to go," said Hank.

"Why don't you do a performance about it?" I asked.

Bill punched the keyboard. His screen froze. Portalia had crashed again. After a pause, the whole cycle started over—the computer restarted and dialed SI. Bill screamed an unholy scream.

A door slammed in the hallway outside. We looked at the front door and saw it was open a crack. Rudy and Roman had left it open on their way out. Our soundproof fortress had a breach; someone had heard Bill's scream and was coming to check it out. We heard feet padding down the hall.

Hank ran for the door. "Run interference!" he whispered to me.

Bill saw the commotion. "HELP!" he screamed.

Hank opened the door just in time for me to dive into the hallway and intercept Solveig. I hopped up and down on one leg and moaned.

"WHAT IS HAPPENING IN THERE? WHAT IS ALL THAT SCREAMING?" she yelled.

"I HAVE TERRIBLE GAS!" I cried, doubling over and clutching at my stomach. I forced myself to fart. Solveig held her nose and hurried back down the hall in disgust. I banged on the door. Hank opened it and I dove back inside, safe.

33

HANK MADE FINAL ADJUSTMENTS TO his video camera while I sat on the couch and watched Bill glare at us.

"You should type something," I said, nodding to his keyboard.

"I'm busy," said Bill.

"You don't look busy."

"I'm thinking."

"About what?"

"First, if you two are fucking."

"That was only one time," I joked.

Bill crawled forward to the chain-link in his homemade skirt and put his mouth up to one of the holes so his lips and teeth were framed by the metal. "And second, I'm thinking about how when I finally get out of here, I'm going to have you ground into meat by a sick third-world mercenary who'll love a shot at a quick million in exchange for supplying a billionaire's poodle with fresh feed."

"What makes you think you'll get out of there?" said Hank.

"And if you do get out, what makes you think you'll still be a billionaire?" I asked.

Bill's lips quivered.

"I think we're ready," said Hank, aiming the camera at the cage. "Plug her in and let's shoot some footage."

I rose from the couch and hunted for the camera's power cord.

"Have you seen the cord?" I asked.

Hank and I searched for it. It wasn't on the floor or under the couch or in the kitchen.

"I must've left it at my apartment," said Hank.

I groaned. We turned on the record player, cranked up the volume, and headed out.

* * *

We climbed the stairs to Hank's apartment, opened the door, and entered to find the rug salesman kissing Sherry on the living room floor. They stopped what they were doing, sat up, and looked at us. Both were naked except for the rugger—he was still wearing his socks and toupee. He twirled his mustache. His pecker was the size of a gherkin.

Hank took in the scene, then walked to the kitchen, came back with plastic garbage bags, went to the bedroom, found the video camera's power cord, grabbed some clothes and a blanket from the bed, and headed to the den. He stuffed as much of his Bill shrine into the sacks as he could— photos, cutouts, books, videos, T-shirts—and in less than a minute his bags were full and I was following him out of the apartment, down the stairs, and outside.

Hank paced the sidewalk with his bags and began to cry.

"I don't know what to say," I whispered.

"Say you'll help me get a performance going," he sputtered.

"Of course I will."

"I don't even care what it is."

"I've been dying to put on a show. We'll find a venue and do it. Something small at first, maybe, then we'll work our way back up."

Hank nodded, took a deep, shuddery breath, and stood up straight.

"All right," he said, forcing a smile through tears. "I—I'll see you later."

He turned and started down the sidewalk with his bags, then stopped.

He had nowhere to go.

I walked to him, took him by the arm, and led him back up the street to my place.

* * *

Hank and I put in our earplugs, unlocked my apartment door, and went in. The yoga record was deafening. Bill was stomping around the cage with his hands over his ears. "TURN IT OFF!" he yelled.

We ignored him. Hank walked to the farthest corner of the living room to unpack his sacks while I sat down on the couch and checked the computer's logs. The machine had restarted itself three times while we'd been gone, costing Bill millions; his fortune was disappearing.

"PLEASE!" Bill begged, waving his hand at me through the chain-link. "PLEASE! I'LL GIVE YOU HALF OF WHAT I HAVE! BILLIONS! YOU'LL NEVER HAVE TO WORK AGAIN! PLEASE, I'M GOING CRAZY—"

"DO A PERFORMANCE ABOUT IT!" I yelled.

"I DON'T KNOW WHAT THAT *MEANS!*" Bill screeched, pulling at his hair—then a look of horror crossed his face and he fell silent. Something over my shoulder had caught his attention. I turned and saw Hank pinning up his shrine in the corner. There were Bill pin-up dolls, Bills with scratched-out eyes, Bills with no heads . . . it looked like the work of a psychopath. When Hank was finished, the shrine covered the corner of the living room from floor to ceiling.

Hank stepped back to judge it. "IT'S NOT AS BIG AS THE LAST ONE," he shouted. He sounded disappointed.

"BUT NOW YOU HAVE HIS WALLET," I yelled, pointing to the center of the shrine where Hank had stuck Bill's tarred wallet to the wall, "WHICH MAKES THIS ONE MORE AUTHENTIC."

Hank put his hands in his pockets and smiled.

34

NIGHT FELL. HANK SHUT OFF the living room lights, turned up the cage's spotlight, removed his boots, adjusted his earplugs, and curled up on the floor beside the shrine to sleep.

I stretched out on the couch. Hours ticked by. I tossed and turned. Sleep wasn't coming. I finally sat up to find Hank lying wide awake on his side. He was staring at his shrine. I strained to see where he was looking, then spotted it—

Down near the baseboard, hidden among the cutouts and pin-ups of Bill, was a little wallet photo of Sherry.

* * *

I heard a crash and jumped up to find Hank crouched over the record player. It was broken and in pieces all over the floor. I took out my earplugs.

"He knocked the player off the shelf," said Hank, holding up a telltale chunk of red brick. We'd included a brick in Bill's stack of props; somehow he'd broken off a piece, squeezed it through the chain-link, and flicked across the room with his fingers to hit the player.

"Pretty good aim," I said. "Did you sleep any?"

"No," said Hank. I saw him steal a glance at the Sherry photo.

"Were you looking at that thing all night?"

"It's just a souvenir."

"What you need is to get her out of your system."

"I will."

"Right now. Perform her out. It'll do you good. And no wax this time. Keep it simple."

Hank swallowed. He knew I was right.

We went outside. Heavy traffic was already speeding past the apartment building, though it was still early. Hank covered his eyes, stood on the street curb facing the sun, and breathed deeply.

"Don't rush it," I said.

Hank swung his arms to warm up, took a big suck of air, bent over, said Sherry's name into the gutter, straightened up, cracked his knuckles, watched the cars fly past, took another breath, then said "Sherry" into the gutter, but he held the name longer this time.

He straightened up and wiped sweat from his forehead. Traffic lights at the end of the block turned red. Cars slowed, then stopped. Drivers looked at us. Hank nodded hello to them, wiped more sweat off, took another air swig, then did it again, blowing Sherry out as hard and as long as he could into the gutter. Drivers opened their windows to hear what he was saying. Hank continued blowing: "Sheeeeeeeeeeee . . . ." He was deep into the E and deflating toward R. Thirty seconds passed, then sixty. His face turned red. His neck veins pulsed. He was running out of air. He bent over at the waist, pushing it out, forcing it, blowing it out into the gutter like a sick trumpeter until Sherry's air was gone.

Drivers whooped and applauded, then the light went green and traffic moved. Bathed in sweat, Hank straightened up and nodded to me.

We both felt better.

* * *

We walked to a coffee stand for two cups of joe. Hank bought a newspaper and flipped through the business section.

"Looks like Redsoft just expanded its cover story," he said, showing me a headline article about Bill:

REDSOFT ANNOUNCES CEO ON SABBATICAL

SAN FRANCISCO, CA—Software maker Redsoft announced today that CEO Bill Kunstler was away on sabbatical at an undisclosed location in order to continue work on what insiders are calling a breakthrough technology.

"As a visionary, Bill is very hands-on," said Don Zeila, Redsoft Senior Executive for New Product Development. "None of his staff knew he was leaving, but I've been told that this opportunity was unexpected and needed immediate attention. I doubt he even had time to call his wife. I haven't talked to him since he left, but all of this just proves his dedication to innovation."

Zeila could not say how long Kunstler would be gone, but he did confirm that the CEO was still running the company with daily direction to key members of the board.

The story was accompanied by an archival photo of Bill waving to the camera.

"Have a great trip," said Hank, toasting the photo with his cup.

"The board must be running the whole show," I said.

"But for how long?" Hank took a sip of coffee, then spat it out.

"Bad beans?"

"Tastes like metal," he said, wiping his mouth on his arm.

I took a sip from my cup. "Mine's fine."

Hank tasted his again. "I don't think it's the coffee. It's something in my mouth. Maybe one of my fillings came loose. Do you see anything?"

I looked at his teeth. "Nothing unusual."

"It's probably just a filling," he said, spitting.

"Maybe revenge tastes like cavities."

Hank laughed, dribbling coffee all over his shirt.

35

THE WEEK WORE ON. PORTALIA crashed multiple times daily, and each was followed by a brand new Bill antic. He tried stomping tirades, screaming and ripping his hair, assaults on the chain-link, threats of legal action and arrest, inane ruses and trickery, pleading frenzies, bribes, and even vomiting into the toilet, which without water for flushing was slowly filling up.

It was feeding time. Hank topped off Bill's water bottle while I pushed a raw potato into the cage. The chain-link shredded the potato's skin off so only the meaty part mashed through. Bill looked at the skin stuck to the chain-link with distaste as he crawled to the skinless potato and gnawed into it with ennui. Hank and I fed him whatever leftovers we had in the kitchen and secretly snickered at the messes we cooked up: wet cereal kibbles on brown lettuce, orange peel dipped in molasses, mashed raisins in gelatin. . . .

"I'm still hungry," said Bill, swallowing the last of the potato.

"That was dinner," said Hank.

"I'm not a HAMSTER!" Bill cried, rattling his water bottle. "I'm sick of your raisins and rotten vegetables!"

"Come on! That was some gourmet shit!" I said.

Bill darted to the toilet and vomited up the potato. "THERE'S YOUR GOURMET!" he yelled.

"Vomit is the performance artist's leitmotif—the symbolic turning-inside-out of the gut—the Hierophant lifting his skirt for the viewer's pleasure," I said. "It's a powerful sign that should never be used in anger."

"And it's no way to treat your audience," said Hank.

We slid the canvas over the cage and left it there as punishment.

* * *

A day passed. Bill yelled from under the canvas that he was hungry. We ignored him. Another day went by. Bill cried anytime Portalia crashed. We heard him breaking props, and later, trying to pick the chain-link's padlock, but the canvas stayed on.

A third day passed. Bill's only light came from his computer monitor, which he complained was too bright. He tried covering it with duct tape, but when he realized the tape made it impossible to see how often Portalia was crashing, he ripped it back off.

On day four we heard fewer tantrums, but occasional sobbing and several complaints about the toilet, which he swore was almost full.

Day five brought whimpering and screams over the death of his freedom as he passed through the stages of bereavement.

Day six was filled with moans and impassioned pleas for a toilet flush.

"PLEASE!" Bill screamed. "I'M DYING! THE AIR IS POISON!"

Hank rose from the couch, sauntered to the toilet's water supply valve, and turned it on. Water rushed through the hose to the toilet. We heard Bill scramble to the commode and flush. The tank refilled and he flushed again. He told us the bowl was clogged and begged us for a plunger. We decided to give him one. I pulled the cage's cover off.

Hank and I gasped. Bill looked like a different man. He'd dropped ten pounds and his acne was flaming—his whole face was in revolt.

Bill grabbed the plunger and attacked the toilet, willing the water down, pumping like mad until the bowl emptied. Then he collapsed in the center of the cage and glowered at us.

"You'll die in prison," he said. "Redsoft will be looking for me. They'll dispatch agents. They'll break down your door—"

"No one is coming for you," said Hank.

"How would you know?" asked Bill.

Hank pushed the sabbatical newspaper article through the chain-link. Horror crept across Bill's face as he read it and realized he wouldn't be missed by the public, at least not for a while; Redsoft's sabbatical angle had concealed the kidnapping perfectly.

Bill slumped down and started to cry. He was out of gas. He tore off pieces of the newspaper, daubed his tears, and refused to look at us.

36

I OPENED MY EYES. IT was morning and the sun was up. I rose and looked for Hank. He wasn't in the living room. I walked to the bathroom. The door was open. I turned the light on and found him shivering in a tub of water.

"What are you doing?"

"My skin's on fire and there's metal in my mouth," he quivered.

I went over and felt the tub's water.

"This water's ice-cold!" I said.

"How long has it been since we had an audience?" Hank asked through blue lips.

I tried to remember our last performance, but couldn't.

"Get out of there," I said. "Let's go find a gig."

* * *

The most popular art galleries in the Tenderloin were along its edge nearest Union Square and the theater district, so we left the apartment and headed over there.

"I don't want to get my hopes up," said Hank as we walked.

"We'll find a place," I said. "There must be thirty galleries down here."

The first gallery we saw was called The Master's Tendrils. We looked in the window and saw a Rembrandt hanging on one wall and a Van Gogh on another.

We went in. The owner stepped out from behind a desk that was shaped like a pubic hair. "May I help you?" he asked.

"Do you ever show performance art here?" I asked.

The owner looked confused.

"We're looking for a place," said Hank.

"To . . . purchase a painting?" asked the owner.

"To do performance art," I said.

The owner sniffed. "I only deal in works of historic significance—painting, sculpture, and the other high arts—and preferably the Dutch Masters."

"They have performance art in Amsterdam," I said.

"I would not call red-light ladies crushing apples with their crotches high art," said the owner.

Hank spat on the floor.

"What are you doing?" asked the owner.

"I had metal in my mouth," said Hank, smearing the spit with his shoe.

"GET OUT!" yelled the owner.

Hank and I stepped outside.

"I want to pound him," Hank growled.

"That was only the first one," I said. "There are plenty more. Come on."

We visited several more galleries without luck, then saw one called Prance Prance that looked promising. We looked in the window and saw paintings of white-skinned nudes eating fruit on velvet couches.

"Let me do the talking," I whispered.

Hank nodded and sneaked in a quick spit.

We walked in. The gallery owner came over and introduced himself. His name was Vaughn. He looked artsy in a ruffled shirt and striped knickerbockers.

Vaughn's frilly outfit reminded me of my father. While stationed in Paris during a stint in the Army, Abe had earned extra francs by giving farcical lectures about the beloved French playwright Molière. Wearing a white peruke, pancake make-up, and a yellow jumpsuit, Abe had treated bystanders along the Pont Neuf to hour-long talks in broken French that always climaxed with a reenactment of Molière's death, which amounted to Abe collapsing in the gutter mid-sentence. The Parisians found him ridiculous, of course, but when they nicknamed him *le professeur manqué*—French for "the failed professor"—he mistakenly translated the moniker as "professor monkey," which he believed was not only a compliment on his animal antics and ferocious wit, but also an obscure reference to Molière's family crest, which featured monkeys prominently. Invigorated, Abe donned the title like a badge of honor and, upping the ante, began dragging his knuckles along the ground during his lectures. He was eventually arrested and deported.

"What sort of performance art do you do?" Vaughn asked.

"If you like that," I said, pointing to a painting of a nude, "you'll LOVE us."

"Really?" said Vaughn, eyeing the nude. "You can do that? Something as intense as that?"

"Absolutely," said Hank.

"I don't know," said Vaughn. "The last performance artist I showed did horrid things to my hardwood floor. There was confetti and gasoline everywhere and it took a week to scrape the deer carcass off of the wall."

"We'll be good," said Hank coyly.

"Well," said Vaughn, "I do have a new show opening next week; it's called Lovers in Gentle Paradise. What do you think?"

"It sounds brilliant," I purred.

"I can pay you an honorarium of one hundred dollars—plus I'll throw in whatever props you require if they aren't too expensive."

"We'll take it!" said Hank.

"And you promise not to wreck the place?"

"We promise," said Hank. He clicked his heels and offered a salute.

We were in.

37

DAYS PASSED. HANK AND I stayed up nights drinking and making flyers to advertise our Prance Prance gig. When our flyer stack was tall enough, we went around town, taped the ads up, then came back and made more.

One night we ran out of wine. We walked down to the local liquor store.

"I'm out of everything cheap," said the clerk behind the counter. "No dollar wine, no vodka, no rum. Next shipment arrives tomorrow."

"You must have something," I said.

The clerk rooted around behind the counter and came up with a dusty bottle. He handed to us. We read the label: COOKING SHERRY.

"You're kidding," said Hank.

"Fifty cents," said the clerk.

"Let's drink her!" I said.

We bought the bottle and drank it on the walk home. Sherry gave a putrid buzz—we felt nauseous, yet elated.

We went up to the apartment. Hank fixed the broken record player with duct tape, then put on the yoga record. The needle dragged over the scratched vinyl, then clawed over the tape with terrible popping and hissing. It was lovely. We put our earplugs in, cranked up the volume, and danced around while Bill ransacked the cage in search of ear protection. Digging through his props, he pulled out his own roll of duct tape and a pair of menstrual pads. He taped the pads to the sides of his head.

Hank picked up a black marker and danced toward his Bill shrine. He stalked the little picture of Sherry like a tiger, back and forth, back and forth, then dove at it pen-first, leaving his mark in a single stroke: an upright penis scribbled on her forehead.

"I DREAMT IT WOULD BE THERAPEUTIC," he yelled over the yoga.

Hank stepped back to admire his handiwork while I laughed and ran to the bathroom to let some Sherry out.

* * *

We played the yoga record nonstop. Bill's mental state worsened. He stopped sleeping and his days were increasingly punctuated with severe emotional breaks. He'd go comatose for an hour standing up, bang around the cage like a drunk, talk to himself, pick at his acne, cry whenever Portalia crashed. . . . We told him to use his depravation as choreography—write it down, work it out, make a performance out of it—but he resisted, night after night, until finally, after days of our prodding, he cracked.

"FINE!" Bill screamed, storming around the cage with his menstrual pads on. "YOU WANT ME TO WRITE IT DOWN? I'LL WRITE IT DOWN!"

Hank and I turned the yoga down, ran to the couch, and watched our computer screen to see what he'd type.

"DON'T LOOK AT THE SCREEN! I'LL MAIL IT!" Bill yelled.

Hank and I looked away. Bill pounded out something on his keyboard.

"THERE!" he screamed. "I HOPE YOU'RE HAPPY!"

We looked at our screen. There was a new piece of mail in Bill's inbox.

"Why look, Hank!" I said. "We have mail!"

Hank pushed a button and the mail opened:

From: Bill
To: You

FUDK YOU!

Hank eased back on the couch. "What do you want me to do with this?" he asked, letting his disappointment hang out like a paunch. "I suppose this counts as some kind of beginning, and I'll give you a point for the misspelling, but really, the content's commonplace. Trite. Right up there with shitting yourself."

Bill screamed and ran at the cage door. He tried to ram it with his shoulder, but missed and connected with his face instead. The force of the impact sent him flying backward onto his ass, but he jumped up and did it again, skipping the shoulder this time and going right for his mug. Hank and I watched with our mouths open, flabbergasted.

"IT'S ROUGH, BUT IT'S LOOKING LIKE PERFORMANCE ART!" Hank screamed.

The phone rang. I ran to it.

"Hello?" I huffed.

"Larry!" said Mouse. "How are you?"

"Oh, man, you should see it!" I said, keeping an eye on the cage as Bill did another screaming face smash.

"Who is that yelling?" Mouse asked.

"It's Bill!" I said. "He's working up to his first performance piece!"

Mouse laughed. "You and Hank really need to lay off the wine."

"Where are you calling from?" I asked.

"A payphone at our hotel," said Mouse. I could hear slot machines dinging in the background. "There are twenty kickboxers waiting in line behind me, so I'll let you and Hank get back to whatever you're doing. I just wanted to hear your voice and ask about Blanche."

Oh, shit.

"How's my little doggy?" asked Mouse.

"He's . . . swell," I said. "Frisky—and a big eater."

"Oh, that's a good sign," said Mouse. "I was worried for nothing. Thanks again for feeding him. All right. People are waiting for the phone, so I'll go. Say hello to 'Bill' for me. Ha. And," she whispered, "I miss you." She giggled and the line went dead.

I missed her too, I thought, slipping the phone back into its cradle.

"Who was it?" Hank asked.

"Mouse," I said. "She wanted to know how Blanche is doing."

Hank laughed and waggled a finger at me.

38

I DROVE TO MOUSE'S HOUSE and let myself in. Blanche was running around in circles. I ran to the kitchen and saw that his doggy door was locked. I unlatched it and he bolted into the backyard to squat.

I walked through the house and surveyed the damage. After polishing off the contents of his food bowl and water dish, Blanche had survived by eating half of Mouse's plants. There were leaves, potting dirt, and urine puddles in every room.

Blanche's trail led to Mouse's bedroom. Her vanity and dresser were undisturbed. I ran my hand over the vanity's marble top. It was home to Mouse's boxing mementos—medals, trophies, admission tickets from fights she'd attended, and framed photos of her in cheesecake fighting poses.

Mouse's top dresser drawer was filled with boxing shorts. I took out a pair, held them up to my waist, and looked in the mirror. They might fit. I slipped my pants off and wriggled into them. The shorts were snug, but the silver metallic material and black waistband were handsome. Returning to the dresser, I opened the next drawer: sports bras. I pulled off my shirt, put on a bra, and threw a few punches in the mirror. Not bad, even with my gut hanging out.

I padded to the kitchen in my new outfit, found a water pitcher, and watered Mouse's surviving plants. I had to make six trips to the faucet to get them all. There were floradendrums on the floor, tulips on the tables, violets on the sills, and an unidentifiable bush by the kitchen window. The bush was half-eaten and covered with gnats. I put it in the sink and ran water over it. The gnats flew up and landed on my bra. I tried to brush them off, but only managed to smear them into wings and black flecks.

Unsure of when I'd return, I took all of the bowls out of Mouse's cupboards, filled them with water, and set them around the house. Food was next. Mouse had left me a fifty-pound bag of dog chow. Singing a little song about it being dinnertime for Señor Blanche, I laid the bag flat on the kitchen floor, then ripped a hole in it just big enough for Blanche's head. Dinner was served.

The doggy door squeaked. I looked and saw a stray cat had wandered in. It had yellow fur and eyes, pointy alien ears, high cheekbones, and a broad nose. It trotted past me and into the living room. I followed. It jumped onto the windowsill, gazed out the window, then turned and looked at me with a controlled deliberateness. It wasn't just a nonchalant gaze or a simple-minded response to stimuli; the cat was looking at *me*. I took a step toward it. Its eyes widened. We both froze.

I made a peeping sound. The cat darted into the kitchen. I hurried after it. It circled in a panic, then threw itself against the kitchen's back door repeatedly, up and down, up and down, over and over, slamming its little body against the wood, paws scrabbling for purchase, and then it was yowling and hissing and pissing, spray flying onto the door and the floor. I wasn't going anywhere near an animal like that—it was a wildcat, all eyes and urine and fur with its little penis spouting willy-nilly until finally it found the doggy door and pushed through, slick as shit, sprinting fast and over the fence before Blanche could even get a bark out.

39

NEW PENISES APPEARED ON SHERRY'S photo in black marker, and they were no longer confined to her forehead: tiny dicks multiplied and overlapped to cover her cheeks, eyes, and ears.

"Pretty soon you won't be able to see her face at all," I said.

"Lovers in Gentle Paradise," Hank mumbled sourly as he drew a cock on her nose. "Which reminds me—I came up with an idea for our performance."

He handed me a crumpled scrap of paper from his pocket. I read it. It was a finished choreographic performance score.

"Shit, this is genius," I said. "Let's do it!"

Bill sat scratching his belly on the floor of the cage. His tits sagged. His acne had spread from his face to his chest. He looked like hell. We watched his eyes droop, then close. His head bounced.

"Don't fall asleep now!" said Hank, rattling the cage. "It's time for you to do a performance!"

Bill jerked awake. "I'm not performing anything," he muttered.

"Watch," Hank whispered to me, "this is just like training a dog."

He turned his attention back to Bill. "PERFORM!" he ordered, clapping his hands.

"No!" Bill squealed, scratching his legs.

I laughed. Hank was undeterred. He took Bill's refusal as a chance to cobble Bill's unconscious behavior into an ad hoc performance art lesson: "Look at yourself," said Hank, pointing to Bill's belly and legs. "You protest while scratching; that's two actions at once. Ask yourself: how do they relate? Is one more significant than the other? Does one inform or critique the other? Make a note of it! Self-awareness is a performer's greatest asset!"

* * *

Hank and I took turns ordering Bill to perform, but nothing we did convinced him to focus on becoming a performance artist; in fact, he seemed unable to focus on much of anything for long. His attention span wavered. The sleep deprivation was starting to have deep effects: his tics became uncontrollable, he scratched, he rubbed his eyes, his limbs trembled, his own body became alien to him, his tolerance for pain dropped. His brain embarked on a strange serotonin dance and little hallucinations set in: in one episode, he thought he had lice; in another, he was sure he'd spotted a rat under the props. He wandered the cage, babbling about the stink of the toilet that was burning up the room; he complained of dehydration and announced he was dying; he said he wanted to talk to his people, to give the company board a call, and most of all, to check his stocks, which were disappearing rapidly.

We decided to appease him a little. Hank went out and brought back a newspaper that reported Redsoft was down two points. The news set Bill to tears, exhausting him even more.

40

THE DAY OF LOVERS IN Gentle Paradise arrived. Hank and I practiced our piece in the living room while Bill sat in the cage and watched.

"How long have you been doing this performance crap?" he asked.

"Crap is nothing new for us," I said. "We've been avid students of crap for years, if by crap you're referring to the psychological detritus, epistemological ruins, and cultural offal that drop in the wake of our constantly emerging *bildungsroman*."

Bill responded by spitting on the floor.

It was time to get ready. We called Vaughn with last-minute additions to our performance prop shopping list, drank a little wine to kill the nerves, and doused on cologne.

I pulled our formal performance art uniforms out of the living room closet piece by piece. The white cotton karate pants came out first. They were stained with blood, grease, and other viscera of past performances. The fact that they fit three inches too short made them all the more charming. The white T-shirts with their yellow armpit stains came out next. Veteran performers knew that yellow meant the cotton had thickened with deodorant and sweat into a barrier that protected the underarms from harm during acrobatics, kung fu, and other risky choreography—a real convenience. My cowboy boots came out last. They were black—not as fancy as Hank's red ones, but they did the trick.

We dressed and checked ourselves in the bathroom mirror. We looked terrific. The uniforms were classics, real crowd pleasers. I noticed the wax burns on top of Hank's head were fading; his hair was growing back in little tufts.

It was time. We headed for the front door. Hank paused to turn the video camera on. He aimed the lens at the cage.

"What are you doing?" Bill asked, bleary-eyed.

"You can't become a performance artist without an audience," I said. "The lens is like an eye—"

"You don't have permission to film me," said Bill. He scrambled around the cage in an effort to stay off camera, but quickly realized it was hopeless.

As the apartment door closed behind us, I saw Bill pace the cage again, then slick his hair down for the lens.

Vanity, even now.

* * *

Hank and I walked down to the gallery. A hundred people were shuffling toward Prance Prance's main doors when we arrived. We joined the crush. There was a drinks table on the sidewalk up ahead. I pushed my way over to it and saw pink champagne in a punchbowl. I grabbed a cup, dipped and drank, and waved to Hank. He came over and had a drink. The crowd moved forward. We grabbed the bowl and brought it with us so we could shuffle and drink at the same time.

Vaughn was greeting guests at the front of the line. I looked through the window at the art crowd inside. The gallery was packed. People stood elbow to elbow. A jazz quartet struggled to play in a corner without getting knocked over.

We reached the front. The punchbowl was empty—Hank and I had each downed nine cups. Vaughn saw the bowl and laughed. He grabbed our hands and we saw he was drunk.

"Oh my!" he slurred, ogling our dirty white uniforms, "don't you look like a couple of art butchers!"

We all laughed, then Vaughn led us inside. We weaved through the crowd. I saw chatty high society types, men in pinstripe suits, women in furs and diamonds, painters, poets, benefactors, collectors, and gallery assistants in knickerbockers running in all directions with bottles of champagne. . . . Then I saw the art—the walls were covered with framed paintings of cherubic cupids with wings and rosy cheeks and big hairy dongs . . . lovers in paradise indeed. Vaughn led us to the lobby's performance area. It was a ten-by-ten section of hardwood floor bounded by stanchions and red velvet rope. A chair with a thick white vinyl cushion, a red heart-shaped candy dish filled with thumbtacks, and a microphone sat on the floor facing the audience in the middle of the clearing.

"Start performing whenever you're ready," Vaughn purred as he sashayed away into the crowd. "I can't wait to see what you'll do with those tacks!"

Hank turned the microphone on and stood in front of the chair, facing the audience. I stood beside the chair, facing Hank. We each stared straight ahead with blank expressions. A minute passed. Some people noticed us and gravitated closer with their drinks to watch.

We begin. Hank sits down on the chair, knees together, eyes looking straight ahead. The chair's cushion flattens out under his weight with a high-pitched hiss. The microphone picks it up. The sound's barely audible over the noise in the room. A few people in the crowd hear it and look up at the gallery's loudspeakers overhead, but the noise is not enough to hold their attention for more than a second. Hank stands up. The vinyl cushion re-inflates. He sits down again. The cushion flattens out with a hiss. The mic picks it up. More people in the crowd look around. Hank stands up again, then sits with another hiss. A rhythm builds. Stand, sit-hiss. Stand, sit-hiss. The microphone gets it all.

The audience drifts closer. People are still chattering, but fewer than before. I see their faces out of the corner of my eye. A few look interested. Others are ambivalent. Some haven't seen performance art before. Others have, but look like they don't want to see it again. I spot a few bums from our old performance art days—here for the free booze, no doubt. Standing behind them is Jean Gateau, a tough art critic from a local rag. She's five feet tall with black hair, funky glasses, and white teeth. She waves hello.

Hank sits, stands, sits, stands, then stops. He grabs his pants, shoves them down to his ankles, snaps back up to attention, then resumes sitting and standing while I pick up the candy dish. The audience is really watching now. I spot expressions of mild amusement. People murmur and wonder what the performance has to do with love.

Hank sits, stands, sits, then stands. I take a tack from the candy dish and place it squarely in the middle of the cushion. After a beat, Hank sits right down on it and stops—then he stands. The tack is gone, apparently stuck to his ass. Some people gasp. Others laugh.

Hank sits, stands, then stops. I take another tack and put it on the chair. He sits down, the cushion hisses, then he stands. The tack's gone. That's two tacks. People grimace. A woman covers her mouth.

Hank sits and stands some more. We get into a rhythm. Every two or three stands, I put down a tack, he sits, and *voilà*, it's gone. The tacks are disappearing as fast as I can put them down.

A man gasps and points at the cushion. I glance down and see a drop of blood. We ignore it and continue. More tacks vanish. More drops of blood appear.

We're really feeling the moment. I feel a burp coming from the champagne, so I let it rip. The counterpoint to the cupids is elegant—a real study in the pangs of love, though spectators' reactions are mixed: some look ambivalent, others are disgusted. Jean seems to like it, though the collectors and benefactors do not—one holds up his glass of Merlot and slowly pours it onto the floor in protest.

Finally, the last tack vanishes. The candy dish is empty. The piece is done.

We turned to the crowd, bowed, and said thank you. There was some scattered applause, then the quartet resumed playing and the audience returned to socializing and gossip and cupids as if nobody had just witnessed anything at all. Their lack of interest was a little troubling, but we were rusty, and high-brow art crowds were notoriously fickle.

"That was incredible," I whispered to Hank.

"I'm so excited I'm shaking!" he whispered, pulling up his pants carefully over his rear.

Jean, the reporter, came over.

"Hi, Jean," I said.

"That was amazing," she said, clapping. "Where the hell have you been? The last piece I saw was that thing you did with the ice cubes and the motor oil—oh man! You used to be famous!"

"We still are," said Hank.

There was an awkward pause, then Jean laughed. "Of course you are. So really, where have you been?"

"Touring," said Hank.

"Well, welcome back!" she said. "I can't wait to see more of you. And good luck with that," she added, checking out Hank's ass with a wink before walking away.

Vaughn stumbled over to us. He was more inebriated than before.

"That was highly experimental," he slurred, waving his hands. "The blood maybe I didn't like so much, but it was a critique of cherubic bliss, no doubt about it!"

"Thanks," said Hank.

"Come back again in a couple of weeks," said Vaughn. "I have another opening called Scenes of Fairy Woodsmen if you'd like to perform."

"We'll be here," I said.

Vaughn kissed Hank's forehead, then floated off to find some vodka.

* * *

Hank and I walked home.

"Jean was rough," said Hank. "We USED to be famous?"

"She was just teasing."

"It wasn't our fault the audience didn't get it."

"I think they got it," I said. "The piece was just too powerful. It hit them straight in the gut and they didn't know how to respond. We'll have to train them."

"Or give them something so outrageous they'll have to respond," said Hank, glancing over his shoulder.

"Somebody following us?" I asked.

"I don't see anyone," he said, "but I feel it all over—eyeballs pressing down on me like a blanket of grapes. Do you ever feel that?"

"Sure," I said, but in truth I wasn't sure that I did.

* * *

We unlocked the apartment door and went in. Bill was red-faced and pacing the cage. His breath came in short hisses.

"Why are you all worked up?" asked Hank. "Look at you. You're sweating bullets. You'll give yourself a heart attack."

Bill clenched his teeth so hard they squeaked, then attacked the chain-link with wild punches and sweat flying until he was winded. He backed off, then resumed pacing. What was wrong with him? Hank and I looked the cage over. The chain-link seemed intact. The room's temperature was comfortable. Bill had plenty of food and water. Aside from a few scrapes and bumps, our prisoner seemed perfectly healthy.

I grabbed a bottle of wine from the kitchen. Hank pulled the tacks out of his ass, then tried to find a sitting position on the couch where his rear wouldn't hurt.

The camera was still running. I removed the videotape, slid it into the VCR, rewound it, and pressed the play button. Video footage of Bill came on. He walked around the cage, glanced at the camera a few times, then seemed to forget it was filming.

I fast-forwarded. Time code numbers at the bottom of the screen raced forward as video flew past of Bill lying down on his side . . . Bill taking a nap . . . Bill eating . . . Bill drinking . . . Bill sitting down on the toilet . . . Bill getting off of the toilet . . . Bill bending over and talking into the toilet. . . .

"Wait a minute," said Hank.

I stopped the tape, rewound to Bill on the toilet, and pressed play. We watched Bill sit down on the toilet seat—then he tilted his ear. He'd heard something. He stood up, turned around, looked down at the toilet, waited, listened, then knelt and put his ear over the bowl. Yes, he was definitely hearing something.

"Turn up the volume," said Hank.

I turned it up, rewound, and played. We watched Bill get off the toilet again, then we heard it: voices talking.

"They must be coming through the sewer pipe," I said. "Probably the newlyweds who live on the fifth floor."

"HELLO?" yelled Bill into the toilet.

There was silence, then a male voice yelled back: "HELLO?"

"Oh, shit," I muttered.

"I'VE BEEN KIDNAPPED!" yelled Bill. "Please help me! They locked me in a cage!"

"Sure ya are!" answered the voice.

"Please! I'm not kidding!" said Bill. His voice sounded frantic.

"Which apartment are you in?" the voice asked.

"I don't know!" pleaded Bill. "Please—"

"What's your name?" asked the voice.

Bill yelled his famous name into the toilet.

There was a pause—then laughter.

"IF YOU'RE REALLY BILL KUNSTLER," yelled the voice, "I'D PREFER IT IF YOU STAYED IN MY TOILET." The voice laughed its ass off. I stopped the tape. Hank and I tried to keep our faces straight, but it was hopeless. We laughed so hard that wine came out Hank's nose.

"DON'T YOU LAUGH AT ME!" Bill screamed. He banged against the chain-link, threw props, then grabbed the base of his toilet and lifted, dumping it. A torrent of shit-piss gushed across the living room's hardwood floor.

"Oh, no," said Hank, waggling his finger at Bill. "Oh, no! The performer learns his boundaries! Performance is nothing without an audience! Alienate the audience, and you might as well perform for yourself!"

Hank and I grabbed the canvas and slipped it over the cage.

41

HANK BURST INTO THE APARTMENT with a morning newspaper. "THE REVIEW IS OUT!" he screamed. "IT'S OUT AND JEAN
LOVED IT!"

He marched around the room and read bits aloud: "'Known mainly as Hank and Larry, the duo shocked the audience with visceral work and
raw, shoot-from-the-hip originality . . . a stark contrast to the city's polished
provincial works . . . deceptive in its simplicity . . . a harsh critique of mecha-
nistic repetition, human suffering, and the agonies of our vanity. . . .'"

"FAIRY WOODSMEN WILL BE PACKED AFTER A RE-
VIEW LIKE THAT!" I yelled.

Hank and I danced around the room, pausing just long enough to
open a new bottle of wine.

* * *

A week passed. We played the yoga record around the clock. Bill
remained in solitary confinement under the canvas. He tried sending mail

to get our attention.

> *From: Bill*
> *To: You*
> *I can't urinate. My mouth is dry. I'm nauseous. I think I need a doctor. Please? Hello?*

> *From: Bill*
> *To: You*
> *I'm so tired of the yoga. PLEASE, WHY ARE YOU DOING THIS? I'm experiencing abnormal persistence of vision—my retinas are holding images for minutes at a time like a bad movie. What's wrong with me? You're giving me hypochondria, you fuckers!*

> *From: Bill*
> *To: You*
> *Shaking. Spasms in my lower extremities are working up to my head. Might be suffering malnutrition. I'm biting my own teeth.*

When sending mail didn't work, he tried screaming. He begged us for something to eat, pleaded for us to let him out, cried that it was too dark. I slid a flexible plastic tube under the chain-link so we could send in food without taking the cage's cover off, packed my mouth with diced arugula, and blew it in. Bill howled for an hour.

Eventually, the dark became too much for him. He rooted through his performance art props in the dark, discovered a butter knife, and dug at the canvas until he'd carved a little hole through the fabric so he could see out. His eye followed us around the apartment while we prepped our Fairy Woodsmen performance. When he wanted to speak, he put his lips up to the hole and flapped them. They begged us for exercise, pleaded to see the financial section of the newspaper, cried for a drop of Châteauneuf or Yquem ... and when all of that failed, they went back to howling.

* * *

It was night-time. Hank and I sat on the couch drinking beer and making flyers for the Fairy Woodsmen show.

A light outside flashed across the living room window.

"Did you see that?" whispered Hank.

"Probably just a reflection from some car's high beams," I said.

Hank stood up. "It looked more like a flashlight," he whispered.

"Go see," I said, swallowing beer.

Hank tiptoed toward the window, slowed, then stopped ten feet from the glass. His legs were shaking. He began to hyperventilate.

"What is it?" I whispered. "Your fear of heights? Acrophobia?"

Hank nodded. "I—I'm flapping in the wind here," he wheezed. He started backing up. "Look at that window—there's no railing, no handhold, nothing! A man could trip and fall right through that glass!"

He backed all the way across the room until he bumped into his shrine, which was as far from the window as he could go. He tried to slow his breathing. "Could you go look?" he asked.

I went to the window and looked out. The street was dark. I saw a few parked cars. Trash blew past in the wind. Otherwise, nothing.

"Nothing," I said.

"Are you sure?" asked Hank. "Are you positive? You hardly gave it a glance...."

I needed another drink. I went to the kitchen, washed my face in the sink, dried it on my T-shirt, and opened a bottle of wine. Hank was going to go crazy if he couldn't see out that window.

"Maybe we could hook up the camera to the TV," I called out. "We could aim the lens at the street and you could just watch from the couch—it'd be easy."

Hank didn't answer. I returned to the living room just in time to see him headed for the window. His back was pressed against the wall perpendicular to the pane, palms out flat against the drywall, his face a frenzied frown-smile as his feet inched sideways toward the glass like a crab's. He rested, then crabbed some more.

"Look at me go," he whispered, grimacing.

"Only ten more feet!" I said.

"I must look really paranoid," he sputtered with a tense little laugh.

I sat down on the floor to watch. Hank crabbed another six inches, rested, then crabbed again.

The whole trip took five minutes. When he was a foot away from the glass, he reached out, grabbed the window frame, and—shaking so hard I wondered if he could even see straight—craned his upper torso sideways until he could push the window open.

"All right." He shuddered in his window-sill-death-grip. "Let's see what the hell's going on."

He looked out and spotted some action right away. "I see a motorcycle . . . there's a delivery truck . . . wait . . . here comes a man with a briefcase . . . he's walking with a limp . . . he's passing us . . . heading down the street . . . he's turning the corner . . . he's gone . . . he might come back . . . I'll let you know. . . ."

Bill watched all of this through the hole in the canvas.

"What's he looking at?" he asked.

"Nothing," I said, but I could sense that Bill didn't buy it. His eye narrowed. It made no sense for a man with acrophobia to fiddle with a sixth-story window.

"My people are looking for me, aren't they?" said Bill.

"Unlikely," I said.

"Oh yes they are! How does it feel to be hunted? IS THIS CAN-

VAS PROTECTING ME OR YOU? IT'S ONLY A MATTER OF TIME!"

"Don't bet on it," I said, slapping a piece of duct tape over Bill's hole.

* * *

The phone rang. It was Rudy.

"Bill's wife is on Franky Burn!" he said. "Turn it on!"

Franky was a New York tabloid jock with a syndicated call-in radio show. I grabbed a portable radio from the kitchen and hustled Hank out of the apartment and into the hall.

"What's going on?" Hank asked.

"His wife's on Franky Burn," I whispered. I turned the radio on and dialed in. The show was already in progress.

"So what it's like, sleeping with one of America's richest men?" asked Franky.

Bill's wife guffawed. "I'm not telling you that!"

Franky put his sly lips up close to the mic and coaxed in a sonorous whisper: "Come on. You can tell me. He's not listening. It's just us—you and me—"

"Sure it is," she laughed.

"What's it like doing it with a tycoon? Come on. Give us a just a taste. . . ."

"Well . . ." said Bill's wife, "I wouldn't really know."

"What do you mean?" asked Franky.

"I never see him. How long's it been? A month? Two? He sends a telegram every week from his so-called sabbatical, but—"

"You sound skeptical," Franky prodded.

"Well. . . ."

"Has he skipped town for sabbaticals before?"

"No."

"Are you saying you don't think he's on a sabbatical?" Franky whispered.

"I don't know what to think," said the wife.

"What are you saying? You think he's having an affair?"

"He's a bastard if he is," she said.

"What are you going to do?" cooed Franky. "You could leave that heartless billionaire. Leave him, if that's what you think he's doing. You could run away with me. You and me in the tropics, rubbing on the oil. . . ."

The wife laughed. "I've never really considered leaving him. . . ." Then, with all the Hollywood starlet sensuality she could muster: "But maybe I should."

Franky Burn let out a long "Woo!" and the show cut to commercials.

"Should we tell Bill about this?" I asked with a smile.

"Let's save it for a tender moment," said Hank, grinning.

42

THE NIGHT OF OUR FAIRY Woodsmen performance arrived. We walked down to Prance Prance. A mob of three hundred people waited outside to get in. They pushed and shoved and cursed and spat as Hank and I threaded our way to the front of the crowd where Vaughn was waiting. He unlocked the lobby doors and hurried us in.

"It's crazy out there!" he said, locking the door behind us.

"Who are those people?" I asked. "They look a little rough."

"I was going to call you," said Vaughn, clapping his hands, "but I ran out of time."

"Call us about what?" I asked.

"This was a bad week in the neighborhood with all of the drug busts and murders—I'm sure you saw it in the news. Patrons are afraid; it's hard to get them to come to the Loin. So . . . I couldn't sell any tickets to the show."

My mouth fell open.

"But the *good* news," said Vaughn, clapping his hands again, "is that we still have an audience because—you'll thank me for this!—I gave the tickets away for free! I know it's not our usual suits-and-furs gang, but they look plenty game."

Hank and I scanned the faces in the crowd. Most were neighborhood addicts and bums who'd come for the free wine. The others were art critics who were angry they hadn't been invited to the tack show, and now here they were, ready for their chance to pan us. A critic and I locked eyes. He shook his notepad at me with a sneer while a junkie shot up beside him.

"I wanted you to perform in the lobby like last time," said Vaughn, "but it'll never hold all these people. We'll have to use the theater in back."

"You have a theater?" asked Hank.

"Oh, yes—four hundred seats. You'll love it!" he said, leading us past paintings of winged lumberjacks to a large door at the gallery's rear. He opened it, handed us each a bottle of wine, and pushed us through. "The props you requested are on stage. Come out swinging!" he sang, slamming the door shut.

It was dark backstage. The only light came from a dim lamp resting on a set carpenter's workbench and, thirty feet away, the hairline crack in the stage's tall red curtains.

"This stage is huge," said Hank. "We'll never be able to use all of this space."

"We could try to make it smaller," I joked, nodding to a handsaw hanging above the workbench.

Hank giggled, tiptoed to the workbench like a loon, and picked up the handsaw. "Looks too dull," I whispered. Hank nodded in agreement, tossed it aside, then began rooting through tools—hammers, chisels, and a shovel came flying out, and then, from a dark corner, a small chainsaw. Hank made a few sample cutting motions in the air.

"Oh, YES!" I cried. We laughed silently with tears streaming down our cheeks. Our choreography had just been revised.

We downed more wine and readied our props, then heard Vaughn stumble onto the stage. He welcomed the crowd. The audience responded with catcalls and ridicule. It didn't matter. We were ready for them.

The curtains part and we step out. The crowd's already restless: spectators are yammering, men are drunk . . . it's like a goddamn kung fu theater. A bum sucks booze from a flask and walks across a row of laps to reach his chair. Junkies are passed out in the aisles. A woman in a cowboy hat lobs a half-eaten chicken leg at us. Critics scribble madly in their notebooks; I smile at one and he scowls.

I climb into a shopping cart that's packed to the top with dirt. I have a golf club in one hand and an air horn in the other. Hank's holding the chainsaw.

Hank pushes the shopping cart a few feet toward the audience, then collapses onto the floor. I blow the air horn. Hank pulls himself up by the cart's handle, pushes the cart forward a few more feet, then collapses. I blow the air horn again. We repeat this over and over as we slowly make our way across the stage. The audience grows restless, then annoyed. The crossing is taking forever and the horn's wearing on their nerves.

We near the foot of the stage. I leap from the cart, dump the dirt out into a mound, and get to swinging the golf club like a sand trap pro, over and over, spraying dirt across the stage and into the audience as Hank goes to work with the chainsaw, cutting into the stage floor and ripping out planks.

My swinging uncovers a golf ball in the dirt. I pick it up, blow off the dust, set it on the mound, then tee off, blasting it over the audience to the rear of the theater where it pops through the drywall, leaving a black hole behind. I leave the dirt mound and, still swinging, strut around the stage with my legs bowed mountain-man style. Pretending not to notice one of Hank's chainsawed holes in the stage, I fall in, smacking my chin on the hole's edge on the way down. I catch myself with a hand and pull myself back up as Hank gets to cutting out a new section of floor.

I crawl to the mound and dig with my hands until I uncover a paper sack. I throw it. It trails dust as it arcs across the stage, hits the floor, and rips open. Out rolls a human skull with a bloody cow liver dangling from its mouth.

The audience is steamed; they don't understand the piece. They rush the stage and attack. A critic throws a punch and Hank's nose gets popped. It swells up and blood drips on his shirt. "They popped by dose, goddabbit!" he growls.

A grizzled, long-haired bum in a denim shirt runs up, grabs the chainsaw from Hank, and starts sawing through the stage's curtains.

"It's a goddab lynch bob!" screams Hank. "Let's get out of bere!"

We run for the doors, bleeding and laughing. It's so beautiful I can hardly breathe.

* * *

Hank's swelling went down as we sang and danced our way back toward the apartment.

Suddenly, he grabbed my arm. "There's a man following us," he whispered.

I turned and looked behind us. "I don't see anyone," I said.

Hank pulled me into a supermarket. Music blared from the store's loudspeakers as he led me down an aisle to the tinfoil section, opened a box, pulled out a sheet of foil, and began shaping it.

"What are you making?" I asked.

"Hats," he said, glancing up at the security mirrors that ran the perimeter of the store's ceiling.

"Do you see him?" I whispered.

Hank nodded. "He's here—he followed us into the store."

I scanned the mirrors, then froze. A man in sunglasses and a wrinkled white suit was watching us from an adjacent aisle. He saw me looking and walked quickly out of view. I jogged over to his aisle. He was gone. I raced down the aisle, then back up to the checkout stand, but he was nowhere to be found. I returned to Hank.

"You were right," I huffed. "He took off as soon as he saw me."

"I knew it," said Hank. He blinked a few times in slow-motion.

"What's wrong with your eyes?" I asked.

"They feel gummy," he said, working on the foil.

"Are you taking your vitamins?"

"I stopped."

"What? Why?"

"I don't like them. I can't think when I'm on them. Numbs me out smooth like a shaved hand—I have no grab."

Hank finished two foil hats. We each put one on.

"What do these do?" I asked.

"They keep our brainwaves from leaking out and deflect light to aid in invisibility."

"Invisibility? So the critics can't see us?"

"Him too," said Hank, pointing at the mirror where we'd seen the white suit watching.

43

THE ART CRITICS HAD THEIR way with Fairy Woodsmen the next morning. The newspapers blamed us for the Prance Prance melee, then went on to deride our piece as ". . . idiosyncratically dense . . . an inebriated study in literal deconstruction . . . eighteen Freudian holes of slow-playing prepubescent fetishism. . . ."

"The critics want to kill us!" cried Hank.

"Don't hate the critics," I said. "We overwhelmed them, that's all. We were too intense with too many ideas. Training them will take time."

Hank thought about it. "You're right," he said. "It was a mistake to jump from blood tacks to full-bore chainsawular re-org of proscenium space-time in a single step. Maybe we need to regroup."

"Simplify," I said, nodding.

* * *

Another week passed. Bill was quiet under the canvas. The light and sleep deprivation had taken the fight out of him. He no longer screamed.

The yoga record no longer made him cry. He received his raisins and orange peels through the tube without complaint, though we couldn't be sure if was eating them. We didn't know if he was shitting either, for that matter, because he stopped asking for permission to flush the toilet.

Vaughn refused to take our phone calls, so we spent our days searching for a new performance venue. We marched from gallery to gallery, from the Tenderloin to the financial district, but word of the Prance Prance riot had spread. Curators were nervous; nobody wanted to talk to us.

We even tried Neptune's Underwater Grotto, a tourist stop on the city's wharf that specialized in paintings of whales and blown-glass starfish.

We went in. The sound of crashing surf played over loudspeakers.

A woman sat a desk. We walked up to her.

"Are you the curator?" I asked.

"Yes," she said.

"Hi. I'm Larry and this is Hank," I said. Hank smiled and offered a zany bow at the waist, then I continued: "We're searching for an art venue that might—"

"You're the performance artists," said the curator gravely.

"Yes! That's right."

"We're not interested in that kind of art."

"I . . . what kind of art, exactly?" I asked.

"Yours, exactly," said the curator.

Hank offered her another bow.

* * *

"Are you awake?" Hank whispered.

"No," I mumbled, opening an eye. I'd fallen asleep on the floor. I looked at the clock. It was five a.m. "When was the last time you slept?"

"Never mind that," said Hank. "Let me show you my new invention!"

Shimmying along the wall, Hank led me over to the window where he'd built an intruder alert system: ten wine bottles dangled from our window ledge on long pieces of string that reached almost all the way down to the ground. I poked my head out and saw the bottles swinging just above the sidewalk in front of the apartment building like a glass curtain. A few pedestrians walked through them. The bottles glinted and clinked.

"Now we don't have to keep watch at the window anymore," said Hank. "We'll hear anyone who comes near the building."

It occurred to me that an intruder could easily sidestep the bottles, but somehow this made Hank's experiment all the more beautiful, and surely a basic test of our elusive spy's ingenuity.

"There's something else," Hank whispered. He glanced at the cage to make sure the duct tape was still intact over Bill's hole, then gestured for me to follow him.

We tiptoed to the couch and sat down in front of the computer. I looked at the screen and saw a list of the mail that Bill had sent over the past week. Hank pointed to one piece in particular. It looked like all the others, but for one minor detail: it was addressed to Bill instead of us; for the very first time, he'd sent one to himself.

"I found it this morning," said Hank in a low voice as he opened it. "I don't think he meant for us to see it."

> *From: Bill*
> *To: Bill*
> *Too dark in here. Can't sleep. Feel docile like a patient. It's hard to eat through the tube. I've grown a beard. My paunch is gone. Lost weight. Even my shins are thinner. Wait—my beard is gone! Where did it go? It was just here! They're playing tricks again.*

"He's becoming a performance art machine," Hank whispered.

44

BILL SENT ANOTHER PIECE OF mail to himself the next day, two the day after that, then five the next. Soon the typing in the cage never seemed to cease. He was up to fifteen by the week's end, then thirty by Monday. Hank and I read them as fast as we could. Sometimes Bill pretended to be different people when he wrote—his wife, maybe, or a Redsoft customer—and occasionally he even wrote back: *Dear Wife . . . Dear Customer . . . Dear Stockholder. . . .* It was sheer lunacy, oneirophrenia, irrefutable proof of increasing hallucinatory duress:

> *From: Bill*
> *To: Bill*
> *Can't sleep. / And it's your fault, fucker! / MY fault? / That's what I said, you rip-off artist! / Me? / Yes, you! This is payback for all the companies raped! Consumers swindled! Ideas stolen! Workers abandoned! The fact your flaccid body appears constituted of equal parts oatmeal and dried sperm makes the ferocity of your crimes all the more shocking, you*

unfuckable pimp! This cage is so apropos! How does it feel to be despised by the whole world, O King of Redsoft? Even your LAWYERS—you earn those sycophants MILLIONS and even THEY despise you! / That's a lie. My lawyers like me. / No, they don't. You make them brown-nose. You're the butt of their jokes—they even have a song:

> *Bill has a hemma-roid*
> *And I am surely it—*
> *Dangle from his rear*
> *Like a ruddy little shit*

> *'Cause he puts my counsel nose up*
> *Inside his royal ass*
> *To hail Redsoft*
> *And sniff his golden gas*

You'll always be remembered as a greedy bastard, Billyboy. A hard case. A cut-throat. When they tear you open on judgment day, all they'll find is shit. Why do you have to be so hard all the time? You're like a goddamn pelvis! Rub off some of that hip and check for yourself! Go ahead! Did you do it? Good! See that bone? You're just like that!

"Do you think he really rubbed off some of his hip?" asked Hank.

"I don't know," I said, "but if he did, I hope he'll do the other one so we can get it on video."

* * *

Another week passed. The frequency of Bill's mailings climbed. One day it was fifty . . . then eighty. We stopped sleeping. Hank drank coffee. I refused to leave the couch. The faster they arrived, the shorter and more erratic they became:

From: Bill

To: Bill

Lady Penance bangs my golden gavel / It's midnight and I guzzled all the oil / There'll be no wedding now.

The pace increased. Before long, detached words were all he could manage: *vent . . . corset . . . devoid. . . .* His coherence decayed. Soon even words were too much—he could no longer control his fingers. He defaulted to short, repeatable strings, easily typed: *iiii . . . memememe. . . .* The letters read like secret codes but Hank and I were too busy reading to slow down for decipherment.

When Bill finally reached a hundred mails per day, his fingers spasmed, failing him entirely. He resorted to sending blanks, one after another, filling his inbox with empties for days on end. We opened every single one—we would read them all!

Then . . . nothing. The mail stopped.

We waited. Three days passed. No new mail arrived. Was he dead? We shook the cage and called his name, but there was no answer.

We tore the canvas off. Bill had hit rock bottom. We were shocked at what he'd become: a monster, crazy. No longer captive, nor free, nor CEO, nor performance machine, he was now all fringe, scatology intermezzo, mentally dismantled and lying beard-up on the pile of scattered performance props like an albino cave fish with dilated eyes and his skirt still on . . . white skin and all ribs, pimpled with acne, raggedy hair, teeth rotting, lips chapped, hip bone bloody and gristled with a skin flap missing. . . .

We scrambled into the cage and helped him to his feet. He began to shit. It came out long and dry and white like cigarette ash.

"WHY IS IT DRY?" Hank screamed.

"I DON'T KNOW!" I yelled.

The heat under the spotlight was sweltering. We scurried out of the cage to the safety of the couch as fast as we could.

Bill stood in the cage, pigeon-toed and shaking, half-crying and sucking for air as he tried to focus on us through his matted hair . . . then slowly, looking down at himself under the light, he took in the view of what he'd become.

"I—I'm gonna be sick," he said, shivering.

"Do a performance," I encouraged.

"No," said Bill. "Look at me! What have you done?"

"This is normal," said Hank. "You're not a performance art machine yet. You're still on the fringe. Do a performance! Continue your transformation!"

"Your mind is anew!" I said. "See with your stomach! Taste with your anus!"

"No," said Bill.

"DO IT!" yelled Hank.

"PICK UP THAT CLOTH!" I commanded, pointing to a dirty handkerchief that was lying on the floor of the cage.

"What is it?" asked Bill, eyeing the cloth.

"It's your power animal," said Hank.

Bill began to cry in earnest. "I'm humiliated!"

"Humiliation is initiation!" said Hank. "PICK IT UP!"

Bill picked up the cloth.

"Now perform with it!" I said.

Bill's head lolled around as he tried to focus under the bright light.
"I—"

"PERFORM!" commanded Hank.

"I don't know how to start," Bill cried.

"MOVE THE CLOTH!" I yelled.

Bill put his hand under the handkerchief and flapped it around like a dancing ghost puppet.

"YOU'RE DOING IT! KEEP IT UP! THAT'S IT! YOU'RE DOING IT!" screamed Hank.

"NOW EXPAND IT! ABSTRACT! MOVE YOUR BODY!" I yelled.

Bill started jumping up and down with the cloth.

"Good! Now add some text!" Hank encouraged.

"Text?" cried Bill, still jumping, "I don't know what to—"

"TEXT!" I screamed. "SPEAK!"

"Bang," said Bill. "Spit." He jumped and danced the cloth. It was lovely.

"Keep going!" said Hank.

"Bang! Spit!" said Bill again, crying harder and drooling. He looked down at his bouncing bony ribs and bloody hip. "What is wrong with me?"

"You're a little hysterical," I said.

"I DON'T HAVE A WOMB!" Bill cried.

"But you made a baby," I said, pointing at his dancing cloth.

Bill stopped jumping and looked at the handkerchief over his hand. "Oh," he said.

Hank and I stood and applauded. Bill smiled like a simpleton.

How often dramas of men begin with flapping hands under cloth.

45

WE STOOD ON THE SIDEWALK outside Prance Prance. It was Monday noon and the gallery was closed. We put our faces up to the window and peered in. It was dark, but we could see Vaughn working inside. His back was to us. I pressed my lips to the glass.

"VAUGHN!" I yelled. Vaughn jumped, saw it was us, and ducked down.

"We saw you!" Hank taunted.

"Are you getting ready for a new opening?" I asked.

"GO AWAY!" yelled Vaughn.

"Talk to us. Just five minutes, we promise," I pleaded, tapping on the window.

Vaughn reappeared, shook his head, and waved us away.

There was a mail slot in the door. I knelt and put my lips up to it. "Let us perform," I said.

"You chainsawed my stage!" said Vaughn.

"It wasn't us! That crowd you invited was crazy! Things spun out of control. No more chainsaws, we promise!"

"Let's make up," said Hank.

Vaughn shook his head. "Paying patrons will stay away if they know you're performing."

"We'll surprise them!" I said. "We'll just step out and do our thing unannounced! It'll be tame, I swear. They'll love it!"

Vaughn held his head in his hands. "I have to sell some art at my next show or I'm dead. I'll go bankrupt—"

"We'll play for free!" said Hank.

"When's the opening?" I asked.

"When is it?" Hank repeated with his lips against the glass.

"Please?" I begged.

Vaughn looked at us for a long time.

"No shopping carts or chainsaws," I promised. "Brand new pieces. Minimal. Short. No mess."

"The show's Friday," said Vaughn with a sigh.

Hank and I whooped. We were back in business.

"What's it called?" I asked.

Vaughn pointed to a flyer that was taped to the gallery window.

Hank read it aloud: "Trotsky's Shoes: Revolutionary Socialism in Footwear Portraiture."

Hank and I cheered, pulled off our boots, folded them flat, and shoved them through the mail slot. Vaughn opened the door and handed them back to us. I saw him crack a smile as we ran away barefoot.

* * *

Bill sat on the floor of the cage pushing props around like Mahjong tiles and babbling to himself with his back to us. He was struggling to come up with a performance. I looked at the clock. Hank and I had been waiting on the couch for five hours.

"He's moving the props around faster," I whispered.

"He's building up to something, I can feel it!" Hank whispered back.

Suddenly, Bill spun and faced us. He picked up an empty cat food can, sniffed it, dropped it, picked it back up, licked it, put it down, dug around in the prop pile, found a hairbrush, combed his hair, lifted his cellophane skirt, brushed his pubic bone, poked the brush's handle into his belly, then threw the brush down, finished.

Hank and I whistled and applauded.

"What's that piece called?" I asked.

Bill looked at us blankly. "I don't know," he said.

"Give it a name," said Hank.

"I don't know what to call it."

"Simple names are best. Just say what you did, or what props you used."

Bill looked at his props. "Pubic Bone Hairbrush and a Tin Can?"

Hank and I applauded. Bill sat down on the cage floor and began to cry. "My head hurts," he said.

"Pain is normal," I said. "We've broken your brain. It'll take you a while to put it back together."

"My brain's not broken," said Bill.

"Sure it is," said Hank. "You have to learn how to think and see all over again. What do you see here?" he asked, pointing to the chain-link.

"A cage," said Bill. "Chain-link."

"No, there's more. Do see the material repeating? The same patterns of metal over and over again? Look through it but focus on me. What do you see?"

Bill studied Hank from behind the chain-link. "You in little diamonds?"

"Little diamonds. The patterns break my body up into segments, into pieces. They fragment me. I am disfigured. It is both structure and dismemberment."

"You're broken apart?" asked Bill.

"Yes. But am I really broken apart?" asked Hank. "Truly?"

Bill stared at the chain-link. "No."

"The breaking apart is only what you are seeing, in your mind."

Bill nodded.

"So who is the one really broken apart?"

Fear registered on Bill's face. "Me?"

"You. I put the breaking apart in your mind. When you go shamanic, you'll be able to break any mind apart, including your own. It's the highest level of performance art. Your choreography will stick in people like diamonds."

"I want to go shamanic," Bill whispered.

"You're almost there," said Hank.

"Are you hungry?" I asked.

Bill nodded. He was still weak, so I brought out the tube. I fed one end to him through the chain-link. He slid it down his throat, hand over hand, until it reached his stomach. Hank poured a can of fruit in my mouth. I chewed it, then dribbled it down the tube into Bill until he signaled he was full.

"I like fruit," Bill gurgled with the tube still in him.

46

IT WAS TIME TO CHECK on Blanche. I drove to Mouse's house, found a parking spot two blocks away, parked, hiked to the front door, let myself in, put out food and water, locked the front door, and started back to the car.

"That looks like a fast car."

It was a male voice. I looked across the street. A heavyset man in a wrinkled white suit stood on the curb looking at me. His skull's shape—square with an overbite, his lower incisors clearly visible—hinted at savage determination and acrimony. A saggy glabella, thinning straw hair, and a flushed complexion suggested monomaniacal concentration occasionally interrupted by bouts of apprehension, dehydration, and kidney stones. Most unmistakable of all were his piggy eyes—sure signs of hyperthyroidism mixed with cunning, duplicity, and sadism.

"That a five-liter?" he asked, nodding at Mouse's car. A toothpick dangled from his mouth.

I gave a nod and kept walking.

"That's a fast one all right," said the man. He began keeping pace with me on his side of the street. "Burn rubber like hell, those Impalas."

I walked faster.

"Are those Firestones?" he asked, pointing at the Impala's tires.

I reached the car, fumbled with the keys, found the right one, slid it into the lock, then stopped: the door was already unlocked. Had I forgotten to lock it?

"My name's Stark," said the man. "What's yours?"

His voice sounded closer. I found his reflection in the car window and saw he'd stepped off the curb and was crossing the street toward me.

I opened the door, jumped in, fired the engine, shifted, and floored it. I looked in the rearview. Stark was standing in the middle of the street with his head down like a bull ready to charge.

I accelerated to forty, made two quick turns, and stopped at a red light. I was bathed in sweat. The man in the suit was the same we'd seen at the supermarket. Hank's intuition had been right all along. What evidence did he have? He couldn't know for sure we were the kidnappers—he didn't know where we were holding Bill—he didn't have any physical evidence—

I looked down and saw an unmarked manila envelope sitting on the passenger seat beside me. I glanced at the stoplight—still red. I picked up the envelope, opened the flap, and gave it a shake. A picture slid out. It was a black-and-white photo from a surveillance camera that showed the Impala parked behind the convention center's loading dock. I exhaled with relief. Only the back of Hank's head was visible through the car's rear window; there was no way it could be used to identify us.

There was another photo in the envelope. I pulled it out. It was a close-up shot of burnt tire treads on asphalt. Firestones. I swallowed. Stark had taken a print of our car's skid marks, made a few phone calls, obtained a list of Impalas in the area, and from there, it had only been a matter of checking their tires, a process of elimination—and once he knew Mouse's car was the one, he'd simply staked out her house until I'd shown up. I felt sick—then I turned the photo over. On the back in black, handwritten ink:

SEE YOU SOON.

A horn blared. The traffic light was green. I pressed the accelerator and looked back. There was a BMW behind me, and behind that, a beat-up tan Camaro with a man at the wheel. I squinted.

Stark.

I turned onto Van Ness Avenue and headed north. The Camaro turned too. Traffic was heavy. I changed lanes after a light. So did the Camaro. I drove a mile, turned right onto California, gunned it down to Polk Street, made another right, then floored it hard to Post. I checked the rearview. Traffic was bogging down the Camaro two blocks back.

I turned left, made another left on Taylor, then floored it to the top of Nob Hill where the menacing wyvern grotesques of Grace Cathedral, an architectural jewel reminiscent of France's gothic Cathédrale Notre-Dame de Chartres, stood watch over the city. I parked behind the cathedral's quire in a stall reserved for clergy, ran inside, grabbed a bible, hurried back to the car, and set the book carefully on the dash so the vehicle wouldn't be towed.

I made my way back to the apartment through a maze of alleys, shredding and tossing the photos as I went. Even if Stark found the Impala, he'd never trace it back to my apartment.

I decided not to mention any of it to Hank.

47

DAYS PASSED. THERE WAS NO predicting at what hour Bill's next piece would come. He kept his back to us, babbling and scattering props, sometimes for hours, then suddenly he'd spin and perform without warning. Each piece was short, lasting only seconds before decaying away, yet his nascent work was becoming more complex, like disparate primordial cells coalescing into protoplasmic ooze. He was building momentum, experimenting. It took time for a new performer to gain endurance and twiddle the props. In one piece he spun around to drop fifty marbles into a bucket of lard one by one with satisfying plops; in another he folded a glowing pocket flashlight into a wet chicken skin.

Hank and I watched the cage in shifts so we could each catch some sleep. If Hank saw a piece he liked during the night, he performed for me when I woke, and I did the same for him.

"Look at this," said Hank one morning. "It's called Facial Contortions with Crackers and Butter."

He stepped back, pulled his eyelids straight out until they snapped back, rubbed his nose violently with his forearm, wiped peanut butter on his cheeks, pasted crackers on the butter, and made me eat them off.

"That was great," I said, swallowing cracker. "Did you come up with that?"

"Sure," said Hank with a wink. It was Bill's piece, of course, but we'd made him—he was our machine—and besides, it took a professional like Hank to really pull off a butter-and-crackers piece. Hank struck a pose and ran his peanut-buttery hands over his scabby head like a Hollywood star. I shook my head and laughed.

"That piece reminds me of the performance we did with the wigs and petroleum jelly a couple of years back," I said.

"I still have those wigs!" said Hank. "We should go pick them up from Sherry's. In fact, all of my props are still over there. You don't think she'd throw them out, do you?"

I bit my lip. Sherry was exactly the type to do something like that.

"Let's go," I said.

* * *

Hank and I headed for Sherry's. It was dusk. The Tenderloin side-walks were crowded with bums and tourists.

We ducked into the alley beside Sherry's building, looked up at her apartment window, and saw it was dark.

"This'll only take a minute," said Hank, wiping sweat from his brow. He looked shaky.

"Maybe you should just let her keep the props," I said. "You can always get more."

"No," said Hank. "It took me years to build my collection."

"What if she comes home while we're up there?"

"You keep a lookout," said Hank. "Whistle if you see her coming."

I went to the alley's mouth and surveyed the passing pedestrians for Sherry. There was no sign of her—then something: a man walking in our direction about two blocks away. He was moving slowly. There was something familiar about his gait. He passed under a streetlight and I saw he was wearing a suit. He was studying buildings as he passed them, scanning lit apartment windows for activity, casing the neighborhood like he was looking for something—or someone.

Stark.

I grabbed Hank and pulled him back into the alley.

"Sherry?" he gasped.

"No," I whispered, my heart pounding. "There's a man headed toward us on the sidewalk a block and a half away. He's wearing a suit. Look, but don't let him see you."

Hank stuck his head around the corner. "I see him," he whispered.

"His name's Stark," I said. "I think he might be a detective. He showed up at Mouse's. He had surveillance photos of the Impala parked behind the convention center."

Hank covered his mouth. "He's the one who's been following us? Do you think he knows where—"

"No," I said. "He would've knocked on our door a long time ago if he knew where we're holding Bill. He traced Mouse's car to her house, staked it out, and tried to tail me back to the apartment."

"Where'd you park the car?"

"Up on Nob Hill. He must've spotted it and figured that we had to be somewhere close by—he's probably hoping to get lucky beating the pavement."

Hank took another peek around the corner. "He's getting close. We could run—"

"I can't—he saw my face at Mouse's. There has to be another way."

I ran to the far end of the alley—a dead end. I looked up. It was nine stories to Sherry's window—sheer brick all the way up.

"Can you climb it?" Hank asked.

"There's nothing to grip," I said, feeling around on the wall.

"I'll get the fire rope!" whispered Hank. Before I could protest, he darted out of the alley and into the apartment building. I waited. A minute passed. I jogged back to the alley's mouth and looked out. Stark was only a half block away and closing.

Hank whistled. I looked up and saw the fire rope descending. It reached all the way down to the ground.

I ran, jumped, caught it, and climbed as fast as I could into the dark with my knees banging against the brick. Pedestrians walked past the alley's mouth. I climbed faster. My hands began to burn. I passed the seventh floor, then the eighth, then, just as my arms turned to jelly, my fingers touched Sherry's windowsill. I hooked an arm over and pulled myself up, falling through onto the floor inside. It was pitch black. I rose to my feet. Hank was on the far side of the room, keeping well away from the window.

I turned and looked out. Crowds passed the alley's mouth in both directions on the sidewalk—then Stark walked into view. I held my breath. He looked down the alley and saw it was empty. He scanned the other side of the street, then continued walking, passing out of view.

"He's gone," I whispered.

The lights in the apartment came on. We spun and saw Sherry in her bathrobe.

"WHAT ARE YOU DOING HERE?" she screamed. Her voice rattled around the apartment, out the window, and down the alley to the street. I looked out and saw pedestrians on the sidewalk look up. One of them pointed at the fire rope. I grabbed it and began pulling it up as fast as I could, hoisting, doubling, coiling—

Stark stepped into the alley. He'd heard the scream.

I followed his gaze. He looked down the alley, searching. His eyes found the alley's dead-end . . . the brick wall . . . then up . . . way up . . . nine stories up . . . to a bright window where a man stood holding a rope . . . and the man was me.

Stark bolted for the apartment building's entrance.

"HE'S COMING!" I warned.

"GET OUT OF HERE!" Sherry yelled.

"I JUST WANT MY PROPS!" said Hank.

"I THREW THEM OUT!"

"YOU DID NOT!" Hank wailed.

Sherry ran away to the kitchen. Hank ran to the bedroom with me right behind him. We caught the bald rugger sitting up naked in bed with his eyes wide open. He grabbed his toupee from the nightstand and held it clumsily out in front of him for protection, but Hank ignored him and headed straight for the dresser. He opened the top drawer. It was empty. He opened all of them. Empty.

"They're all gone," he said with tears in his eyes.

Sherry returned from the kitchen with a carving knife. I dropped the fire rope and backed away.

"GET OUT!" she growled, waving the blade.

Hank and I backed toward the front door.

She inched toward us, then stubbed her toe on the fire rope. "I HATE THIS STUPID ROPE!" she screamed, slashing at it.

"THAT'S PERFECTLY GOOD ROPE!" yelled Hank.

"THIS ISN'T THE TIME TO SHOP FOR PROPS!" I interjected.

"I'M SICK OF LOOKING AT IT!" Sherry screeched. "TAKE IT NOW OR I'LL CUT IT UP!"

She backed away a foot, giving Hank some room. He crept forward and began gathering up the rope. He took his eyes off of her for a second and she lunged, cutting his arm, but he held his ground, piling the rope onto his neck and shoulder as she lunged again with another flailing cut. Blood ran down his forearm. I grabbed his collar and dragged him and his rope out into the hall. Sherry slammed the door shut behind us so hard that its apartment numbers fell off.

We ran to the building's spiral staircase and looked down. Stark was already on the fourth-floor landing and ascending fast. He stopped and looked up. His sweaty face was a twisted mask of veins and teeth. He aimed a revolver at us.

I jerked Hank away from the railing and we ran, punching through the fire door at the end of the hall and descending the emergency stairwell as fast as we could. Halfway down, we heard the fire door bang open—Stark was coming.

Hank slowed. His cuts were leaking blood.

"USE YOUR SHIRT!" I yelled, transferring the spaghetti mass of rope from his shoulders to mine as fast as I could. Free of the rope, Hank ripped off his shirt and wrapped it around his arm. We took off down the stairs. Hank pulled ahead by ten steps, then twenty—the rope was slowing me down—coils were sliding down my front. I slowed to gather them up, but it was too late: a loop caught my ankles and locked. I tripped, went airborne, and crashed onto a landing.

I got to my feet—no broken bones. Tasting split lip, I bear-hugged the rope, hoisted it over my neck, and threw myself down the stairwell, slamming into walls, rebounding, descending like a maniac until I crashed through the stairwell exit door and onto the sidewalk. Pedestrians scattered. I looked for Hank, but he'd vanished into the crowd—no time to find him. I sprinted across the street, darted into an alley with my fire rope albatross, and disappeared.

* * *

I limped into the apartment and dumped the rope on the floor.

"HANK?" I yelled. There was no answer.

Bill was working on a new piece in the cage. He sat staring at a pile of rocks.

"Has Hank been here?" I asked.

Bill turned and looked at me. He opened his mouth to speak. A rock fell out. No help there.

I went to the kitchen for wine. The cupboards were bare. I walked back to the living room. Bottles littered the floor around the couch. I picked one up. There was a little wine at the bottom. I sniffed it. It smelled like vinegar and curdling had set in, but it was all we had. I drank some. Black lumps of sediment slid down.

I paced the room. My legs were weak with adrenaline. The back of my neck burned. I touched it. Blood. The rope had scratched it raw.

I went to the living room window. Pedestrians passed under the streetlights below, but the window's narrow view made it hard to watch for Hank. The roof would make a better lookout. I wrote a note for Hank, left it on the couch, grabbed the wine bottle, and stepped out of the apartment.

There was a door at the end of the hall marked ROOF EXIT. I pushed through it, climbed the stairs up to the roof's tin access shed, and stepped out onto gravel. A cold wind whipped my face. I grabbed the safety railing in front of the shed to steady myself, then inched across the roof until I could see over the edge. Car headlights cut silently through the dark six stories below. I watched awhile, but no Hank.

The wind was freezing. I walked around behind the shed and found a sheltered spot where I could warm up. I sat down on the gravel, leaned against the roof's parapet, and had a sip of wine. I looked out across the city. A sea of rooftops stretched out as far as I could see under a black sky.

* * *

I opened my eyes. It was morning—I'd fallen asleep. The sun was up and the wind was howling. I stood, walked across the roof to the edge, and looked down. The streets were empty. It was still early.

I heard a whimper. I turned and saw Hank, shirtless and barefoot, his arms and legs wrapped tightly around the safety railing in front of the shed. He was shivering in the cold with his eyes scrunched shut, his tinfoil hat mashed down on his head, and his bloody T-shirt still wrapped around his arm. He opened his eyes when he heard crunching gravel and saw it was me moving toward him.

"Hi," he quivered, teeth chattering. "I saw your note . . . and . . . thought I'd come up . . . I didn't know . . . it would be so high . . . I had a little panic . . . and thought . . . I'd just hang on right here." He turned his head an inch, saw the dizzying rooftops all around, and clenched the railing tighter.

"How long have you been out here?" I asked.

"A few hours . . . I don't know . . . all night . . . it's cold up here, eh?" he rattled.

"You can't stay up here. The Trotsky Footwear show is tonight."

"I know," he chattered with a shaky smile, lips chapped, the sun rising across his face.

I knelt down beside him, pried his pinky from the cold railing, moved it to my forearm, then started on his ring finger. His T-shirt fell to the gravel and I saw his knife wounds were still bleeding.

"How long before Stark finds us, you think?" asked Hank.

"I don't know," I said, transferring his middle finger to my arm. "If he goes back to Sherry's and she gives him our address, it won't take long at all."

"He won't go back. She was crazed and screaming her head off; I doubt he'll want any part of that."

Hank was right. I stood him up, tied his T-shirt around his cuts, walked him three feet to the shed, and down the stairs.

* * *

Hank sat down beside me on the couch, removed his foil hat, and held out his arm. I daubed the bloody cuts with rubbing alcohol.

"She's deadly with a knife," I said. "You're lucky she didn't dice an artery."

"I can't believe she threw away my props," said Hank, wiping a tear from his cheek. "I think she wanted to kill me!"

"Really? It looked like flirting to me."

Hank sputtered a laugh and wiped away another tear.

Bill moaned. We looked and saw he was face down on the floor of the cage. "My head hurts," he said.

"Your brain's still healing," I said. "Drink some water."

"I think I'm going shamanic," said Bill.

"I doubt it," I said. "Going shamanic takes a long time."

"But I'm seeing things," Bill slurred. His eyes were rolling around in his head.

"Look at him," said Hank. "He looks half-asleep."

"I think we're talking directly to his subconscious," I whispered.

Bill flopped onto his back and gave Hank a pained look.

"What do you see?" Hank asked.

Bill writhed, wiped drool from his mouth with his fist, then squinted at Hank with a gaze that burned in a way I'd never seen before.

"I see a man watching you," said Bill.

The hair on my arms stood up.

Hank looked at me. "Did you tell him about that?" he whispered.

"No," I said.

"You should get into birds," said Bill. "Nobody can spy on birds when they're high in the sky."

"Birds," Hank's lips repeated.

Bill's eyes rolled around. "Like a sparrow," he said, "or a hawk . . . or a pigeon . . . or a stark. . . ."

"Did he just say Stark?" whispered Hank.

"I don't like this," I whispered.

"GET INTO BIRDS!" Bill screamed.

Hank grabbed his tinfoil hat and put it on.

48

A HEAT WAVE DESCENDED OVER San Francisco. The Tenderloin hit ninety degrees by noon. The apartment was sweltering. Sweat ran down my face. Hank sat slumped on the couch wearing his foil hat and thinking about birds. Our lips were parched.

"I'm going out for wine," I said.

"Stark might be out there."

"I know, but we're dying in here."

"I'll stay," said Hank. "Bill's doing a piece."

I looked at the cage. Bill was struggling to pull a fat beach towel through one of the chain-links inch by inch. It looked like it might take all day.

"That's good work," I said.

"I'll video it," said Hank. "Maybe he'll say more about the birds." He went over and turned the camera on.

I stepped out of the apartment, locked the door, and headed down the hall toward the stairs.

Solveig's door opened and she came out in a blue bathrobe. A black trash bag dangled from her fist.

"You're going downstairs?" she rasped.

I nodded. She thrust the bag into my hand. It must've weighed twenty pounds. "You take for dump," she said. I opened my mouth to protest, but her door was already closing in my face.

I took the stairs down to the basement. Nobody was around. Furnace and gas pipes hissed overhead. The air reeked of sewage. I turned a corner and found the trash cans buried under a mountain of slick garbage. Flies circled in the air. I heaved Solveig's bag onto the pile, then wondered why it was so heavy.

The bag was sealed with a twist tie. I untied it and looked inside. I saw two empty whisky bottles, an old can of beans, wilted spinach . . . and something heavy at the bottom. I rooted around, pushing the spinach aside to find a half-roasted pig's head smiling at me with beady eyes, a charred snout, and sharp little teeth. I smiled back at it.

Then I noticed something odd: the pig's forehead was wrinkled. I didn't know pigs could wrinkle their foreheads. I looked closer. There was tension in the pig's temple and jowls. The pig looked worried. "What's wrong?" I whispered. The pig didn't answer, but a worried pig seemed like a bad omen. I thanked the pig, then hurried out of the basement, leaving the flies free to feast on the contents of the bag.

I walked to the supermarket. The store's air conditioner was broken. I gritted my teeth, mopped my brow, grabbed a shopping cart, and rolled toward the liquor section. A woman looked at me intently as I passed.

I came to the wine aisle. A stock boy eyed me while I loaded three of the cheapest jugs I could find into my cart.

I rolled to the checkout line. The clerk stared at me as I unloaded the jugs onto her conveyor belt.

"WHAT THE HELL IS EVERYONE LOOKING AT?" I yelled.

The clerk pointed at my shirt. I looked down and saw I was covered in pig blood.

"Just give me the wine," I growled.

The clerk rang it up. "Six dollars," she said.

I reached for my wallet. My pocket was empty.

I'd left my money at home.

* * *

I returned to the apartment to find Hank kneeling beside the couch with a black pen and a ream of blank paper. He took the top sheet from the ream, dirtied it with a black scribble, fluttered it across the room, then repeated the move with the next sheet on the stack. I picked up a dirty and looked at it. The scribble was inky and violent.

"They're blackbirds," he said proudly as he flipped a new scribble over his shoulder. "I thought we could hand them out to the audience as souvenirs at the Trotsky show." Hank paused and looked at my shirt. "Is that blood?"

"Don't ask."

Hank sniffed the air. "And do I smell ham?"

"Never mind!"

Hank licked his lips. "So. Where's the wine?"

"I forgot my wallet. Don't make me go back out there. It's too hot."

I fell onto the couch. Sweat ran down my neck. "We'll have to drink these," I said, picking up one of the near-empties from the floor. Black flecks of dried wine floated in an inch of vinegar. I drank them down.

Hank crawled to a bottle and held it up.

"There's gunk in here," he said.

"That's all we have," I said.

Hank sipped a little, then chewed.

49

NIGHT FELL. IT WAS TIME for Trotsky's Shoes. Hank and I made our way through the alleys toward Prance Prance. We were disguised in blond wigs and sunglasses so Stark wouldn't recognize us if we encountered him on the street. An afternoon rain had left the asphalt passages humid and slick. I slipped around in the dark, sweating and cursing under the weight of the eighty-pound prop bag slung over my shoulder, while Hank darted between muddy puddles like a nervous cat with his stack of blackbird scribble handouts held tightly under his arm. He kept a steady hand on his tinfoil hat, which he'd insisted on wearing over his wig as protection against Stark and, if necessary, the Trotsky critics.

My wig itched. "This bag weighs a ton," I huffed.

"You shouldn't have brought so many props," Hank taunted, his tinfoil bobbling.

"I didn't know how many we'd need," I growled. "Those Russians had better appreciate this."

"Careful," said Hank. "You don't want to antagonize the Russians—especially their women."

"What do you know about their women?"

"They're crazy in the sack."

"You never had a Russian woman."

"I did so," said Hank. "She was a blonde just like you—and dirty."

"Dirty how?"

"Dirty like this!" yelled Hank. He whipped mud off the ground, slapped it on my face, and ran off down the alley, screeching.

"I'LL KILL YOU!" I screamed and ran after him.

We burst out of the alley, crossed a street, jumped a curb, and sprinted down the sidewalk laughing until I caught him and we crashed to the ground, rolling into the gutter with the props. I jumped on him, scooped up gutter sludge, and shoveled it into his mouth.

A man gave us a disgusted look as he walked past on the sidewalk. I recognized him—it was the owner of the Master's Tendrils gallery. I pointed him out to Hank. Hank spat out sludge, grabbed a scribble handout, and ran after him.

"Hey!" Hank yelled.

The gallery owner stopped and turned around. He took in Hank's wig, hat, and dirty mouth with a frown.

"You're that performance artist I chased out of my gallery," said the owner.

"Yes," said Hank, out of breath. "We finally found a gig at Prance Prance—"

"I read about it in the paper."

"Oh—good—well—we're doing a brand new piece there tonight. You should come! Here, have a blackbird," said Hank, offering up one of his handouts as a token of peace.

The gallery owner took it, cocked his head, and studied the scribble. "Well well," he said generously, "I'd have to say. . . ."

Hank nodded and beamed with a sure smile.

" . . . that this is utter shit!" the owner finished. He spat on the handout, crumpled it up, and tossed it into the gutter before walking off with a smirk.

Hank kicked and screamed as I dragged him away down the street.

* * *

The Prance Prance lobby was packed when we arrived. Critics, reporters, Communists, Marxists, art collectors, and socialites were crammed into every square inch. Everyone was drinking vodka. Hank and I threaded through the mob in our wigs and sunglasses and kept an eye out for Stark.

The critics and reporters were clumped in the center of the gallery with their notepads, dyed black hair, and indifference. We tried to sneak past them, but Jean Gateau spotted us and stumbled over with her vodka.

"Hello, boys," she slurred, "don't you just love this Commie art? So, tell me: will tonight be as violent as your chainsaw performance?"

"Do you want it to be?" I asked.

"Of course!" Jean laughed. "And they do too."

She pointed across the room. Hank and I looked. A surly gang of leather-clad bikers stood glaring at us.

Hank squirmed. "Who are they?"

"S&M motorbikers," said Jean. "They heard about the brawl at your last gig and they're pretty upset they missed it."

"Who the hell invited them?" I asked.

"I did," said Jean with a giggle.

Hank and I found the vodka table. We poured some drinks, hid a couple of bottles in our pants for later, and set out to look at the exhibit.

The first painting showed Russian workers in black boots trudging through snow. We walked to the second painting. It was identical to the first. We looked around the gallery. All of the paintings were identical.

A woman was studying one of them. Hank went up to her.

"Which one's your favorite?" he joked.

The woman insulted him in drunken Russian and walked away.

Vaughn came over with a drink in each hand.

"Hello how are you and yes I'm on my fifth vodka already," he babbled.

"These Russians are a tough crowd," said Hank.

"They take their shoes and their Trotsky VERY seriously," said Vaughn. He looked around the room, then grabbed our shirts and pulled us close. He smelled like booze. "There are two neo-Marxist critics here," he whispered. "Watch out for them! They're driving me crazy! They're spies, wreckers, saboteurs! I haven't heard a kind word from either of them! They hate the show, they hate each other, and they're determined to sit in the front row for your performance!"

It was time to get ready. Hank and I made our way toward the stage door at the rear of the gallery. We passed a history table that was stacked with old Russian shoes and hats. A beefy Russian wrestler stood behind the table guarding the artifacts. He nodded hello to us. Hank and I picked up a pair of dark felt hats. The wrestler nodded and pointed at them with a sausage finger.

"Those are Kamilavka hats," he said with a thick accent. "Worn by Russian priest."

Hank and I tried them on.

"No!" said Wrestler, pointing at our heads. "You may not wear! For priest only!"

Hank and I put the hats back on the table and casually sipped our drinks. A woman stepped forward and asked Wrestler about some shoes on display. As he turned his attention to her, we grabbed the hats and hustled through the backstage door.

The light behind the curtains was dim. We put on the hats, then took out the vodka bottles and got to drinking while we changed into our costumes and readied our props.

The audience began filing into the theater. Hank pointed to the vodka bottle in my hand and laughed. I looked down and saw it was empty—I'd polished it off. I looked at Hank's. It was empty too.

"How much vodka was that?" I asked, doing sloppy Russian kicks low across the floor.

"Probably not enough," said Hank.

I pointed at Hank's stack of handouts. "When are you going to pass out your blackbirds?"

"I don't feel like it now." Hank pouted, kicking the papers across the stage. "That asshole from Tendrils thought they were shit."

"I like them," I said quietly.

The audience sounded belligerent. Everyone was talking at full volume. Vaughn climbed onto the stage and tried to introduce us, but it was impossible to hear him over the crowd's drunken Slavic banter.

Hank and I step out through the curtains as the stage lights come up. We spot the two neo-Marxists in the front row right away; both are wearing gray button-up Mao shirts. Behind them are the socialites, then the critics and reporters, then the Communists, then the collectors and buyers. The bikers are last—they're standing against the theater's back wall in leather chaps and vests with their arms crossed. One adjusts his crotch and hucks a spit of chaw onto the carpet.

Hank and I are dressed in drag—knee-length Russian peasant dresses, white gloves, fur coats, purses, and tap shoes. Hank takes an egg timer out of his coat pocket, turns it to ten minutes, sets it on the stage, and begins tap dancing. I take out a tape recorder, press play, set it down, and start tapping too. The tape plays. It's a recording Hank found at the library of a stutterer reading Trotsky aloud: "WHEN THE COUNTER REV-REV-REVOLUTION COMES, THE PROLETARIAT WILL SUH-SUH-SING. . . ."

Hank and I tap it out like a pair of white-ass Sammy Davises complete with shuffles, slides, splits, the works. A minute passes. The audience watches the timer. Another minute goes by. The audience grows restless, but we tap on. At three minutes we raise our purses waist-high, tap tap tap, and open them wide to the crowd like spread-eagle vaginas. Rubles spill out. The audience roars in horror . . . the neo-Marxists thumb their noses . . . the Russians shake their heads . . . the socialites fall out of their chairs laughing and make fucking motions in the air . . . the bikers glare and crack their knuckles . . . the egg keeps ticking . . . everyone is talking . . . I feel sick. . . .

A minute passes. "HOW MUCH LONGER?" I yell.

Hank squints at the timer. "SIX MINUTES," he yells as the stutterer goes on stuttering, the neo-Marxists stand and boo, and the bikers remain attentive and patient, confident their time will come to kick some performance artist ass.

I grab Hank and pull him behind the curtains.

"I know I'm drunk, but this is crap!" I slur. "We've lost it! The piece is too much! They don't get the jokes, the references. . . ."

"They hate us more than ever!" Hank cries, hiding his face behind his white gloves.

I consider it. "I think they might actually kill us."

"Let's junk the tap piece," says Hank. "It's not getting us anywhere."

"You want to improvise?"

"Let's do one of Bill's."

"I'll do it if you hand out your flyers," I say.

Hank looks at his scattered handouts. He knows I'm right.

The egg timer dings. Hank steps out on stage with his flyers. "THESE ARE BLACKBIRDS," he announces, chucking them out into the crowd. The papers flutter down to the seats. People grab them and study the black scribbles.

Hank kneels and sets the egg timer to an hour. It starts ticking. The audience groans. Hank disappears behind the curtains, then I step out wearing nothing but a black Kamilavka priest hat and dirty white underwear. The audience gasps. A Russian woman faints. The neo-Marxists look horrified. The S&M bikers stare at my crotch.

I walk to the foot of the stage and begin marching in place, barefoot, knees high, fists pumping. A minute passes, then Hank comes out. He's
wearing the same outfit as me: priest hat, underwear, and nothing else. He
walks to the foot of the stage and begins marching like me.

Nobody in the crowd speaks. People look at each other.

The timer ticks off ten minutes. Nobody says a word.

Twenty minutes. We continue marching. People murmur. Critics
and reporters take out pens and make notes. The piece has something . . .
intrigue . . . flair. . . . People study the flyers, the scribbles.

At thirty minutes the critics point and whisper. People exchange
ideas and possible references in our work. The two neo-Marxists in the front
row begin arguing about the significance of the marching.

By forty minutes the discussions have grown heavy. Critics call out
ideas. The murmur builds to a low roar. Dissension mounts. Theory camps
form and disband. The neo-Marxists are really going at it.

At fifty minutes the neo-Marxists can't stand it anymore. Neo-
Marxist One jumps up and starts yelling at neo-Marxist Two.

"LOOK AT THOSE HATS!" One yells. "Combined with the
underwear, the reference to Russian priesthood is a Dadaist affirmation of
Trotsky's fight to demystify religious and other pie-in-the-sky appropria-
tions of the Revolution!"

Neo-Marxist Two has never been so insulted. He jumps up and yells
back: "*NIET!* I am Russian, and yours is only a superficial treatment! First,
we are all given equal pieces of paper in a thinly veiled gesture of repetition.
Second, we are treated to orderly, yet strenuous, marching in place. Together
these invoke the egalitarian aims of the Revolution, its rational and strategic
teleologies, its cyclical periods of struggle. But as swiftly as it appears, this
invocation is undone: first, when we are told these harsh black marks on
the paper are birds, which they are not; and again, when the marching becomes a show of emperor's new clothes—the barefoot marching in a show
about shoes! We are shown truths, only to have them obfuscated by word-

play and fancy hats! In this they argue that the act of perceiving may be dangerously veiled by romantic lies and half-truths as surely as blackbirds fly starkly against white Russian snow. How you cannot SEE this, I DO NOT KNOW!"

Neo-Marxist One throws a punch and the two of them go down, wrestling and beating the shit out of each other.

The egg timer dings.

Hank and I slip backstage. The audience goes crazy with cheers and applause. Tears stream down our faces as we stumble back out and give a bow.

The neo-Marxists cheer loudest of all.

* * *

Hank and I ran around the apartment, blurting out ideas and talking about the future. We were back in full swing. The morning papers carried reviews of the show. The critics hated the tap piece but loved the hat march. Bill's work was a hit.

We sat down on the couch and encouraged Bill to perform as much as he could. Bill fought off his headaches and tried to oblige us. Having a steady audience seemed to energize him. He babbled to himself constantly, trying things, testing ideas, discarding some, and keeping others while Hank and I took notes.

Hank watched the clock. Bill seemed to be averaging a new piece per hour, but it was hard to tell—sometimes the pieces ran together, so it wasn't always clear when one finished and the next began.

"Is that the end?" I'd ask. If Bill nodded, Hank and I would applaud.

Hank offered some advice: "You should always signal the end," he said. "Give a little bow. Say thank you."

Bill tried it and liked it. He started bowing and saying thank you after each piece. It was repetitive, but at least we knew when to clap.

* * *

The phone rang. It was Vaughn.

"I CAN'T STOP THINKING ABOUT THE SHOW!" he yelled. "Have you seen the papers? The reviews are still rolling in! People are talking! My phone won't stop ringing!"

I screamed with excitement. Hank asked me who was on the phone. "VAUGHN!" I screamed. Hank screamed and laughed.

"I have another show Saturday night," said Vaughn. "I know it's short notice, but you'd be perfect for it—and I CAN PAY!"

"WHAT'S IT CALLED?" I screamed.

"BALLETA ANONYMOUSA!" screamed Vaughn.

"WE'LL BE THERE!" I screamed and hung up.

50

HANK HANDED ME A NEWSPAPER article about Horace Lipschitz.

Horace was the billionaire CEO of Invinciblesoft, Redsoft's fiercest
competitor. Although software industry players feared his business tactics,
he was reviled more for his temper tantrums, shameless vanity, and infantile
drive to amass more wealth than Bill.

Horace's Bill-obsession was legendary. He employed a team of
economists to monitor Redsoft's moves around the clock. He used his press
tours to promote his financial exploits and advertise Bill's losses. There were
even rumors that he'd diverted Invinciblesoft funds to acquire private com-
panies in which Bill's money was invested just so he could personally kamikaze them into the ground.

Well aware of Horace's obsession, Bill had chosen to play the game
with nonchalance. When *Billionaire Magazine* named Bill Man of the Year,
a reporter at the awards ceremony asked Bill how he felt about beating Horace for the title.

"Horace who?" asked Bill. "Oh—you mean Lipshit? I don't think about him at all."

The very next week, Lipschitz bought an eighty-foot yacht, changed her name to *The Billdown*, paid fifty sailors to piss on her bow, then scuttled her off California's coast with six sticks of dynamite.

* * *

Bill performed day and night. We egged him on, told him he was brilliant, and commended his innovation. Naturally, his ego grew. It was inevitable. He tore through pieces as fast as he could and finished performances like an impresario with flourishes and bobs of the head; he was gaining mastery and he knew it. Hank and I stayed awake for three days straight videotaping, cataloguing, inventorying, and appropriating, and by the end we had enough material for the Balleta Anonymousa performance and maybe twenty more.

And just when we thought we'd seen it all, Bill announced that his billions no longer held meaning for him. He prayed on his knees for poverty. He crashed Portalia intentionally to flaunt his disdain. He loved the millions going down the tubes, the decrementing dollars flashing on the monitor, the pretty pixels in monochromatic green. He watched the machine crash over and over, threw his head back to laugh, and jiggled his tits at the screen like a drunken Vegas biddy winning at the slots.

* * *

The phone rang. It was Mouse.

"You sound dead tired," she slurred.

"I am. How's fight camp?"

"I'm drunk. All we do here is fight and drink. And not always in that order," she teased.

I pictured Mouse running around drunk in her silver boxers and smiled. A lump rose in my throat.

"Are you ready for the big bout?" I asked.

"I hope so. I've beaten everyone here, so they're kicking me out. I'm coming home. I'm so nervous; I have butterflies constantly. Do I sound drunker than last time? No, wait—don't answer that. Tell me about what you're doing."

"The three of us are working on new material, and some of it isn't half bad," I said, glancing at the cage where Bill was sculpting a wet mound of refried beans.

"The three of you?"

"The two of us and Bill."

"Ah yes, 'Bill,'" Mouse laughed. "Do you have any performances coming up?"

I told her about the Balleta Anonymousa show while I watched Hank play with his fire rope. He coiled it into a human-sized bird's nest, then climbed in. The nest was so deep he practically disappeared in it.

"I love ballet," said Mouse. "Would you mind if I came? There's a bus leaving for San Francisco tomorrow."

I told her to come. She said she would. We said goodbye and hung up.

Hank was busy taping magazine photos of hawks, sparrows, and crows to his shrine. I noticed that the tufts of hair growing back over the wax burns on his head made him look like a baby bird.

It made me laugh. And that made him laugh.

* * *

I walked to the liquor store, bought a fifth of whisky, and caught a bus to the cemetery.

The afternoon was warm. Blades of freshly cut grass stuck to my cowboy boots as I walked through a field of headstones to the place where my parents were buried.

I walked to my father's grave. The headstone read ABE FROM-MER. I rested the whisky beside it gently in the grass. "Happy birthday," I whispered. I choked back hot tears, wiped my nose, offered a wave goodbye, then turned and started back across the lawn.

A gravedigger in a hole paused his digging to wipe his brow. He rested on his shovel, adjusted his hat, and nodded as I passed.

"Abe your daddy?" the digger asked.

"Yes. Did you know him?"

"I've known them all in my fashion," said the digger, tapping his shovel in the dirt. He nodded to the whisky. "Will Abe be drinking all of that tonight?"

"Feel free to take what's left," I said.

"You should visit your daddy more often," said the digger with a tip of his hat.

* * *

I opened my eyes in the night. The apartment was dark except for the spotlight over the cage. I sat up on the couch. Bill was churning out performances behind the chain-link at breakneck speed. He finished one called I Tie Myself to the Roof of the Cage with Shoelaces, bowed, said thank you, then launched into Wrapping High Heels in Toilet Paper While Eating Apples and Peaches. I looked at the clock. He'd conceived two pieces in less than three minutes—I'd never seen anyone work that fast.

Something moved in the dark. I dove to the floor, grabbed a flashlight from under the couch, and flicked it on. The beam found Hank clutching the living room window.

"What are you doing?" I asked, crawling over to him with the light.

"Watching for Stark," Hank whispered. "Do you think he saw the newspaper reviews of the Trotsky performance?"

"He doesn't look like the type to read the arts section."

The wallet photo of Sherry was in Hank's hand. I noticed the dicks he'd drawn in black ink were gone.

"What happened to your dicks?" I whispered.

Hank started to cry. "I decided I didn't like them," he said. "I showed them to Bill and he said they were evil."

"Where'd they all go?"

"I took them back."

"Took them back?"

Hank stuck out his tongue. It was black with ink.

I shined the light in his eyes and saw they were at half-mast.

"Hank?" I asked.

"Yes?"

"Are you asleep right now?"

Hank nodded, smacked his lips, crawled back to his rope nest, and passed out.

* * *

The phone rang in the morning. It was Rudy.

"TURN ON CHANNEL SIX!" he yelled. "BILL'S WIFE IS ON!"

I ran to the couch and turned the TV on. Bill's wife was being interviewed by a talk show panel of feminists.

"The problem isn't that he's off on some sabbatical," said the wife.

"Then what is the problem?" asked a feminist.

"The problem," said the wife, "is that since he left, our fortune—which is tied up in stock, of course—has been, well, *disappearing*. I can only assume he's cashing it in on this new technology thing he's working on, and if that's what he wants to do with his money, fine, but—"

"But—*billions*? What do you think he's buying?"

"I have no idea. Computer equipment? Programmers? Beer? Who knows?"

"Could you freeze the accounts?"

"Absolutely not. He's a grown man. If he wants to piss it away, fine. Our pre-nup prevents me from touching it anyway. Let him diddle it off! I don't care. Why should I?" The wife pointed at her ample breasts. "What do you think is in these breasts? Silicon, that's what. And guess who paid for them? He did. And why, do you suppose? Do you think it was because he wanted bigger boobs on his wife so he could fondle 'em?"

"It wasn't so he could fondle 'em?" a feminist asked.

"No. He wanted to be able to fondle silicon. He wanted to be reminded of computers."

"No!" gasped the feminists.

"It's true. He named them his Fabulous Flesh Chips."

The feminists hissed and shook their heads.

"He just doesn't care," cried the wife.

Hank and I looked at Bill. He was busy performing Scraping Off Bunions with Half-Eaten Onions.

The interview hadn't fazed him a bit.

51

HEAT SHIMMERED UP FROM THE asphalt as Hank and I threaded through the alleys toward Prance Prance with a bag of performance props. We took our time and watched for Stark. As we neared the gallery, we saw a line of hundreds waiting to get in.

"Look at that crowd," said Hank. "Not a bad turnout."

We approached a man at the end of the line. "Do you know what time the doors open?" I asked.

"Oh, they're open," said the man. "They've been open for an hour."

"Why isn't everyone going in?" I asked.

"The gallery's full. I don't know how they're going to fit all of us in there."

"This is the line for the Balleta Anonymousa painting show?" Hank asked.

"Yes," said the man, "but I couldn't care less about the paintings. I'm here to see the performance. So is everyone else in town, apparently."

We ran to the front of the line and saw it was true. The doors were open wide and Prance Prance was jammed with people.

We pushed our way into the lobby. People stood elbow to elbow. The air was humid. We could hardly move. Sexy bespeckled women in lipstick and big hair, goateed men in hip plaid suits, and socialites in strapless gowns were mashed into corners and pressed against the windows. Everyone seemed in good spirits. Cheers and applause went up each time the crowd pushed forward an inch toward the theater entrance at the rear of the gallery. Liquor passed from hand to hand. A few people recognized us; they smiled and congratulated us and we shook hands all around. We were back in the game with full force. There'd be no more begging, no more hanging flyers, no more idiots in berets. The fans were hungry. I grinned under the lights.

I looked at Hank. He was white as a sheet.

"What's wrong?" I whispered.

"Critics," he hissed.

"Where?"

He pointed to a herd of people wearing tan raincoats in front of us. The coats were suspicious, considering how hot it was outside, but it didn't mean they were critics.

"Why do you think they're critics?" I whispered.

Hank gave me a push so I collided with the herd. The people turned around. All of them were wearing press badges, cameras, notepads, and audio recorders tucked discretely under their coats.

Something was wrong. Reporters usually flaunted their equipment. They dangled microphones and press passes from their necks with braggadocio to impress or intimidate a subject. The camera and recorder were their genitalia, and just as neurotic: powerful, yet needy; sophisticated, but petty; impartial, yet narcissistic; discrete, yet eager to be thrust in front of a subject's flapping mouth. But here, right in front of us, was a group taking great pains to keep its half-cocked tools of the trade hidden from view.

I began to sweat. How many were there? I stood on my toes and counted ten right in front of us, but I could see more critics up ahead. I looked past those and saw more critics—and more critics after that. It was raincoats all the way to the theater entrance. I shook my head and chuckled. Leave it to us to get stuck in line behind them!

Then I looked to my right. Critics. Lots of them. A thick herd that extended all the way to the gallery wall. I nodded hello and they stiffened like they didn't want to be seen. I looked to my left. More critics. Some darted and ducked behind patrons to avoid my gaze. I turned and looked behind us. There were critics all the way back to the windows and more critics out the door. The room had suddenly become a shark tank.

"They're everywhere!" I whispered.

"They seem fidgety," said Hank, "and why are they incognito?"

"I'LL TELL YOU WHY," yelled a woman behind us. We turned and saw Jean Gateau, the art critic. "These reporters are NERVOUS, my boys, because they're NOT SUPPOSED TO BE HERE. Look at them! It's like a goddamn critic convention! They all want a piece of the up-and-coming performance art scene EVEN IF THIS ISN'T THEIR BEAT!"

All the critics heard her. Their conversations died down. They shuffled around. Some looked at the ceiling. Some whistled. They tried to appear nonchalant, but it was impossible; Jean had them cornered.

She took out a flask and had a hit of gin. "SO," she yelled, "since they're INTENT ON STEALING MY STORY, LET'S AT LEAST INTRODUCE TONIGHT'S CROWD, SHALL WE?" She began pointing out the critic cliques all around us. "There's a FASHION critic over there! And over there's a DANCE critic! Miserable DRAMA critics wearing pompous ascots are in the corner—New York is EAST, boys! CULTURE and GENERAL UNSPECIFIED HOLLYWOOD CRITICS are standing over there beside the LIT-CRITS with their multicultural THEORY CRIT sidekicks. And there's a FILM critic at nine o'clock . . . and ten o'clock . . . and eleven o'clock . . . best cut back on the popcorn, FAT MAN! And oh, look! Even the MUSIC critics are here, TONE DEAF AS THEY ARE!"

She pulled us close. "You'd better watch out. All the people smiling and shaking your hands are looking to eat you alive. You boys are going to get critted up the ass!" she whispered before shucking us off for another sloppy hit from her flask.

Conversations started up again and the crowd shuffled forward.

One of the Balleta Anonymousa works on exhibit hung on a wall beside us. It was a painting of an airborne ballerina in a white tutu crashing to the stage before a sea of frowning critics in tuxedos. Her right leg was cracked backward at the knee from the impact, and her shoulder, bony and angled downward scapula-first, was ready to hit next. Despite the coming wreckage, she smiled gaily under the hot lights, arms and chin up, white feathers in her hair, pearly bodice slicing through air, fingers lightly extended, noble to the end.

Hank eyed the painting and swallowed. "I think I'm going to be sick," he whispered, clutching at his stomach.

We shoved our way to the rear of the gallery and ducked through the backstage door. Hank ran for the restroom while I peeked out through the curtains. The theater was crammed. Every chair was taken. Critics stood and sat in the aisles and more people were pouring in.

Vaughn climbed onto the stage, thanked the show's sponsors, then began introducing us. The critics went wild with screams and applause. Hank and I were dead. I closed the curtains.

"How's it look out there?" asked Hank from behind the restroom door.

"They're going to kill us," I said plainly. "Are you sick?"

I opened the door and looked in. Hank was splashing water on his eyes at the sink.

"My eyes itch," he said. "Must be the nerves. The water helps." He dried his eyes off with a paper towel. "Maybe it's an allergy. Do you see anything?"

I looked at his eyes. "They're bloodshot from the washing, but that's all. You look a little pale, though. Are you sure you're up to this?"

"I'm fine," he said, swallowing. "Let's go get killed."

The curtains open. Hank and I come walking out in pink tights with our feet turned out like ballet dancers. I'm carrying a shovel; Hank has a bucket of lard. We head for the foot of the stage. Our naked chests flash white under the hot lights. Our tights fit snugly in the ass and show off our balls. Our expressions are serious, like this is the best thing since Balanchine.

We reach the edge of the stage and stop. We wait a beat—then suck in our guts.

Spectators chuckle. Cameras flash.

Hank sets down the bucket, then slowly pushes himself up onto the balls of his feet. As he reaches full height, he squeals in French with a surprised expression: *"Moi?"*

He holds the pose. I jam the shovel into the bucket, scoop out a grapefruit-sized blob of lard, and flip it up into the rafters. It hits a spotlight and sticks. The fat starts melting on the bulb. Golden drops of lard sprinkle down on us as Hank lowers himself back down to his feet.

Hank grabs the shovel as I repeat his move—I squeal a *Moi?* and rise up onto my toes while he flicks another fat blob onto the lights. Half the fat sticks; the other falls and splats onto my head as I lower myself back down.

Hank goes next, then me, demi-pointe, a *Moi?* while the other slings the fat, then down, then him, then me, then faster, demi-pointing and shoveling as quickly as we can like two slick pigs under a golden shower.

Each *Moi?* lasts longer than the one before. Our voices begin to overlap. Soon the sound is constant, a variegated moan, an oscillating man-tra reminiscent of Tibetan throat singing . . . hypnotic . . . eerie. . . . The air vibrates. The audience watches. They know we're up to something, but they haven't caught on yet. Then they see: something's moving in Hank's tights, in the crotch—he's getting an erection. A few critics laugh, then they look at my tights and see it's happening there too. A woman gasps. I look and see her nipples are hard. A few men shuffle erections in their seats as we go on. Our tights are bulging. The moaning chant grows longer, then louder. Pressure's building . . . up-down-up-down. We're drenched in buttery goodness and I'm sweating like a hog—

We stop. We're breathing hard. The audience is quiet. The piece is over. We step back to bow.

Hank lurches and sprays vomit all down his pink tights. He tries to stop it, but the gush runs through his open fingers, little pools puddling in each hand. He looks up and smiles at the audience with breakfast in his teeth. Critics recoil but love it. The sound and smell are overpowering and my stomach goes sour. I try to hold back, but can't. I lurch and vomit gushes down my legs. The audience jumps up with deafening applause as we wipe our mouths and bow.

We laughed as the crowd rushed the stage. A critic mopped up some vomit with his handkerchief and made a run for the door, but a female reporter in a dress and heels tackled him and fought for the souvenir as photographers went crazy with snapping and flashing.

"WHAT'S THIS PIECE CALLED?" yelled a reporter.

The crowd hushed for the answer.

"DEMI-POINTES, THEN VOMIT," yelled Hank.

The crowd roared. Champagne bottles popped, music cued, critics danced, Hank and I were delirious. . . .

Vaughn ran up to us. "INCREDIBLE!" he cried. "I have another opening next Thursday—you must perform!"

"What it's called?" asked Hank.

"CIRCUS FREAKS!" screamed Vaughn.

Hank and I laughed.

Mouse pushed toward us through the crowd. She was tan with lean muscles and wearing a bright-yellow dress. I jumped down from the stage and kissed her.

"I loved your piece," she slurred, drunk.

"It was all Bill's idea!" I said.

Mouse shook her head and laughed.

Hank waved to her.

"Hello, Hank!" said Mouse. She started toward him.

"Don't mention Sherry," I whispered.

"No?"

I shook my head with a sad face.

"Oh, no!"

I nodded. Mouse covered her mouth, then went to Hank. They hugged. She touched his burnt scalp. "What happened to you?" she asked. Hank laughed and hugged her again for the cameras.

When the night was over, I walked Mouse up to Grace Cathedral. The Impala was right where I'd left it.

"What happened to my car?" asked Mouse, running her hand over the scratched hood and peeling paint.

"It saw a little action," I said. "We drove it to kidnap Bill—"

"I kind of like it," she said, cocking her head.

"You do?"

"It looks like something a performance artist might drive."

"And we did," I blurted out, "we drove it all over—"

Mouse smiled and held up a hand. "Let's just leave it at that," she said.

I shut up and drove her home. She was fast asleep by the time we arrived. I parked, gathered her up, and carried her inside. The house was a wreck—even worse than before. Blanche barked and came running to greet us. Mouse stirred in my arms. "Just sleep," I cooed, carrying her past the mess as fast as I could.

"You were really good," she whispered, slipping under her bedcovers as I tucked her in. I kissed her on the forehead. She giggled, mumbled something dirty about tutus, then drifted away while I hurried off to clean the place.

* * *

Hank ran into the apartment the next morning with a stack of newspapers. "WE'RE EVERYWHERE!" he screamed. He thrust an arts section at me and there we were, right on top in bold black caps: PERFOR-MANCE ART STAGES DANCE-ATTACK COMEBACK.

"Holy shit!" I said.

"THEY LOVE US!" yelled Hank, shaking his fists. He whipped the paper out of my hand and began a slow prance around the room on his toes as he read: "'The performers' absurdist movement invoked the years of unoriginal choreography ballet dancers must endure. The tutus, retracted bellies, and repeating *mois* delivered searing blows to the vain choreographers and socialite cults that continue to promote Dance's darker dysfunctions of starvation stardom, self-indulgent suffering, and freakish mutilations of the body.'"

I could barely breathe. I flipped through more reviews, but they were the same. The critics adored us.

I ran to the kitchen, brought back wine, and we got to drinking.

"Stark's going to see these reviews for sure," I said.

"We'll be careful," Hank sang.

We looked at the cage. Bill was performing faster than ever. He pounded away on a stuffed donkey with a hammer, bowed, said thank you, then started on a new piece involving a hairnet.

"Look at him go," said Hank.

"Maybe we should take him to Prance Prance next time and cut out the middleman," I joked.

Hank walked to the cage. "How would you like to perform?" he asked. Bill looked up at Hank while his hands continued working the hairnet. "It would be a real show," said Hank, "a real audience!"

There were dark circles under Bill's eyes. He looked exhausted. He blinked, struggling to focus. "It sounds nice," he said weakly.

Hank turned to me. "I think he's ready," he said.

I bit my lip. Hank saw I needed more convincing. He turned to Bill.

"Your piece would have to be professional quality," said Hank. "Something totally new."

"I could do it," said Bill, shaking his hairnet.

"How long would you need to prepare?" I asked.

Bill's performing slowed. He saw we were serious. He shrugged.

"A week?" asked Hank.

Bill nodded.

"I'm still not sure he's ready," I said.

"I'm ready," Bill said, trembling.

"Prove it," I said.

Bill swallowed. "What day is today?"

"Monday."

"Monday is Redsoft's weekly board meeting," said Bill.

"And?"

"Let me call in."

"You're crazy. You'll cry for help."

"I won't," said Bill.

"You're crazy," I said. I looked at Hank. "Crazy."

But Hank considered it. "Would it really be that risky for him to call in? What could he tell them? He doesn't even know where he is."

"They love me," Bill babbled.

"What if they trace the call?" I asked.

"We could route it through SI's phone line," said Hank.

"I'M THE CEO!" Bill yelled.

He was semi-conscious at best—it was impossible to say what might come out of his mouth—but Hank was convinced. He unplugged the telephone, walked it to the couch, and plugged it into the back of the computer.

"You'll have five minutes once you make the call and not a second more," I said.

Bill nodded.

Hank enabled the phone's external speaker, then dialed SI. Once he had a connection, he handed the handset through the chain-link to Bill.

Bill dialed Redsoft. We heard the number ringing, then an automated voice came on: "Welcome to the Redsoft Conferencing System. Please enter your conference code."

Bill punched his code into the phone. "Thank you," said the automated voice. "You will now be connected to your scheduled meeting. There are forty-three callers already in conference."

After a series of a beeps, Bill was connected to the conference call. The meeting was underway. We heard a man's voice reading a financial report. He paused.

"Hello?" he asked. "Did someone new join the call?"

"It's Bill," said Bill, his nasal whine unmistakable. "Is that you, Gil?"

"Why, yes it is! Hello, Bill!" Gil stuttered. "This is a nice surprise. Tell us how your sabbatical is going. It's mighty hush-hush around here—the top brass are tiptoeing around with their lips sealed!"

The other callers chuckled politely. Bill chuckled too.

"Everything's fine, fine," said Bill. "You all know I'm working hard on something new—something exciting—but I can't say any more just yet. Please, Gil, continue with your report."

Bill's eyes rolled around in his head. He gritted his teeth and fought for focus.

"Sure thing," said Gil. He resumed reading. A minute passed. We watched Bill trying to concentrate, but his eyes were glazing over. He wiped away drool. The report was very dry. Profitability ratios . . . earning assets . . . preferred securities. . . .

Bill snickered.

Gil heard it and stopped reading. "Did someone have a question?" he asked politely.

"Did you say 'preferred' securities?" asked Bill. "Because I'd swear I heard you say 'furred.'"

Gil laughed. "Maybe I did say 'furred,'" he joked.

Bill chuckled. "I thought so. You have me imagining a 'hairy' security."

The callers on the line cackled.

"I think you're going to need to 'shave' that from your report," Bill quipped.

"You got it, Bill!" said Gil.

"Good. I think you should. Because you know," said Bill, "when people think of 'hairy,' the first thing they think of are testicles."

Gil was silent.

Bill laughed. "Sure, sure, I suppose a man's balls are a form of 'security' as you said, you know, a symbol of procreation and so forth, but—"

"Bill, oh, I, pardon me, I didn't really say—"

"DON'T INTERRUPT ME, GIL! All I'm saying is I don't think it's a good idea to mention HAIRY BALLS in a financial statement. Or is it? Is that the common practice now? My God, am I that far behind the times?"

The phone was silent. Bill was on a roll.

"Eh, *amigo*?" asked Bill. "Is everyone dangling the sack in financial statements these days?"

"I . . . no! Bill, sorry, no, the report doesn't actually say—"

"Because, Gil, right now I can't stop imagining your hairy balls bobbing up and down on some fat financial analyst's eyes while his secretary looks on in horror. Ha! Look at you, standing on that poor sap's desk! Bouncy, bouncy, bouncy—"

"Bill, please, I—"

"So that's why I say it, Gil: you really need to shave it!"

Silence.

"We understand each other?"

"Of course, Bill, but—"

"Good," said Bill. "I'm sorry, but I have to run to another meeting."

"It was . . . nice of you to call in," said Gil.

Bill hung up the phone, gave us a sloppy wave, and went back to his hairnet.

The Prance Prance Bill Show was on.

52

"THAT'S THE LAST OF IT," Hank announced, holding up an empty wine bottle.

"I'll go buy more," I said.

"Get something French this time," said Hank. "Fancy."

I stumbled out of the apartment building barefoot. The streets were dark and a cold wind whipped papers and trash into the air. I hurried past dark storefronts, a park, a bar called The Hog Tie, and a gas station.

The liquor store was open. I went in. The clerk behind the counter saw my bare feet.

"You'll freeze to death," he muttered.

"Not with these," I said, setting two bottles of three-dollar Bourgogne down on the counter.

The clerk bagged the wine and rang it up. A stack of old magazines sat in a cardboard box behind the register.

"Are you throwing those out?" I asked.

The clerk shrugged. "They're old. You want them?"

"Performance art props," I said.

The clerk handed me the stack. There was no room in my grocery bag, so I tucked them into the front of my pants and covered them with my T-shirt.

I left the store and headed back toward the apartment. The wind howled. I saw The Hog Tie just up ahead.

Suddenly, the bar's door burst open and a man stumbled out. He lurched and threw up in the gutter. He looked familiar. I squinted and tried to make him out.

Stark.

I backed into a dark doorway and held my breath. A minute passed. I peeked around the corner. Stark was doubled over in his wrinkled white suit with his hands on his thighs. When he was done, he stood up—then fell back down.

He glanced in my direction. I ducked back into the shadows. Had he seen me? I heard him stand up. There was shuffling on the sidewalk, then the sound of the bar door opening and closing. I peeked and saw he'd gone back inside.

I crept up to the bar window and looked in. The joint was nearly empty. Stark sat on a stool right beside the window. He hadn't shaved in a week. A united front of whisky shots sat before him. He knocked two back, then hung his head. The stress had to be getting to him. The Redsoft executives running the search for Bill were undoubtedly ruthless, with endless power and money. Stark was probably thinking about what would happen to him if he didn't find Bill, and soon. He lifted another glass, swallowed, and set it down.

Suddenly, his fist shot out and hit the window. He held it there, then slowly opened his hand.

There was a dollar in it, flattened out against the glass.

It was a bill.

I dropped the grocery bag and took off running. The bar door banged open. I looked back and saw Stark hurtling after me. I sprinted across the street with the sound of his boots right on my tail, cut down an alley, accelerating, arms pumping—then the sound of his boots disappeared. Where was he? I looked back just in time to see him diving for my legs. We collided and went down hard. I hit the asphalt with my shoulder, skidded five feet to a stop, rolled onto my back, and saw Stark rising. He was muddy with asphalt and the fall had ripped his suit.

He lunged. I scrambled backward on all fours onto a pile of trash and rose to my feet. I could run left or right. Stark crouched with his hands out, ready to move in either direction.

"Where is he?" Stark growled.

"Who?" I quipped, smiling blood.

Stark flicked his wrist and a six-inch stiletto clicked open. He aimed the point at my belly and made sickening cuts in the air.

"What the hell are you doing with him?" he spat. "You haven't asked for anything—not a single demand. We can't figure it out. Is it some kind of power trip?"

"We're making him into a performance art machine."

"A performance art . . . what? Are you insane? HE'S NO MACHINE! HE'S MY MILLION-DOLLAR MEAL TICKET, YOU IDIOT!"

"You'll get your money. I doubt we'll keep him forever—"

"Let me educate you about stocks," Stark hissed. "I am being paid in SHARES. The men on Redsoft's board are all paid in SHARES. These things called SHARES ride on the perception of value. And value tends to fall when you hear the beloved CEO isn't running the company because he's busy being TORTURED—"

"Torture is—"

"What?" asked Stark, waving his knife closer. "A strong term? How would you term it? If not torture, then what? What, other than torture, would make a billionaire celebrity who revels in the admiration of his peers spout off about TESTICLES on a CONFERENCE CALL? When TES-

TICLES enter the discussion, value tends to go down, which means stock prices go down, which means, as SHAREHOLDERS, we end up with SHIT!"

"We didn't tell him to say testicles—"

Stark slashed at my face with the knife. I raised my arms, blocked the blade, and kicked him in the gut, forcing him back. Blood dripped from my elbow. I glanced down and saw the stiletto had flayed open a six-inch gash in my right forearm. Stark charged again. I jumped aside, but too late—the blade crashed into my chest, slamming me backward against the alley wall. Stark slipped and fell, then looked up at me from the ground. He laughed. I looked down. The stiletto was sticking straight out of my sternum.

"THERE'S SOME PERFORMANCE ART!" Stark jeered. I pulled up my shirt. The magazines had taken the blade. I turned and ran. The knife bobbed up and down.

53

I SAT ON THE LIVING room floor and held a towel against my forearm. Dark blood dripped out. Hank tried not to look as he paced the room with a bottle of bourbon.

"Do you think he knows where we are?" asked Hank. "It's only a matter of time—"

"I know," I said. "You should've seen him. He looked insane."

"I don't want to see him!" Hank shuddered. He crept along the wall to the window and looked out. "Are you sure he didn't follow you?"

The cage rattled. We turned and saw Bill on all fours with his face mashed up against the chain-link. He was slack-jawed and sweaty. His eyes closed, opened, then rolled around behind his glasses. "Am I shamanic yet?" he asked, trying to aim his eyes at us.

"Don't use your eyes," said Hank. "Break up your mind! Break up the cage! Me! Larry! The apartment!"

Bill stood, ran to the end of the cage, turned around, and ran back in the other direction.

"FASTER!" Hank yelled.

Bill picked up the pace. Sweat ran down his face. Chain-links flashed across his view of us. "I'm breaking you up!" he gasped as he ran and sucked air.

"See with your cheeks, your lips, your mouth!" said Hank.

Running to his left, Bill aimed his right cheek at us and tried to see with it. The cheek dragged along the chain-link. When he reached the end of the cage, he switched cheeks and dragged again, faster this time, then again, one cheek after the other while his slack lips bounded over the links. He started to cry. The cage rattled. His teeth clicked over the metal. Finally, his legs gave out and he collapsed.

"That was beautiful," I said.

"Did you break us up?" asked Hank.

"I think so," Bill sobbed.

"Then look at us! Tell us what you see! Use your hair, your arms, your mouth!"

Bill rolled onto his side, arched his back, opened his mouth wide, and pushed it up against the chain-link. The mouth looked at me, then Hank.

"Ehhh," said the mouth.

"Try harder!" said Hank.

"What do you see?" I begged.

The mouth licked the air and struggled to speak. "You . . . you're being watched," said the mouth.

"That's right!" Hank encouraged. "And who is it? Who is watching us?"

"A detective," said the mouth, licking the air again.

A chill ran up my back; Hank and I hadn't told the mouth anything about Stark.

"Tell us about him," said Hank. "Where is he now?"

"Get into birds," said the mouth.

"I am into them," said Hank, pointing at his rope nest and the bird pictures he'd taped to his shrine.

"Get into them more," said the mouth.

Bill convulsed, fumbled around in his prop pile, grabbed something small and black, and pushed it out through the chain-link. It was a woman's compact case. Hank picked it up. It was old and beat-up with a piece of chewing gum for a clasp. Hank slid the gum aside and opened the lid. There was a small mirror inside.

"What's this for?" he asked.

"Watch your back," said the mouth.

Bill's eyes rolled back in his head and he fainted.

"BILL!" yelled Hank, shaking the chain-link. "BILL!"

It was no use. Bill was out.

Hank grabbed the bourbon, took a hit, and paced the room like a maniac.

"Hey," I said, shivering, "let's wake him up and make him do that thing with his cheek again."

* * *

I awoke in the night. I went to the kitchen, removed the bloody towel from my arm, wrapped gauze around the wound, secured it with duct tape, opened a bottle of bourbon, poured half a glass, washed my mouth out with it, then poured another.

Mouse's flyer for the kickboxing title fight was taped to the refrigerator. I threw a few punches. Bourbon splashed onto my arm. I licked it off, padded back to the living room, grabbed the phone, went to the couch, pulled a blanket over my head, and dialed Mouse's number.

"Hello?" she answered.

"Hi," I whispered.

"Why are you whispering?" she whispered back. "Is this a heavy-breathing sex call? Because if it is, I must warn you that I'm wearing very unsexy flannel pajamas."

"My mother wore flannel," I whispered.

"Then I'm burning these in the morning," said Mouse with a laugh. "Are you drunk?"

"A little," I said.

"And you called to share your stupor? Wait." She put the phone down, then returned.

"Where'd you go?"

"You should never drink alone," she said.

I heard ice clink in a glass.

"What do you have?"

"Tequila."

"To your flannels," I toasted.

"To your mother," she toasted.

We drank.

"So," said Mouse. "Why are you really calling?"

"There's a man watching us."

"A man you know?"

"No."

"Who, then? Some kind of voyeur? A pervert?"

"We're not sure. Probably."

"You make it sound like he might be dangerous."

"Perverts usually are."

"You're a pervert."

"You think I'm dangerous?"

"You're an incorrigible Mouse molester."

"Don't forget performance art kidnapper."

"Oh yes, right—you and Hank will have to show me your 'Bill' sometime. Maybe we can all have a drink together," she laughed.

"Thanks for the talk."

"Sure. I hope you catch the voyeur in the act."

"Me too," I said.

"Pervert."

54

WHEN THURSDAY NIGHT ARRIVED, HANK unlocked the cage and Bill crawled out in nothing but his cellophane skirt. He grabbed the chain-link and slowly pulled himself up, hand over hand, until he was standing. He looked down at his forearms, ribs, and legs like he'd never seen them before. The forty pounds he'd lost in the cage had left him gaunt.

He looked out at the apartment's high ceilings and clothing-covered walls. The living room was cavernous compared to the cage. He began to hyperventilate.

"Take it slow," said Hank.

Bill turned and looked back at his prop pile. "Can I take those?" he asked.

"They'll be waiting for you when we get back," I said. "Here, put this on." I handed him a paper bag. He slipped it over his head and we led him out of the apartment and down the stairs to the lobby.

I stepped outside and surveyed the street. There were plenty of pedestrians, but there was no sign of Stark. I motioned to Hank. He walked Bill outside. The sidewalks were bustling with tourists, but with all the crazies in San Francisco, nobody gave Bill's paper bag a second look.

Hank pulled out his compact mirror and looked behind us as we walked.

"Are we being followed?" I whispered.

Hank nodded.

"Is it Stark?" I asked.

"I don't know," Hank whispered, "but somebody's back there."

We ducked Bill into an alley and hustled him toward Prance Prance as fast as we could.

* * *

The gallery was jammed with people when we arrived. Hank and I waved and smiled to our fans as we pushed Bill through the lobby. Critics patted our backs. Reporters snapped photos of the paper bag and demanded to know who was under there, but Hank and I just laughed and said it was a surprise.

Vaughn was dressed in a ringmaster's coat and top hat. He took a hit from a champagne bottle as he stumbled over to us.

"WELCOME, CIRCUS FREAKS!" he yelled over the noise. "THE THEATER'S PACKED, I'VE SOLD FIVE PAINTINGS SO FAR, AND MAYBE I'M DRUNK, BUT I COULD SWEAR SOMEBODY'S STANDING IN FRONT OF ME IN A CELLOPHANE SKIRT WITH A BAG OVER HIS HEAD. WHAT'S YOUR NAME, MYSTERY MAN?" he asked, flopping a sloppy hand onto Bill's chest.

"I'M BILL," said Bill from under his bag.

"ARE YOU PERFORMING?" Vaughn asked.

Bill nodded.

"HE'S NEW," said Hank.

Vaughn wished Bill luck, then looked at his watch. "IT'S AL-MOST TIME. LET'S GO LOOK AT YOUR PROPS."

Vaughn led us toward the rear of the lobby. As we pushed through the mob, Hank and I craned our necks and spotted black-velvet circus freak paintings hanging on the walls. There was "Black Goat Woman with Three Teats," "Opposably-Thumbed Bonobos," and "Armless Sad Clown Whose Suspenders Won't Stay Up."

We slipped backstage. A handheld spotlight, a roll of duct tape, a taxidermied yellow canary, a pogo stick, five feet of twine, a custom pair of bulletproof Kevlar underwear, and a four-foot pea shooter with twenty dried peas were lined up on a table for us.

"They're perfect," I said, stroking the canary.

"If you like those, get a load of this," said Vaughn. He parted the curtains an inch and we peeked out. An antique-wood circus podium with hand-carved scrollwork sat on the stage.

"Gorgeous, isn't it?" he slurred. "I bought it at auction for a small fortune. Built in nineteen twenty-three. It belonged to a sideshow master with an act called Hernia John and His Singing Truss. I must go touch it now. Break a leg." He downed some champagne, stepped out through the curtains to thunderous applause, and strutted to his podium to warm up the crowd.

Hank slipped the bag from Bill's head.

"Are you ready?" Hank asked.

Bill nodded that he was.

We hear circus music begin to play, then Vaughn ballies like a crackerjack showman: "STEP RIGHT UP AND SEE THE MAN WHO PO-GOS WITH A PEA SHOOTER AND A DUCT-TAPED LEG, THE BALLISTOPHOBIC BIRDMAN WITH A TWENTY-INCH WAIST IN KEVLAR UNDERPANTS, AND THE GYMNASTIC GENT PER-TURBED BY HIS INABILITY TO FLIP!"

I run out through the curtains with the spotlight, pogo stick, duct tape, pea shooter, and a mouthful of peas. I turn the spotlight on, lie down on the stage, contort until my left foot is folded behind me, duct tape it to my ass, stand up on my right leg, cram the shooter down my pants, grab the spotlight, climb up onto the pogo stick, and begin hopping up and down on my one free leg. The pogo stick clicks each time it hits the stage as I struggle to steady the spotlight.

Hank marches out wearing the Kevlar underwear and nothing else. He counts twenty paces, turns, faces me, pulls the dead canary out of his underwear, perches it on his head, pulls out the twine, ties it around his waist, and cinches it tight until his middle is only twenty inches around. A rope descends behind him from the rafters.

Still pogoing, I reach into my pants, fish out the shooter, pouch a few peas in my cheek, and pogo a one-eighty-degree turn until I'm facing Hank. I aim the shooter and spotlight at him. Hank sees me aiming and scrambles to hide behind the rope dangling from above. The rope is tied to a motorized wagon wheel up in the rafters. The wheel begins turning with a slow squeak. Hank grabs the rope. It drags him around the stage in a centrifugal arc. I keep the light on him as he picks up speed; Tarzan shadows flash across the theater's walls. I push a pea into the shooter with my tongue and fire. The pea ricochets off Hank's Kevlar ass with a dull ping. Hank likes it; he throws his head back and groans like a sex maniac.

The wagon wheel squeaks faster. Hank's flying just inches from the floor in a blur. I pogo as fast as I can. My spotlight bounces around in a drunken light-and-shadow play. I load and fire again. Hank takes another pea on the ass and groans—then the circus music stops.

The curtains part. I make a pogo-turn and aim the spotlight at the figure walking out. It's Bill. The audience recognizes him right away. People gasp. A hundred lips whisper his name. He walks to the foot of the stage and stops. He's gaunt and his acne's on fire and the bags under his eyes are dark, but his cellophane skirt glows like magic under the lights.

"I can't flip," he says earnestly in a screechy baby voice, pacing.

The audience laughs. What the hell? Is it really Bill?

"I can't flip," Bill repeats, wringing his hands.

The audience laughs again. It just can't be! Bill Kunstler? Here? Preposterous!

"I can't flip," Bill says again.

The audience cracks up. Writers scribble. Women slap their thighs. A circus midget in the front row sits transfixed.

"I can't flip," says Bill. "So I'll flip."

And he flips: a quick backward run and suddenly he's flying in a delightful arc, backward like an Olympic diver, cutting through air, high and long, head first, then neck, shoulders, then upside down and still going, hips passing over, then feet, finishing now, descending, then a crash as he lands squarely on Vaughn's podium, crushing it into a thousand splinters in a cloud of dust.

The audience remained silent. Ten seconds passed. People grew concerned; was Bill alive?

Suddenly, Bill popped up in the middle of the rubble, bowed, and said thank you. The audience erupted with a roar. Reporters threw notepads into the air. Cameras flashed. Vaughn cried silently in the corner. Hank and I joined Bill and bowed. The applause was deafening.

A reporter stood up on a chair. The crowd quieted so he could speak.

"WHAT'S YOUR PIECE CALLED?" he yelled, pointing his pen at Bill.

Bill looked at me, unsure. I gave him a nod.

Bill looked at the reporter, then said it: "I Can't Flip, Then Break the Podium."

The audience roared. Bill took another bow.

"How did you like that?" asked Hank over the applause.

"I put choreography in them like diamonds," said Bill.

People started running toward the stage—they were desperate to touch the circus freaks for themselves.

Hank and I grabbed Bill and disappeared behind the curtains.

* * *

I'm sitting on a barstool in my mother's bar.

Abe is behind the counter, digging with a shovel.

"What are you digging for?" I whisper.

"Your mother's buried here somewhere," says Abe.

I look down at my arm where Stark cut me. My bandage is gone and maggots are crawling on the wound.

I lean over the counter and watch Abe shovel. He digs through the hardwood floor, breaking through to dirt, and keeps digging. The hole grows deeper; it's starting to look like a grave.

"I found her!" Abe says, popping his head out of the hole. He smiles. He's wearing my mother's dentures. "Sha sha sha," he says with her big teeth. I fall on the floor, laughing.

"Don't tell your mother," says Abe, putting a finger to his lips to shush me.

I wait for the shush. When it finally comes, it's the rush of freeway traffic amplified a hundred times. The walls shake. Beer glasses shatter. The mirror behind the bar cracks. I cover my ears. It's deafening. I taste exhaust and soot. The lights overhead explode in a shower of sparks, plunging the bar into darkness as the shush goes on.

I opened my eyes. Cars and trucks rushed past my face. I raised my head an inch and saw I was lying in a gutter beside a half-empty bottle of whisky. The sun was up.

"I think I'm drunk," I slurred, sitting up. We were on Market Street. Traffic whipped past us. Hank was sitting on the curb with his eye on a newspaper stand across the street where a newsboy waited for his morning supply of papers to arrive.

"What's taking them so long?" asked Hank, chewing on a fingernail. "It's already six o'clock." He bit a piece of nail off, swallowed, washed it down with the whisky, then handed me the bottle. I took a gulp.

"How long have we been out here?" I asked.

"Since four."

I looked at my arm. Blood seeped through the bandage.

"What'd we do with Bill?" I asked.

"Put him back into the cage, then came down here to wait," said Hank. He blinked, then cupped his hands over his eyes.

"Your eyes again?" I asked.

"They itch," said Hank. He crawled over and showed me. "They've itched since the Balleta show. It comes and goes."

"I don't see anything," I said. "They look like they always look."

A newspaper truck pulled up across the street. The driver stepped out and handed the newsboy a fresh stack of papers.

"THEY'RE HERE!" Hank yelled. He jumped up, swayed, steadied himself, then took off in a dizzy run across the street, dodging bicycles and honking cars. Traffic swerved and screeched to a halt. Hank reached the stand, tackled the fresh stack, and scanned the headlines.

"WE MADE THE FRONT PAGE!" he screamed.

The newsboy held out his hand for payment.

Hank pointed at him. "THE KID WANTS A QUARTER!"

I rolled over, fished into my pockets, found a quarter, and threw it. Bad throw—the coin clinked and rolled into the street. I ran after it. Drivers hit the brakes. I stumbled, laughed, searched, cars honking, found it, crossed halfway toward Hank, spun, ran back for the whisky, more honking, drivers cursing, snagged the bottle, ran back, made it across, jammed the coin into the kid's sweaty hand, grabbed a newspaper, and opened it flat on the sidewalk so we could read:

REDSOFT CEO FLIPS, STOCKS JUMP

SAN FRANCISCO, CA—Redsoft shares rose in early trading Friday after reports that Bill Kunstler, the software giant's CEO, made his performance debut before a surprised audience at the city's Prance Prance gallery Thursday night.

"He did a backflip," said San Francisco art critic Jean Gateau. "I was in the front row. He came out, looked at us, said he couldn't flip, then flipped."

Ronald Berett, a technology sector analyst for Wilson & Barley, remained skeptical. "It couldn't have been Bill on that stage," Berett said. "Redsoft insiders have assured me that he's still away on sabbatical—probably at the company's manufacturing base in Europe. It seems unlikely he flew back to the US for a little flipping."

Still, Berett believes the antics could bode well for Redsoft.

"My phone's been ringing all night," he said. "The story's all over the wires. Investors certainly seem excited by the prospect of a CEO hip enough to let his hair down for a little performance art."

"WE'RE FAMOUS!" whooped Hank. We jumped and spun. Blood dripped off my arm onto the newspaper stack. The newsboy looked horrified. Hank pointed at the blood and yelled, "THAT'S FAMOUS BLOOD!"

The boy jumped out of the booth and took off running. Hank grabbed our paper and we stumbled into an alley, dancing and trailing blood all the way home.

* * *

Hank shimmied to the window with a handful of quarters and looked out. "I want more copies of our flip article," he said, jingling the coins, "and there's a full newspaper rack down there. I could run out, buy the whole stack, and come right back. The chance of running into Stark is pretty small, don't you think? If I ran?"

I was about to answer when movement in the cage caught my eye. I looked and saw Bill doodling furiously on himself with a pen.

"What are you drawing?" I asked.

Bill turned and showed us. His torso and limbs were covered by a black tattoo of his skeleton. There were a hundred bones drawn in painstaking detail: humeri, clavicles, scapulae, tibiae and fibulae, a sternum, ribs, phalanges, carpals, taluses, a pelvis, and more, as if he'd gained the power to render his flesh and organs invisible. It would have taken an osteopath days to draw with that precision, yet Bill had done it in an hour.

"We can see right into you," said Hank.

"And I can see right into you," said Bill with a blank look that gave me chills.

* * *

The phone rang. It was Vaughn.

"WHAT DID YOU DO?" Vaughn yelled in my ear.

"Hi, Vaughn, hey, we're sorry about your podium. We didn't know he would—"

"FORGET THE PODIUM! WHERE HAVE YOU BEEN HIDING HIM? HE WAS BRILLIANT! HE CAN SMASH ALL THE PODIUMS HE WANTS! I THOUGHT HE LOOKED FAMILIAR WHEN HE CAME OUT, BUT I HAD NO IDEA! IS IT REALLY HIM? NO WAIT, DON'T TELL ME—I DON'T WANT TO KNOW!"

Vaughn paused for air, then went on: "They want another performance! The critics are going crazy! TV stations! Reporters! They want your man! They're in love! They're begging! They're willing to pay! We'll make a bundle at the gate! Let's do it! Friday night! They'll eat it up!"

"Is that Vaughn?" Hank whispered.

"The critics are going crazy," I said. "They want another performance Friday night—and they'll pay."

Hank put his itchy eyes up to mine. "We're famous," he whispered.

"Should we do it?" I asked.

"What's the theme?"

"NOTHING!" came Vaughn's scream from the receiver.

We looked at the cage. Bill was busy performing. He stopped and looked at us.

"What do you think of Nothing?" Hank asked.

Bill blinked.

"Nothing," Hank repeated.

"Nil?" Bill asked.

"WE'LL DO IT!" I screamed into the phone.

Vaughn screamed and hung up.

Hank circled the room, jingling his quarters, then bolted for the front door. "I have to buy more papers or I'll go crazy!" he said, slamming the door shut behind him.

The phone rang again. It was Rudy calling from a payphone.

"I saw the morning newspaper—was this flipping thing you?" he asked.

"Maybe."

Rudy laughed. "Redsoft shares were up three points this morning. You should've seen Roman. I told him he should've bought some, but he didn't want to hear it."

"We have another gig Friday night."

"Really? I'll call my broker. Look, I'm sure you have this all under control, but I wanted to warn you: a detective showed up at Belly's cubicle yesterday."

"What? Why—"

"You know the phone line we patched through SI for your hack job?"

"Yes."

"Apparently, some prankster pretending to be Bill used it to join a Redsoft conference call and raised a real ruckus. You wouldn't know anything about that, would you?"

"Maybe," I said.

Rudy laughed. "I thought so. Well, Redsoft discovered the patch and they're out for blood. The detective asked Belly for a list of all employees named Hank or Larry."

So Stark had our names—or at least our first names.

Rudy went on: "The dick went crazy when Belly told him employee records were confidential—he dumped Belly's desk and punched out a programmer."

"Did Belly give him anything?"

"Like your address, you mean? Probably not, or the dick would be kicking down your door right now. But watch your backs."

Rudy hung up. I swallowed. Stark was getting closer.

The front door opened. I jumped. It was Hank.

"You scared me to death!" I said.

"Sorry," said Hank. He was holding a fresh stack of newspapers and a crumpled brown paper bag.

"What's in the bag?" I asked.

Hank reached in and pulled out a dead crow covered with lice. Most of its feathers were gone. Its bumpy skin looked like chicken.

"Not bad," I said. "Where'd you find it?"

"In the gutter right out front!" Hank sang, running for the kitchen to wash the bird.

The phone rang. I answered.

"Is this Hank or Larry?"

"Yes."

"Hello, I'm a reporter with the *Bayview Daily*. I'd like to interview you—"

I slammed the phone down and backed away. If a reporter could get our number, so could Stark.

Bill whimpered. I looked at the cage and saw him covering his ears with his hands and crying.

"What's wrong?" I asked.

"I think I'm going shamanic," he quivered.

I opened my mouth to offer advice, but a knock on the door made me jump. I looked through the peephole. It was Mouse.

"I hear you in there," she said. She was sweaty in jogging shorts, a T-shirt, and boxing hand wraps. She knocked again. "Come on, it's me."

I opened the door a foot, being careful not to flash the cage.

"It's him, isn't it?" she whispered, trying to peer inside.

"Who?"

"You know who. I read about it in the paper."

"I—"

"Oh my God, you really did it? You really kidnapped him?"

I held a finger to my lips.

"He's really in there?" she whispered, grabbing my shirt. "This is crazy! I thought you were joking."

Her eyes looked past me at the clothing on the walls and ceiling.

"Why are your clothes—"

"Soundproofing."

"*You* did that?"

"It was Hank's idea."

"Oh, man."

"It's necessary, believe me."

"This is crazy!" she whispered. "You are so going to jail! When he gets out—"

"No, no," I whispered. "He's not like you think he is. You should see his performances."

Mouse let out a snort, then saw I was serious. "How in the world did you get him up to your apartment?" she asked.

"In a sack."

"In a sack, of course, sure. You just walked up to Bill Kunstler, tossed him into a sack, and carried him home over your shoulder."

"We drove him."

Mouse's eyes narrowed, but Hank's face appeared at the door before she could interrogate me further.

"Mousey!" said Hank.

"Hi, Hank."

Hank held up his crow. "Look! I washed the lice off!" he said, dancing the bird around.

Mouse stared open-mouthed at the bird, then watched as Hank tucked it under his arm, pulled out his compact case, held the mirror up over his shoulder, looked to make sure the living room window was safe from intruders, returned the compact to his pocket, and danced his crow away.

"Is he all right?" asked Mouse.

"He's fine."

"He doesn't look fine. Clothing on the walls? A crow with lice?"

"He's really getting into birds—"

"I'M GOING SHAMANIC!" Bill screamed from somewhere behind the door.

Mouse looked at me. I looked at her.

"Who was that?" she asked.

"SHAMAN BOY WASHING OUT HIS BRAINS!" screamed Bill.

Mouse licked her lips, then looked down at my arm. She saw the bloody bandage. I moved the arm behind my back.

"So," I said, changing the subject, "your fight's next week!"

"That's why I came over," said Mouse, trying to focus. "I wanted to know if you'd ride with me. I'm going to be so nervous. You and Hank could be my cheering section."

"Of course! I wouldn't miss it."

"Will you drive me home if I get knocked out?"

"I'm sure you'll be the one doing the knocking."

Mouse stepped forward and put her face up to mine with a wry smile. "Good. All right. Well." She planted a peck on my nose. "You are so going to jail," she whispered, before boxing me in the gut and jogging off down the hall as Bill let out a blood-curdling scream.

55

HANK READ THE NEWSPAPER BESIDE me on the couch while I fast-forwarded through videos of Bill's performances.

"How about this one?" I asked. The video showed Bill applying lipstick, slowly at first, then faster and harder. The lipstick broke off in his teeth, and then he was eating it—biting off whole pieces with blood-red lips.

"What else do you have?" asked Hank.

I fast-forwarded the tape, then hit play. Bill climbed out of a plastic trash bag, stretched fifty rubber bands around the top of his head one by one until they formed a thick headband, forced his hand into a jar of honey, pulled out a glob, and drizzled it on his chest until he'd written a goopy HONEY HO in upside-down letters.

"That's perfect for Nothing," said Hank. "The crowd will love it. By the way, look at what I found." He handed me a newspaper ad featuring an obnoxious two-page headshot of Horace Lipschitz.

The ad said that Horace planned to give a free speech at Pier 32 where he'd detail his plans to open a new Invinciblesoft distribution center in Hawaii. He'd obviously chosen to make his announcement in San Francisco in order to steal some of Bill's limelight; Horace was smiling in the photo, but all the attention on his nemesis had to be boiling him raw.

Hank looked at the clock. "His speech begins in an hour," he said.

"Let's go have a look at him," I said.

Hank donned his wig disguise while I watched Bill put the finishing touches on a shaman's rattle he'd fashioned from a tin can, a chicken bone, and hair. He tied it to his ankle and walked around in a circle. The can clanked and rattled.

"What did you put in there to make it sound like that?" I asked.

"Fork tines," said Bill.

"Is that all?"

Bill pulled down his lower lip. Two of his teeth were missing, freshly pulled.

The sight of it made me dizzy.

"What's wrong?" Hank asked.

"I need air," I croaked.

* * *

Hank and I cut through alleys to San Francisco's piers. My legs felt shaky.

"You sick?" asked Hank.

"Nervous stomach," I said, wiping my mouth. I looked at Hank's foil hat glinting in the sun. "Did you have to wear that?"

"It's for our own protection," said Hank.

"But it calls attention to us. Stark's surely seen the newspapers by now. He'll be on the lookout for anything unusual."

"Do you think he'll show up at Prance Prance?" Hank asked.

I stopped in my tracks. Prance Prance was the first place Stark would go after reading the morning's paper—if he wasn't there already.

"We have to warn Vaughn," I said.

* * *

We found a payphone. I dialed Prance Prance. Vaughn answered.

"Larry! I was just thinking about you two," he said.

"Hank and I want to stop by with our prop list for the Nothing show," I said.

"Sure," said Vaughn, "come on by, but don't use the front entrance. Meet me in the alley behind the gallery instead."

"Why?"

"We have a little problem."

"What problem?"

"Come see for yourself."

* * *

Vaughn was pacing and smoking a cigarette in the alley behind Prance Prance when Hank and I arrived.

"Did anyone see you?" he asked, exhaling smoke.

"I don't think so," I said.

"Then take a look at this," said Vaughn. He led us past a dumpster to the mouth of the alley. Hank and I peeked around the corner at the gallery's entrance. A hundred people with sleeping bags and tents were camped out on the sidewalk under the hot sun.

"Who are they?" whispered Hank.

"Reporters . . . critics. . . . They're desperate for tickets," said Vaughn.

"So? Sell them tickets," I said.

"We're sold out," said Vaughn. "We sold every single seat—plus fifty more."

Hank and I looked at each other. We'd never oversold a show.

"Just look at them," Vaughn whispered, his eyes narrowing. "I had no idea there were so many critics in this city. Where do they come from? And camping—how rude!" He went on blathering and pacing like he was doomed.

Hank poked me in the ribs and pointed to a bus stop across the street. I looked and saw a man waiting for a bus. He was reading a newspaper. He turned a page and I caught a flash of his face.

Stark.

He was watching the gallery. He'd probably talked to the reporters camped out front, which meant by now he knew Bill would be performing at the Nothing show Friday. All he had to do was wait.

Vaughn continued smoking and pacing. "I've never seen this kind of demand," he said. "Everyone wants a seat. I don't know if I'll be able to handle the crowd. What if things get out of hand?"

"What you need is a little security," I offered.

"Security?" said Vaughn like he'd never heard the word before. Cigarette ashes fell unattended from his fag.

"Security guards to take tickets at the door and keep out the riff-raff," said Hank. "You know—bouncers. Bodyguards. Big, burly men."

"Big, burly men," Vaughn repeated, nodding.

"Sizable," I said.

"And everywhere," said Hank. "Your front door, back door, outside, backstage. . . ."

Vaughn nodded. "Now why didn't I think of that? Of course. I'll start calling around right now. Big, burly men. In the phonebook, you think?" he asked, snuffing out his cigarette. We watched him amble into the gallery to begin making calls.

"I hope the burly men are bigger than Stark," said Hank.

I hoped so too.

56

HANK AND I ARRIVED AT Pier 32. Two hundred investors, bankers, reporters, tourists, and Hawaiians waited in front of Horace's podium platform for the speech to start. Polynesian dancers in grass skirts undulated their tanned hips through the crowd and handed out free Invinciblesoft poi balls and ukuleles, while a tiki booth sold watered-down umbrella drinks off to the side.

Dressed in black slacks and a loud Hawaiian shirt, Horace marched up onto the platform at twelve o'clock sharp, punctual as always. He snorted hello with a grimace and clenched his fists in a show of power.

"He's a sadistic-looking fuck," said Hank.

"All he needs is leather chaps and a cattle-prod dildo," I said. Reporters standing nearby heard us and laughed.

Horace began speaking. "Hawaii's long cultural history and seminal strategic position in the Pacific. . . ."

Minutes ticked by. People shuffled around.

" . . . since World War Two . . . revenue stream potential. . . ."

Attention spans waned. The hot sun moved overhead.

". . . distributed supply-chain management . . . multi-tiered vertical models. . . ."

A line formed at the drinks booth. Hank wiped his brow. Flies buzzed in the air.

Horace wrapped up his talk. " . . . and that's why expanding to Hawaii, ladies and gentlemen, will finally give Invinciblesoft the winning leverage to push us ahead of the competition."

A few people clapped. Hank raised his hand. Horace called on him.

"When you say 'competition,'" said Hank, "are you referring to your personal nemesis, Bill?"

Reporters chuckled. Horace stiffened. "I don't consider Bill competition," he said. "I think it's obvious by now that anything Bill can do, I can do better."

"Really? Even performance art?" Hank taunted.

"Performance art? Why yes, I'd say I definitely have the upper hand there."

"I didn't know you did performance art," said Hank.

"I do," said Horace. "In fact, it just so happens that I prepared a little something to show you how it's really done!"

Horace jumps off the stage and runs to the clearing in front of the crowd. Assistants deposit performance props on the lawn in front of him while an oiled, four-hundred-pound Samoan in a grass skirt marches forward carrying a flaming torch.

Hawaiian rock music begins playing. Horace pumps his pelvis in and out like Elvis and counts down from five, then all hell breaks loose: he rips open his shirt, jumps into a barrel of slick mahi-mahi, climbs out, unzips his fly, pours a can of macadamia nuts down his pants, ignites his shoes with the torch, flicks his tongue in and out like a Polynesian warrior, pulls a live mackerel from a tank, bites the head off, yells something unintelligible about sushi, dabs each of his nipples with fish blood, spins in a dizzy circle, then thrusts out his chest just in time for the Samoan to smash him in the chest with a twelve-foot ceremonial oar.

Horace falls to the ground, squirming. The Samoan messed him up good. The audience is aghast—investors and Hawaiians shake their heads and walk away. Horace doesn't try to stop them. Hank and I shrug; the piece wasn't bad. We grab handfuls of macadamias in the chaos and head home.

The story made the news on TV that night. Horace was shown limping down a hospital corridor—he'd cracked three ribs.

Shares of Invinciblesoft stock would slip two points the next day.

* * *

Hank and I returned to the apartment to find Bill shaking in the corner of the cage. He looked pale.

"I swear I'm going shamanic," he said, shivering so hard his tin can rattled. Sweaty lines of skeleton tattoo ink ran down his arms. He turned his head, threw up in a jar, wiped his mouth, dug around in the props, found a dirty blanket, and wrapped himself up.

There was nothing Hank and I could do for him, so we sat down on the couch to watch as the sun set outside.

* * *

I opened my eyes. The apartment was dark except for the spotlight. Bill was asleep on his back in the cage. I could hear him breathing. Sometime during the night he'd undressed himself and pulled a paper bag over his head. His cellophane skirt dangled on a hanger above his naked body.

Suddenly, Bill's breathing stopped. I froze. He slowly raised his head and looked at me. He had no eyes—his paper-bag face was featureless . . . alien . . . devoid . . . a faceless Kachina doll capable of gnashing a man's soul to pieces. My heart pounded in my chest. I squeezed my eyes shut for protection and didn't make a sound. A minute passed, then I heard the paper bag crinkle. I opened my eyes. Bill had lowered his head back down. He fell back asleep while his skirt, turning slowly in a draft on the hanger above him, sparkled in the light.

* * *

I awoke on the couch. Bill was singing in the cage like a bird. He'd cut a hole for his mouth in the paper bag and was twittering with his lips raised up toward the spotlight. A strand of white string dangled from his mouth like a worm.

I sat up and looked for Hank. His rope nest was empty.

I stumbled through the dark to the bathroom. Hank was curled up beside the toilet with his sunglasses on.

"What are you doing?"

"My eyes hurt."

I sat down beside him. The floor was cold. Bill's twittering floated in from the living room.

"He's singing my spirit song," Hank whispered. A tear ran down his cheek.

"How do you know?"

"I just know," said Hank, trembling. "Will you stay here with me?"

I nodded and leaned my head against the wall.

* * *

The rattle of Bill's tin can shook me awake. I sat up. The bathroom light was bright. Hank was snoring on his back beside the toilet. I rolled onto my belly, slithered across the tiles to the doorway, and looked out.

The living room was still. The spotlight cast a hot glow over the cage in the dark.

Something moved near Hank's shrine.

I squinted into the black and saw Bill standing there in the shadows, bent over at the waist, naked except for his tin can. How had he escaped from the cage? He stared at me, wide-eyed.

"What are you doing?" I whispered.

Bill didn't seem to hear me. Was he sleepwalking? He shook his ankle. His tin can rattled, but the sound came from the cage across the room.

I looked at the cage. Bill was there, asleep on his side, naked and twitching under the spotlight with the paper bag over his head.

I looked back at the shrine. The figure in the shadows had vanished. Could Bill have been in two places at once? I rubbed my eyes and looked at the cage. Bill was still there, fast asleep.

It was said that gifted Tungus and Ojibway shamans were capable of bilocation, but only after years of apprenticeship and practice. I chuckled and crawled back into the bathroom. It was ridiculous to believe Bill had already mastered such a feat, even if he was gaining some shamanic skill. The doppelgänger I'd seen had only been a dream, or a trick of light and shadow, or maybe pareidolia, like spotting the Virgin Mary in a bowl of oatmeal.

* * *

"Larry," Hank whispered. "Wake up."

I sat up on the bathroom floor. Hank was wearing his sunglasses and holding a flashlight. I scrambled to my feet and he led me into the pitch-black living room.

"The spotlight's bulb burned out," said Hank. "And look at this."

He shined the flashlight on the cage. Bill was sprawled naked, face up, with the paper bag still over his head. His arms and legs were covered with hundreds of cuts.

Bill groaned.

"What happened?" I asked. "Why are you all cut up?"

Bill pulled his bag off. His face was smooth and white—the acne was gone and his eyes were larger than I remembered. He looked at us with a gaze that was plain and direct like an animal's.

"Birds came," he said. "They bit me and broke my bones." He held up his arm and showed us. The cuts looked like bird bites. "They washed my brain, then put me back together just like you said they would."

"Where are your glasses?"

"They put them in my feet so I can see better when I fly."

"In your feet?"

Bill raised his feet. They were wet with blood. He'd crushed up his eyeglasses and pushed the shards into his soles. They glittered like diamonds.

"You're a shaman," Hank whispered.

My armpits were soaked.

57

THE SUN ROSE, THEN SET. It was Friday night. Hank and I guided Bill through the alleys toward Prance Prance. He wore his paper bag and insisted on walking barefoot so he could adjust to his new magic feet; fresh skin was already growing over the slivers.

We ducked into the alley behind the gallery. A burly goon in a black T-shirt guarded the theater's backstage door.

"Who are you?" he asked, nostrils flared.

"We're the talent," said Hank.

"You don't look like talent," said the muscle man. He put his face up to Bill's bagged head. "Where's your backstage pass?"

Bill babbled something under the bag, bent down, and spat tenderly on the bouncer's shoe.

"WELL, AREN'T YOU A SICK LITTLE NUT!" the burly man growled, clenching his fists.

Vaughn emerged from the theater door. "Down, Clarence," he cooed, squeezing the big man's bicep. Clarence looked down at the ground and mumbled an apology.

"Sorry about Clarence," said Vaughn as he led us backstage. "He's a little nervous; the theater's absolutely packed. We're making a killing. At forty dollars a head—"

Hank and I stopped walking. "You charged forty bucks?" I asked.

"Of course!" said Vaughn, clapping his hands. "We could've charged a hundred!"

Hank and I looked at each other. We'd never paid more than ten for a show, ever. Forty was unheard of.

"We'll have to perform all night to give them their money's worth!" said Hank.

"No, no," said Vaughn, smoothing out Bill's cellophane, "you don't understand: you're stars now. THEY pay YOU. Don't worry—I warned them the show's about nothing and not to expect much, just a couple of short performances and that's all. A little goes a long way. You three could burp in a tin can and toss it into the crowd, and reporters would trample their own children to get their hands on it." Vaughn took a step back and looked at Bill's getup. "You know, most performers wouldn't dare wear the same skirt two performances in a row, but kudos to you for bucking the trend. Oh—and your rattle is fabulous."

"He made it himself," said Hank.

"It looks like he did," said Vaughn with a wink as he stepped out on stage to warm up the audience.

Hank readied our props while I peeked out through the curtains. Vaughn was right—the theater had never been more crowded. All four hundred seats were taken, plus another fifty critics squatted in the aisles.

"How's it look?" Hank whispered.

"Vaughn oversold it all right," I said. "We should ask him for a raise."

"Any sign of Stark?"

"There are too many people—he could be anywhere," I said, shutting the curtains. "We'll just have to be careful."

I turned and saw Bill performing for himself with his paper bag still on. He'd taped a black housefly to each of his fingers and was twiddling them as if playing a trumpet. I slid the bag from his head, but he was too engrossed in his trumpeting to notice.

Hank and I listened as Vaughn brought the audience to a boil.

"Ready?" Hank whispered.

I nodded.

"AND NOW," Vaughn boomed, "HERE'S A LITTLE NOTH-ING!"

Hank and I walk out carrying suitcases. We march to the foot of the stage, open our cases flat, and strip down to our underwear. As we pull our shirts off, the audience sees we're each wearing a leather chest harness with a slack rope tied to its back. The two ropes trail behind us across the floor to a parting in the curtains, where they disappear somewhere in the dark backstage.

Hank pulls goggles out of his underwear, straps them on, and steps into his suitcase. I do the same. We smile. Our cases are roomy and comfortable.

Suddenly, our ropes go taut. Hank and I jerk backward out of our suitcases, fly twenty feet through the air, and disappear through the parting with a crash. The audience laughs. Flashbulbs pop.

I come sprinting out through the curtains, aim for my suitcase, leap, fly, and land in a crouch like I'm trying to pack myself in, but the fit's all wrong—I'm square on all fours and the suitcase is rectangular. I pick myself up and adjust my goggles, then my rope goes taut, jerking me backward again through the curtains.

Hank comes sprinting out. He aims for his case, jumps, flies, and lands on all doggy fours, but like me, he doesn't fit. He stands back up, smiling, nose bloody—then a jerk and he flies backward into the dark.

I bust through the curtains and leap, this time aiming in midair for a rectangular shape, but no cigar—I crash into my case on bony elbows as Hank sprints out behind me. He leaps and flies, but he's the wrong shape too. He crashes. The audience laughs. Hank and I just aren't fitting.

Maybe it's a lube problem. We reach into our cases, pull out jars of honey, unscrew the lids, and hold the jars high. Amber goodness drizzles down our hair, faces, and chests until we're globbed. I write HONEY on my chest, Hank writes HO on his, then the ropes go taut—we jerk, fly, crash, and run out again flinging honey globlets willy-nilly as we leap and fly. I tuck tight and land first, but it's not tight enough; my shins bang on the floor as Hank crashes chin-first into his luggage with his knees hanging out.

We jump up, pull out jars of lard, slather on the fat, then taut rope, jerk, crash, and we bust out again, sprinting. Hank's ahead of me; he leaps, flies, rotates in the air, tucks, and lands in his case perfectly, but my greasy feet slip; I crash and slide, then a taut rope and a jerk and I fly backward through the curtains.

I step out on stage with determination and a can of motor oil. The audience laughs. I dump the can over my head. Oil runs down me and puddles on the floor. There's a jerk and a crash, then I'm sprinting out with black tar slopping off my thighs like arterial spray, faster than before, beating the floor like a bushman. I leap, fly, rotate, tuck, and crash into my case perfectly.

Bill walks out on stage. His cellophane skirt shines under the lights. The audience applauds madly.

A microphone descends from the rafters and stops just above him. Bill bows his head and begins running his fingers through his hair. Sand falls out. It's pretty in the light. The microphone picks up the rustling of his mane and the ticks of grain hitting the floor. The crowd sits in awe. The novelty of Bill's presence and the enormity of his fame double the meaning of anything he does.

The audience sees Bill's lips are moving and realizes he's speaking in a low voice. People strain to hear as the microphone picks him up: "One . . . zero . . . one . . . one . . . zero . . . one. . . ."

Critics murmur and quickly figure it out: the ones and zeroes are binary code, the native tongue of computers. Reporters write the numbers down and discover a pattern. The string of ones and zeroes is repeating—it's some kind of message!

A critic with a calculator converts the binary to English letters, then jumps up and yells it out: "NUMBERS DO LIE!"

People whisper. Numbers do lie, numbers do lie—what does it mean? Pens move on paper. Critics work the letters: numbers . . . do . . . lie. . . . The whole audience murmurs. . . .

"I THINK IT'S AN ANAGRAM!" a critic yells. "IT'S IN CODE! AND THE CODE IS. . . ." He quickly rearranges the letters. "EMBED SOUR NIL!"

"WHAT THE HELL DOES THAT MEAN?" another critic roars. The audience tries to figure it out. Embed . . . sour . . . nil. Interpretations run rampant, then a man in the front row stands and announces his: "EMBED SOUR NIL: WE MUST ALWAYS IMBUE THE COLD, MUTUAL EXCLUSIVITY OF ONES AND ZEROS WITH THE TRANSCENDENT FLAVORS OF HUMAN EXPERIENCE!"

The audience laughs at his exuberance, but likes it. Pens scribble. Letters are rearranged again.

"BLEED IS MR. UNO!" someone calls out.

A young critic interprets it: "EVEN A CEO AT THE TOP FEELS PAIN!"

Skeptics familiar with Bill's cut-throat business tactics shake their heads; they aren't sure Bill feels pain, ever.

The letters are rearranged again. "BED LONER I SUM!" someone cries. The audience murmurs.

"IT COULD MEAN HE'S AN EXISTENTIALIST!" yells a lady.

"OR THAT HIS BILLIONS HAVE COME AT THE EXPENSE OF HIS INTIMACY!" hollers a man in back.

"OR MAYBE HE JUST LIKES TO CUM ON HIS OWN!" bellows another.

The crowd laughs. The letters move once more.

"MUSE BLED IRON!" suggests a man from the side.

"THAT'S EASY," announces a critic from the middle of the crowd. She stands up on her chair. "THE BLEEDING MUSE IS A DIALECTI-CAL SYMBOL: THOUGH STRONG LIKE IRON, BECAUSE MEN-STRUATION IS FERROUS, SHE IS PERSONIFICATION HELD CAPTIVE FOR HER PRODUCTION OF IDEAS. THE MALE IMAGINATION DEMANDS SHE PERIOD-ICALLY BLEED FOR HIM. IMPRISONED AND SEXUALIZED BY HIM, SHE SUPPLIES EROTICALLY CHARGED INSPIRATION IN THE NOUMENAL REALM TO BE TRANSMOGRIFIED INTO THE 'IRON' OF HIS CREATIVE WORKS IN THE PHYSICAL WORLD, WHERE HE SEEKS TO PERPETUATE HER SENSUALITY FOR HIS CON-TINUING PLEASURE. A MALE MANUFACTURER OF HEAVY MACHINERY, FOR EXAMPLE, CASTS HIS IRON FIGURATIVELY AND LITERALLY BY PERPETUATING HER SEX IN THE FORM OF CARS, BOATS, TANKS, AND OTHER 'GENDERED METAL' FE-TISH OBJECTS OF HIS DESIRE."

The critic is brilliant. All the men in the audience want her.

"HOWEVER," the critic concludes, "THE PERFORMER'S USE OF THE PAST-TENSE 'BLED' INSTEAD OF 'BLEEDS' BREAKS THE CYCLE: IF THE MUSE LIVES IN HIS MIND AND SHE NO LONGER BLEEDS—I.E., SHE BLED, BUT HAS SINCE BECOME BARREN—THEN IT'S REALLY HIS IMAGINATION THAT NO LONGER BEARS FRUIT; HIS IMPOTENCE SERVES TO CRI-TIQUE MAN'S OBJECTIFICATION OF WOMAN IN THE POST-INDUSTRIAL AGE!"

Bill bowed and said thank you. The crowd launched into thunder-ous applause. Critics screamed and stomped their feet. Reporters hugged each other in tears. Hank and I let Bill have his moment, then we rose from our cases and joined him. We all bowed. Bouquets sailed through the air. Tears stung our faces while the clapping went on.

Interviewers rushed the stage. A lanky woman with a platinum bob, black eyeglasses, sharp elbows, and big teeth reached us first. She wore a short skirt despite her middle management legs, and said hello out of the side of her mouth with a presumptuous New York accent she employed at every opportunity to remind people she was from Manhattan. Her pointy nose and beady blue eyes behind black intelligentsia frames said that if she was rude, it was because she was from New York, and if she was kind, it was because she was feeling exceedingly magnanimous.

"I'm Deidre Stein from New York," she whined, shoving reporters out of the way and handing me her business card. "I'm a performance artist like you . . . well, I haven't actually done any performances yet." She laughed. "But I plan to do one soon. I'd love to interview the three of you on my TV show."

Hank and I smiled and said yes, absolutely. A TV show! We were famous—no doubt about it.

"Wonderful," said Deidre. "The studio address is on the card. Let's make it Thursday. My assistant, Beth, will meet you in the lobby just before six."

As Deidre turned and marched away, the mob of reporters folded into the space where she'd been, crushing against the stage and yelling for interviews with Bill. We grabbed him and darted through the curtains before things got out of hand.

"WE'RE GOING TO BE ON TV!" I squealed.

"Do you think Stark will see it?" asked Hank.

"Probably," I said. "But here's an idea: let's have Bill pretend he's not Bill. It'll confuse the hell out of everyone and maybe throw Stark off the scent."

Hank laughed and nodded as we opened the door leading to the main gallery. We looked out. Critics chatted as they filed out the gallery's front door—then something odd: a man pushing toward us through the crowd like a salmon swimming upstream.

Stark.

Hank shut the door quietly, I grabbed Bill, and we hurried out the rear.

58

I TELEPHONED MOUSE IN THE morning.

"WE'RE GOING TO BE ON TV!" I yelled.

"When?"

"Thursday, and you have to come. I need you for a demonstration."

"I'd love to be on TV!" squealed Mouse. "What show is it?"

"Her name's Deidre Stein—"

"Oh, I've seen her. Watch out—she's tricky. And she's not fond of men. Will Bill be there?"

"Sure! You can meet him."

"I can't wait!" squealed Mouse.

I gave her the TV studio's address and we hung up.

* * *

The next morning Hank and I donned our wigs and sunglasses and sneaked out for a newspaper. The sidewalks bustled with delivery men making their rounds and junkies in search of scores. Hank and I blended into the throng and headed for the newspaper rack on the corner.

I looked over and saw Hank walking herky-jerky with his arms out in front of him.

"What are you doing?"

Hank laughed. "I don't know. I can't focus my eyes—it's hard to walk in a straight line."

"Are they still itchy?"

"Everything's blurry. I think I'm seeing double."

"You'll be fine. You're probably just hung over."

We hurried to the newspaper rack. Hank took out a quarter and aimed it at the machine's coin slot, but missed by an inch. He tried again, but missed. His eyes were having trouble.

"Where's the slot?" he muttered. He crouched down, concentrated, found the slot, pushed the quarter in, and pulled out a paper. "This is going to be good," he said, opening it up. He tried to read the front page, but couldn't. He held it out at arm's length, but that didn't help either. "You do it," he said.

I grabbed the paper and found our headline right away: "'CEO UNVEILS NEW PERFORMANCE ART!'" I yelled. Hank screamed with delight.

I read as fast as I could: "'The Nothing audience thrilled to Kunstler's titillating translucent skirt, zany anagrams, and real-time binary collaboration with critics while WILD DYNAMOS HANK AND LARRY from San Francisco's Tenderloin scene beat themselves up trying to land perfect jumps into a pair of suitcases with delightfully compulsive repetition . . . bodies at terrible risk . . . bloodied knees and elbows . . . and though the cases seemed a somewhat heavy-handed symbol of modern life's transitory nature, the performers' hyperkinetic rally against obsessive adherence to arbitrary norms that are based on nothing was as beautiful as it was harsh.'"

We danced and sang. Hookers came over and joined us.

"LOOK AT THEM!" Hank screamed, pointing at the hookers.

"THEY LOVE US! WE'RE POSITIVELY INFECTIOUS!"

The hookers frowned; they didn't like the sound of that.

We started back toward the apartment. Hank weaved left and right across the sidewalk with his arms out.

"Be careful," I said.

"I will," he said, before walking into a tree. "I didn't see that coming," he laughed. He took off his glasses and blinked. His eyes were crossed.

"Stop that," I said.

"Stop what?"

"Stop crossing your eyes."

Hank ran to a storefront window, saw his reflection, and gasped.

"You're not doing that on purpose?" I asked.

"Of course not! Holy shit—"

I started laughing. I felt bad, but I couldn't help myself.

"Do you think audiences will like it?" he asked, modeling his eyes in the window.

"Are you kidding? THEY'LL LOVE IT!" I yelled.

59

HANK AND I HEARD A knock. I looked through the peephole and saw Rudy puffing on his pipe. I opened the door.

"You three are all over the papers," he said. "How the hell are you lying low?"

"Disguises and luck," I said. "What brings you around?"

"I needed air. The bomb shelter is driving me crazy," he said, exhaling cherry smoke rings. "How are you and Hank doing? How's Bill?"

"He went shamanic."

"No!"

"Yes!"

"Incredible! I studied a little anthropology in college, but I've never seen a shaman up close. May I see him?"

I let Rudy in and closed the door.

"Hi, Rudy," said Hank.

Rudy smiled, nodded hello, exhaled smoke, and tried to figure out which of Hank's crossed eyes to address—then he noticed the bandage on my arm.

"What's that?" Rudy asked.

"Knife fight," I said, unwinding the bandage to show him. The bandage pulled off gooey and the blood was still wet.

"That looks infected . . ." said Rudy, his voice trailing off. Something in the cage had caught his attention. I looked and saw Bill crushing beer cans with his bare feet.

"He's working on a new piece," I explained.

Bill stomped down on a can with his heel so hard the whole cage rocked. He babbled something unintelligible, spat on the floor, then gave his ankle rattle a shake.

"I'm no expert," said Rudy, "but the way he's talking to himself and the cage—how it shakes—reminds me of shaking tent ceremonies used for spirit contact by shamans of the Innu tribes along the Québec-Labrador peninsula. I'm impressed. He's very skilled. Who taught him?"

"He taught himself."

"Some shamans are like that—intuitive. You should get him to heal your arm."

"You think he could?"

"Sure—he's a shaman. Hello? Bill?"

Bill stopped performing and looked at Rudy.

"Sorry to interrupt you," said Rudy, "but Larry's arm is infected." Rudy held up my arm. Bill looked at it. "Will you fix it?" asked Rudy. "I'll trade with you—here, take my pipe as an offering."

Rudy slid his pipe through the chain-link. Bill took it.

"Every shaman should have a pipe," said Rudy.

Bill sniffed the pipe, then gave it a tentative puff. Sweet cherry smoke rose in the air. Bill nodded; it was a fair trade. He began circling the cage. His ankle rattle clanked. His lips moved. He talked to himself in a low voice and felt the air with his hands.

"He's going into a trance!" whispered Rudy.

Bill circled around to the toilet, lifted the tank's lid off, reached in, scooped out a handful of thick brown mold, wrapped it in a dirty dust rag, dropped the package on the floor, flattened it with his slivered feet, then passed it through the chain-link to Rudy along with a pair of shoelaces.

Bill shook his rattle while Rudy tied the fetid pack to my arm with the laces. The pack gushed brown water and stank like shit.

"It's a poultice," said Rudy, "from the Latin *pultis*, meaning 'porridge.' It's very shamanic. You're going to feel great!"

60

HANK AND I HUSTLED BILL through a maze of alleys. Deidre Stein's national talk show was broadcast live from a TV studio in North Beach, a neighborhood popular with tourists where San Francisco's Italian and red-light districts intermingled in a surreal embrace of sin and marinara—especially in the alleys. Dumpsters overflowed with congealed restaurant pasta, strippers stood around smoking cigarettes on break, drunks stumbled out of gambling dens to buy dessert from short Sicilians manning gelato carts, thick cuts of prosciutto crudo bobbed overhead beside socks and underwear on laundry lines slung between tenements. . . . Hank zigzagged under the meat with his arms extended out in front of him so he wouldn't collide with anyone while I brought up the rear. Bill whispered new performance texts to himself the whole way over.

Deidre's assistant Beth was waiting for us in the studio lobby.

"You're on in five minutes," she said curtly in a New York accent as she led us backstage. "You want hair and makeup?"

"Do you think it'll do any good?" I asked.

Beth pursed her lips, shook her head sourly, and walked off.

Mouse arrived, kissed me hello, then greeted Hank.

"What happened to your eyes?" she asked.

"I was double-crossed," said Hank, smiling.

Mouse laughed, then asked about my poultice. I held it up so she could smell it. She wrinkled her nose.

"It smells like mold," she said.

"It is," I said proudly. "Bill made it."

Mouse smiled at Bill. "It's a thrill to meet you," she said, extending her hand. Bill was still talking to himself, but he managed to put out his palm. Mouse took his hand and shook it.

Hank and I peered out. A studio audience sat waiting in stadium seats. The floor of the brightly lit stage glowed a deep Prussian blue. Five armchairs were arranged in a semicircle around a coffee table. A pink neon DEIDRE sign buzzed overhead. Down in front, in the dark between the stage and the crowd, TV cameras on wheeled tripods waltzed mutely across the floor like ghosts.

The show's theme song began to play—Deidre was on the air. She jogged out on stage in black stretch pants, a purple turtleneck, and red boots. The audience cheered.

Beth ran over to us. "Three minutes!" she whispered, holding up three fingers.

Deidre bows, greets the crowd, tells a few jokes, then walks to a chair and sits. She talks about performance art, plays a short video clip of famous performances, then invites us out.

"Ready?" I whisper.

"Performance time," Hank replies.

Mouse, Hank, Bill, and I walk out on stage. The audience applauds. Bill's ankle rattle shakes and clanks as we cross the set to our seats. The crowd laughs.

"Welcome to the show!" says Deidre. "As I said earlier, our guests tonight are Hank and Larry—two longtime performance artists of San

Francisco's infamous Tenderloin district—and of course Bill, a recent addi-
tion to the troupe whose face I'm sure you all recognize."

Somebody in the audience yells Bill's name. Hank and I smirk.

"And who are you?" Deidre asks, turning to Mouse.

"Their bodyguard," says Mouse.

The audience laughs. Deidre offers Mouse a nod hello, then turns
to the camera. "As you all know by now, I'm something of a performance
artist too, so this is especially exciting for me," says Deidre. "If you've seen
any performances by these gentlemen, you know how potently primal their
work is—and how minimal—which are two aesthetics I try to achieve in my
own work."

Deidre turns to Bill. "So, Bill. Do you have a last name?"

"I used to," says Bill quietly, "but I can't recall it."

"Right," Deidre says with a wink. "Tell us: where did you perform
before joining the troupe? In galleries, theaters, or—"

"In a cage."

"A cage?"

"Yes."

"What sort of cage?"

"Chain-link."

"Did you enjoy that?"

"Not always. Performing barefoot in there can be uncomfortable,
but on the other hand, not having an audience lets me perform pieces as fast
as I want."

"What do you do when you're not performing?"

"I stay busy getting brainwashed and tortured."

"What? That sounds terrible!"

"Repetition of the absurd is transformative. Keep it up long enough
and eventually you thin out until your bones begin to show." He stretches
out his arms to show her his skeleton tattoos.

"Your bones . . . I see . . . so you're turning inside out?"

"Or they are," Bill says, looking at us. Something in his eye makes me nervous.

Deidre turns to me. "Larry, where do you get all of your ideas?"

"From my muses."

"Muses?"

"She's one," I say, pointing at Mouse.

"She's your muse?"

"Yes."

"Really? How does she inspire you?"

Mouse jumps up and knocks me out of my chair with a punch across my face. I get up. My nose is bleeding. The crowd gasps. I laugh and sit back down in my chair.

"I . . . see," says Deidre, "but you said muses—plural. You have others besides her?"

"Him," says Hank, pointing at Bill.

Deidre turns to Bill. "So you're the one who pulls ideas out of the air?"

"Oh, all of us are mildly psychic," says Bill.

"So you're not the idea man?"

"They are." Bill points to me and Hank.

"Really? Only them? Not you?"

"I don't have ideas. I'm a performance machine, an automatic. Every few minutes, a piece just comes out. *Res ipsa loquitur*—the thing speaks for itself."

"Really? So if I asked you to make a performance right now, you—"

Bill sprints to her, jerks her up to standing, rips her chair's arm off, whips a little grease from the bottom of his foot, wipes it across her upper lip, and shoves the chair arm down her stretch pants. He bows to the audience, says thank you, and sits back down.

Deidre blinks. "That was certainly fast," she says, disheveled. "What would you call a piece like that?"

"Alice B. Toklas's Mustache, Then Stein's Arm Down Her Pants,"
says Bill.

The audience laughs. Deidre forces a smile, sits, and tries to retake
command.

"So you . . . you're obviously a performance art savant. I can't believe
how quickly you. . . . Now, look. Bill. Let's be real. Aren't you really the famous 'Bill' we all think you are? Level with us."

"No."

"But you look just like him."

"Maybe I'm his baby."

Everyone laughs.

"There's a rumor that Bill's wife is dating other men. Do you know
if that might be true?"

"That sounds like performance art," says Bill calmly, "but it isn't. It
could be, maybe, if she washed her brain, but I doubt she has."

"That's . . . ahem, yes. Changing topics now: as a budding performance artist, I'm always looking for more exposure. So, let me ask: have you
ever thought about expanding your show? I mean, it's tremendous, performing
for almost nothing at little galleries like you do, but there's so much more out
there. There's Vegas . . . you could add some variety acts . . . maybe circus . . .
dance . . . ."

None of us answer. Deidre's pressing her luck. She turns to Hank.

"Hank, does your group have a manifesto?"

"No," says Hank. "We're constantly chewing through our own con-
ventions."

"Really? No set rules? You don't have an aesthetic?"

"Anesthetic? Well, we drink plenty—"

The audience laughs. Deidre grimaces.

"No," she says, "*an* aesthetic—an art aesthetic."

"Oh yes, we have that," says Hank.

"For example?"

Hank leans forward and spits on the floor.

"Interesting. Was that literal or—"

"That's up to you," I say.

Hank and I rise to leave.

"How is it up to me?" Deidre asks.

Hank puts his cross-eyed face up to hers and chews in the air in front of her eyes.

The audience doesn't know what to make of it, but people laugh and stand and applaud anyway as we grab Bill and exit stage right.

* * *

Hank and I kicked open the apartment door and danced into the living room with a case of wine. We ushered Bill into the cage, uncorked a pair of bottles, and guzzled.

"WE WERE ON TV!" Hank screamed, rebounding off the chain-link while I twirled, fell, and swigged.

"I THINK BILLY NEEDS A DRINK!" I sang.

Hank giggled, grabbed a fresh bottle, and passed it through the chain-link. Bill crawled over to the bottle, sniffed it, pushed the cork in with his thumb, looked inside, said hello to whatever spirits might be in there, then poured the wine into the toilet to see what would happen. The toilet bit cracked Hank up—he hollered and danced, blind as a bat, then pratfalled over the back of the couch. "WE'RE UNBEATABLE!" he hollered, holding up his bottle to show he was still in one piece.

The phone rang. I crawled to it.

"Hello?"

"Hallo, this is Favio. I saw you on the TV—"

"OH MY GOD, IT'S FAVIO!" I yelled to Hank.

"SCREW YOURSELF!" Hank screamed toward the phone.

"Oh, I will," said Favio. "You and Billy Bill come perform for me and I'll screw anything you like—"

I laughed and slammed the phone down. Hank and I danced and drank some more.

The phone rang. I answered.

"Hello, this is Barry Evans with the Western Talent Agency in Hollywood. Is Bill there? I'd like to talk about a possible movie deal—"

"IT'S A TALENT AGENT!" I howled with glee.

Hank ran over to me, giggling, grabbed the phone, and slammed it down. We drank and jumped up and down on the couch.

The phone rang. I answered. It was Vaughn.

"I SAW YOU ON TV!" he screamed. "IT WAS TREMENDOUS! THE PHONES WON'T STOP! THEY ALL WANT YOU! BROAD-WAY PRODUCERS! NEWS MAGAZINES! SPERM BANKS! THEY WANT TO KNOW WHERE YOU FOUND BILL! THEY WANT TO KNOW WHY HANK'S EYES ARE CROSSED! THEY WANT TO KNOW WHAT THAT WET THING WAS ON YOUR ARM! ARE YOU HEARING ME? I CAN BOOK YOU SOLID! WE COULD CHARGE A HUNDRED AND FIFTY PER SEAT OR MORE! THE CRITICS ARE WET AND READY TO PAY! I WANT TO HOST A TWO-NIGHT GALA EVENT JUST FOR THEM! CRITICS AND REPORTERS ONLY! I'M CALLING IT *THE VERBOSE CRITIC*! WILL YOU DO IT? SAY YES! WE'VE GOTTA RIDE WHILE THE STALLION'S IN HEAT!"

"When?" I asked.

"WE COULD START TOMORROW NIGHT!"

"Vaughn might have a two-night gig called The Verbose Critic," I said to Hank. "Are you interested? It's a gala."

"A gala," Hank cooed with dreamy eyes.

"Do we have enough material?"

Hank held up a sheaf of performance art ideas we'd copied down from our videos of Bill. It looked like plenty.

"What about you?" I asked Bill. "Any new material?"

Bill gave his empty wine bottle a lick, then jammed a baby toe into its opening.

"We'll do it!" I said into the phone.

"GOOD," yelled Vaughn, "BECAUSE I ALREADY SOLD ALL OF THE TICKETS!"

I laughed and hung up.

61

THE SUN WENT DOWN. HANK and I drank and danced on the furniture while Bill performed nonstop in the cage.

"You should take a break once in a while," I said.

Bill ignored me and went on performing.

Solveig banged on our door. I opened it a crack.

"WALKING BY, I HEAR RACKET!" she yelled. "YOU ARE TOO LOUD!"

I slapped a fresh bottle of wine in her hand and slammed the door in her face. I looked through the peephole and saw her padding away down the hall in her slippers, happy as a clam.

Hank and I drank and danced some more.

"What time is it?" I slurred.

Hank checked the clock. "Four a.m."

"The gala's tonight!"

"TO THE GALA!" roared Hank, toasting the air.

I rattled the cage. "Are you excited, Bill?"

"No," said Bill.

"Of course not," said Hank. "You've probably been to a thousand galas—the rich and famous have galas all the time. But you mustn't think of those now because performance art galas are entirely different. This'll be your first gala as a shaman! You must be a little excited. . . ."

Bill shook his head.

"Come on," said Hank. "You're a star!"

Bill shook his head again.

"What does that mean?" I asked. "Do you need more time to pre-pare?"

"No," said Bill.

Hank's smile fell. "What's wrong? Are you sick?"

"The audience slows me down."

"You don't have to wait for them. Just do your piece."

"I'm faster alone."

"Then use that—pretend you're alone when you come out on stage. Do your piece as fast as you want tonight."

"I won't be there," said Bill plainly.

"Sure you will," I said, trying to control my voice.

Bill shook his head. "I don't need a stage anymore."

"You have to go," said Hank, his voice cracking.

Bill shook his head.

"You're going," I said.

Bill rolled his eyes back into his head and opened his mouth.

"DON'T YOU IGNORE US," boomed Hank.

Bill sniffed the air, picked up a bell he'd made from coins and a dirty sock, and shook it. It jingled. He shook it like a divining rod, circling around the cage until he came to the toilet. He lifted the lid, knelt, and looked in. The pot was filled with shit. Bill whispered something to it, then waited for a response.

"It's spatilomancy!" I whispered to Hank. "He's telling the future with his own droppings!"

Bill shook his bell. He was in a trance. He stared deeply into the shit. The shit stared deeply into him. "The white suit man is looking for you," Bill said. "He knows about tonight's performance."

"Shit," said Hank.

The word startled Bill. He turned, slowly training his animal gaze on Hank's forehead. Hank swallowed, backed away, found his tinfoil hat, and put it on.

Bill's eyes narrowed. "You need more birds," he commanded.

"I've been getting into them," said Hank.

"Get into them more."

Hank ran to his rope nest, grabbed his flea-bitten crow, lifted his shirt, and tied the bird to his naked chest with twine.

"Now will you perform?" Hank asked.

Bill shook his head—the answer was no.

Hank paced the room. "What are we going to do?" he whispered. "We can't perform without him!"

"Maybe we can," I said. "We could do our piece, then his."

Hank thought about it. "You really think that would work?"

"It's a great gimmick! We do our piece, then we perform Bill's piece as Bill—we'll BECOME Bill—we'll BE Bill—I'll be half of him and you be half!"

We looked at the cage just in time to see Bill put his hand into the toilet.

"You can be that half," said Hank.

* * *

Hank and I lay sprawled on the couch under a mountain of videotapes and performance notes.

"Are there any more tapes?" I asked, nursing a wine bottle.

Hank sifted through the pile. "No. We watched them all."

"How long until the show?"

Hank looked at the clock. "Thirteen hours. And get that thing away from me," he said, pointing at my poultice. I lifted my arm and saw the bandage had left a green stain on the couch.

I let my head loll against my chest. "Put together some material for us."

"Like what?"

"Anything. The Verbose Critic—what does that mean to you? They'll love whatever it is. Just throw it together. A couple of pieces."

"You do it."

"I'm too drunk."

Hank laughed. He grabbed a random page of notes and threw it at me. "There's the first piece," he said, then he grabbed a second page and threw it. "And there's the second. One for us and one for us as Bill."

"That's pretty random," I slurred.

"They'll love it," said Hank.

I read one of the pages. "You think Vaughn will be able to find these props in time? Shit, this is a lot of material; it's not very minimal."

"We'll tell them Bill's branching out," said Hank. "We'll say minimalism's dead; everyone knows there's way too much of it."

"To maximalism!" I sloshed, toasting the air.

* * *

Dusk fell.

"How much did we drink?" asked Hank.

"Five bottles," I said. "There's only one left. We'll have to pick up more after the show."

We cracked open our last bottle, poured over our performance notes, practiced a few moves, donned our wig disguises, and set off for Prance Prance. The alleys were dark. Hank wore his foil hat and, heeding Bill's spatilomancy, used his compact mirror to watch behind us for signs of Stark. We ducked into the alley behind the gallery. Clarence was dressed in a tuxedo.

"You look fancy," I said.

Clarence blushed. "Good luck tonight," he said, ushering us through the theater's backstage door.

Prance Prance stagehands ran around frantically. Hank and I removed our wigs and sunglasses and saw our performance costumes had been laid out on a table. An assistant ran up to us, slipped beers into our hands, and ran off. So far the gala was first class all the way.

We peeked through the curtains. The theater was bursting at the seams. All the seats were taken. The aisles were crammed. Critics and reporters chatted in evening gowns and bowties. I saw a flower in every buttonhole. Ladies fanned their faces and men daubed their foreheads. Blue cigar smoke wafted in the air. Waiters weaved champagne through the crowd. It might as well have been the opera.

"Hello, my little cash cows!" Vaughn sang, swooping down on us. He was wearing a red velvet suit. He saw Hank's crossed eyes and laughed. "You should really see yourself," he joked. Then he sniffed the air. "What is that stink?"

"My poultice," I said, holding up my arm.

"I see. Well, make sure the audience gets a whiff; they'll want to get their money's worth!" he guffawed, pulling a flask out of his coat. He took a hit, then leaned in close. "I still can't believe you called me at dawn with that crazy prop list. You must be nuts. Look at my crew running around! They're ready to kill you!"

"Did you get everything?" I asked.

"Of course. Your costumes and props are ready, and we managed to find the special item you requested," he said, walking us across the stage to a large mass covered by a bed sheet. Flies buzzed in the air over it.

"It smells worse than my arm," I said.

"I had it trucked in from Fresno," said Vaughn. "It's a little old. I hope it'll do."

Hank peeked under the sheet. "Oh, it's perfect," he said.

"Good," said Vaughn. "The lighting is set, the cameraman and sound are ready, and the audience is primed." He looked around. "So . . . where's Bill?"

"He couldn't make it," I said.

"What?"

"He's sick," said Hank.

"I don't understand. What are you saying?"

"He's not here," I said. "But don't worry—we're going to do his piece as him."

"WHAT ARE YOU SAYING TO ME RIGHT NOW?" Vaughn yelled.

"They'll love it," I said.

"WHAT ARE YOU TALKING ABOUT?"

"He's really sick," said Hank.

"THEY ALL THINK BILL WILL BE PERFORMING!"

"I know—"

"HE'S THE MAIN DRAW!"

"We're the draw," said Hank. He lifted his shirt and showed Vaughn his crow. "THIS is the draw. Not Bill. Us."

Vaughn looked at Hank like he was nuts, then turned to me like I was the more rational one.

"Look," he said in a low voice, "I wasn't going to tell you this, not with all the excitement, but critics have been calling me all day. They saw your performance on the Deidre Stein show and they're boiling. They're saying you disrespected one of their own."

"One of their own? She's a two-bit talk show host."

"But she's also a critic," said Vaughn. "I'm just telling you. They didn't like Hank chewing in her face."

"That was brilliant!" I said.

"I'm just passing along what they said," said Vaughn. "I hope I'm wrong, but some of the critics tonight might not be as 'amicable' as you might like." He looked at his watch. "Please. Clarence has a car. Let's go see Bill. Let me talk him—"

"Impossible," I said. "He's out of commission."

"What about for tomorrow's show?"

"I doubt it."

Vaughn shut his eyes and clenched his jaw. He stood like that for a while, then pressed his flask to his forehead. "White light," he whispered. "White light, white light, white light." He counted to ten, put the flask to his lips, drained it, wiped his mouth, then gave Hank's shoulder a pat. "Forget what I said," he said. "I was just nervous. By God, if anyone can beat them, you can, right? Screw amicable! You're Hank and Larry!" He put away his flask, wiped his forehead, then backed away from us. *"MERDE!"* he called as he disappeared into a flock of scurrying assistants. *"MERDE!"*

"Isn't 'merde' French for shit?" I asked, remembering Bill's spatilomancy.

"I think it is," said Hank.

"French shit's the best kind," said one of Vaughn's assistants in passing.

Hank and I readied our props, then took our positions near the curtains as Vaughn whipped the audience into a frenzy.

"WELCOME TO PRANCE PRANCE!" yelled Vaughn as the crowd roared and applauded. "TONIGHT WE'RE FEATURING TWO FABULOUS FULL-LENGTH PIECES PRESENTED ONE BEFORE THE OTHER, OR IF YOU'RE LUCKY, ONE AFTER THE NEXT."

"Are you ready?" I whispered.

Hank nodded. "Should we give them the kind or evil version?"

"Definitely evil," I said. "For those 'not-so-amicable' ones."

"LADIES AND GENTLEMEN," Vaughn boomed, "WITH-

OUT FURTHER ADO, HERE THEY ARE, OUR VERY OWN PER-
FORMANCE ART VIRTUOSOS, LIVE HERE TONIGHT, GROW-
ING MORE FAMOUS BY THE DAY, I GIVE YOU: THE VERBOSE
CRITIC!"

The curtains rise. The audience screams and applauds as Hank begins pushing a red couch onto the stage. He's barefoot and wearing white underwear and a short Japanese kimono that lets his crow hang out the bottom.

"I LOVED YOUR PERFORMANCE! ADORED IT! STUN-
NINGLY BEAUTIFUL! DELICIOUSLY MOVING!" Hank shouts like
a smarmy East Coast critic. He smiles gaily, licks his armpit, and pushes the
couch forward another few feet. "I ATE IT! GOBBLED IT UP! A VERI-
TABLE FEAST! EVERYONE SHOULD SEE IT! REALLY SANK
MY TEETH IN! PICKED THE BONES RAW! SHUCKED AND
SUCKED IT! PALATABLE TO THE END, AND MAYBE EVEN
THEN SOME!"

The critics stare at his crossed eyes.

"OH, DON'T LOOK SO WORRIED," he assures them. "I'M
NOT LOOKING AT YOU."

The crowd laughs.

The couch reaches center-stage. Hank stops pushing and sits down.
The couch's wooden legs creak. A bucket, an electric drill, and a pile of
screws sit beside him. He lifts the bucket high with a flourish and dumps
it. Greasy eggrolls spill out onto the floor. A man with a video camera runs
onto the stage and zooms in on an eggroll. The close-up appears on a video
screen hanging from the rafters; the eggroll looks five feet tall.

Hank whips a spatula out of his kimono and scrapes up the roll. He
bites off half, takes up a screw, picks up the drill, and screws the uneaten half
of the eggroll to the couch's cushion. The camera zooms in to show it. The
audience chuckles.

Hank's fingers move into view on the video screen, caressing the
roll, feeling the grease. "YOUR PERFORMANCE WAS BRILLIANT!"

Hank screams to the eggroll, his neck veins popping. "SEARINGLY BRIGHT! AN ECLIPSE OF PURE, RADIANT JOY! HELEN KELLER WOULD'VE BLINKED! SIZZLING MOLTEN DAZZLE! HOT LAVA ON MY FACE! ICARUS FRYING IN A BUCKET OF WINGS!"

Hank grabs the screwed eggroll and pulls. The screw inches out of the couch's fabric with a sickening rip, then snags on the cushion's stuffing. He pulls harder. Six inches of fluffy white cotton stream out of the hole like a lamb's umbilicus. He holds up the whole greasy mess up for the camera, then gingerly sets it on the head of the spatula. He raises the spatula up, pulls the head back like a slingshot, and fires. The ammo skids ten feet across the stage, leaving a greasy trail.

I run out on stage in cowboy boots and my underwear, slide on my ass across the floor, reach under the couch, fish out a spray bottle and a scrub brush, scramble on all fours to the eggroll, toss it into my mouth, chew, spit out the screw with a clink, then swallow the rest. The roll's greasy trail on the stage floor shines under the spotlights. I spritz it with the spray bottle and get to scrubbing with the brush while the cameraman hurries in for a close-up.

"MAY I HAVE YOUR AUTOGRAPH?" I yell. "WILL YOU SIGN THIS? WILL YOU SIGN THAT? WILL YOU SIGN MY WIFE'S ASS? THAT'S REALLY YOUR SIGNATURE? NOBODY WILL BE-LIEVE IT. I CAN'T READ IT. THE INK'S TOO FAINT."

Hank picks up another eggroll, bites off a piece, screws the remain-der into the couch like before, pulls it out with a trail of stuffing, and spatula-flips it across the stage. It flies and skids to a stop. I toss the spray bottle and brush aside, scramble to the couch, reach under, pull out a new spray bottle and brush, sprint to the new eggroll, drop it into my mouth, spit out the screw, chew the eggroll and fuzz, and get to scrubbing the grease on the floor.

"YOUR PERFORMANCE WAS SO INTENSE!" I scream with eggroll in my mouth. "SO TIGHTLY WOUND! SO DENSELY COILED! SO WELL PACKED! SO TENSELY TAUT! TENDONS IN A STRAIGHTJACKET!"

Hank bites, screws, and flips another roll. I fish out a new bottle and brush and get busy cleaning. He flips another. I grab a new bottle and brush and scrub. He flips another. The floor's littered with brushes and spray bottles. Cleaning fluid vapor hangs in the air. Hank picks up the pace even more as I eat and spit and spritz and fish out new cleaning supplies as fast as I can. "YOUR PERFORMANCE WAS ELECTRIFYING!" I scream. "VOLTAIC! HAIR-RAISING! BLOW-DRYER IN THE BATHTUB!"

I slide around. The floor's soaked. My boots are greasy. I slip and fall on my ass; this just won't do. I throw down the bottle and brush, slide a small hacksaw out of my underwear, and go to work on two of the couch's legs, sawing off the front left one and then the rear right one so the couch conks down cock-eyed. I borrow Hank's drill, screw the legs to the bottoms of my boots like stilts, and clop around like a Texas hooker.

Hank cocks the spatula with his tongue hanging out and really lets one fly. It sails into the audience and plops into a woman's lap. She gasps. Her dress has a grease stain. I grab three new brushes and a spray bottle, jam them into my underwear, and scan the crowd. The woman is three rows back. I climb down from the stage with the cameraman in tow, scramble up onto a man's chair, step over his head to the chair behind him, and stilt down the row until I reach her. I give her lap a spritz. She covers her mouth to keep from choking on the cleaning fumes.

Hank fires another long shot. It lands on a man's coat, row six, seat thirteen. I clop over to it, my stilts shooting out at critics' eyes and teeth. I find the roll and spritz. I look at the stage. Hank is running out of rolls.

He flicks another. The eggroll sails, lands. I clop to it and spritz. He sends another one, faster this time. I go for it, stilts shooting out in all directions, find it, spritz. Another roll sails, lands. I clamber over to it and spray. Cleaning fluid mist floats in the air. The audience laughs, fighting for oxygen.

There's one eggroll left. Hank scoops it up, smiles at the crowd, waves the drill around like a drunk, and nonchalantly sinks a screw into the roll. The audience gasps. Hank looks down and sees he's accidentally screwed his hand to the couch. He giggles and puts the drill in reverse, drops the roll onto the spatula, and lets it rip. It sails over the crowd and lands on a lady's hat.

I wobble knock-kneed toward the lady, screaming, "WHAT DID YOUR PERFORMANCE MEAN? TELL ME! I HAVE TO KNOW! TELL ME WHAT YOU MEAN! I MEAN IT!"

I reach the woman. The cameraman zooms in. A bit of Hank's blood is on her hat. I spritz it.

"SAY SOMETHING FAMOUS!" Hank yells, jumping up and down on the couch, sweat flying. "GIMME AN EPITAPH! AN EPI-GRAM! SAY SOMETHING EPIC—ANYTHING! LET'S TALK! LET'S CHAT! JUST BETWEEN US! YOUR FANS WANT TO KNOW. MAY I HUG YOU? LET'S HANG OUT! I'LL BUY YOU A DRINK! ARE YOUR BREASTS REAL?"

"HOLD ME," I beg like a starlet.

"MOLD YOU?" Hank beams.

"LIKE A TUMOR," I sob.

"LIKE A GROWTH?" Hank cries in horror.

"LIKE A CYST," I hiss, stretching out on a row of critics' laps like a diva on a piano.

"A BUMP?" screams Hank.

"A LUMP," I say, squeezing a critic's crotch.

"LIKE A CORN?" says Hank.

"AN EAR," I reply, giving the woman's hat another spritz. The camera zooms in. The blood stain is still there.

"IS IT PIERCED?" asks Hank.

"A NEEDLE," I say.

"A PIN?" screams Hank, tap-dancing on the couch.

"A STICKER," I say, and I clop across the theater, grab a red fire extinguisher from the wall, and stilt back toward the lady.

"YOU MEAN A PRICK?" Hank trills.

"YOU STICK," I reply.

"I STAB?" asks Hank.

"MUR-DER!" I scream, squeezing the extinguisher's trigger. Thick, wet, white fire retardant sprays out, gushing the hat, the lady, and everyone in a fifteen-foot radius. Critics yelp and jump out of their seats as the lights fade. Pandemonium reigns. The theater's pitch black. People yell and climb around on the chairs in the dark.

The lights come up. Hank and I are back on the stage. We take a long bow. The extinguished audience is a white, sticky mess—people wring their hands and pick curdled retardant off their clothes while the others stand and offer polite applause like they're at the ballet. Hank and I take another bow, then disappear behind the curtains.

The backstage crew applauded. Hank laughed and gunned his drill in the air like a maniac.

Vaughn stumbled toward us, reeking of bourbon.

"You didn't tell me your piece was going to be so . . . verbose," he whispered.

"Does verbose worry you?" I asked.

"I can't believe the critics put up with it."

"You think maybe we should've emptied two fire extinguishers?"

Vaughn grimaced at the thought of it. "You're not worried? You don't think they'll turn on you when they realize Bill's not coming out?"

I smiled. Vaughn's lips quivered; he realized Hank and I had prepared for that eventuality. Vaughn closed his eyes, whispered something about white light, and took another hit of his flask.

Our second piece begins. The stage lights dim. A mariachi band begins playing on the floor beside the stage. The audience jumps up with a roar and applause—everybody is ready for Bill. Critics whistle and holler. Photographers ready their cameras.

Hank and I step out through the curtains wearing sombreros, white underwear, and our cowboy boots.

Hank is clutching the end of a rope that trails off somewhere backstage through the parting in the curtains. He walks forward. As he walks, the rope goes taut behind him; it's caught on something. He turns around and pulls. The rope doesn't budge. He pulls harder. His boots slip and slide on the floor. Whatever's anchoring the rope backstage is heavy.

I walk to the foot of the stage, reach into my underwear, and pull out a reporter's tape recorder. The mariachis stop playing. I aim the recorder at the audience, click the record button, and wait for someone to say something interesting.

The critics watch me. Thirty seconds pass.

"WHERE'S BILL?" a critic yells from the back of the theater.

The audience laughs. Everyone is obviously thinking the same thing.

"I'M BILL," says Hank.

The audience laughs.

"COME ON," moans the critic in back.

"I'M BILL," I say.

The audience laughs again.

"WHERE IS HE?" yells a woman in front. I get her on the tape.

Hank: "I'M BILL!"

"IS HE HERE OR NOT?" the woman roars.

Me: "I'M BILL!"

Hank: "I'M BILL!"

And so it goes . . . Hank and I say it, back and forth, him, then me, then him. The mariachi band strikes up as Hank and I pick up the pace: "I'M BILL I'M BILL I'M BILL." The words start running together. The critics scan the stage. Is this all some kind of build-up? When is Bill coming out? Is he even in the theater?

Hank and I speed up: "IMBILLIMBILLIMBILL." Then we stop. The mariachis strike up. I do a little solo Mexican hat dance. Stomping to the music, I slide a bottle out of my underwear and hold it up. It's full of gold tequila and twenty dead worms. The audience gasps. I uncork the bottle with my teeth, guzzle until I get a worm, tuck the bottle back into my underwear, remove the worm from my mouth, and drag it across my bare chest, animating it. Tequila and worm juice seep down my belly into my underwear.

"REVIEWS ARE WRITTEN ON PAPER," I hiss in Spanish as I slide the worm around. An English translation appears on the video screen overhead. "PAPER COMES FROM TREES. TREES ARE MADE OF WOOD. SPANISH REVIEWS, SPANISH WOOD. VERBOSE CRITICS, VERBOSE WOOD. I THINK YOU'RE STARTING TO GET THE PICTURE: THERE'S A WHOLE LOT OF WOOD GOING ON."

I let go of the worm. It sticks to my chest.

Without warning, Hank and I launch into "I'M BILL" again, screeching it, screaming it, "IMBILLIMBILL," picking it up even more, our voices high-pitched and squealing, "UMBLAUMBLAUMBLA," veins popping, Hank pulling on the rope like crazy, "LUMBALUMBALUMBA." All of the lights come up. The crowd squints. Spotlights, flashlights, and houselights shine on the stage in holy glory. The audience claps. Bill is sure to emerge at any second. Hank and I keep it up, lips moving as quickly as they can, faces turning blue, spit flying; "LUMBERLUMBERLUMBER" we scream, until, unannounced, a two-by-four falls from the rafters overhead.

The audience watches it fall. It's yellow and reflecting light like lumber from Heaven. It passes through different angles—vertical, a forty-five, horizontal—then crashes to the floor with a crack that makes the whole house jump. A reporter's camera goes airborne, a shocked writer's specs bobble off his face, champagne glasses tumble. The two-by-four bounces once, then rests. It's a miracle nobody was killed. The crowd looks annoyed, but everyone claps—with Bill sure to emerge any minute, everyone is determined to brave everything we have in store with a smile.

I take another swig of the tequila, suck out a worm, and animate it like the last one while the dust settles and Hank keeps pulling on his rope.

Another two-by-four falls. The band strikes up as the wood hits the stage. I take another tequila hit. Another two-by-four falls. Then another. The wood keeps coming. I keep drinking.

The applause dies down. Reporters look at each other. Where's Bill?

More two-by-fours fall—one, two, three at a time. I take out the tape recorder, aim it at the audience, and wait for the next critic's mouth.

Hank keeps pulling the rope. He's making progress. Whatever he's pulling onto the stage is massive, but still behind the curtains. He sweats and curses in Spanish with a terrible accent. I crack up.

"NOBODY KNOWS WHAT THE HELL YOU'RE SAYING," I laugh.

"NEITHER DO I," he says in Spanish. An English translation appears on the screen.

"WHERE IS BILL?" a man in the crowd booms. I get him on tape.

"I'M BILL," I tell him.

"I'M BILL," Hank says, pulling harder on the rope. Something on the other end of the rope starts to slide through the curtains into view. It's big. Very big.

Me: "I'M BILL!"

Hank: "I'M BILL!" And so it goes again: "I'M BILL I'M BILL I'M BILL." The words start to run together. The audience is restless. People scratch their heads. A reporter flips us off. More two-by-fours fall. Hank's really pulling on the rope now, digging in with his heels. He wins a foot, then two.

We pick up the pace. "IMBILLAIMBILLAIMBILLA." We relax our lips. The vowels grow deeper, looser. We speed up even more. The audience realizes that Bill is not coming out. A critic takes off his bowtie. A photographer lowers his camera.

"THIS IS A SWINDLE!" yells a reporter up front.

We ignore him and keep the pace going so fast we can hardly breathe, but we push it even faster: "ABULLABULLABULLABULLA...."

Hank gives the rope a final tug and a bull slides out through the curtains on its side, ass-first. It looks terrible . . . dead of old age . . . gray and gristled . . . legs sticking straight out from rigor mortis. The rope's tied to its tail and flies buzz and land on its black anus.

Hank keeps pulling the rope. The bull slides toward center-stage and the band strikes up while I do the sultry hat-and-tequila-worm dance all over again.

"THIS IS HORSESHIT!" a woman shouts.

"IMPOSSIBLE, LADY!" yells Hank. "IT'S A BULL!"

Hank and the bull reach mid-stage. Hank drops the rope, walks to the bull, reaches under its spine with both hands, and tries to lift the beast up onto its legs. It doesn't work—the bull's too heavy. There are piles of two-by-fours all over the stage. Dodging falling wood, I run to a pile, push it over to the bull, grab a two-by-four, and use the pile as a fulcrum to jack the beast up.

"WITH ENOUGH WOOD, THE BULL STANDS UP!" Hank announces in Spanish.

The mariachis keep playing. The two-by-four is still in my hands. I take a few steps back, then make a run at the bull like a pole vaulter. I plant the board into the wood pile and vault over the animal, land on my feet, and bow. Hank applauds. I drag him back to the starting point, put the two-by-four into his hands, and give him a push. He takes off running and lowers the pole in preparation for the vault, but his crossed eyes misjudge the target and he doesn't lower the wood far enough; it sinks straight into the bull's gut with a dry pop. Dust rises. Hank lets go of the pole. The wood sticks, impaled in the bull's ribs. Reporters groan and throw down their notepads. Hank responds with a Mexican hat dance.

I run to the bull's tail, untie Hank's rope, circle it around the bull's torso, then throw the loose end up into the rafters. A stagehand catches it, wraps it around the theater's wagon wheel, and pushes a button. The wheel begins turning with a squeak. The rope goes taut and starts lifting the bull into the air. The rope creaks. I rewind the tape recorder, press play, and shove it up the bull's ass. The critics' voices play out of the butt as the animal rises.

Hank grabs a two-by-four and swings at the bull like a baseball bat-ter under a piñata. He misses by a mile. I crack up. His crossed eyes make him a terrible hit.

The bull inches up little by little: six inches . . . twelve inches. The two-by-four is still impaled in its side and sticking straight out.

I walk to the front of the bull, light a cigar, and set it in the bull's mouth so it looks like it's taking a drag. I give the bull's forehead a hard push. The animal swings out toward the audience ass-first, then back toward the curtains. I step aside to avoid the horns as the beast swings past. The bull's cigar embers glow. It swings back out over the audience, then returns. Smoke trails in the air.

Hank bats the air with the wood, misses the bull, tries again, and connects with a meaty thump. Critics wince. The bull bobbles on the rope, but continues swinging—out, then in. The band plays on. Hank dances around, swings his two-by-four again, and connects.

The bull swings toward me. When it reaches the end of its arc, I remove the cigar from its mouth and take a puff. The bull swings out over the audience, then back to me. I whip out my bottle and pour tequila into the bull's mouth before it heads back out toward the audience. It swings out, then back. I put the cigar in its mouth and give its forehead another push. The beast is really swinging now, ass-first out over the crowd, then back over the stage, then back out. Tequila dribbles from its lips. The cigar burns bright orange. The tape recorder is still playing. The critics' voices come and go with every pass of the bull's ass.

The flywheel keeps turning. The bull is four feet up and still rising. I toss the tequila bottle to Hank. He takes a hit, shuts his eyes, runs, jumps, catches the bull's rear, and pulls himself up onto the animal's back. He's fac-ing the audience like a cowboy riding backwards. The bull's tail sways with each swing. Hank looks down at the crowd and his jaw tightens when he sees how high up he is.

There's a whoosh. Hank looks over his shoulder and screams—the bull's head is on fire.

"RIDE IT!" I scream in Spanish as more two-by-fours fall. "RIDE THE BULL!" I grab wood and take a swing at the animal.

A reporter throws his champagne glass at the stage in disgust. The glass hits and explodes in a shower of slivers. Another glass flies from the crowd and smashes, then another. Glasses whistle through the air.

Black smoke billows from the bull's head. Some joker pulls the theater's fire alarm. All of the critics are yelling.

A champagne glass flies and explodes against Hank's chest. He looks down and sees broken glass glinting on his stomach. He picks up a shard. It's sharp and shiny under the spotlights. He looks down at the crowd and sees the bull has risen higher. He swallows and clutches the rope tight.

"CLIMB DOWN!" I bellow.

"I CAN'T!" he cries.

"HACK IT DOWN BEFORE IT GETS ANY HIGHER!" I yell. For an acrophobe, falling ten feet is worse than rising to twelve. Hank starts sawing on the rope with the glass shard.

"HE'S SAWING THE ROPE!" a woman screams. Critics seated under the bull's swing trajectory look up, see what Hank's doing, and scramble en masse over the chairs to the safety of the theater's side aisles.

The bull keeps swinging. It rises another foot toward the rafters. It's fifteen feet off the stage. The nose and ears are ablaze. Orange flames lick a fire sprinkler in the rafters and set it off. Water gushes out. Critics yell and raise their notepads like umbrellas while the mariachis play on and the fire alarm clangs away.

Hank saws faster. It's only a matter of time. The smoke's heavy. Reporters choke and hack. The mariachis speed up. The rope creaks. Hank saws as fast as he can. His shard's a blur. Rope strands fray. The band speeds up even more. I go wild with the wood, batting the air, smashing the stage, the curtains, until, just as the bull is at full extension ass-first over the crowd, the rope snaps.

Critics part like gazelles as Hank and the bull sail through the air and descend, down over the first row, passing over row two, then row three—on final approach, Captain. The impact sends Hank crashing into the fourth row. He lands on his back, unharmed. He sits up. The smoke's thick. The sprinkler's gushing. The bull's lying across a row of seats with its head still burning and the tape still playing out of its ass.

"FIRE!" I scream.

I leap from the stage with a pair of two-by-fours, climb over the seats to Hank and the bull, and hand Hank a plank. We jump onto the bull and get to beating out the fire with full overhead swings. Charred head meat flies. Somebody kills the fire alarm. The mariachis pick up the pace. A stage-hand shuts off the sprinkler. The tape recorder reaches the end of the tape and clicks off. The mariachis build to a crescendo. We drop the two-by-fours and do a final hat dance on top of the bull. We're exhausted and covered in soot. The band strikes a big finish with a final bass note and it's over.

We bow and say thank you.

The theater was quiet. The sprinkler dripped. We eyed the audience. Half the crowd was soaked. Photographers glowered. A reporter set her jaw. Nobody said a word. Hank and I sensed a turning.

"Should we do it again?" I asked in Spanish.

The crowd rushed us. Hank and I jumped over chairs, climbed onto the stage, and darted through the curtains, leaving the bull behind as sculpture.

"THEY'LL KILL YOU!" screamed Vaughn. "GET OUT, GET OUT! TAKE THE BACK DOOR!"

Clarence held the backstage door open for us as we sprinted to the prop table, threw on our wigs, and raced out into the alley. The theater door slammed shut behind us and we slowed to catch our breath.

"You think they liked it?" Hank asked, huffing.

Before I could answer, the backstage door opened and Stark stepped out. I grabbed Hank's shirt and pulled him backward toward the sidewalk.

Stark shut the stage door and slowly started toward us. His hair was disheveled, he hadn't shaved, and there were dark circles under his eyes.

"I have to admit the performances were interesting," he said. "But you seemed to have trouble connecting with the crowd."

"How'd you get in?" I asked. "It was a press-only show."

"I'm with the *Stark Daily News*," said Stark, holding up a forged press pass. "I read in the paper that you've been doing minimalist pieces lately, but tonight's work didn't seem minimalist at all. In fact, it seemed a little . . . overwrought. It was missing something. Maybe you should've brought your friend along. I was disappointed he didn't perform. Wasn't he on TV recently?"

The backstage door opened and Clarence came walking out holding trash bags. He nodded hello, carried the bags past us to the curb, and set them down for collection.

"Everything all right out here?" he asked.

"Everything's swell," said Stark.

"I wasn't asking you," said Clarence. He stepped between us and Stark.

"Take your dandy pecs back inside," growled Stark. His hand inched toward his gun pocket.

Clarence crouched into a fighter's stance, whipped a six-inch collapsible steel baton out of his waistband, and waited. Stark eyed the weapon. Six inches didn't look like much. Clarence flicked a button on the baton and twelve more inches of skull-cracking steel snapped out with a click. Stark slowly lowered his gun hand.

I grabbed Hank and pulled him away quickly down the sidewalk.

"WHAT'LL HAPPEN TO REDSOFT'S STOCK WHEN THE TRUTH COMES OUT?" yelled Stark after us. "WHERE WILL THAT LEAVE ALL OF ITS INVESTORS? OR THE EMPLOYEES? OR HIS WIFE?"

Hank and I found an alley and took off running.

62

HANK LEANED AGAINST THE CAGE and took a swig of wine. "You missed a good night," he said, pressing his face against the chain-link to watch Bill pour rice into a pair of underwear.

Bill didn't respond. He stood up, mumbled some performance text, and slid the underwear up his legs. Rice poured from the crotch.

"It was a great turnout," said Hank. "The critics were dressed to the nines—you should've seen them."

Bill still didn't respond.

Hank leaned in closer. "I wore the bird," he whispered, lifting up his shirt to show the crow was still tied to his chest.

Bill spun in circles. Rice sprayed out in spiral orbits around him.

Hank took another swallow from the bottle, then trudged over to the couch and flopped down beside me. The chain-link had left indentations on his forehead.

* * *

I awoke on the couch. It was morning. Wine bottles littered the floor. Hank was sitting beside me.

"Did you sleep?" I asked, noting the bags under his eyes.

"Too hung over," he rasped.

I left the apartment and bought a newspaper from the rack down on the corner. Our performance had made the front page: "PERFORMANCE ART AUDIENCE SUFFERS RETARDANT AND BULL."

"How bad is it?" asked Hank when I returned.

"It's not good."

"How not?"

"Very not."

Hank grabbed the paper, skimmed to the meat, and read aloud: "'The evening proved a disappointing departure from the trio's recent work . . . a shocking, disjointed assemblage of half-baked performance art mini-bites undone by shameless tantrums, bleeding, and flying eggrolls . . . reminiscent of a one-bull Pamplona where victims are trampled under hoof without having to leave their seats . . . highly recommended if drenching your finery in rusty sprinkler water sounds like a good time . . . spectators were treated for retardant and smoke inhalation, thanks to stunts that blurred the line between reckless endangerment and attempted murder . . . the only show in town where the featured performer is absent, and afterward, the gallery's owner hands out coupons for free dry cleaning. . . .'"

"They shredded us!" Hank cried.

"We can't perform those pieces again, ever," I said.

Hank's eyes welled up. He looked around the room and started breathing hard.

"Don't panic," I said. "We'll come up with new material—"

"By tonight?" Hank gasped. He rose and paced the room, then went to the cage. Bill was performing with a porno magazine and a black plastic garbage bag.

"Bill," said Hank, his lips dry. "Please—we're in a bind."

Bill shook his head.

"Please," Hank whispered. "Just a small piece—a little performance—it would only take a minute."

Bill dropped the porno mag into the plastic bag and shook it.

"Please?" Hank cried.

"I can't," said Bill.

Hank blinked. "Why not?"

"I'm too fast now."

"I'm sure the critics could follow you," said Hank. "They see fast performances all the time—"

Bill jumped into the bag, stomped around to rustle the plastic, pulled out the magazine, tore out a page, read random text from it fast like an auctioneer, shoved it into his mouth, chewed and swallowed, tore out another page, read it, crumpled and ate, then again, page after page, running them together like surreal porno poetry until he'd eaten them all. He bowed and said thank you.

He'd finished the whole piece in minutes. I tried to analyze it, but my mind failed. It was like I'd just awakened from a dream about hungry auctioneers having sex with poets on plastic sheets and . . . and . . . Bill was right: his speed made him hard to critique.

The phone rang. I answered. It was Vaughn.

"How's Bill?"

"Still sick. It might be terminal."

Vaughn sighed. "I think we should cancel tonight's show," he said.

"That's crazy! You saw last night's crowd! The response was tremendous until the end. We overwhelmed them, that's all."

"What about the man who threatened you?"

"What man?"

"The man on the sidewalk. Clarence told me."

"He's just a crazy fan. He follows us around and pretends to be a paparazzo—"

"I don't want that element around the gallery."

"He's harmless."

"Clarence didn't think so."

"Forget about him. Tonight'll be a hit—you'll see."

"You know it's mostly the same crowd—the same critics—the same reporters. They'll be there in case Bill shows up. You know that, right?"

"Sure—"

"Which means you can't do the same material you did last night. They'll kill you if you try."

"We couldn't possibly. Hank's out of eggrolls and the bull's burnt."

"I'm not joking," said Vaughn. "Don't even think of dragging out a bull again—or any other animal, for that matter."

"No bull," I said. "It'll be all new material. They'll love it—standing ovations from start to finish."

Vaughn sighed. "All right," he said. "Be there early in case there are problems."

"White light," I told him.

63

HANK AND I SAT ON THE couch and tried to come up with a new performance.

I looked at the clock. "We only have two hours left."

"What do we have so far?" Hank asked.

I picked up a notepad and read aloud:

1. Build a brick outhouse on stage with a big toilet inside.
2. Put a critic in the toilet.

It was terrible. I threw the notepad on the floor.

Hank shut his eyes and let his head fall back. "Two hours," he whispered. "Two hours . . . two me . . . two you. . . ." His voice became light. He was drifting off. I let my head fall back and did the same.

I see my mother Marilyn tap-dancing on a glitzy Vegas stage. It isn't the young Marilyn of her early casino days, but the old Marilyn—the Marilyn with the frizzy hair and the nicotine-stained fingers who tended bar. A cigarette dangles from her lips as she taps and flaps like a hoofer until a cymbal crashes and she strikes a cock-eyed finale pose with her arms outstretched toward the audience.

Nobody claps. Dust floats in the air. Marilyn frowns. What is going on? She inches to the foot of the stage, squints against the spotlights, and looks out.

Two hundred spectators sit motionless in their chairs with their eyes and mouths wide open. Marilyn waves at them. Nobody moves. She climbs down from the stage in her dress and walks up the theater's center aisle in her tap shoes. The spectators are frozen, she sees, and gray like they've been gassed.

Something moves in a dark row up ahead. Marilyn walks to it and looks.

Abe is halfway down the row on his knees, shining spectators' shoes with a cloth and polish. He looks up, sees it's her, and gets to shining faster.

"You," she growls.

I jerked awake on the couch and looked at the clock. We only had an hour left. I looked at Hank. His eyes were shut but he was drenched in sweat.

"Are you asleep?" I asked.

"I dreamt they beat us," Hank mumbled.

"Who?"

"Critics."

"With their fists?"

"Baseball bats . . . golf clubs . . . hammers. . . . And you wouldn't shut up. You kept saying that you can't beat a dead bull. That really pissed them off. . . ."

I chuckled. "Maybe we *should* give them the bull piece again."

Hank laughed. "They'd never see that one coming."

The idea floated in the air. Hank and I sat up.

"Where would we get a bull?" he asked.

"Where's the one from last night?"

"Burnt," said Hank.

"But where is it?"

"I don't know . . . probably in the trash. There's a dumpster behind Prance Prance."

"Let's go get it."

Hank shook his head. "If it's in there, we'll never get it out. It weighs a ton. You'd have to move it in pieces."

I jumped up, ran to the kitchen, dug around in a drawer, and came back with a hacksaw.

"That'll move it," said Hank.

64

WE STUMBLED TOWARD PRANCE PRANCE. The late afternoon sun was still up and the sidewalks were busy. Hank and I had disguised ourselves as bums in torn shirts, soiled pants, and dirty faces so Stark wouldn't recognize us, and we played the parts to the hilt—I made wild gestures and screamed into my hand while Hank hurled one of his boots into traffic and darted between honking cars to retrieve it. Crowds parted and gave us a wide berth.

"Do you have the hacksaw?" Hank whispered, limping along in one boot.

"It's in my pants."

Hank nodded, then checked behind us with his compact mirror one last time as we ducked into the alley behind the gallery's theater.

We walked to the dumpster. The lid was shut, but I could smell charred bull from ten feet away.

We lifted the lid and looked in. The bull stared back at us.

"You or me?" I asked.

"You," said Hank.

I climbed in and pulled out the hacksaw.

"Where should I start?"

"Start small—maybe a hoof."

I sawed off a hoof and handed it out to Hank. "Make a pile," I whispered.

Hank walked over to the theater's back door, laid the hoof on the ground, and came back.

"Now something bigger," he said. "Maybe a shank."

"Which part's the shank?"

"I don't know. Try near the leg."

It was hot in the dumpster. Sweat ran in my eye. I ran the saw across a leg. Chewy gristle split open like jerky.

"Shit," Hank whispered.

"Stark?" I asked.

"No—the first critics are starting to arrive. I just saw two walk by."

"Where?"

"Right past the alley. They're probably headed for the gallery entrance. I think they recognized me."

I raised my head and looked out. Pedestrians walked past the alley. I didn't see any critics—then a tall man in a suit walked into view. Tall sensed that he was being watched and looked over at us. He looked like a critic. He slowed his pace and squinted—then a flash of recognition crossed his face.

I ducked down, sawed off a leg, and handed it to Hank. He set it on the growing pile of parts by the stage door.

"How much is left?" Hank whispered.

"Almost all of it," I said. "I haven't even started on the head yet!"

I raised my head and peeked out. Tall was back, this time with four other critics.

I ducked down. "Critics!" I squealed. "Get rid of them!"

"Is the performance going to be here in the alley?" asked Tall.

"We're just preparing our props," Hank stuttered.

Tall nodded, then he and his pals sniffed the air. They smelled bull.

"Is Bill here tonight?" asked one of the critics.

"I'M BILL!" I yelled from inside the dumpster.

"Hey, is that Bill in there?" asked another critic.

I stuck my head out and smiled.

"Oh," said Tall.

Five more critics entered the alley. "Is the performance back here?" asked one. Then right on their heels, ten more critics appeared.

"I heard the performance is back here," said one of the newcomers.

A reporter ran off to get more critics and returned a minute later with fifteen behind him.

There wasn't much we could do—the show had begun. I ducked down and went back to sawing. I handed Hank another leg and he put it on the pile.

The backstage door opened and Vaughn stepped out. "What's going on?" he said—then he saw us.

"What is this?" he asked in a low voice, wincing at the smell.

"We're recycling the bull," said Hank.

"I said no bull!" Vaughn snapped, nodding and smiling to the crowd like everything was fine. "Is this all you have? Is this your only piece?"

Hank and I looked at him. A gust of wind blew down the alley as word of the bull butchery spread through the crowd. Reporters murmured and craned their necks for a look.

"Is Bill here?" whispered Vaughn. "Is he in the dumpster with you?"

I shook my head. Vaughn pursed his lips.

"THAT IS SICK!" said a critic as he took in the view of the growing limb pile.

"Let's call it off now," said Vaughn. "They might leave and not write any reviews. It'll be like this never happened—"

"It's too late!" I said, sawing through gristle. "They're already here!" I handed Hank an ear.

"IS THIS THE PERFORMANCE?" a reporter boomed as ten more critics showed up.

"You're crazy," said Vaughn. "The reviews will be lethal! How am I going to survive this? I have a business to run!"

"BILL HAD BETTER BE INSIDE THAT DUMPSTER!" a photographer demanded.

Hank was shaking. "Pick up the pace," he whispered. "Let's give them something to look at!"

"I'M BILL!" I yelled, waving the hacksaw around.

"I'M BILL!" Hank screeched, jumping up and down and pinching his nipples while I crouched deeper in the dumpster and sawed like crazy.

"THIRTY MORE SECONDS AND I'M LEAVING!" a critic insisted. His sentiment spread quickly through the crowd.

"Call if off!" said Vaughn. "Please, I'm dying. . . ."

"The show's just starting to come together," said Hank, jumping, his crow bobbling under his shirt. "It's like jazz—let us play it out."

I handed Hank another leg, then went to work on the snout.

"THIS IS ANIMAL CRUELTY!" a reporter cried. "I CAN'T WATCH ANY MORE!" He turned and pushed away through the crowd.

Vaughn took out his flask.

I paused my cutting to rest and peeked out. More critics had poured into the alley. I saw bodies all the way out to the sidewalk where pedestrians were slowing to see what was going on.

Suddenly, Stark stepped into view behind the audience. We locked eyes as he pushed toward us through the crowd. I jumped out of the dumpster with the hacksaw.

"What are you doing?" asked Hank.

"Stark's here," I whispered. I grabbed Hank's arm and pulled him away from the scene and down the alley.

"WHERE ARE YOU GOING?" roared a critic.

"I'M SORRY, LADIES AND GENTLEMEN," Vaughn announced. "TERRIBLY SORRY. IT LOOKS LIKE THE SHOW'S CAN-CELED—"

"Forget Stark!" said Hank. "We've already started! He won't touch us in front of a hundred witnesses!" He pulled away and marched back to the dumpster.

Stark rammed his way toward us through the crowd.

"RUN!" I screamed. I grabbed Hank and pulled, but he grabbed hold of the dumpster and howled like a dying animal. I pried at his fingers until he finally let go.

The din of the crowd fell away as we ran. It was a long alley. The exit at the far end was a quarter mile off—a full city block. I pumped my arms. Hank beat the pavement. Doorways and dumpsters flashed by. Our lungs burned. I looked back. Stark was chasing. His face was beet-red, but he wasn't gaining on us. I threw the hacksaw off to the side and we picked up the pace. Hank and I pulled away.

* * *

We entered the apartment. Bill was performing a new piece with an egg carton.

I uncorked a bottle of wine. Hank took it and paced, working himself into a lather, then he circled around to the cage with his teeth clenched.

"Bill," Hank seethed.

Bill ignored him and went on performing.

"BILL!"

Bill shook the egg carton, sniffed it, gave an approving nod, then opened the lid. There was wet spaghetti inside. He pulled out a strand and held it up to the light. It glistened like a worm. He held it out to Hank. "Hungry?" he asked.

"YOU WILL PERFORM!" Hank screamed, throwing the wine bottle against the cage and punching the chain-link with his fist. "DO YOU

LIKE IT IN THERE? DO YOU LIKE PLAYING HOSTAGE? DON'T YOU WANT TO GET OUT?"

"I don't care where I am."

"DON'T YOU WANT TO PERFORM?" Hank cried, ripping at the cage.

"I am performing."

"OUT THERE? ON A STAGE? IN THE FRESH AIR?"

"Audiences slow me down."

"PLEASE?" Hank begged, throwing himself to the floor.

Bill dangled the spaghetti out through the chain-link. Hank crawled to the cage, pulled himself up, and opened his mouth. Bill dropped the pasta in. Hank gulped it down.

"Now will you perform?" asked Hank, chewing.

"Take refuge in birds," said Bill.

"I HAVE BIRDS UP THE ASS!" Hank yelled, jiggling his crow.

Bill closed the egg carton, picked up a pencil, licked the lead, and began poking little holes in the Styrofoam so the pasta could breathe.

"HOW CAN YOU BE SO CONTENT?" cried Hank. He ran to the record player and flipped it on. The yoga record played. He cranked the volume to max, but Bill went on performing without a flinch. Hank grabbed the player and smashed it on the floor. Plastic scattered everywhere. He picked up what was left and ran at the window like he meant to hurl it through the glass, but the player's cord tripped him up—he fell, slid across the room on his belly, and crashed into the windowsill. The view of the street six stories below made him freeze. He whimpered and began to shake.

"Don't look out the window," I said calmly. "Close your eyes."

Hank shut his eyes.

"Now, slowly back up."

Hank began inching away from the glass. "Today was all my fault," he cried.

"That's crazy," I said. "Stark staked out the gallery—there was nothing we could do."

"I wasn't wearing the foil hat," wailed Hank. "We had no protection!"

"I don't think it would've made a difference."

Hank began to sob. He rolled onto his side, gritted his teeth, ripped out a clump of his hair, and threw it across the room.

I picked up the hair, went to the kitchen, came back with a roll of duct tape, knelt beside him, tore off a piece of tape, and readied to tape the hair back onto his head.

Hank's lips trembled. He looked down at his crow. The bird's head was bare—there wasn't a feather on it. I put the hair clump on the crow's head. Hank nodded with approval. I taped the hair down. Hank stopped crying. I helped him to his feet, walked him to the bathroom, and turned on the light. We looked at the crow's taped-on hair in the mirror. I laughed.

Hank smiled a little.

65

THE NEXT MORNING I WENT to the window and looked out. Hookers strutted on the sidewalks. Junkies passed each other dime bags. Bums drank and sang.

A van pulled up to the corner newspaper rack. The driver stepped out with a fresh stack of papers under his arm.

"The morning edition's here," I said.

"You think Vaughn's read it yet?" Hank asked, biting a thumbnail.

"I'm sure he'll call when he has. I'll go get one."

"Watch out for Stark," said Hank, pulling his tinfoil hat low over his brow.

Trying to look nonchalant, I walked down to the rack, put in a quarter, took out a paper, and opened it flat on the sidewalk. The dumpster performance had only lasted a few minutes; maybe the critics had gone easy on us.

I flipped to the arts section and there it was, in bold capitals at the top: "ANOTHER DUMPSTER-WORTHY PERFORMANCE." The critics had written plenty. I took a breath, then skimmed: "... insidiously bad craft . . . bullish in its frantic incoherence . . . psychotic cut-ups with butter knives . . . recycled props with predictable punch lines . . . wallowed in banal process . . . violated the first rule of coprophagia: don't leave the audience holding the leftovers. . . .'"

I threw the paper away and went back to the apartment.

"How was it?" asked Hank.

I bit my lip.

Hank ran to the phone. "I'm calling Vaughn."

He dialed and waited, listening. "No one's answering," he said.

"Not even his answering machine?"

"It just rings."

We took turns calling. No answer.

We sat on the couch. We polished off more wine. Hank watched Bill perform. I looked out the window for Stark and played with my poultice while the earth turned.

I tried calling again. It rang twice, then finally I heard Vaughn's voice: "Hello?"

"Vaughn! It's Larry. Your answering machine—"

"I unplugged it. The critics are ruthless! You should hear the messages. Insults . . . threats . . . and the reviews. . . ."

Hank came over from the couch. "How is he?" he whispered.

"Vaughn," I said into the phone, "don't worry. The next show—"

"I'm getting out of the performance art business," said Vaughn.

His words were a punch in the gut. Hank saw my face and covered his mouth.

"Vaughn—"

"I have to make some money, Larry. The health department came by about the bull. An asthmatic critic is threatening to sue over the smoke. The fire sprinklers put three feet of standing water in my basement. . . ."

Hank tugged at my arm. "What's he saying?"

I covered the mouthpiece. "He has three feet of water in his basement."

"Tell him we'll pump it out."

"He's not listening."

"Tell him!" Hank whispered.

I shook my head and offered the phone to Hank. He put it up to his ear. Vaughn was still going on about the flood.

Hank interrupted him. "Vaughn . . . Vaughn . . . hi. It's Hank. Look, we'll fix it. I know it's flooded. Yes, but Vaughn, listen, we could do Venice! What do you think of that? VENICE! THINK OF IT! A NIGHT OF PERFORMANCE ART WITH A VENETIAN THEME! ACCORDI-ONS AND MASKS! WE'LL WEAR STRIPED SHIRTS AND FAKE MUSTACHES AND PUSH CRITICS AROUND YOUR BASEMENT ON GONDOLAS!"

Vaughn started shouting. Hank crouched and set the phone on the floor. We got down on our knees and put our ears up to the receiver. Vaughn was still yelling—then he hung up.

"I don't think he likes Venice," whispered Hank.

"He'll call back," I said.

* * *

We slumped on the couch and waited for Vaughn to call. Hank wore his tinfoil hat. I wore a dirty T-shirt. We looked like sad clowns.

The sun set, then rose, but the phone didn't ring. I uncorked a bot-tle of red. Hank leaned against the chain-link and watched Bill perform. Bill picked up a forty-pound chunk of concrete, raised it high, and dropped it. It landed on an old violin, smashing the instrument flat. Bill rolled the chunk around in a crunchy circle with his foot. Bits of concrete fell off and were quickly ground to dust, while underneath, violin strings buckled and snapped with muffled staccato cries.

"What's that one called?" asked Hank.

"Concrete Music by Bill," said Bill, grinding.

"We could get you a music gig—maybe you could open for the San Francisco Symphony."

Bill ignored him. Hank pressed himself harder against the chain-link.

"I'm doing it," Hank whispered, lifting his shirt to show Bill the crow. "See? Birds. I wear it all the time—it's practically an appendage."

"It's about as functional as a fibroma," said Bill without looking up.

Hank looked down at his crow and frowned. "It's functional," he said quietly in protest.

Bill ignored him and went on playing with the concrete.

Hank came and sat down on the couch.

"How functional does it have to be?" he asked no one in particular.

66

THREE DAYS PASSED. I VIDEOTAPED Bill's performances.
Hank took notes and stroked his crow. The air in the apartment grew stale.
I dunked my head in the bathroom sink and combed my wet hair. Hank
added more layers of tinfoil to his hat. Vaughn still didn't call.

"I'm going crazy!" said Hank, jumping off the couch to pace the
room. "We have to find another gig!"

I walked to the window and looked out. A steady wind blew outside. The morning air was crisp. "What about Stark?" I asked.

"I enhanced it," said Hank, pointing at his hat. "It's at maximum
interference. There's no way he'll detect us."

"Let's go," I said.

We left the apartment, sneaked through the alleys to the gallery
district downtown, and ducked into a phone booth. A dirty phonebook
dangled from a chain. I flipped to the gallery section. There were fifty listings. A-A-Art Gallery was first, and it was only a block away. Hank ripped
the pages out and we took off, running.

We found A-A-Art and went in. Empty picture frames hung on the walls. A stuffy academic with a receding hairline and thick glasses stepped out from a back room. "Welcome to A-A-Art," he sniveled, pushing his glasses higher on his nose.

"All of your frames are empty," I said.

"Art is a reflection of the beholder," snorted the academic.

"We're performance artists," said Hank, "and—"

The owner sniffed, pushed up his glasses, and returned to his back room without a word.

Hank crumpled the phonebook listings into a ball. "I'm going to shove this down his throat," he said calmly.

"Relax," I said. "It's a numbers game. We have fifty chances to win."

Hank uncrumpled the listings. "The next gallery is called Always-Already Wet," he said.

We walked to Always-Already and went in. Shag rugs globbed with wet paint glistened on the walls. A man sitting behind a desk stood up to greet us. He was skinny and pale with a black goatee.

"Good morning," said Goatee. "Welcome to Always-Already Wet. The paint on the rugs you see is fresh; we have a rotating staff here day and night to keep it from drying out. Each rug comes with a complimentary one-gallon can of paint so you can keep it going."

Goatee reached under his desk, grabbed a can, walked to a wet rug, and slathered more paint onto it with a brush. The excess ran down and pooled on the floor.

"That's awfully wet," I said.

"Exactly!" Goatee said, setting down the can. He squinted at us. "You look familiar. Have you been here before?"

"We're performance artists," I said. "I'm Larry and this is Hank—"

"WOW!" yelled Goatee. He ran to his desk and came back with a pen and paper. "I love your performances! Could I get your autographs?"

Hank and I smiled and signed. Goatee held the paper up to the light. "I'm going to frame this!" he said.

"A-A-Art has a nice frame selection," said Hank.

"Really? I'll have to stop by," said Goatee.

"Let us perform here," Hank blurted.

Goatee smiled. "Oh, I'm sorry, but we couldn't. We're not set up for that kind of work."

"Your space is perfect."

"My ceilings are too low."

"We can do low-ceiling pieces."

"I don't have a first-aid kit."

"We'll bring our own."

Goatee shook his head. "No, I couldn't."

"But you like our work. . . ."

Goatee blushed. "Yes, well . . . the truth is that I haven't actually seen your work, but I keep meaning to—"

"What? But—"

"I've only read the newspaper articles, you know, the blow-by-blows. That thing you did with the bull? Oh, that made me laugh."

"This is your chance to see us up close!" I said. "You'll have already-wet spectators spilling out the door!"

"It sounds nice. . . ."

"Let's get it on your calendar."

"I can't. I'm sorry." Goatee took a step back to excuse himself, then stopped to reconsider. "But you know. . . ."

"Yes?" asked Hank.

"I might be able to schedule something for your partner."

"Partner?"

"Bill. I might be able to slip him in. Maybe I could get his phone number?"

Hank and I did a slow turn and walked out without a word.

We headed to the next gallery—Balzac's Mustache. The curator rose from her chair as we entered. She was a lanky woman with a long neck and a tight hair bun. She smiled rigidly and remained behind her desk.

Hank introduced us. The curator listened. Her eyes studied Hank's face, then moved down his shirt to the bulge there. She cocked her head. Hank finished his introduction and asked if she'd let us perform. The curator raised a finger at the ceiling as if considering his question, then lowered it until it was pointed right at his middle.

"What is under your shirt?" she asked.

Hank raised his shirt. There was the crow. He jiggled it. The curator's mouth opened.

"Do you think it's functional?" asked Hank.

"Oh, definitely," said the curator, smiling freshly as she crab-stepped over to her telephone. "Pardon me for just one moment." She fumbled for the receiver, dialed a number, waited, then whispered something. Hank and I read her lips—it was either "mend the fleece" or "send the police." We turned and hurried out.

We walked to the next gallery, then the next, working the phonebook listings one by one. We tried Union Square, Maiden Lane, Grant Street, and Sutter, dragging our asses down the sidewalks to painting dealers, rug sellers, lamp hawkers, and antique stores—but everyone said no.

We heard all the excuses. Only the manager can say yes, and he's away on vacation. Our gallery's too small. 'Performing arts' aren't allowed here. You're too wild. You're not presentable to the general public. I don't care if that thing on your arm *is* called a 'poultice'—it smells. The last performers flashed genitals that didn't belong to them. We only show homoerotic nudists, banned third-world videos of multi-culti politico satire, and mouth-paintings by paraplegics.

We paused to rest on the corner of Market Street and Kearney. Wind whipped our hair around. The phonebook listings flapped and rattled in Hank's hands as he poured over them. He flipped the pages over, read the listings, then flipped them over again.

"Hurry and pick one," I said. "I'm freezing."

Hank shook his head. "There's only one gallery left," he said.

"That's impossible! Read them all off," I said.

Hank flipped to the first page and read from the top: "A-A-Art, Always-Already Wet, Balzac's Mustache, Before Breasts, Caustic Delivery, Dogmatic Taco, Earlicker. . . ." He picked up the pace in a clipped staccato, the words running together like surreal verse. I closed my eyes and listened. " . . . Nunchuku Muscle, Operator Error, Penultimate Ultimatum, Potty Polly's Penthouse, Prance Prance. . . ."

He read on until the end.

"That's all," he said.

"Except for one?"

Hank nodded.

I swallowed and braced myself. "Where is it?"

Hank pointed. I turned around and looked. There it was, across the street, with a pink neon sign: Z'Art Brut. A naked, flesh-colored male mannequin stood in the front window. Half his face had been blown off by a shotgun. Not bad.

We crossed Market Street and went in. Twenty naked male mannequins stood around the gallery in different angles and poses. All of them had been shot in the face.

A man-giant jumped up from his desk and ambled toward us. "Welcome to Z'Art Brut!" he boomed with bad breath and an Oklahoma drawl. "The name's Laramie Skillard. Welcome, welcome." He wore a black beret, a polyester suit from the 1970s, and around his neck, a silver steer-head bolo. We shook his hand. It was meaty and wet.

"The gallery's brand new," said Laramie. "I show works of the Art Brut style—do you know it? It's art by criminals, the insane, the self-taught. . . . This is our first opening. The show's called Daddy Does Plastique Surgery Too, and it features the work of Billy Joe Kruger, a pig farmer and militia infantryman from the Midwest. He's a self-made sculptor in the Brut style— very fine work—a real master of the mannequin form. It's right up there with the *Lez Euro-peans*, don't ya think? *Oui-oui?* Ha ha ha."

Laramie grinned, hung his hands on his bolo, and waited for a response. He looked at Hank. Hank smiled and gave a nod. Laramie returned the nod and tried to determine which of Hank's eyes was the good one. Hank smiled and nodded again. Laramie smiled back. Not much was happening there, so Laramie turned to me.

"So! You're looking to invest in art. Let me show you something real special."

He walked us over to a mannequin and pointed at its shotgunned face. "Look at this mannequin. Even though he has four limbs and appears to be looking right at you, he is nothing—a trifle, a department store fixture, a lump of plastique, a body with no organs. We should not give a shit about him—yet!—he horrifies. Why, you ask? The answer is because he has no face. He refuses to acknowledge your gaze. He reflects nothing back to you. Unsettling, ain't it? LOOK AT HIM! He's unrecognizable! Impenetrable! This is what Nietzsche's abyss had in mind. The body goes infinite without a face because its intentions cannot be known. There is only a hole, a gape . . . and so? You're driven. You look. You try to reconstruct what was there, the lost territory, but you can't. His cheeks were blown off in a Kentucky backyard and you can't recall what you did not witness—UNLESS, OF COURSE, YOU ARE ZEE COPS, HA HA HA."

Laramie went on: "And so you suffer, you struggle to reconstruct, to rationalize his indifference and cushion your ego. You ask questions in despair. When was he shot? Who the hell shot him? What was their quarrel? How did things reach a point such as this, so *très serioso*? And what about the others who were shot? Like him over there? And him over there? Why has everybody been shot? Could it happen again? Could the shooter return while you are standing here? COULD HE BE HERE NOW?" Laramie yelled, pointing a finger at me.

Hank and I blinked.

"You replay the violence over and over even though you weren't there. You replay it BECAUSE you weren't there. You assign tragedy to a becoming-territory that never becomes. What you see horrifies because of what you never saw. The disease of defacialization defacializes you. And that, my friends, is the mystique—the horror of plastique."

"Don't you mean 'plastic'?" I asked.

"No—plastique. These mannequins are all made from military grade C-4 plastic explosive. Real nice."

"They could explode?" asked Hank.

"*Oui!* As it always is with great art!" Laramie barked, slapping Hank playfully in the gut. "So! Tell me. You're here looking for some art? Maybe you're even artists yourselves," he said, eyeing my unkempt hair and the bulge under Hank's shirt.

"We're performance artists," said Hank, "from the Tenderloin."

"Why yes, of course, I've heard of you ... the stories in the paper ... you are zee so-called 'weapons of gallery destruction,' no? Ha ha ha!"

"We're looking for a new performance art venue," I said. "Some-place...."

" ... edgy," Laramie finished with a wink. "Sure, I get it: something with padded walls and a drain in the center of the floor, no? Ha ha ha!"

Hank and I forced wooden smiles.

Laramie saw our reaction and bowed regally. "I wish you luck. I'm sure you'll find the perfect place."

"Let us do a show here," said Hank.

"That would be something, eh? Sorry, but no, I'm afraid—"

"Isn't this your gallery?" asked Hank.

"Sure."

"Then you could book us."

"Impossible," Laramie said, waving his hands. "No no, I'm sorry. The bulls, the fire ... they are too extreme. There's the liability, the insurance—"

"I'll assure you," I said.

"Me too," said Hank.

Laramie looked at us, unsure, then decided we were joking. "AREN'T YOU ZEE COMEDIANS!" he yelled, doubling over and cracking himself up so hard tears ran down his face. He slapped me in the chest. I nodded and forced a smile. Hank saw my blood was boiling. He began a slow jog backwards. I smirked.

Laramie was still laughing. "SO!" he screamed, drooling. "IN ZEE PERFORMANCE, WILL THERE BE BLOOD? HA HA HA! BECAUSE IF THERE AIN'T NO BLOOD—"

"OF COURSE THERE'LL BE BLOOD!" Hank laughed.

"HELL, I HOPE SO—I JUST HAD THESE FLOORS REFINISHED!" belted Laramie through his tears.

Hank nodded and laughed as he jogged backward into the maze of mannequins.

"AND WHAT ABOUT A CARCASS?" Laramie giggled with a slap of his thigh. "ZEE CARCASS THAT HANGS FROM THE RAFTERS? BECAUSE IF THERE'S NO CARCASS—"

"ANY KIND YOU LIKE! A DONKEY ON A ROPE'S A REAL GOOD TIME!" I laughed, jumping up and down while Hank backward-circled the mannequins faster, working himself up.

"WE'LL PIN THE TAIL ON HIM, NO?" roared Laramie, doing little bumps and grinds with his pelvis.

"THESE MANNEQUINS COULD USE A LITTLE ASS!" I howled.

Hank picked up speed, then made a wrong turn and bumped a mannequin. The male form bobbled . . . tipped . . . then crashed to the floor. The head popped off and rolled like a grenade across the hardwood floor toward me and Laramie. Laramie dove behind his desk. I froze and held my breath. The head rolled, bumped against my foot, and stopped. We all waited. It didn't blow.

"It's a dud," I said, disappointed. I crouched down beside it. I'd never seen a C-4 head before. It was a phrenologist's dream—

"Stop!" whispered Laramie. "Don't touch it!"

I touched the head. "Can we name him?" I asked.

"Get the hell away from it!" Laramie begged.

"Let's name him Yorick," said Hank.

"Oh, I like that," I said.

"STOP NAMING HIM!" Laramie rasped.

"Will you let us perform?" asked Hank.

"No! Please! Just head for the door! Quiet as you can! The plastique's probably gone unstable!"

"We could do a short show," I whispered. "Just an hour—"

"JUST GET THE FUCK OUT, SEE VOO PLATE!" Laramie yelled.

Hank and I hustled out the door. The wind howled. We walked a few feet, then Hank went weak and collapsed on the sidewalk. I helped him up. The street noise was deafening. Cars flew past. Trucks rumbled. Hank took the gallery listings out of his pocket. They flapped in the wind. He held them up against the sun. They glowed yellow and pretty. He let go and they fluttered away down the street.

We walked a block to a liquor store. Hank went in to buy wine. I waited outside and watched for Stark. Pedestrians walked past. A rib-thin junkie in dirty pants and a torn tanktop stood on the sidewalk a few feet away. He was hunched over and staring down at his crotch. I recognized him. He called himself Junkie John. We'd talked a few times. He'd been on the streets ten years. He'd had a wife once. They'd made the rounds together in the early days, panhandling, scrounging, laughing . . . until one morning he woke up in a parking lot, rolled over in the sack to kiss her, and saw a thief had stabbed her to death for her shoes. He was never the same after. Now he made the rounds alone.

John took a step back and his crotch followed him. He gritted his teeth and brushed at it hard, as if he were flicking off vermin, but it had no effect. He shook his head to clear it, then looked again. Nothing had changed down there. He stared at his crotch so hard he shook, like he was commanding it, willing it to somehow to obey, but it didn't.

People walked past. He looked up at them and began to cry. Pedestrians pretended not to see him. He raised a hand to stop someone, anyone, but nobody cared. He looked down again. His crotch was still there.

John raised his arm, licked his needle tracks for good luck, crouched deep, and sucked in a breath. He held out his hands just above his crotch and waited. Ten seconds passed, then a truck horn honked, firing him off; he grabbed the crotch of his pants as fast as he could with both hands and squeezed, catching it like a rabbit.

I went over to him. "Hi, John."

He looked up. "I ATE A BURGER AND NOW I'M CONSTI-PATED," he cried, shaking.

"It happens," I said, eyeing his crotch. He was still squeezing.

"Not like this shit," he said.

"You have to push."

"I CAN'T!"

"You have to."

"I can't," John mouthed silently, shaking his head. "I can't." Tears ran down his cheeks.

"Why not?"

"IT MIGHT ALL COME OUT!" he cried.

He stepped back for more space, then looked at his crotch and swatted it—then another swat, then another, faster, until he was batting it like it was on fire. He screamed and spun, slap slap slap, then plunged his hands deep into his waistband like two fish diving into water, working them front to back and side to side, searching by touch alone, head turning, feeling around in circles, then out flew the hands and it was back to the slapping.

I stood and watched him go. Did he have the clap? Was something missing down there? Maybe he was crying for his wife, recalling the things they used to do together, their lovemaking in the alleys—or maybe he really was constipated from too much burger, in which case he just wanted to hang on to what little he had, even if it only seemed like shit to everyone else.

67

HANK AND I COLLAPSED ONTO the couch, opened a bottle of Merlot, and watched Bill churn out one piece after another. There was Toenail Clippings Eaten One by One From the Waxy Head of a Lipstick, Slow-Motion Backbends in a Mismatched Set of Women's High Heels, and Ten Lethal Karate Moves for Hernia Patients.

Hank looked at the video camera and saw it had sagged down on its tripod—the lens was pointed at the floor. He went to it, pulled the camera body up, aimed it at the cage, tightened the tripod's screws, and let go. The camera sagged. He ran to the kitchen, returned with a roll of duct tape, taped the camera upright, and let go. It sagged again. The tripod was a piece of junk.

Hank ripped the camera from its mount with a growl, hoisted it onto his shoulder, walked to the cage, and began shooting.

Hours ticked by. Bill was performing a new piece every few minutes. Hank tried to keep up, but shooting video with crossed eyes was difficult and the camera was heavy.

Hank's shooting arm eventually gave out. He lowered the lens and leaned against the cage. His lips quivered like he might cry. He whispered something to Bill. Bill whispered something back to him. Hank hung his head, shuffled over to the couch, and collapsed down beside me.

"What did he say?" I asked.

"More birds," Hank whispered.

Bill went on performing for himself, the cage, the air.

* * *

Days passed. I drank, stewed on the couch, and made rounds to the window. Hank shot more Bill footage until his arm grew tired, then sneaked out to collect padding for his rope nest. Bringing back handfuls of string, leaves, and tree branches from the gutter outside was his new hobby.

I shuffled through piles of newspapers and dirty laundry to the bathroom. I looked in the mirror. I had dark circles under my eyes. With my mussed hair, dirty white T-shirt, and patchy beard, I was starting to look like Junkie John.

My legs itched. I lifted my pant cuff and saw my calves were red and swollen. Performance Art Withdrawal Rash was setting in.

I went back to the living room. Bill was busy performing in the cage and Hank was out gathering more nest material. My forehead felt hot. I curled up on the floor, covered myself with an old blanket, and drifted off.

I'm standing in a dim forest clearing. The ground is soft with pine needles. I hear leaves rustle above. I look up. A human figure crouches on a branch. I squint and see it's my father. He's smiling. I wave. He gives a slow wave back. Leaves rustle behind me. I turn and look, but nobody's there.

I opened my eyes and sat up. Hank was standing in his nest with tree branches tied to his arms and legs like featherless wings; except for a few sparse leaves, the branches were bare and spindly. He stepped out of the nest and marched through the trash on the floor to flaunt his new outfit. The branches and leaves rustled.

"They look like bird bones," I said.

Hank ran around the room flapping his arms and squawking until I laughed.

* * *

I went to the bathroom with a wine bottle and the telephone, sat down on the floor beside the toilet, and dialed Mouse.

"Hello?" she answered.

"Are you nervous about the fight?" I whispered.

"Like you wouldn't believe."

"When is it, again?"

Mouse laughed. "Friday."

"Friday . . . Friday . . . when is that?"

"Tomorrow. Are you drunk?"

"Yes. Are you still training?"

"I've tapered down. We had our weigh-in today."

"How much?"

"One twenty-five."

"Oh, you're light, baby."

"I'm heavy enough to kick your ass."

"How much does Kitty weigh?"

"One twenty-eight."

"I can't wait to see you flush that Kitty down."

"Is that a new boxing term?"

"Flush her down," I whispered, flushing the toilet. Mouse giggled. I flushed again. Mouse laughed.

Finally, I just dropped the whole phone receiver in and flushed.

* * *

I returned to the living room. Hank was sitting on the floor in his bird-bone suit. His pants were pulled up to his thighs and he was scratching his legs furiously—his thighs and ankles were red and swollen. "Performance Art Withdrawal Rash," he said, scratching. "I have to find an audience soon."

"I have it too," I said, pulling up my pants. The swelling on my legs had advanced to full-blown welts—the skin was variegated and puckered. I lifted my shirt. The rash had spread to my stomach. "We should give Vaughn a call," I said. "I'm sure he's cooled off about the Venice thing by now."

Hank didn't answer. I looked up and saw his crossed eyes were wide open. He rolled them to the left as far as he could, then the right.

I laughed. "What are you doing?"

Hank moved his eyes some more. Terror spread across his face. His mouth opened. A whimper came out.

"What's wrong?" I whispered.

"I CAN FEEL MY EYEBALLS MOVING IN MY HEAD!" he screamed.

We couldn't wait any longer—we had to see Vaughn. I helped Hank off the floor, out the door, down the stairs, across the apartment lobby, and through the alleys to Prance Prance.

* * *

The gallery's front doors were open when we arrived. We walked in. The lobby was quiet. A refreshment table bearing wine and cheese stood in the corner of the gallery. Helium balloons floated in the air.

"Where is everyone?" Hank asked. His words echoed around the empty space.

"It looks like a new show just opened," I said, pointing to thousands of Polaroid photos pinned to the gallery's main wall. The words FORMAL-D-HYDE FROGS were stenciled above them.

Hank went to the refreshment table, grabbed an open bottle of champagne, and took a suck. "This bottle was just opened," he said. "There have to be people here somewhere."

We drank and looked at the Polaroids. Each picture showed a frog preserved in a jar of formaldehyde.

Hank cocked his head. "Do you hear that?" he asked.

I listened. A low rumble came from the theater door at the rear of the gallery—it sounded like people talking. We marched to the door and threw it open. The theater was packed. Hundreds of critics chatted. Flashbulbs popped. I spotted Vaughn. He waved and jogged over to us.

"WHAT A SURPRISE!" he gushed over the noise.

"WE WERE JUST WANDERING BY," I yelled.

"WELCOME TO FORMAL-D-HYDE FROGS. I SEE YOU FOUND THE CHAMPAGNE!" Vaughn laughed. "AND LOOK AT YOU!" he bellowed, getting a load of Hank's branches and leaves. "I HEARD SPRUCE-BRANCH FASHION WAS HEATING UP AGAIN—"

"IS SOMEONE PERFORMING TONIGHT?" asked Hank.

"MADEMOISELLE D!" roared Vaughn.

Hank and I looked at each other and shrugged. We hadn't heard of her.

"ALL THE PHOTOS IN THE GALLERY ARE HERS," shouted Vaughn. "INCREDIBLE, AREN'T THEY? THE REPORTERS ARE WILD FOR HER. STAY AND WATCH! SHE'S JUST ABOUT TO START."

"I THOUGHT YOU WERE OUT OF THE PERFORMANCE ART BUSINESS," I hollered.

"I AM! BUT SHE'S PAYING ME—FOR THE SPACE, THE FOOD, EVERYTHING. DOES THAT MAKE ME A WHORE?"

"LET US PERFORM A LITTLE SOMETHING," blurted Hank. "YOU KNOW, GET THE CROWD WARMED UP."

Vaughn laughed and gave Hank a consolatory pat on the shoulder.

"YOU DON'T UNDERSTAND! I CAN FEEL MY EYES!" Hank screamed, rolling his eyeballs around in his head.

"AND LOOK AT THIS!" I yelled, pulling down my pants to flash my rash.

Vaughn smiled and nodded like he hadn't heard us. The house lights flickered. "GOTTA RUN!" he sang, backing away. He pointed to a pair of seats in the middle of the orchestra section. "TAKE THOSE! YOU'LL LOVE HER! SHE'S A HIT!"

Hank and I slunk down to the orchestra seats in full view of the crowd. A few critics spotted us and whistled. We nodded hello, smiled politely, and sat down.

The lights dim. A soundtrack of chirping frogs begins playing. The curtains rise. Mademoiselle D stands behind a table in the center of the stage. Her head is bowed so we can't make out her face.

She starts pushing her table toward the foot of the stage. It passes under a spotlight and we see it's an old metal dissection table. An open jar sits on top. It's filled with formaldehyde. Big frogs float inside. A scalpel rests beside the jar.

Mademoiselle D keeps pushing. The table's stiff legs rumble and vibrate over the stage's floorboards. The jar jitters. Formaldehyde sloshes out.

The table reaches the stage's edge. D looks up at the audience. Hank and I gasp.

It's Deidre Stein, the talk show host.

She leans into a microphone. "FROG," she whispers with bedroom allure, her voice booming over the theater's speakers. A video camera zooms in on her and her image appears on the screen over the stage. The camera tilts down her face, her neck, her chest, to the table, the jar.

She lowers her mouth into the jar and blows bubbles in the formaldehyde. The frogs float and swirl in the bath. She nabs one in her teeth and jerks it out with snap of her head. The frog dangles from her mouth. Formaldehyde runs down her chin. She shakes her head to get the liquid off, then drops the frog onto the table. It lands on its back. The camera zooms in on it.

Hank squints at the video screen. "That's not a frog," he whispers. I look closer and see bumpy skin—he's right; it's a toad. Maybe Deidre doesn't know the difference.

The camera zooms in tighter. The toad has a very large penis.

Toads don't have penises.

"Prosthetic," I whisper to Hank. He nods.

Deidre picks up the scalpel and scans the audience, then looks in our direction. She frowns. Hank and I duck down.

"You think she saw us?" Hank whispers.

Deidre gives the toad a kiss on the lips. "IF ONLY THERE WERE NO PRINCES," she says. "HARK, THEN TARRY." She holds the toad down and chops a leg off with the scalpel. Clear juice runs out. The critics in the front row clap and howl. She looks up and smiles. I swear she's looking right at us.

"WHAT I MEAN IS: WHAT YOU MEAN IS!" she yells into the mic. "HARK! TARRY!" Her blade falls. Another toad leg goes. The audience claps. "I CAN'T HEAR MY DIFFERENCE IN A QUIET ROOM! HARK . . . TARRY!" Chop. Another leg falls. "THE FROGS REIGNED . . . UNTIL NOW! HARK! TARRY!" Deidre makes a final cut and the last leg is off.

"Why all the hark and tarry?" whispers Hank.

I shrug. Her piece is shit.

Deidre picks up the legless toad and hops it around the table. The audience laughs. I'd never seen such a macabre crowd.

She slaps the toad down on its back, slices open the belly, jams her fingers in, scoops out the organs, and tosses them across the stage with a splat. Destroying evidence is sly; it's harder to argue a frog's a toad if there aren't any organs.

Deidre continues with her spew of incomprehensible maxims and theory-drivel: "EPHEBES BLOOM AS THOU WILT! HARK, TARRY! WATCH ME DIDDLE OFF YOUR FIDDLE WITH MY UTTER-ABLE UNARY ULU! HARK! TARRY! I SUBORDINATE YOUR TEXTUAL DADDY IN MY TWOFOLD SOLIPSISTIC VAT! HARK AND TARRY!" She smiles and cracks herself up.

The critics clap and laugh. They have no idea what the hell she's talking about, but they're bent on loving it anyway.

Mademoiselle D slowly lowers the blade over the toad's penis.

Hank slides down deeper into his chair. "Hark and tarry," he whispers out of the side of his mouth.

"What?"

"Hark and tarry! Hark and tarry!"

"What the hell are you talking about?"

"Hank and Larry!"

I look at Deidre. She's fiddling with the knife and staring right at us. She smiles. Hank and Larry. Holy shit—Hank's right. She's making her performance about us. I start to sweat. She's calling me and Hank frogs. But why? To what end?

I start by analyzing the toad. It's constructed. Artificial. Deidre pretends it's a frog even though it isn't. She cuts the legs off so it can't hop. It has a fake gonads so it can't reproduce, as if to say Hank or I could screw like a frog all day long with her sewn-on dick without effect. There'd be no off-spring. No children. Our lineage would croak. I sit up in my chair. Deidre's pushing fake patriarchy . . . impotence in the hope of subverting our progeny . . . a Marxist-feminist plot to trade the loins of our poesy for artifice of her making to prevent us from propagating and to halt the continuation of our performance art in a single generation of fruitless fucking! The hark and tarry serve as both command and warning: hark, but do nothing and see what happens to you; tarry, and listen to what you become: a frog that will never be, a vacuum, a sign with an imaginary referent and no feet in the real world, a false frog without legs and with an impossible cock.

Deidre goes on prattling with more harks and tarries. Her words are meaningless. Of course they are. She's trying to be incomprehensible. It's a strategy: keep everyone occupied while you slip us the fake penis; occupy the mind while you penetrate us with your choreography just as sure as formaldehyde preserves—even as it kills.

A reporter turns around and smiles at us. Look at him! He's enjoying it! The critics are taking the opportunity to band together in the face of our derision! It's revenge for the Toklas-mustache bit! There's no coherent narrative thread in Deidre's piece whatsoever! She probably saw us come in, and now it's all a set-up! Perverse sex education designed to castrate by supplying us with new cocks that will never work! The old bait and switch! Voodoo choreography aimed straight at us! A solipsistic incantation designed for one thing only: castration! The witch! The witch!

I squeeze my thighs together and cover my ears for protection. Hank sees me and covers himself too.

Deidre is poised for the penis cut. She looks up at us one last time and sees our defensive postures. "OH, YOU'RE NO FUN AT ALL," says her mouth with a seductive smile, but of course we don't hear her.

She lowers the blade and separates the penis from the toad. Her choreography sails over the crowd toward us. We wait. It hits, but falls on deaf ears. I shake my head at her. Nice try.

The spectators jump to their feet with applause. Deidre steps in front of her table and bows. The theater roar is deafening. The house lights come up. Deidre holds up a hand. People quiet so they can hear her:

"YOU'RE A BEAUTIFUL AUDIENCE! THANK YOU ALL FOR LETTING ME EXPRESS MY PERFORMING ARTS VISION WITH YOU TONIGHT!"

The crowd goes berserk. Critics climb onto their chairs. Grown men cry. Spectators scream and stomp the floor. A drunken Vaughn waves at the audience from the wings.

Hank and I sit and watch with our mouths open. Words fail us entirely.

We returned to the apartment. Vomit rose in my throat. I covered my mouth and ran to the bathroom. The phone receiver was still in the toilet. I grabbed it and yanked, but it was stuck in the drain trap and wouldn't budge.

I went to the sink and leaned over the basin. I felt acid coming up. I looked in the mirror. Junkie John stared back at me. I thought of him hunched on the corner of Market Street, holding it in:

You have to push. / I can't. / Why not? / It might all come out.

I shut my mouth, gritted my teeth, and, with my nostrils flared, swallowed it all right back down.

68

HANK AND I SAT ON the couch. We polished off two bottles of red, then cracked open two more while Bill performed I Twirl Fish Entrails in Circles Above My Head for Twenty-Four Hours.

Night fell. Hank was still wearing his leaves and branches. He stumbled around the apartment with the video camera shooting footage of himself, his shrine, and the ceiling while I sat on the floor and tried to fix the camera's tripod with duct tape.

The sun rose. We drank on. I scratched my belly. Hank smiled, muttered something unintelligible, stumbled in a drunken circle with loose hips, and shot off video with a lazy hand. I jumped up and shadowboxed. Hank laughed and shot some more tape. We cracked open a red to celebrate. I lost count of the drinks. Some bottles we didn't even bother finishing; we'd drink a little, then crack open a new one for the fresh scent.

The tripod was back in working order. We mounted the camera on top, taped it into place, and aimed it at the cage where Bill was still performing his Fish Entrails piece.

A car honked outside. I looked out and saw Mouse's Impala pulling up to the curb.

Hank and I each tucked two fresh bottles of wine into our pants, then I hurried to the bathroom, dunked my head under the faucet, combed my hair back, and slicked down my shirt.

Hank appeared at the door. "How do I look?" I asked.

"Dangerous," he slurred. He dusted off his cowboy boots, flattened his T-shirt down over his crow, fluffed his branches, and spread his arms. "How about me?"

"Like a performance waiting to happen," I said.

Hank held up a white bed pillow. "I'm taking this along too."

"A performance prop?"

"Just in case. You never know."

* * *

We hurried through the lobby to the street with the wine bottles clanking in our pants. Mouse was double-parked with the engine running. I took the front seat and Hank climbed in back.

Mouse grabbed my shirt and pulled me close.

"One thing first," she whispered.

"Yes?"

"THAT needs to stay outside," she said, pointing at my poultice.

I rolled down the window and stuck my arm out.

"Better?" I whispered.

"Much," said Mouse. She pulled me closer. "I am so nervous."

"Don't be."

"What if I lose?"

"You won't."

Mouse looked back at Hank. She took in his crossed eyes and branches and laughed.

"Hello, Hank," she said.

"Hi, Mousey," he said, scratching his legs.

Mouse began to drive. After a few blocks, she looked in the rearview mirror. Her eyes narrowed.

"What are you eating?" she asked.

I turned and looked. Hank had ripped open the pillow and was eating the feathers.

"It was Bill's idea," Hank mumbled, chewing. "He said the crow wasn't enough."

"It never is," said Mouse gently, shooting me a concerned look. "Feathers?" she mouthed.

"Feathers!" Hank sang, his mouth still full.

* * *

Mouse turned the Impala into the War Memorial Gymnasium's lot, eased into a parking space reserved for fighters, and cut the engine. She grabbed her duffel bag from the trunk, Hank grabbed his pillow, and we set out walking across the asphalt toward the gym's rear entrance.

We heard the thunder of the crowd as we approached. Two thousand spectators had arrived early to watch the preliminary exhibition bouts that were already underway.

An ambulance was parked outside. Two medics sat up front smoking cigarettes with their feet on the dash. Some unlucky fighter would need them before the day was done. They exhaled white smoke and nodded hello. Mouse kept her head down until we'd passed them, then took my hand and quietly folded her car keys into it.

A security guard waved us through the gym's rear door and into a noisy lobby jammed with managers, photographers, and sweaty exhibition fighters. Hank and I covered our ears. Everyone was yelling to be heard over the roar coming from the main arena's fervid crowd.

A school of reporters swam through the mob toward Mouse. She yelled greetings all around, posed for photos, then excused herself to go warm up.

She led us down a dim cinderblock hall to a doorless dressing room that was furnished with a massage table and two metal chairs. A muscular woman in a red tracksuit and flip-flops stood waiting for us.

"This is Liza, my trainer," said Mouse.

Hank and I smiled. Liza looked at Hank's crossed eyes and my dirty T-shirt and frowned. A feather floated out of Hank's mouth. Liza pointed to the two metal chairs. Hank and I sat.

Mouse climbed onto the table and stretched out on her stomach. Liza began massaging her back.

"How much time do we have?" mumbled Mouse.

"Two more exhibition fights, then you're on," grunted Liza as she sank her elbows into Mouse's trapezoids. "You're cut as hell. I've never seen you in better shape."

Mouse nodded dreamily, her eyes shut.

"Let's review the rules and strategy," Liza grunted.

Mouse rattled them off: "Full contact Muay Thai kickboxing rules with five three-minute rounds. Head and leg kicks are legal—so are elbows to the face. No biting. Make sure the judges can see my kicks."

A high-heeled herd of socialites, punk rockers, and D-list celebrities clopped past the dressing room, laughing and cursing and trailing champagne bottles as they pushed each other single file down the narrow hall toward the lobby. One woman clutched a bloody red steak between her fingers. She wore a fur waistcoat, a miniskirt stretched dangerously tight over a pair of muscled white thighs, and a gaping silver blouse that showed plenty of fake tit. She took a bite of meat and looked in at us as she wobbled past on six-inch stilettos. Her hair was a platinum straw mop, her foundation was caked, and her bright-red fish lips were ready to burst from too much injected collagen. She chewed her steak at Hank and me with disdain—then she saw Mouse. She stopped dead in her tracks. Her brow furrowed. She finished chewing, swallowed, pursed her greasy fish lips, and leaned against the doorframe with an edgy coke-fueled mien, the leftover meat in her hand. There was only one woman in the whole world she could possibly be:

Raylene "Razorlegs" Kitty.

Mouse sniffed the air. Something stank. She looked up from the table and saw Kitty. The two women locked eyes.

Kitty: "So."

Mouse: "So."

Kitty: "I heard your old man died."

Mouse: "That he did."

Kitty: "Too bad."

Kitty spat on the ground, turned on her stiletto, and walked off.

Mouse pushed herself up off the table with clenched fists, but Liza pushed her back down.

"Soon, Mousey, soon," Liza cooed. "Concentrate. Review the strategy. Tell me what you're going to do."

"Beat her."

"Tell me how. Visualize her in the ring."

Mouse shut her eyes and pictured it: "Her thighs are thick, so I'll angle my shins downward for deeper cuts. Use straight jabs to keep her away. Her peripheral vision is weak, so shoot under her chin with high front kicks—who knows, maybe she'll bite her tongue off. Throw punches up the middle and beat those fake udders to the ground. Use low kicks until her hands come down, then strike high—try to break her nose early. Did I mention her thighs are thick?"

Mouse took a breath to calm her nerves, then pushed herself up an inch so she could reach her gym bag. She fished out her gloves, then a framed photo of her father. "Here we go," she whispered. She gave her father a kiss, tucked the frame under heart, and lowered herself back down.

"Time for you to go find your seats," grunted Liza to me and Hank.

We rose to leave. "Good luck," I whispered to Mouse. She was smiling, eyes shut, concentrating. Liza gave us a nod. Mouse was ready.

69

THE FIGHT RING GLEAMED UNDER the spotlights in the center of the gym's basketball court. Spectators were already seated on aluminum risers that surrounded the canvas on all four sides, and more people were pouring in through the arena's main entrance. Fight judges, a gong ringer, a timer, and a doctor sat at a ringside table beside a traditional Thai music band.

The next exhibition bout was about to start. The ringer stood and banged his gong as Hank and I climbed the risers to our seats.

People began running in every direction. Sports fans toted beer and hotdogs to their seats. Reporters sprinted past us with notepads. Flashbulbs popped. It was just like a performance art night. My balls began to buzz. The air was filled with the scent of garlands and incense. Hank and I drank it in like it was our very own.

A Thai announcer in a tuxedo steps into the ring. A microphone descends from the rafters. He takes it and greets the crowd.

Two fighters emerge from opposite corners of the arena. Each woman wears boxing gloves, a ceremonial Muay Thai robe, and the mongkon—a crown of stiff cloth woven with silk thread. The fighters weave through the crowd to the ring with their trainers in tow, climb over the ropes, and bow three times in a show of respect.

One fighter goes to the red corner; the other jogs to blue. They remove their robes. Their arms and legs ripple with muscle and sinew. Each fighter wears shorts, a tight tanktop, and a kruang ruang—a braided piece of cloth above the bicep with herbs and good-luck charms pouched inside.

The women warm up by performing Ram Muays—sacred Thai dances that pay homage to the fighters' lineages and offer hints about their respective combat styles. The women circle and stomp around the ring in deep lunges and crouches as the music plays. Blue walks the ring in a circle, reverses direction, then throws an imaginary spear. Red dodges it and fires back imaginary arrows plucked from an invisible quiver.

The women finish their dances and return to their corners. Their trainers say a final prayer over the fighters' heads, remove the mongkons, and blow in the fighters' hair for good luck.

The fighters join the ref in the center of the ring. They listen to his instructions, bow, and return to their corners. The gong clangs. The fighters emerge and circle one another with their gloves raised.

The band strikes up as Red and Blue trade a flurry of punches. The crowd goes wild. The women bob and weave, trading shin kicks to the legs, chest, and head. Red feints left, charges like a bull, leaps, flies, and thrusts a quick knee under Blue's chin. Blue's head snaps back and she falls, limp, to the canvas. The ref starts a ten-count over her head. Blue tries to rise, but her arms just flail sickly in the air. It's over. The ref raises Red's glove high in victory as Blue's trainer and the paramedics scramble into the ring and the crowd roars.

Sweat pours down my face. The gym's roasting. Hank pulls a bottle of wine out of his pants and we each take a swallow.

The Thai announcer steps into the ring and announces the next fight. The women emerge, disrobe, perform their honorifics, and get down to business. These fighters are faster than the last, slugging it out with shins to the head and thighs, uppercuts to the tits, and knees to the ribs. The crowd grows frenzied and the band plays faster.

Mouse's fight is next. My head throbs. Spotlights beat down on the canvas. I take another hit of wine. Sweat courses down my back. Hank sees me and laughs, his mouth full of feathers.

"Thinking about Mouse?"

"It's hot in here, that's all."

"You look nervous."

"I'm not. Mouse will bury her."

"You can't have a burial without dirt," Hank sniffs, then washes feathers down with wine.

His words linger. We stare at the ring. The virgin canvas under the hot lights is like a performance art stage from the heavens. I look at Hank. Choreography passes between us. He smiles crazily. I laugh. Hank grabs his pillowcase and we sneak down the bleachers and out the gym's rear entrance.

We jog through the parking lot. Hank spots a grassy parking strip. We run to it. I get on my knees and tear clumps of grass out of the ground until I reach dirt. Hank holds the pillowcase open and I shovel sandy earth into it, right on top of the feathers, filling it up, mound after mound, until it's full. Hank plucks a dandelion from the grass and tosses it in, then we lug all sixty pounds of the dirt back to the gym, through the crowd, and up the risers to our seats. Hank plops the sack into my lap. It's warm like a baby.

The exhibition fights are over. The announcer steps into the ring and takes the mic.

"LADIES AND GENTLEMEN! GOOD EVENING AND WELCOME ONCE AGAIN TO SAN FRANCISCO'S HISTORIC WAR MEMORIAL GYMNASIUM. TONIGHT'S TITLE FIGHT WILL DETERMINE THE WOMEN'S PROFESSIONAL LIGHT-WEIGHT DIVISION MUAY THAI KICKBOXING CHAMPION OF THE WORLD!"

Rock music thumps. A spotlight cuts an angle on the far corner of the gym where Kitty emerges wearing a blue robe with her name embroidered on the back. She pushes through the crowd with an entourage of trainers, managers, and agents following close behind. She reaches the ring, climbs over the ropes, and bounces around with her gloves raised. The crowd cheers. She's a star. She drops her robe. Her arms are thick and cut, her stomach chiseled, her shins raked with scars. A tasseled kruang ruang containing a pea-sized bulge of magical charms is cinched tight around her bicep for good luck. She flexes the bicep, then tips her mongkon to the crowd like a hat. The audience laughs.

The spotlight swings to the opposite side of the gym where Mouse emerges with Liza in tow. Mouse weaves through the crowd in a red robe, hair in a ponytail, head down. She reaches the ring, climbs over the ropes, bounces to her corner, greets the crowd with a wave, then drops her robe. Her body is stunning: wiry with sharp ribs, a washboard stomach, bulbous shoulders atop sinewy arms, fast-twitch thighs of striated muscle, and a jagged set of shin scars. She smiles and points to her own leather kruang ruang—its good-luck pouch is as fat as a golf ball. Kitty's is puny by comparison. The audience laughs and applauds. Kitty glares and sets her jaw.

The rock music fades. The announcer continues: "INTRODUCING, IN THIS CORNER, WEARING RED TRUNKS AND STANDING FIVE FEET, THREE INCHES TALL, WEIGHING IN AT ONE HUNDRED TWENTY-FIVE POUNDS, THE FORMER WOMEN'S LIGHTWEIGHT MUAY THAI CHAMPION OF NORTH AMERICA WITH A THIRTY-EIGHT-AND-FOUR RECORD, THIRTY-TWO WINS BY KNOCKOUT, DAUGHTER OF THE LATE WORLD CHAMPION PUGILIST 'GENTLEMAN JIM' SULLIVAN, HERE TONIGHT BATTLING FOR HER FIRST MUAY THAI WORLD TITLE, SAN FRANCISCO'S VERY OWN MOUSE 'STEEL SHINS' SULLIVAN!"

The crowd thunders with applause, then the announcer goes on: "AND IN THE OTHER CORNER, WEARING BLUE TRUNKS AND STANDING FIVE FEET, FIVE INCHES TALL, WEIGHING IN AT ONE HUNDRED TWENTY-EIGHT POUNDS, THE FIERCE SOUTHERN BELLE HAILING FROM ATLANTA, GEORGIA WITH A RECORD OF FORTY-FOUR-AND-SIX, FORTY-TWO WINS BY KNOCKOUT, FORMER HOLDER OF THE U.S. LIGHTWEIGHT DIVISION FULL-CONTACT KICKBOXING BELT AND CURRENT WOMEN'S PROFESSIONAL LIGHTWEIGHT DIVISION WORLD MUAY THAI KICKBOXING CHAMPION, HERE TONIGHT DEFENDING HER TITLE, RAYLENE 'RAZORLEGS' KITTY!'"

The crowd roars and stomps its feet on the aluminum risers. We see wisps of incense float up from the seats . . . skinny Thai men with cigarettes dangling from their lips squat in the aisles and bet on the fight with fistfuls of baht . . . Vegas bookies flash cash wads and jabber into cell phones like they're on the floor of the New York Stock Exchange. . . . The sight of it all makes my gut hurt. Hank catches me holding my belly and laughs.

The band strikes up. Kitty and Mouse walk to the center of the ring and begin their Ram Muays, lunging and stomping across the canvas in deep crouches and firing off attacks against imaginary foes. Each woman is careful not to look at the other; glancing at an opponent betrays shaky concentration and invites bad luck.

The band plays faster. Kitty fires off quick elbows and knees, then lobs an uncontrolled roundhouse kick just inches from Mouse's face—an intimidating move usually reserved for amateurs. A hush falls over the crowd. Mouse continues her routine—a few elbows here, a few kicks there—then retaliates with a barrage of windy punches so close to Kitty's skull that the taller woman's hair blows. The audience murmurs. The referee waves his hands and tells the fighters to keep their distance.

As the band mounts its climax, Kitty brings her performance to the chase: she throws a flurry of elbows and kicks into space, turns toward Mouse with a slow burn, and traces a final, ugly arc in the air with her glove—a pantomime of Mouse's throat being slit. Mouse ducks the cut, thrusts her gloves into the air, grabs an imaginary Kitty by the ears, smashes her down into an upward knee thrust, wraps arms around her neck, and snaps her spine with a violent wrench. She lets the ethereal body fall to the canvas and saunters back home to her corner. The audience howls. The referee shakes his head. The fighters' preliminary niceties are over.

Liza removes Mouse's mongkon and blows in her hair for luck. The referee calls the women to the center of the ring, looks them over, recites the rules, then sends them packing.

Mouse inserts her mouthpiece and looks for us in the crowd. I twirl a wine bottle over my head. She sees us and nods.

"Stark!" Hank whispers, ducking down in his seat.

"Where?"

"Near the entrance."

I look across the gym. The main entrance is jammed with spectators. Then I spot him—his white suit pressed against a wall in the shadows. He sips a beer and scans the audience.

"He must've tailed Mouse's car," I whisper.

"Where's my foil hat?" Hank asks, feeling his naked head. He searches behind us, then under his seat, but the hat's not there. He stands up. I pull him back down. He grabs my shirt. "We're unprotected! Stark will see us! He'll find us!"

"Did you wear it on the ride over here?"

"I can't remember," says Hank. He scratches his legs, sits up, looks at Stark, ducks down, takes out his mirror, looks behind us, shuts his eyes, tries to recall. "It must in the car. Give me the keys and I'll go see."

We sit up slowly and check Stark's position. I spot him strolling away along the bleachers with his back to us—a narrow window of opportunity.

"Keep your head down," I whisper, handing Hank the keys. He nods, eases himself out of his chair, and creeps away in a crouch with his hands out, feeling for obstacles.

The gong clangs and I'm on my feet as the fighters come out crouched with gloves up, chins down, lats cinched tight to protect their floating ribs, rear feet coiled, heads snaking left and right as they circle. Then Kitty pounces and they're at it, all kicks and elbows, ducking and weaving with Kitty taking control early, slamming hard hooks into Mouse's gut. Mouse is quick, but Kitty's a beast, pounding the fists home, finding the angles, battering Mouse's washboard as the underdog covers behind her gloves.

Mouse dodges, finds an opening, throws two clean jabs and then a knee, grazing Kitty's eye. Kitty drives a double roundhouse over Mouse's gloves and catches her on the neck. Mouse stumbles back, but it's only a ruse and Kitty swallows it whole, dropping her guard as she rushes in to find Mouse uncoiling a whistling right cross. Kitty ducks, throws a left knee, then a right. Mouse blocks both, jams Kitty's gloves down, and fires a right elbow that cleans Kitty's nose.

Kitty stumbles back with a growl—blood streams into her mouth. She returns a left kick, then a jumping right knee. Mouse steps aside and sends a roundhouse into Kitty's kidney with a wallop. Kitty winces, but converts her momentum into a fast hook kick that knocks Mouse ten feet across the canvas.

The gong clangs and the round ends. The crowd goes nuts. I fall back into my seat; my whole body's shaking.

The women go to their corners. Liza douses Mouse's legs with water, while across the ring a trainer kneads Kitty's shoulders and a medic ices her nose. The women drill holes into each other with their eyes.

The gong clangs and Kitty sprints across the canvas toward Mouse. Mouse leaps from her stool with a high heel kick that catches Kitty under her chin. Kitty shakes it off, throws a three-jab combination and a hook, then darts left and shoots a surprise roundhouse to Mouse's head. Mouse ducks, but the shin connects, splitting her lip—blood runs down her chin.

Mouse drives down the middle with jabs and elbows, beating Kitty's jugs to the ground, giving as good as she got. Kitty's arms are pinned against her chest from the onslaught as she backs into a rope and takes hard hits to her face. She throws up a defensive knee, but Mouse blocks it and sends a hello hook to Kitty's cheek. Kitty reels and converts the momentum into a spinning hook kick, but Mouse is too fast and ducks. She follows with a left knee to the ribs, then jumps back and fires a hard right roundhouse. Kitty takes the kick in the chest with a grunt, wraps her arm around the leg, drops to one knee, and hammers her forearm down onto Mouse's kneecap— illegal, but so quick the judges don't catch it.

Mouse growls and pushes Kitty off as the gong rings and round two is done. The crowd roars. Mouse limps to her corner as bettors swap their bills.

Mouse ices her knee while a medic works on her lip and Liza fans her with a towel. Kitty spits blood into a bucket and glowers at them all from across the ring.

I pull a fresh bottle out of my pants and take in the crowd. All the seats are full. People are standing in the aisles, even up in the nosebleeds. I imagine all of them jammed into Prance Prance cheering and my teeth start to chatter.

The gong bangs and the fighters move in. Mouse's limp is gone and her busted lip is holding. Kitty charges and throws a haymaker. Mouse ducks, comes up with three quick cross-elbows, then a knee. Kitty doubles over, sucks air, covers against the punches, then descends over the top with a hook that cuts Mouse's lip. Mouse swallows the blood and moves in—a left front kick, two quick jabs down the middle, then a high roundhouse right on the nose, snapping Kitty's head so far back she falls. Her beak is broken. Red spots bloom across her tanktop.

Kitty stands, staggers, nods to the ref she'll fight on, and then they're back at it, trading hooks and jabs and shins. The women are huffing. They clinch and circle to rest, gloves wrapped tight around each other, around and around, each fighter wriggling for an opening. Mouse throws a short uppercut under Kitty's chin. Kitty dodges it and sneaks in a headbutt. Mouse blocks it with her shoulder, but Kitty follows with a clean left elbow to Mouse's eye. Mouse stumbles as the gong crashes and the audience roars.

Mouse stumbles to her corner. The doc checks her eye. It's swelling fast. The ref takes a look and asks if she'll go on. Mouse nods. The crowd applauds.

My stomach's in knots. I look down at the pillowcase filled with dirt. My legs itch. I wipe my brow, drink more red, look up at the rafters, and try to steady myself.

A woman seated beside me stares at my hands. I look down and see they're quivering.

"Delirium tremens," I explain.

"Oh, is that a condition?"

"Performance art withdrawals and too much wine in my pants," I laugh, dribbling wine down my chin. The woman makes a face and switches seats with her husband.

The ringer bangs the gong and the fighters stagger out, stooped and winded with heavy arms. Mouse's left eye is swollen shut and Kitty makes quick use of it—she darts right into the blind spot and shoots an unanswered jab that spins Mouse halfway around so fast she only has time to raise a forearm as Kitty circles right with more jabs and elbows, then a brutal knee that smashes Mouse's forearms into her own ribs, knocking the wind out of her.

Mouse fights for air and retreats—she knows now she can't anticipate Kitty's close-quarter attacks fast enough with only one good eye. But Kitty's already on top of her with a blur of jabs. By a miracle Mouse slips the barrage and goes for the clinch, locking her arms over Kitty's and hanging on for dear life. The women two-step a blind figure-eight, gulping oxygen and gripping each other tight, arms sliding over oily backs, both wary of stealth attacks.

I hug the pillowcase as the ref pulls the fighters apart. Kitty circles right into the blind spot again, but Mouse sees her in time and switches to long-range weapons—a roundhouse chaser that smashes into Kitty's left thigh with a crack. Kitty winces and cocks to throw a cross, but crack!—another shin smacks her leg. The crowd roars. Kitty shakes off the pain and throws a few elbows, but Mouse defends like a wounded animal. She fires another roundhouse and crack!—Kitty's thigh is bright red. Kitty limps left, then cuts to the blind spot and slams Mouse to the canvas with a hook to her chin. Mouse rises, shakes her head, then nods to the ref—she's OK.

The fight's on: Kitty circles right again and charges with a front kick and elbows, but Mouse slips them, coils, and fires another shin to Kitty's left thigh so hard it leaves a purple lump. Kitty shakes it off and pumps a knee under Mouse's chin. Mouse jams it down with a glove, ducks a hook punch, slams her shin onto Kitty's thigh, leg-blocks two furious kicks, then fires another shin.

Kitty grimaces—her left thigh's dying. The women trade kicks fast to the head and gut, then another shin lands on Kitty's leg with a sickening thump. Kitty bites down on her mouthpiece with a cry, but manages a hard jab to Mouse's temple. Mouse hits the canvas. The crowd quiets. Mouse rolls onto her side, stands, wobbles, then comes back for more as the audience cheers and I breathe in the terrible beauty of Mouse answering her father's call.

The band picks up the pace. Kitty advances, firing hooks from every angle in a knockout hunt. Mouse takes one to the forehead and another to the cheek, then pops a knee under Kitty's beak. Kitty stumbles, blood streaming from her nose. She charges with heavy jabs. Mouse retreats into the ropes, rebounds, fires a rope-a-dope kick to Kitty's thigh, cocks, fires another, then cocks again. Kitty can't ignore the kicks anymore—she raises her leg to block the next, but Mouse beats her to it: crack-crack!—machine gun shins pound Kitty's thigh.

Kitty screams—her thigh's mottled with black-and-blue welts. Mouse readies to kick again. Kitty raises her left leg to block. Mouse fires.

Kitty braces her shin for the impact, but this kick is high—the roundhouse sails over Kitty's block and smashes into her temple like a baseball bat. Kitty slumps to her knees. Her arms hang limp at her sides. Her chin goes slack like a dullard's. She lists, then falls straight back with her knees bent under her ass, out cold.

I look down and see I'm erect.

The ref runs to Kitty and starts a ten-count over her head as I thunder down the aluminum risers with pillowcase in hand, scramble over seats to the floor, sprint to the ring, and dive under the ropes onto my knees. The canvas is slippery with sweat and hotter under the lights than I'd imagined.

I open the pillowcase. Dirt spills across Kitty's chest and down her sides, burying her deep from belly to chin. I pat it firm in a frenzy, giggling, shaking, and dizzy as performance text flows from my tongue unrehearsed—jokes, poetry, Kabbalah, even goddamn Mandarin—and pillow feathers float up and the light beats down on my hair. I laugh at the erection bobbing in my pants and the ref keeping his distance. I find the dandelion and plant it in Kitty's bellybutton so it stands straight up, complete—

"GET OUT OF THE RING!" growled the ref. "I HAVEN'T FINISHED THE TEN COUNT!" He pointed at me and looked at Mouse. "Is he one of your cornermen?"

Mouse shook her head.

"Do you know him?" asked the ref.

Mouse swallowed and gave a little nod. The ref walked to the ropes and conferred with the judges.

Mouse covered her mouth with her gloves and sank to her knees beside me.

"What did you do?" she whispered.

"It's called You Can't Have a Burial Without Dirt."

"It—what? That was a performance?"

I swallowed.

Mouse stole a glance at the conferring judges. "They're going to disqualify me!"

"What? They can't. You buried her!"

The crowd was growing restless. People swarmed like wasps, fans yelled and shook their fists, gamblers scrambled to reclaim their dough. . . .

"What's happening to you?" whispered Mouse. Her eyes were welling up. "Look at this! Look at you! You're positively manic! And Hank—my God!"

"What about him?"

"His eyes are crossed . . . he babbles . . . he has a dead crow strapped to his chest . . . he's eating feathers!"

"He's just depressed. We haven't had any gigs."

"He's sick, Larry."

I looked at her. She was serious. I turned and looked for Hank in the crowd. Why wasn't he back from the car? How long had it been? Five minutes? Ten? I turned and surveyed the gym's entrance. Stark wasn't there.

"What are you doing?"

"Looking for Hank. He went to the car and should be back by now."

"You gave him my car keys? Are you crazy?"

As I scanned the crowd for Stark's white suit, riots broke out in all corners of the arena. The audience was spoiling like rotten fruit. People left their seats and folded into a mob around the ring as medics lay Kitty on a stretcher and the fight announcer requested house lights. Security guards pushed through the audience toward the ring with their eyes fixed firmly on me.

Tears ran down Mouse's cheek. She untied her leather kruang ruang with her teeth and dropped it into my hand. "I think you need this more than me," she whispered.

The security guards were closing fast.

"Go," Mouse said, tears falling.

I shook my head. "I can't—"

"GO!" she pleaded.

I rose and stepped toward the ropes, then Mouse tugged my arm. I stopped and looked back.

"Aren't you supposed to bow after a performance?" she whispered, folding her gloves in her lap. "And say thank you?" She sat upright and waited, shaking but regal, trying not to crack.

I stood frozen. She'd never looked more beautiful. What had I done?

"Bow," she whispered.

I bowed solemnly, then whispered a thank you.

Mouse smiled a little, nodded graciously, then covered her face so I wouldn't see her cry.

The guards reached the ring—there was no more time. I ducked under the ropes and pushed through the audience. A woman in overalls yelled, "HE'S THE ONE WITH THE DIRT!" and the crowd went crazy, pelting me with beer cans, popcorn, and sucker punches. I gasped for air, pushed through bodies, broke free, dove for the rear lobby, hit the doors, and sprinted across the parking lot to Mouse's car—

But her parking space was empty. Hank and the Impala were gone. I looked out across the sea of cars. There were hundreds. Every parking spot was taken except for Mouse's and, I saw, one other—an empty space five cars away.

Stark.

I ran into the street. Traffic whipped past. I flagged a taxi. It stopped and I jumped in. "Post and Leavenworth in the Loin," I pleaded.

The cabbie floored it. The speedometer climbed to forty. I clutched my gut and hung my head. I should never have let Hank go to the parking lot alone.

The cabbie lit a cigarette, exhaled, and watched me in his rearview.

"Open the window if you have to be sick," he muttered.

I rolled my window down. My whole body was shaking. I looked down and saw I was still clutching Mouse's kruang ruang. The round leather pouch was damp with her sweat. I tied it around my left bicep for good luck.

The cabbie hit the brakes. "Traffic jam," he said.

"How close are we?"

"Two more blocks," he said, inching forward. I sat up and looked out. Cars were sandwiched bumper-to-bumper ahead. I watched drivers jockey for position, then spotted Mouse's car parked at a curb half a block ahead on the right.

I paid the cabbie, jumped out, and ran to the Impala. I touched the hood. The metal was lukewarm—the car had been parked for at least ten minutes, I figured. I jogged toward the apartment and scanned the street for Stark's Camaro, but I didn't see it anywhere. Maybe he hadn't followed Hank home after all.

A crowd had gathered on the sidewalk up ahead. People were watching some kind of street performance and laughing. I slowed for a look. The spectators in back were too tall to see over, so I squatted and peered through the forest of legs to the center of the crowd. The performer was wearing red cowboy boots.

"HANK!" I cried, fighting my way into the mob. People were shoving and I joined them, throwing elbows and swimming over jackets and purses until I broke through to the center—

It was Bill. He was performing in his cellophane skirt and Hank's boots. A can of hairspray, a cigarette lighter, and a pile of crow feathers lay at his feet. He picked an old cigarette out of the gutter, unfolded the butt, dumped out the tobacco, and rolled a pinch of crow feather into the paper. "There's nothing hotter than flying the coop," he said, sealing the feather fag with spit. He spritzed the cigarette with hairspray, stuck it in his mouth, and flicked the lighter. The butt ignited with an orange flame that shot up twelve inches. His eyebrows began to singe. The audience laughed.

"What's your performance called?" a woman asked.

"Burning My Eyebrows Along With My Parole," Bill answered, taking a drag from his burning-feather nub. The crowd chuckled. Nobody could believe it was really him.

I grabbed Bill's arm. "How'd you get out?" I whispered. "Where's Hank?"

Bill looked at me blankly. His cigarette sizzled and popped. He was so focused on his performance that he seemed to have no idea who I was.

A TV van pulled up onto the sidewalk across the street. The rear doors flew open and a cameraman jumped out.

It was too much heat. I bolted from the crowd, ran to the apartment building, unlocked the security gate, and rushed in toward the lobby stairs. The door leading down to the basement caught my eye as I passed—it was cockeyed at a strange angle. I gave it a push. The door tipped straight back, then crashed down the basement steps. Someone had pried it right off its hinges.

I stepped down into the basement. Florescent lights buzzed overhead. "Hank?" I whispered. There was no answer. I sneaked along the concrete corridor past the gas meters and trash cans. The passage ended at a door that led to the alley behind the building. The door was usually locked tight, but it was plenty unlocked now—afternoon sunlight beamed through a six-inch hole where the door's bolt lock had been sledgehammered out.

I put my eye up to the hole and looked. The alley was quiet. A breeze blew newspapers around. An abandoned shopping cart sat rusting in a bed of yellow weeds beside a dumpster—and behind the dumpster sat Stark's tan Camaro. He'd followed Hank home, circled the block, then stashed his car out back—probably so he could extract Bill quietly out of the building through the basement. It was a fine strategy except for the fact that Bill was now performing free as a bird on the sidewalk out front for a growing crowd, TV cameras, and Lord knew who else. After realizing Stark was tailing him, Hank must have arrived first, hurried upstairs, and ushered Bill down and out the front doors before Stark entered through the back. It would have taken Stark at least five minutes to circle, park, and break through the two basement doors—

But that didn't make sense. Hank never would have driven back to the apartment if he'd known Stark had been tailing him, so he would have taken his time—park the Impala out front, enter the building, climb the stairs, enter the apartment, pick up the tinfoil hat, maybe sing a little tune. . . . So why, being under no duress whatsoever, would Hank walk to the cage, unlock the padlock, and let Bill go? It was absurd. I had to be missing something.

I raced back to the lobby and up the spiral stairs, slowing as I neared the sixth floor. I paused, caught my breath, then flattened myself against the stairwell wall and inched up to the landing.

I could see down the hall to my apartment. The front door was ajar and the TV was blaring. The videotape of Bill's I Twirl Fish Entrails in Circles Above My Head for Twenty-Four Hours was playing at full volume.

I crept forward toward the noise. The rash on my legs itched. I was sweating like a pig. The whistle of twirling fish guts echoed in the hall.

Reaching the door, I saw it was open an inch. I put my mouth up to the crack and called Hank's name. There was no answer. I pushed the door open. The TV was deafening. I covered my ears and stepped into the living room. No one was there. I tiptoed across the floor. The cage door stood open. Mouse's car keys were on the couch. I dropped them into my pocket, then pressed the VCR's pause button. Bill's fish guts froze in mid-twirl on the TV as the apartment fell silent.

"Hank?" I whispered.

No one answered. Cars were honking outside. I went to the window and looked out. The crowd around Bill was plainly visible—it had doubled in size and was starting to block traffic. Another TV van pulled up across the street.

The floor behind me creaked. I spun and saw Stark standing in the bathroom doorway with his revolver aimed at my chest.

"Your toilet's broken," he growled.

"It's old," I chirped.

"THERE'S A PHONE IN IT!"

I took a step back. Stark sniffed the air. "I can't believe you kept him in this shithole. There's mold in the basement, your landlady's crazy, the stairwell reeks of piss . . . and what is that?" He pointed at Bill's computer monitor. "Is that for real? Are those his accounts? What happened to his stocks? WHY ARE HIS BALANCES ZEROED OUT?"

We stood there looking at each other.

Stark squeezed his gun tighter. My throat went dry.

"Have you seen Hank?" I croaked.

"NO, I HAVEN'T SEEN HANK!"

Then where could Hank be? He wasn't in the alley. He wasn't with Bill. Mouse's car was still parked on the street. Was he still in the building? I had to buy time.

"Where is Bill?" Stark seethed.

I blinked. He was serious. He honestly didn't know Bill was right outside.

"Sometimes Hank lets him out for exercise," I lied.

"Bullshit!"

"It's true. Bill likes the sun . . . he suns . . . because he's so pale . . . so he takes walks . . . around the block. . . ." I babbled on. Stark stood there and listened. Apparently, he was unaware his quarry liked to sun so.

I lifted my right foot and moved it an inch toward the front door, slowly, imperceptibly, then set it down. Stark didn't notice.

"How long is he usually gone?" Stark asked.

"Thirty minutes, an hour . . . it's hard to say," I said.

I yammered on about Bill's diet, the raisins, the orange peels, the constipation. Stark listened. I took another step toward the front door, then another, slowly. Three inches, then six. I was on the move. *Adiós*, motherfucker! You just stand there while I crab sideways right out the door. . . .

My shoe settled on something soft. I looked down.

I was standing on Hank's tinfoil hat. I swallowed. Hank never would have left the building without his hat—not after driving halfway across town to get it.

I bent down. The hat had drops of fluid on it. I touched one. Blood.

My knees began to shake.

"STAND UP!" yelled Stark.

I stood up.

"WHERE IS HE?"

I couldn't speak. My knees started chattering.

Stark saw them. "What the hell's wrong with you?"

"Nothing," I said, shaking my head—then I puked. Red wine gushed down my shirt to the floor. Stark covered his nose. I knelt and tried to clean it up—

"STAND UP!" Stark yelled, squeezing his gun so hard it shook.

"What'd you do with Hank?"

Stark knocked me onto the couch, pounced onto my chest, de-cocked his gun, and jammed it into my cheek.

"Oh my God, you reek!" he said.

"It's probably my poultice—"

"SHUT UP!" Stark shouted. "Shut up, shut up! Tell me where Bill is! Why are you stalling? Is he dead?"

The question was laughable. I smiled a little.

Stark flipped the gun around and cracked me in the forehead. I screamed. He jammed his hand over my mouth.

"DID YOU KILL HIM?"

I shook my head.

"DID YOU HURT HIM? TORTURE HIM?"

I shook my head again.

"THEN WHAT THE HELL'S THIS?"

Stark smacked the play button on the VCR and Bill resumed twirling entrails. "THIS ISN'T STANDARD BEHAVIOR FOR A BILLION-

AIRE," yelled Stark over the noise. Bill twirled faster, spinning like a dervish, until he hit full speed and let the entrails fly. The guts slapped against the chain-link and fell to the floor. Bill bowed, said thank you, then turned his back on the camera and started callisthenic backbends and toe-touches. His skirt rode up each time he bent over, exposing his ass.

"Oh, that's precious," Stark snorted.

"He's become a performance artist—"

"SHUT UP!" Stark jammed the gun barrel under my chin and pointed to the video time code running at the bottom of the TV screen. "This footage is only minutes old. He was just here. This is your last fucking chance—"

I swallowed.

Stark moved the revolver down to my thigh.

"He's right outside the building," I said quickly.

"I WAS JUST OUT THERE," yelled Stark. He pushed the gun hard into my leg.

"IN FRONT! HE'S OUT IN FRONT!"

I heard the revolver cock.

"No no no, please don't," I babbled, squirming, "you don't understand—"

"Understand what?"

"Getting shot in the leg is a performance art cliché—"

BAM! Meat was cooking. Smoke was in the air. Flecks dotted the TV screen. Blood was seeping through my pants. I heard myself scream and tried to stand but Stark held me down. I pointed to the window.

"BULLSHIT!" Stark yelled. He pushed the revolver against my chin. "This is a .38. It makes itty bitty holes. I can shoot you ten times before you'll bleed to death. Maybe I'll even shoot you in the same hole twice."

"Please, oh God, please no—"

The gun went back to my thigh.

"HE'S RIGHT OUTSIDE!"

BAM! My ears rang. I reached down and touched my leg. My fingers came away wet with blood.

"WHERE?"

"ON THE SIDEWALK!"

Stark studied me, unsure, then rose from the couch with the gun trained on my head. He backed across the floor to the window and looked out. His mouth opened when he saw the crowd.

Stark ran toward the front door. I threw an arm over the back of the couch and grabbed his coat as he tried to pass. "Please," I gasped, "where's Hank—"

"I haven't seen him," muttered Stark, trying to pull away. "Let go."

"Please—"

"I SAID I DON'T KNOW!" Stark roared, jamming his revolver into my temple. I let go and he ran out of the apartment.

I inspected my thigh. There was only one wound—Stark had shot me twice in the same hole. I rolled onto my side, slid my pants off, tied them into a tourniquet, and lay there bleeding in my underwear.

I looked at the TV. Bill had started a new piece. He was squatting beside the cage's toilet and swallowing a forty-foot strand of dental floss inch by inch as fast as he could. He kneaded his belly with his fingers to help the string pass unbroken through his gut. He paused and lifted his skirt. A three-foot section of floss already dangled from his rear. He tugged it and another six inches descended from him.

Suddenly, the apartment's front door on the TV screen crashed open and Hank raced into the living room.

I moved closer and turned up the volume. I could hear Hank gasping for air—he must've sprinted up all six stories. Searching for his hat, he kicked through dirty laundry, overturned newspaper piles, ran to the kitchen, returned empty-handed, hurried to his rope nest, saw it was empty, then spotted his hat on the couch. He picked the tinfoil up and turned it in the light. It seemed to be in order. He lowered it down onto his head.

Hank's lungs wheezed. He put his hands on his hips, walked in a circle around the couch, then stopped. He pulled his hat down tighter. His brow furrowed. He swallowed, took out his compact mirror, opened it, held it up, and surveyed the living room over his shoulder. His lip curled like he might cry but he shook it off, stood up straight, wiped his nose, ambled to the cage, and leaned against the chain-link to watch Bill.

Bill gobbled more floss, kneaded his stomach, and teased more string out from under his skirt. The performance was hard not to like. Hank turned and looked at the empty living room . . . there was no audience but him . . . then he saw the video camera.

Hank walked to it. I watched him approach. His face came within an inch of the lens as he picked it up and carried it back across the room. Hank's shrine flashed by as the camera swung around, then the nest, the couch, the ceiling, then the cage as he hoisted it onto his shoulder and aimed it through the chain-link at Bill in a wide shot.

The videotape rolled as Bill swallowed more floss. Balancing the camera in one hand, Hank took out his mirror and held it up at arm's length. I could see part of his reflection. His crossed eyes were bloodshot and puffy. He scanned the living room over his shoulder. Nobody was there.

"I don't think my hat is working," whispered Hank into the mirror.

"Why do you say that?" asked Bill, gobbling floss.

"I feel like I'm being watched everywhere I go."

"You are," said Bill.

"I am? But Stark—"

"No. There's another."

"Another what?"

"Another man watching you."

The color drained from Hank's cheeks.

"Since when?"

"Since the beginning."

Hank swallowed. "I think I've sensed him," he whispered.

"I know you have," said Bill.

"Who is he?"

"You know."

"What? No—"

"You do."

"I don't! I swear I don't!"

Bill looked down at Hank's compact mirror.

Hank looked too. His crossed eyes stared back him.

"Me?" Hank whispered.

"Yes."

"I'm watching me?"

"Yes, you, but worse: you watching audiences watching you," said Bill, studying Hank's eyes. "Your fear of performing without an audience has grown in you like a tumor."

"But I've gotten into birds—"

"A bird's eyes grow on the sides of its head. To see forward it looks with its left eye, then it turns and looks with the right—it never trusts just one, even though it knows what it's doing. But you watch audiences because you don't trust what you're doing with your own two hands. Even when you know there won't be an audience, you still look for one—and because that's not enough, you watch yourself looking. You pile eyes on eyes on eyes. . . ."

Hank couldn't take his eyes off of himself. He started hyperventilating.

"A bird knows never to look at itself," said Bill. "A bird that looks at itself crashes into windows. Looking has nothing to do with flapping; flapping always comes before looking. You've been driven by what audiences *saw*; cut out your fear and you'll be driven by what *you do*—before any seeing—and audiences will become optional. Without looking, without the middleman, you'll succumb to your own dazzling shit as fast as you can make it. You'll perform in the third person, a stranger, like jacking off with your left hand. You'll no longer anticipate your own intentions . . . you'll be surprised by everything you do . . . you'll horrify yourself, crack yourself up, gain speed, and lose your need to be seen. Acts of creation will pass like flashes as you gain confidence—just look at me."

Hank looked at Bill.

"Please don't look at me," said Bill, eating floss.

"Sorry," said Hank, looking away.

A minute passed. Hank waited, gathering courage, then he whispered: "Will you cut out my fear?"

Bill continued chewing but said nothing.

"Please?" begged Hank. "You can have whatever you want—here, look!" He ran to the cage door, unlocked it, and threw it open.

Bill eyed the gaping exit. His chewing slowed, then stopped. A piece of floss dangled from his mouth. Hank walked back to the front of the cage. He had Bill's full attention.

"Cut it out and you can go," whispered Hank.

Bill just sat there staring at the exit.

Hank began to sob. His head drooped and the camera followed—it slid forward off his shoulder and down, wedging to a stop between his chest and the chain-link with the lens pointed down his front. I saw his shirt . . . pants . . . boots . . . and his hand with the compact mirror in it. His fingers relaxed. The mirror fell to the floor and broke. He nudged the glass with his boot, then knelt down. He picked up a shard and fingered it. It was ugly and sharp. He drew it across the toe of his cowboy boot. It made a cut.

Suddenly, Hank stood and raised the camera. Bill was crawling straight toward him on all fours. I jerked back. Bill's eyes were blacked out with gruel from the toilet—it was a shaman's trick for seeing into a man's gut.

Bill wriggled a hand through the chain-link with his palm face-up. Hank laid the shard on it. Bill pulled the shard into the cage, closed his hand around it, and squeezed. The shard snapped, then crumbled. Bill opened his hand. There was blood and his palm was covered with kernel-sized bits of mirror. He slapped his palm to his mouth. Bloody mirror kernels stuck to his lips like jagged little teeth. Hank gasped and almost dropped the camera—it bobbled, then slipped, but he caught it, lifted it above his head, and jammed it high against the chain-link with his left forearm, lens down, aimed at the both of them from above.

Bill twittered a few bars of Hank's spirit song. Hank shut his eyes and cried. Bill pushed a hand through the chain-link, extended a bloody index finger, and drew three red lines across the bridge of Hank's nose. Hank responded by raising his shirt; he showed Bill his soft tummy and the crow still tied to his chest.

Bill stopped twittering. He pushed another hand through the chain-link and felt Hank's abdomen. Hank braced himself.

"Cut it out," Hank whispered.

Bill appeared to plunge his hand into Hank's gut and a pint of yellow fluid gushed out. Hank gasped like an old man dying and tried to pull away, but Bill drilled him deeper. I knew it had to be sleight of hand, but the illusion was perfect—it would have its intended psychosomatic effect without a doubt. Hank spasmed and cried out like a baby, then jammed his thumb in his mouth and sucked it. His hat fell to the floor. He let it go.

Bill fisted further into Hank's middle. Hank screamed and his spasms worsened. I heard Bill caw like a crow so loudly that it registered as distortion on the camera's microphone, then, with a sucking finale gush, he pulled a quivering, bloody-and-white gelatinous blob of feathers and chicken fat from Hank's stomach.

"THIS WAS THE FEAR IN YOUR GUT!" Bill screamed.

He offered the blob to Hank. Hank took it. The bird fat jiggled in his hand. It was pretty. Hank smiled. His eyes were sleepy. The surgery had sapped his electrolytes. His grip on the camera slipped. Bill caught the camera before it fell, turned it around, and focused the lens on Hank.

"How do you feel?" Bill asked.

Hank took a step backward. His legs were wobbly and he was loose in the hips. He worked his elbows up and down a little. "I'm lighter," he said.

He took a few bird hops, then lifted his shirt up and looked at his gut. There was no wound, but his abdomen was damp with blood. "Is that my blood?" he asked.

Bill pulled floss out from under his skirt, broke off a piece, and handed it to Hank.

"Go get a needle," said Bill.

Hank nodded and hurried to the bathroom.

The video cut to snow. Pain shot through my thigh as I rose from the couch. I grimaced, tightened the tourniquet, and limped to the bathroom.

I turned the light on. There was a small cardboard box on the counter and a bloody towel draped over the sink bowl. The box label read CARPET NEEDLES IN ASSORTED SIZES. I reached in and drew one out. It was C-shaped and four inches long with a barbed tip. Steadying myself against the counter, I looked in the mirror. I was a mess. There was blood spatter from the gunshot on my T-shirt and underwear—then I raised my thigh. Burnt skin and dry, black blood peeked out from behind the tourniquet. Dizzy, I lowered my leg back down and vowed not to look at that again.

The bloody towel stared at me from the sink. I gritted my teeth, braced myself, and whipped it aside. A six-inch carpet needle rested in a pool of pink blood at the bottom of the basin.

The ceiling creaked. I froze and listened.

It creaked again. Someone was on the roof.

I tore from the bathroom to the living room, out the front door, down the hall to the fire escape exit, and then up the stairs, climbing, bleeding, throwing the bum leg in front of the other, pushing through lactic acid all the way up to the tin shed door at the top. I slammed it open into a blast of wind and sun so blinding my eyes watered. I felt my way forward, found the safety railing by touch, grabbed it, and held on tight.

I forced my eyes open. Hank was standing twenty feet away on the roof's edge. He was barefoot and his shirt was bloody from the surgery. His red fire rope was coiled beside him with one end tied to his ankle and the other end knotted around a water pipe.

He turned and looked at me with his crossed eyes.

"Look at me on the roof!" he said, spreading his arms wide.

I nodded and tried to smile. Freezing wind whipped across my legs. Hank looked at my underwear and the blood and blinked, trying to make sense of them. He swayed on the roof's edge—

"Careful!" I yelped.

"Don't worry. The rope'll catch me before I hit. I measured."

"It's too dangerous, Hank! Please—"

"My fear's gone. Bill cut it out."

"I know. I saw the videotape."

"I'm sorry I had to let him go."

"It's OK. He's doing fine. I ran into him on the street. He's doing hairspray tricks for hookers."

Hank smiled, but it was forced—his brow was furrowed and his teeth were clenched.

"Don't do this," I said, inching toward him. "We made it. We're famous."

"We're not," said Hank. "It was Bill. All those performances."

He started to cry. His legs wobbled. I raced at him and grabbed him by his belt.

"Let go," he whispered, shaking.

"Don't do this," I said.

"I—I'm not doing so good, Larry. I'm wasting away . . . I'm so paranoid . . . and Sherry. . . ."

"What about her?"

"I can't remember what she looks like."

"Let's go see her."

"No," cried Hank. "Bill was right—I'm a mess. I can't perform unless I'm being watched. I can't take my eyes off myself."

"I'm the same way."

Hank shook his head. "No, I'm worse. I'm lots worse."

"It's my fault," I said.

"No—"

"It is. Sherry was right. I'm always egging you on. I'm a criminal."

Hank sputtered a laugh. "We could make a piece out of it," he said, wiping his nose.

"What kind of piece?"

"You be the criminal on the roof—but I'll take the fall."

"Let me grab the video camera," I said, trying to stall. "We can tape it."

Hank shook his head and cried harder. He put his hand on mine. There was no stopping him.

"Did you measure the rope?" I whispered. "Six stories is—"

"I measured."

"Is it tied on tight?"

"Yes. Now let go."

"I can't."

Hank leaned in close to my ear. "You can't have a burial without feathers," he whispered. He lifted up his shirt. A bloody white pillow feather was sewn to his stomach with dental floss. I touched it.

"It's so beautiful," I whispered.

I began to cry. Hank started prying my fingers from his belt one by one.

"Let go," he said, shutting his eyes. "And don't watch."

"Hank—"

"All right, you can watch, but only for a second. Promise."

"I promise. But—"

"The rope will hold. It's a fire rope."

He pulls the last of my fingers from his belt, then tips backward on his heels.

Time slows as he falls. I watch him plummet like an upside-down Icarus past the sixth story, then the fifth. Red rope races over the roof's edge after him as he drops face-up, eyes pinched shut, sunlight angling on his forehead, sweat dripping from him like molten wax, feathers spitting from his shirt as he grows smaller, receding—then I remember my promise to him. I turn away from the edge and see my father Abe standing in the wind.

"He's falling," I say.

"It's a good piece," says Abe.

"It won't make us famous."

"It's still a good one. Your mother would've liked it."

I can't breathe. Abe points to my bicep. I look down. The kruang ruang's leather has split open and I see Mouse's good luck charm inside. I reach in and pull it out. It's my doll's head.

"Keep an eye on that rope," says Abe.

I look at the rope uncoiling. It would've driven the critics wild. They would've called it a red-hot performance art prop . . . a study in deconstruction . . . a rope transformed into a means of escape precisely by its use as a self-imposed restraint . . . a subtle refiguring of the maternal–fetal umbilicus by the performer into an axis mundi that attaches him to the belly of his fate in a masculine display of self-reliance . . . a phallic etymology joining warrantor to supplicant, father to son, the knotter of both ends, dangling by his guts . . . a one-act descent between fear and falling, irreversible without means of egress, unrepeatable in its wind resistance, shear, torque, and precession. . . .

I catch a glimpse of Hank reflected in the windows of an adjacent building. White feathers trail in the light as he shoots past the fourth story, then the third. Only two stories remain. If the height of an average story is ten feet, then Hank has only twenty more feet to fall. Twenty more feet. I look down at the rope.

There's a lot more than twenty feet of rope left.

I blink. How is that possible? Hank said he measured, and he's better than I am with the numbers.

I think back to the night we stole the rope from Sherry's apartment—how Hank lowered it down to me from the window—how it seemed like a miracle when it reached all the way down to the ground—how I scaled the side of the building with Stark less than a block away—how Sherry ran screaming after us with a knife—how she slammed the door behind us so hard the door's apartment numbers fell off—a nine, a one, a three.

Apartment nine thirteen. Nine thirteen is on the ninth floor. If the average story is ten-feet high, and nine times ten is ninety, then Hank's falling sixty feet with a ninety-foot rope.

I chuckle and shake my head. Ninety feet of rope! Hank's a genius with the math; he must've worked the extra thirty feet in somehow. There's the run from the water pipe to the roof's edge—that's ten feet right there. And then there are the knots—one around the pipe and another around his ankle—he probably used five feet each for those. Thirty extra feet minus ten feet from water pipe to roof edge minus two five-foot knots equals . . . ten feet of rope left over.

I swallow. Ten extra would put Hank right through the sidewalk. How could he have miscalculated? He's a genius with the numbers—

But the genius hasn't been taking his vitamins.

And a crow's tied to his chest.

And a feather's sewn to his gut.

And Sherry left him.

Maybe he hasn't miscalculated after all.

I lunge and grab the rope. It slides through my palms, burning and taking off bits of skin without slowing. I scream and squeeze tighter. My hands catch on the line and jerk me forward into a run. I anchor my heels, yank back, slip, fall, and land on my ass, roaring forward, skidding on both cheeks across the asphalt and gravel, twisting and backpedaling until my feet jam to a stop against the lip of the edge. The rope slows, but it's still sliding. I straddle the line and choke it with everything I can find: crooks of arms, lats, legs, thighs as the rope slows more—

I feel a thump and the rope stops. The air's still. I'm shaking. I look at my hands. Skin hangs from my palms. I roll onto my belly and crawl to the roof's edge—but I can't bring myself to look.

"HANK!" I yell.

I wait. There's no answer.

I rise and hobble across the gravel to the tin shed, ram through the door, and run—down the staircase, the hallway, the spiral stairs, the fifth-floor landing, then the fourth, limping, crying, spent, bleeding on the carpet but still moving as I reach the third, the second, then through the lobby and out the front door.

The sun's bright. The rope's dangling from the roof. A crowd's already gathered on the sidewalk around Hank. People see me bleeding in my underwear and move away. "GET BACK!" I scream, pushing through the groupies to the center.

Hank's lying on his back with the rope around his ankle. His nose is bleeding, an arm looks broken, his eyes are closed—

"HANK!" I sob.

He doesn't move. I shake him—then he stirs. *Alive.*

I help him up. He weaves, gritting his teeth, then slowly stands with a pained grimace and his eyes squeezed shut.

He pauses.

"Hank?" I whisper. "Hank?"

He swallows, then bows at the waist . . . slowly . . . formally . . . deeply . . . ever the professional.

"Thank you," he says.

He slowly opens his eyes.

They're no longer crossed.

EPILOGUE

A TAXI PULLS UP TO the curb and Mouse jumps out in a sweatshirt and shorts.

"Hi, Mouse," says Hank.

"Hi, Hank. My God, what happened to you?" she says to him while making a beeline for me. She slams me backward, pinning me against the apartment building. "WHERE'S MY CAR?" she yells.

I give her the keys and point. She looks and spots her Impala parked down the street.

"You are so lucky," she growls.

"You're not going to kill me?"

"Maybe later."

And with that, she lets go, steps back, and lifts up her sweatshirt to reveal a gleaming gold championship belt.

"OH MY GOD!" Hank and I shriek.

"They didn't disqualify you?" I ask.

"The judges decided that *you* weren't my fault. I just told them you were insane and they believed me," she says.

I caress the massive belt. "You know this will never keep your pants up," I say.

"Hey," says Mouse, beckoning me closer.

I take a step and suddenly she's a blur, kicking my legs out from under me. I collapse on the sidewalk in a heap. I get back up just in time for her to grab my shirt, pull me close, kiss me on the mouth, shove me away, then run off to get her car, leaving me and Hank standing there like a couple of ninnies.

* * *

A mob is coming up the street. As the crowd nears, we see Bill in front—he has silver streamers in his hair and is leading an impromptu parade. He leads the crowd past us with knee-high kicks, stops, picks up an old cigarette butt, spritzes it with the hairspray, ignites it, and takes a drag. A twelve-inch flame shoots up. The mob laughs and claps.

Suddenly, Stark stumbles forward into view. He pulls a fifth of rum from his coat, takes a shaky hit, throws the bottle away, runs a hand through his matted hair, staggers, and draws his gun. People scream. "EVERYBODY BACK!" he snarls. The mob parts.

Stark bows to Bill. "Hello, sir," Stark slurs, waggling a finger at no one in particular. "My name's Stark . . . and . . . and . . . I've fantasized about this moment for a long time. It's truly an honor. I was hired to find you . . . and bring you home . . . and now I've found you . . . and so . . . I will bring you home." Stark bows again.

Bill takes a drag. His cigarette sizzles. This isn't the response Stark expected.

Stark looks around at the crowd. Is this a joke? Maybe Bill doesn't understand.

"You're free to go," says Stark. "I have a car waiting. I can escort you—"

Bill steps forward, whips the gun out of Stark's hand, and tucks it into his skirt.

Stark looks like he's just been slapped. Bill gives the revolver a little pat—he's never had a gun before. He does a little bowlegged cowboy walk in a circle, pulls the six-shooter out, mock-shoots Stark's feet as if to make him dance, then spins the gun's chamber for fun. The chamber pops open and the bullets fall out. Bill crouches, picks up the bullets, blows the dust off, and rattles them hard in his hand like dice.

"Sir," pleads Stark, reaching his hand out for the bullets, "careful, please. Maybe I should—"

Bill pops the bullets into his mouth and swishes them around so they click against his teeth. "The rain in Spain," he mumbles, drooling, mouth full, then he swallows. The ammo goes down. The audience chuckles.

Stark backs away slowly in horror.

* * *

A black limousine honks and creeps through the crowd. It rolls up to the curb, the passenger door flies open, and Bill's wife steps out.

"BILL!" she yells as reporters' flashbulbs begin popping all around.

Bill turns and sees her. He tilts his head. I can't tell if he recognizes her. He circles around to her side of the car.

"WHERE HAVE YOU BEEN?" she growls. She waits for him to come closer, then gets a load of his cellophane skirt and cowboy boots. She tries to appear casual, but takes a step back behind her car door for safety. "WHAT DO YOU HAVE TO SAY FOR YOURSELF?" she yells. "YOU'VE DIDDLED AWAY MOST OF OUR FORTUNE! YOU'VE BEEN VOTED OFF THE BOARD! DID YOU KNOW THAT? DO YOU EVEN CARE? WHAT A DISGRACE! HANGING ME OUT TO DRY! WASTING YOUR TIME IN THE PERFORMING ARTS! AND NOW SMOKING CIGARETTES, I SEE! WHAT IN THE WORLD

ARE YOU DOING?"

"Nothing," Bill replies with a half-smile. "Everything."

A man steps out of the limo behind Bill's wife. He looks familiar—tall and lanky with dark sunglasses and long, curly, black hair.

"FRANKY BURN!" yells Hank.

"The one and only," says Franky in his bassy New York radio voice. He turns and addresses Bill. "Hey, look, no hard feelings, but I wanted to tell you to your face like a man: I've been screwing your wife."

Bill smiles dandily and takes a drag. His wife removes one of her four-thousand-dollar heels and throws it at him. It misses by a mile. Bill picks it up, sprays it, lights it, winds up, and pitches it like a Yankee fastball into the limo. The car catches fire. Bill bows and says thank you. Franky scrambles to help Bill's wife to safety; she limps away down the sidewalk on her one good shoe.

The limo's carpet is going up. The reporters and TV cameras back away as flames lick the upholstery—the gas tank is next for sure.

I put my arm around Hank to hold him up.

We stand there and watch the limo burn.

It's a perfect, perfect piece.

ABOUT the AUTHOR

SCOTCH WICHMANN GREW UP IN Fresno, California. While in college, he joined L.A.'s underground performance art scene with his debut pieces, *Snorting Mouse Fur* and *Having A Ball: One Testicle's Puppet Show*. His live work continues to be featured at galleries and fringe festivals around the world.

A two-time finalist in Northern California's largest comedy competition, Scotch also performs standup at comedy clubs across the U.S., and writes and directs short films.

He and his wife KayDee live in Los Angeles. *Two Performance Artists* is his first novel.

For more, please visit www.seescotch.com